Dreams & Expectations

By Wendi Sotis

First draft was written in 2009 and 2010, and posted serially beginning August 21, 2010 and ending October 31, 2010

Several passages in this novel are paraphrased from

the works of Jane Austen

ISBN-13:

978-1466307964

ISBN-10:

146630796X

In memory of my father,

Charles Leisenheimer,

and to my mother,

Lillian Leisenheimer,

who never stopped encouraging me

to love reading,

though dyslexia made it so

difficult for me.

Prologue

August 25, 1796

Have I not waited long enough? Sighing deeply, the twelve-year-old boy made an effort to still his impatience. Surely being summoned to his mother's bedside now was an assurance that better times would soon return! Nothing had been the same during the endless weeks of her recovery.

His gaze wandered over the sitting room—each corner and every piece of furniture conjured happy memories. Whenever he heard the word *home*, his thoughts made their way here, to his parents' chambers.

This is where he had always felt most loved.

When appearing in public as the Master and Mistress of this great estate, as well as the daughter and son-in-law of an earl, his parents' behaviour was reserved and indifferent. But here, out of sight of the servants and far from the eyes of society, those masks were cast aside. After crossing the threshold to these rooms, the love and respect that each held for the other was openly displayed; their witty banter had always been a delight to observe. Those occasions always ended too soon.

His attention was caught by the door to his father's rooms. Recollections took shape in his mind—great stretches of time had been devoted to examining the process of his father being shaved, observing the addition of the many layers of finely tailored clothing that was proper for a gentleman to wear, and dreaming of the day that *he* would undergo similar preparations to be considered presentable. While there, they discussed many subjects, ranging from the everyday management of the estate to politics or philosophy. Father had always shown an interest in his son's opinion, challenging him to expand his mind.

The young man grinned, remembering the time that Father had allowed *him* to be shaved, even though he had not yet had whiskers! It had been a struggle to remain still as the valet requested. The amusement in his father's eyes as he looked on was a cherished memory. Afterward, he had even been permitted to splash on a bit of cologne.

A noise emanated from his mother's chambers. He could almost hear his mother's gentle voice reminding him, "A gentleman does not slouch, dear." Automatically, he sat up straighter, anticipating a servant about to call him in. Still the door did not open.

The young man reclined against the cushions and sighed once again.

Oh, all the pleasant hours had he spent watching magic being performed as the maid had arranged his mother's hair! They two would take advantage of that time to discuss any subject that came to mind. His mother would instruct him in the typically unspoken laws of their level of society—the highest circles of the *ton.*

When once he had expressed his feelings that a rule seemed ridiculous to him, she had explained, "Even if we personally do not agree, we must follow these rules. If not, all of our relations shall suffer dire consequences! It is essential that we avoid catching the attention of the gossips whenever possible."

One of his favourite pastimes had always been watching his mother brush out her waist-length hair before she tucked him in at night. He would marvel at the many different shades of gold that wound through her locks—as if each strand were a colour all its own.

The sound of the door to his mother's bedchamber pulled the boy from his reverie. The housekeeper stepped aside, and the nurse to his sister exited the room, carrying the wiggling babe.

Smiling widely, he moved toward them and pulled the blanket away from his sister's sweet face. Adoration welled up within his chest at the sight her. The blue of her eyes and the gold of the miniscule wisp of hair upon her head were similar to their mother's, but that is not what endeared her to him so greatly. Though the adults told him she was yet too young, he was convinced that she smiled whenever she saw him.

He slipped his finger into her tiny hand, and she grasped it firmly. "Good morning, Georgiana! Have you been to visit with Mother?" Bending, he kissed the fist that tightened further around his finger.

Glancing at the housekeeper, his grin disappeared when he noticed her eyes were filled with tears. Before he could ask if all was well, she spoke. "Master Fitzwilliam, Mrs. Darcy will see you now."

Young Darcy kissed his sister's soft cheek before wrapping the blanket more securely around her. The nurse bobbed a curtsey and left the room.

Though he wished to throw open the door and rush into her arms, the boy caught himself. Determined to impress his mother with his gentleman-like conduct, he smoothed his coat, corrected his posture, and walked slowly to the door. He had almost passed through it when he recalled the wildflowers that he had collected for his mother.

A few steps into the room, he stopped, shocked at the dark and gloomy atmosphere. The scent that accosted him was frightening, though there were even more arrangements of roses than was usual.

Empty was her customary place at the dressing table, as was her favourite window seat where she would read at this time of day.

At a nudge from the housekeeper, he turned; she nodded toward the bed.

*Mother is **still** unwell?* The young man approached the bed, but the woman who rested there he did not recognize. About to order her from his mother's rooms, he felt his heart stop when she opened her eyes. They sparkled like blue diamonds.

He gasped sharply. *No!* his thoughts screamed. *Why has no one informed me?!*

Lady Anne tried her best to smile and lifted her hand, holding it out toward him.

Young Darcy's hand lifted automatically in response. Only then did he realize that he had stopped several paces away from the bed. He moved quickly toward her, using care to be very gentle when taking her hand. Because her appearance was more pale and sickly than he had thought possible for anyone, he was afraid that he would crush her bones if he applied too much pressure.

She whispered hoarsely, "I have missed you, William."

The young man swallowed hard past the tightness that had developed in his throat. "I missed you very much as well, Mother."

"You have met your sister?"

He nodded. Her voice was so soft, more like a whisper—he had to hold his breath to hear it. "I cannot help but love her dearly already."

Her smile widened. "I am happy to hear it." She coughed, and he helped her take a sip from a glass of water that the maid handed to him. "Will you sit with me for a while? I wish to speak to you..."

"Yes, ma'am," he agreed when her voice trailed off, and then pulled a chair closer. She held out her hand once again. Her skin was so fragile, almost like the outer layer of the onions the cook used.

Remembering the flowers in his other hand, he held them up.

"They are beautiful, William. Thank you."

Lady Anne made a slight gesture, and the maid scurried off, returning with a vase. His flowers were displayed in a place of honour—upon the small table at the side of her bed. Her next motion sent the servants out of hearing range.

She spoke in short bursts. "My son, I have always been proud of your every accomplishment. You are so good, and so very kind. My love for you has grown stronger as each day passes." She hesitated. "William... I – I will not have the opportunity to tell your sister..."

He could not breathe. *Mother is dying!*

Lady Anne paused a few moments to catch her breath before she continued, her voice weaker than ever, "Will you explain to Georgiana? She and I have spent only a short a time together, but I love her very much."

His throat had constricted to a point that would not allow speech. The young man nodded.

"Promise me, William... take good care of your father and sister." Falling into a severe fit of coughing, she grasped his hand tighter than he thought possible. Her eyes communicated a desperate need to go on. She barely wheezed, "You *must* marry well! Promise me that you will marry well."

Realizing that it would be better for her if she rested before he begged for an explanation of the meaning of the last promise, he decided to inquire the following day. Young Darcy vowed, "I promise that I will, Mother!"

Soon after, her cough quieted, and Lady Anne fell into a deep sleep. Mrs. Reynolds, the housekeeper, caught his eye and motioned toward the door.

The boy tenderly kissed his mother's cheek and gazed upon her for a few moments more before leaving her to rest.

Lady Anne Darcy née Fitzwilliam did not awaken again.

~%~

The day following Lady Anne's death, her sister Lady Catherine de Bourgh entered the library in search of her brother-in-law. The room seemingly empty, she turned to continue her search elsewhere. A noise caused her to hesitate.

"Who is there?"

Something halfway between a gulp and a sob was heard, and then all fell silent. Lady Catherine moved in the direction from which she perceived the sound. "I demand that you show yourself this instant!"

The figure of a boy emerged from under a desk in a far corner of the room and swiped at his face with his sleeve.

"Fitzwilliam George Darcy! How *dare* you bring shame upon the memory of your mother?"

Wide-eyed, he gasped. "I did not mean to... I would never..."

Her eyes tightened. "Nephew! Are you so weak-minded that you cannot recall anything that you have learned? A *true* gentleman must not display his emotions for others to see."

A crimson flush crept up young Darcy's face.

Lady Catherine sat down; her form rigid, she folded her hands in her lap. With a slight nod of her head, the corners of her lips turned slightly upwards. She murmured under her breath, "Yes... I can see it!" Her eyes gleamed in a way that sent a chill down her nephew's spine. The young man shrugged off a feeling of impending doom. Though he had no warm feelings for this aunt, he was certain that his mother's sister would do nothing to harm him.

"Well then, nephew. It is lucky that it was *I* who came across you and not Mr. Darcy. If your father had found you crying, he would have been deeply ashamed—his son and heir behaving in such a disgraceful manner!" She shook her head from side to side. "A gentleman does *not* cry, ever!"

Mortified, young Darcy bowed his head and silently swore that he would never cry again.

"You must be properly directed in the customs of the *ton*... now, before you are too set in your ways." She nodded. "I shall see to it."

Since his aunt seemed so well informed in the ways of society, he asked quietly, "Aunt Catherine? Perhaps you will..."

"This is precisely the type of situation in which I shall do you good. You must enunciate *clearly*, Fitzwilliam, or you will never garner the respect that your birthright deserves!"

Young Darcy straightened his frame. "Aunt, can you explain what my mother meant when she told me to marry well?"

Lady Catherine smiled strangely. Looking down her nose at him, she said in a voice full of condescension, "Of course I can! You must marry for wealth and consequence, Fitzwilliam. Your mother was confident that you will do your duty to all the family. You have been chosen for a noble task—to continue the alliance between three great families. The Darcy, Fitzwilliam, and de Bourgh lines will be irrevocably bound into the next generation through your marriage to your mother's namesake, my daughter Anne."

His brow furrowed. "But..."

"Your mother expected it of you, Fitzwilliam... as do we all."

The young man spent much of that day wondering why his mother had gone to the trouble of saying "marry well" when she had really meant "marry Anne." But, surely his aunt would not utter a falsehood!

Since he had no reason to distrust his aunt's word, before the sun had set that day, he believed all that she had said.

Devastated by his wife's passing, George Darcy was never quite the same thereafter. In his grief, he neglected those special moments the father had devoted to his heir in the past.

Being but a child, his son could comprehend only rejection, and had no idea what he could do to accomplish the first promise he had made to his mother. It seemed that no matter what he did, he caused his father additional pain.

The son became overly cautious in his behaviour as a result. Pride being the single emotion the older Darcy would vocalize in reference to his son, from then on the young man did his best to mirror that emotion and behave perfectly, hoping to please his father.

Any time they spent together was centered on reviewing the details of estate management. In rare instances, they would discuss a book they both had read. Though before his mother's death those had been subjects that young Darcy looked forward to talking over with his father, after his mother had passed on, he was too filled with an anxious need to seek his approval to enjoy those occasions.

As the years passed, Mrs. Reynolds had often noted aloud that while Georgiana grew to resemble their mother very closely physically, the young master had many of the same mannerisms and facial expressions as his mother. Young Darcy speculated that being near his children was too painful a reminder of all that his father had lost, but the son's understanding alone could not bring about reconciliation.

Ten years after his wife had passed on, Mr. George Darcy was laid to rest beside Lady Anne in the family graveyard within the grounds of Pemberley. At the tender age of two and twenty, their son became master of one of the grandest estates in all of England, and co-guardian to his much younger sister.

You were made perfectly to be loved – and surely I have loved you, in the idea of you, my whole life long.
--Elizabeth Barrett Browning (English Poet 1806-1861)

Tuesday, October 15, 1811

As he slowed his horse to a walk, his gaze swept across the landscape of the place he believed to afford the perfect prospect. The lake reflected a beautifully clear sky and a mirror image of Pemberley House. His eyes were drawn toward the vision of loveliness that strode in his direction. The sight of her never failed to take his breath away; skin glowing with health that came from long walks in the sunshine, eyes sparkling with intelligence and wit. At the moment she noticed him nearing, a bewitching smile spread across her lips.

"Perfect!" he breathed.

He allowed the reins to fall to the ground as he dismounted and drank in her form, reveling in the grace of her movements as she approached him.

She came to stand before him, their bodies almost touching, and her eyes captured his. His breath quickened; her scent nearly overwhelmed his senses.

She raised a hand to caress his cheek, and he bowed his head to meet her touch. Bestowing upon him the gentlest of kisses, she then pulled back to look in his eyes. His heart rejoiced to recognize his own feelings reflected within her soul.

Winding his arms around her waist, he delighted in the feel of every inch of her body pressed against his. Lips met again and again. As he savored the taste of her love for him, her delicate fingers laced through his hair. The kiss deepened.

Though he felt he should never need to breathe again as long as she was near, his lungs rebelled. They pulled apart after one last gentle kiss.

Her saucy grin reached her eyes. "Have you had your fill of exercise for one morning, or would you rather join me?"

"A walk, perhaps, or would you like to receive the riding lessons I promised you?"

"I think not today, my love. My mind was turned more toward indoor activities. You are in desperate need of a bath, and I was looking forward to... assisting. I am certain the opportunity of other forms of exercise will soon present itself."

The expression in her eyes made him gasp softly. "I do believe that can be arranged," he responded, his voice husky, whilst bending closer for another kiss...

Fitzwilliam Darcy awakened with a start and turned away from the glare of dawn's rays filtering through the open window. He burrowed further into the bedding and fought to hold on to the fading memory of the way *she* had felt in his arms. In the end, he had to reconcile himself to the truth—it had been only a dream.

As his gaze swept the room, recognition seeped through his sluggish musings. He sighed. *Netherfield... and yet **another** day of enduring Caroline Bingley's relentless attentions.*

Although willing to put up with much for his good friend's sake, he had to admit that after spending a fortnight at Charles Bingley's new home, the situation was becoming almost too difficult to bear.

Bingley's elder sister Mrs. Hurst's habit of invariably repeating the opinions of those around her had long since become excessively annoying. The observation of her husband's seemingly permanent state of inebriation had, at first, proven distracting, but he soon found this diversion to grow monotonous.

Still, the notion of shortening his visit would never have occurred to him if not for the presence of Bingley's other sister. After two weeks of suffering through Caroline Bingley's relentlessly enthusiastic pursuit of him, Darcy was tempted to escape to London—to be blissfully alone.

The only housemate who exhibited the smallest of sense was Bingley himself, but even this good fortune seemed to be coming to an end.

Last evening, his host had said, "I believe I will enjoy country living. All of the gentlemen in the area are quite sociable. Since our arrival, they have paid more visits than I had expected, and we have received many invitations. In answer to your references to a lack of activity, Caroline, you should be pleased to know that during my ride into the village today, I purchased tickets to the local assembly so that we may meet the families of all of our new neighbours. Sir William promises a superior time will be had by all!"

Once Caroline had recovered from tittering laughter, she answered, "Yes, of course! The local populous must be *overjoyed* to have true gentlemen such as Mr. Darcy and you in the neighbourhood." A slight sneer appeared upon her features, "But I do not believe that attending this assembly is at all necessary! While a country assembly might be considered 'superior' to *this* society, I have no doubt that it would seem primitive when compared to what we are accustomed to in London. If nothing else, think of Mr. Darcy, brother. He dislikes dancing so completely."

Darcy remembered thinking that if Caroline had thought as highly of *his* comfort as she pretended to do at that moment, she would have excused him from dancing with her as she knew he disliked the activity.

"And *I* think that going out into society is just the thing to break Darcy's gloomy disposition of late! I insist that we shall go. Besides, I have already purchased the tickets... we cannot back out now."

Darcy shook his head—how did Bingley expect *this* event to resolve his gloomy disposition? He was aware only that Darcy was "uncomfortable with strangers." Darcy wondered how his friend would react if his true level of discomfort at events such as these was known to him.

An evening which promised being surrounded by strangers—matchmaking mamas and mercenary young ladies certain to be among them—was not Darcy's idea of a pleasant time. It tended more towards torture from his perspective.

Darcy moaned aloud and buried his head under a pillow. Every fibre of his being was yearning to escape into sleep, eagerly craving to be delivered into the arms of the woman who had haunted his dreams for a fortnight. But Morpheus had no intention of obliging his desire.

His thoughts wandered to the day that he had arrived in Hertfordshire.

Soon after departing London, he had come to understand why Bingley had hinted at riding alongside the carriage instead of within it. Three hours never seemed to take so long to pass! After Caroline Bingley's non-stop chattering and blatant attempts at flirtation, he had been in desperate need of fresh air and exercise to recompose himself. One of Netherfield's stable boys had suggested he ride to Oakham Mount, which he promised would offer the best view of the area.

Even now, Darcy was uncertain whether the lady he had observed there had been real or an illusion. Her eyes had been closed, her face tilted upward. As the light breeze played with a number of chestnut brown curls which had broken free from their confinement. Her arms had been extended slightly from her sides. To him, she had seemed an angel about to take flight, and he almost had expected her to sprout wings.

She was the most beautiful thing he had ever beheld.

As if by enchantment, he had felt as if he were being drawn toward her, but he had encountered difficulty in discerning a path through the thicket that separated them. His disappointment had been great when he reached the top and discovered no trace of her.

Darcy returned to Oakham Mount daily, even varying the time of the day after being unsuccessful in his quest, but had not come upon her a second time.

Sighing again, he decided that the stress of the past few weeks, followed by that horrid carriage ride, must have affected him more than he had realized, causing him to imagine the vision of perfection at Oakham Mount.

Has it not been proven that there is not a woman alive who could make me feel the way I did when I saw her? I must be content with simply spending time with this idealized vision in my dreams alone!

The familiar sounds of his valet making preparations for the day pulled Darcy from his reverie.

Whether he would rather to stay in bed amongst the memories of his dream-lady mattered not; the time had come to rise and face the day—it was expected of him.

~Meryton, Hertfordshire

Elizabeth Bennet carefully ascended the stairs to the assembly room, following behind the other ladies of her family.

It had been a hectic day at Longbourn—a day filled with ribbons, lace, dresses, and shoes while six ladies rushed to and fro in preparation for the evening's activities. Mr. Bennet could not manage at all in this atmosphere, consequently, about halfway through breakfast he left his wife and daughters to themselves for the relative peace of having the commotion muffled by the thick wood of his library door—behind which he would remain until his family had returned from the ball.

Upon her arrival in the ballroom, Elizabeth noted that she would need to find a private place to make a few minor repairs to her gown. Her youngest sister, Lydia, in her state of anticipation of the dancing that was soon to be had, had fidgeted about in the cramped carriage and had torn Elizabeth's hem. Once civilities had been properly attended to, Elizabeth found the proprietor's wife, Mrs. Jones, and was led to a small room in which she could make her repairs.

The light that lies in woman's eyes, has been my heart's undoing.
--Thomas Moore (Irish Poet 1779-1852)

The Netherfield party entered the assembly room. All sound and movement ceased as all eyes were turned toward the door.

Darcy managed to hold his blush at bay by raising *The Mask*—a severe, aloof expression behind which he usually hid when out in society to keep others as far away as possible. Though his expression may have been under good regulation, his thoughts and emotions were not. *This is worse than I had expected—even Bingley looks uncomfortable. How can anyone breathe with such a horde crushing in on him? Why must so many people crowd into this small room?*

Sensing their eyes upon him, his skin crawled, and his heart began to pound. Anxiety threatening to overwhelm him, Darcy hoped that none of these strangers would dare approach him. A clock on the far wall caught his attention, and he concentrated on the second hand to assist in breathing at regular intervals.

After what seemed like hours, but was in reality only a few moments, the crowd began to stir and converse once again. As soon as the attention of the room was no longer directed solely at their party, his anxiety lessened. Darcy carefully moved his attention from the second hand and began to take note of his surroundings. He perceived Sir William Lucas moving forward to greet them, offering to introduce the party to the neighbourhood. Darcy followed Bingley, though the remainder of their party did not deign to do the same.

Bingley chatted easily with his new neighbours in his usual cheerful manner, happily diverting attention away from him. He listened to Bingley's conversations, but could not avoid hearing the whispers around them. Darcy recognized the usual gossip of the matchmaking mamas. *Ah, so it is five thousand for Bingley and ten thousand for me this time, eh? I wonder how they make their estimations.*

They neared a petite, but very *loud,* woman with graying auburn hair who was soon introduced as Mrs. Bennet. Darcy smiled internally when he recognized the puppyish look fall over Bingley's face the moment Bingley spotted the blonde beauty standing next to the matron. It was the same expression that overtook Bingley's countenance whenever he found a new object of infatuation, rendering him forgetful of all the other ladies on a seemingly never-ending list of those he had admired for brief intervals in the past.

The open manners and amiability which Bingley displayed at all times would always endear him to the loveliest lady at any gathering—and to all the other ladies as well. Bingley's good temper never allowed him to notice that these ladies battled for his attention, in a competition that was especially ruthless up until he made his preference known. Darcy sighed in relief that, this night at least, Bingley had made his selection obvious in a timelier manner than was usual. He despised witnessing the incivility that ladies displayed toward one another when they were vying for the attentions of an eligible gentleman. Darcy had noted in the past that the more amiable or rich the gentleman, the more callous the ladies became. In the five years since his father's death, some of the behaviour he had witnessed in pursuit of his inheritance had disgusted him. It was bewildering to him that Bingley observed none of it—ever. He felt it was as if it were impossible for his friend to think badly of ladies, though he seemed capable enough of recognizing abhorrent qualities amongst those of his own gender.

Taking note of the time, Darcy wondered how long it would be before he heard Bingley exclaim that this blonde beauty was "the most beautiful creature I ever beheld!" as he had with countless other ladies to date.

Mrs. Bennet went on to introduce her daughters to the gentlemen. Bingley's newest obsession was the eldest, Miss Jane Bennet.

Miss Mary, the third-born, was sitting nearby reading a book. It was a strange occupation for an assembly room, but one in which Darcy would rather be engaged. A bit envious, Darcy was disappointed that he was too distant to be able to make out the title.

The two youngest, Miss Catherine and Miss Lydia, were dancing with enthusiasm—a great deal more than was proper—attracting quite a bit of attention to their antics. Darcy was amazed at the matron's decision to allow these two out in society at so young an age since they apparently did *not* know how to comport themselves. Perhaps their behaviour would be acceptable for children playing in a field, but, even in the country, at public affairs ladies were expected to behave as *ladies* and should not be giggling loudly and running about.

Mrs. Bennet mentioned her second eldest, but she could not locate her daughter among the crowd. "Well, it matters not; you will see Lizzy at some other time, I suppose! *She* is of no import when my Jane is before you!" She was smiling at Bingley as if these statements were the most natural thing to say in polite society, shocking Darcy with her coarse manners. At least Miss Bennet had the decency to blush.

As Bingley applied for her favourite daughter's hand for the next dance, followed immediately by Miss Bennet's acceptance, the matron turned to Darcy to ask if he enjoyed dancing as well. Darcy was so involved with his fear of having to stand with a blatantly crass mama who had five unmarried daughters whilst Bingley enjoyed himself that he failed even to notice that Mrs. Bennet had spoken! He bowed to Mrs. Bennet and turned to join Caroline and Louisa. *Better the devil you know than the devil you do not!* Darcy thought to himself.

Unfortunately, the distance he had retreated from her was not far enough to avoid hearing Mrs. Bennet telling anyone who would listen about his rudeness in walking away without answering her question.

I did not hear her ask me a question! Blast! If I attempt to apologize, it would bring attention to the fact that I can hear her from such a distance, which might insult her further.

Upon joining the ladies of his own party, Darcy became the object to whom Caroline Bingley addressed her opinions of her new neighbours. As was usual, Louisa readily agreed to every word her younger sister uttered.

Seeking a distraction was usually the way that Darcy coped with Caroline Bingley's diatribes, and so the young man briefly pondered how it could have come about that the younger of Bingley's sisters dominated the elder. He speculated that Caroline had such a demanding nature that anybody with a less forceful manner could easily be intimidated by the lady. Louisa did seem to lack the self-confidence necessary to resist her overbearing sister. In all of their acquaintance, he did not remember ever hearing Louisa voice an opinion not first belonging to her husband or sister—more often the latter.

Caroline Bingley's complaints about boorish country manners were incessant enough to outlast his contemplations: the inferiority of society in Hertfordshire compared to Town, the highest ranking person in the neighbourhood was *only* newly knighted, the decided lack of fashion, and the failure in the *attempt* to be fashionable were among the subjects of her critique. After taking a sip from her glass, she continued, noting the lack of excellence of the refreshments, the low quality of the musicians, the insufficient size of the rooms, and her imagined shabbiness of the furniture—for, though of an older design, he saw nothing lacking in its quality. These and other ceaseless grievances were grating on him excessively.

The gentleman wondered if Caroline Bingley had anything favorable to say about, or a kind word to say to, anyone whom she thought "beneath" herself. He could not recall one occasion on which she had.

She continued to prattle on, even though Darcy did not give any indication of listening. When she began to deprecate the quality of wax used for the candles, for they did not burn evenly enough for her taste, he ground his teeth to keep himself from interrupting. When she finally paused to take a breath, he excused himself immediately.

Darcy began to wander around the outskirts of the dance, looking intently at Bingley's neighbours. *NOT with the hope of seeing **her**, of course; only out of curiosity. **She** exists only in my imagination,* he told himself. And yet, his eyes continued to search the crowd.

Who ever loved that loved not at first sight?
--Christopher Marlowe (English poet 564–1593)

The damage to her gown was more than Elizabeth had previously realized, and, even with Mrs. Jones's assistance, it had taken longer than she had expected to repair it well enough to avoid falling before the whole of the neighbourhood as she danced. She took one last look in the mirror before rejoining the assembly. Her curls never seemed to behave in the way she wished them to, and she tried to rearrange the ones that had been left loose to frame her face, but with little success. Her white muslin ball gown was well-worn, and Elizabeth was unsure whether or not it would survive another washing. For this evening it had been refreshed with deep green ribbons around the hem, sleeves, and neckline, and was passable. She looked well enough for her purposes, she supposed.

Judging from the bits of conversation that she overheard as she returned to the assembly room, she realized that she had missed the highly anticipated arrival of the Netherfield party. Elizabeth had her own reasons for looking forward to their joining the neighbourhood. Since she and her father enjoyed character study as a hobby, new arrivals to such a small village as Meryton would no doubt offer the opportunity for many hours' worth of diverting observation and conversation for the pair.

Elizabeth had missed part of the first set, and so she sat out the second dance. She spent the time studying the faces in the crowd looking for anyone unfamiliar and smiled when she spotted two ladies wearing elegant dresses along with sour expressions. *They obviously think themselves far above their company and are not afraid of displaying their opinion!*

One lady was very tall with dark eyes and copper hair piled upon her head under a turban adorned with long feathers protruding from the top, which seemed to increase her height considerably. Though she had an air of fashionable beauty at first glance, upon further consideration Elizabeth decided that her nose, chin, and jaw line were too pronounced. Even her cheekbones seemed to have sharp edges, making her appear quite shrewish. Her expertly fashioned orange silk dress was not complementary to her hair colour or skin tone in the least, and Elizabeth was surprised that a lady so obviously interested in the latest fashions would put so little thought into colour. Whether or not orange was *the* colour this season should not matter if, when worn, it caused one to look as if her person clashed with her clothing.

The lady beside her was more petite than her companion. She had beautifully arranged hair the colour of buttered toast. Elizabeth had to stifle a laugh when she noticed the feathers that were interlaced into the arrangement of her hair, as the general impression they produced reminded Elizabeth more of a peacock than a woman. The lady was critically eying the crowd in the assembly hall, especially the other ladies. It seemed that she was examining the fashions of the local populace and was not at all happy with what she found. The green silk of her beautifully crafted gown well-suited this lady, though it was unfortunate that the shade did not go well with the colour her friend was wearing since they seemed intent on standing together.

Jane was dancing with a pleasant looking, tallish, golden-haired gentleman. His light blue eyes shone with admiration as he gazed at Elizabeth's sister. *Ah, another man madly 'in love at first sight' with my Jane! If he will be paying his attentions to her, I certainly hope he is more intelligent than Mr. Smythe was!* He had a smile which was so genuine that one could not but feel that he was a good-natured young man. Even from this distance, Elizabeth could plainly see by the way Jane was smiling that she was taken with him as well. Jane had not moved her eyes from the gentleman's face since her sister had begun her observation of them.

And there, sitting quite close to the refreshment table, was a dark-haired, red-faced, heavyset man, fashionably dressed, who seemed to be taking more pleasure indulging in the available food and drink than in any other entertainment offered this evening.

Elizabeth saw one other unfamiliar gentleman, facing away from her at present, standing near where she sat. Judging from what she could see of him from *this* angle, Elizabeth was quite interested in observing him from other aspects. He was very tall and attractively built, extremely well-dressed with unruly curls in his chocolate brown hair. She kept her eyes upon him, hoping he would turn so that she could see him better.

When he did turn to look about, she was not disappointed, her breath catching in her chest. Elizabeth was taken aback by how strikingly handsome he was, even though she perceived that he appeared to be struggling to keep strong emotions hidden from his features. She speculated on how his countenance would improve when graced with a smile and was interested in seeing it happen. She felt oddly drawn to him in a way she had never before experienced—it was an urgent, almost physical, need to be near him. Elizabeth felt she would have to guard her actions carefully or she would find herself drifting closer to him to satisfy this impulse.

Elizabeth watched as the man closed his eyes for a moment, as if in painful sadness. It shocked her because, briefly, she *felt* the strong emotions that flitted across his face. Quickly, his expression darkened and as he opened his eyes, she wondered what thoughts could be causing such a deep scowl.

Being extremely shy, Darcy would normally rather avoid situations such as these. His foul mood was not helping, especially now that *she* did not magically appear before him (NOT that he was expecting her to, of course). Darcy wanted only to melt away into the background. Tuning out his surroundings, he became lost in his own thoughts, contemplating his sister's state of mind as a result of the events at Ramsgate which had transpired several weeks prior.

The guilt over his failure to protect his sister was intense. What Georgiana's companion, Mrs. Annesley, had said about the effects of his more recent actions on his sister was also deeply disconcerting. Darcy had not realized that his almost constant attentions to his sister ("hovering," as Mrs. Annesley had termed it) were making Georgiana even more ashamed of what almost had happened. His acceptance of Bingley's invitation to Hertfordshire was based upon Mrs. Annesley's recommendation that a separation would do them both good.

At the time Bingley had informed him of his newly leased property, Darcy had been torn between the need to assist his sister through her difficult recovery and the ability to offer the benefit of years of experience with his own estate to his good friend. After Mrs. Annesley voiced her concerns, his choice was clear. He would attend Bingley in his new enterprise.

So absorbed was he in his pain that he almost forgot where he was. No matter what Mrs. Annesley had said, tonight, in this jovial atmosphere, he was becoming overwhelmed with the thought that he had abandoned Georgiana in her time of need. As this feeling enveloped him, Darcy closed his eyes and *The Mask* fell away. His expression ended as a scowl as he contemplated his perceived inadequacy.

Just then, Bingley walked over to him. From experience, he knew what was coming next, and Darcy sighed. Being in these surroundings was enough to make him irritable, but in addition, the subject of his thoughts had made Darcy considerably cross, and he would have said *anything* to have Bingley leave him be at that moment. Later, when he had taken time to reflect on the evening, he realized that none of this excused what happened next.

"Come, Darcy," said Bingley, "I can see what you are about. You had much better dance."

Oh please, Bingley, LEAVE ME ALONE! Darcy's inner voice screamed, but he said aloud, "I certainly shall not. You know how I dislike the activity. It would be a punishment to stand up with anyone in this assembly."

After Bingley's assertion that there were several uncommonly pretty girls in the room, Darcy tried to distract him by commenting upon Bingley's partner.

"Oh! She is the most beautiful creature I ever beheld!" Darcy discreetly glanced at the clock, noting it took little more than twenty minutes to make the declaration this time, a shorter time than all previous records. Bingley continued, "But there is one of her sisters, Miss Elizabeth, sitting down just behind you. Do let me ask my partner to introduce you."

Darcy played his part and made a show of looking around him, but he was not interested and so did not look at anyone in particular. He coldly replied, "She is tolerable, but not handsome enough to tempt me. I am in no humour at present to give consequence to young ladies who are slighted by other men. You had better return to your partner and enjoy her smiles, for you are wasting your time with me."

Bingley followed his advice and returned to the dance.

Soon after this exchange, a lady came from behind and passed close in front of him. It was the Angel of Oakham Mount! Her hair was more elaborately arranged, and she was much more formally attired than she had been when he last had seen her, but he had dreamt of her every night and had seen her face in his mind at any time he closed his eyes for the last fortnight—there was no doubt that this was the same woman. It seemed impossible to him, but she was even more beautiful in person than in his memory.

As she passed, their eyes met for the briefest of moments; his breath caught in his chest, and he would swear his heart had stopped beating.

Those eyes! He had never before seen that shade of green—it was exquisite! How could any earthbound creature not want, not *need*, to become lost in those eyes forever? Her eyes were also extremely expressive. From them, he was certain that Bingley had been speaking of her, and that she had overheard what had been said, especially Darcy's insulting phrases. Those eyes were sparkling with intelligence and wit, but they were also laughing—at him.

Miss Elizabeth, Bingley had said—Miss Bennet's sister. Miss Elizabeth Bennet. *Elizabeth!* Even her name had a sensuous, celestial quality about it! How magnificent she was! No, he would never think upon her as Miss Bennet or even Miss Elizabeth. After the way she had made him feel in the two brief moments he had seen her thus far, it was simply impossible to think of her as anything but *Elizabeth.*

When she turned and crossed the ballroom, a part of his heart felt as if it had been torn away, to be *hers* forever. He could not take his eyes from her form as she stopped near another young lady and whispered to her. The two of them laughed as Elizabeth's gaze found his—and his heart sank.

Ridicule was the very last thing Darcy wanted to attract from anyone, but to be ridiculed by Elizabeth as a result of the most deceitful comment that had ever passed his lips was insupportable, though he felt it was rightly deserved.

OH! What an utter fool I have been! How could I have voiced those words? What blasphemy! There is only one thing to do. I must seek her out and apologize immediately! Remembering the earlier incident with Mrs. Bennet, he shook his head. *Oh, yes, good going, Darcy! Not only* *have I insulted **her**, but I have also insulted **her mother**!*

The situation caused a rare and long buried side of his personality to surface, the dreaded "Darcy Impulsiveness," which, after a most embarrassing incident as a young man, had been under strict regulation for so many years that even Bingley had never been witness to this behaviour. Before he knew what he was about, he had crossed the room and stood before her.

It was then, albeit too late, that he recalled that he had never been introduced to the lady. Talking to her would be a major breach of propriety and would only make the situation worse than it already was. Nor had he any idea of what to say! He blushed profusely, knowing he was standing before her in a stupid manner. At a word from her friend, Elizabeth turned toward him.

~%~

Elizabeth's disappointment had been great upon hearing that this extremely attractive man, whom she had been admiring for the past minutes, had thought her "not handsome enough to tempt him." She tried to push this thought aside by jesting about it to Charlotte, but as she did this, Elizabeth looked across the room toward the gentleman. The pain that she had seen displayed upon his countenance earlier in the evening seemed mild compared to what she saw there now. Though she remained deeply wounded by his statement, she could not help but feel guilt for laughing at him.

Elizabeth quickly looked away as she softly confessed, "Charlotte, I should not have behaved so rudely! I know it was wrong of him to speak of me in that way, but I saw how something terrible was troubling him earlier. I have now succeeded in making the evening worse for the gentleman."

Charlotte saw that Darcy had crossed the room and was standing close by, staring at Elizabeth, and displaying the brightest blush Charlotte had ever seen. She motioned toward Darcy while saying, "Lizzy?"

Confused, Elizabeth turned toward her friend, only to find herself facing the gentleman in question, and she became completely mesmerized by the sight of him standing before her.

~%~

Darcy's air was one of apprehension. When Elizabeth turned and met his eyes, he was pleasantly surprised as a wave of tranquility washed over him. He had expected to feel even more nervous in her presence than he did with others unknown to him, but being near her calmed him instead. He felt as if he had come home after being away for a great length of time. *She has already proved to be the most fascinating person I have ever met, and I have yet to hear her speak!*

As the two continued staring at each other in silence, Charlotte took pity and made the introduction. "Mr. Darcy, may I introduce my good friend, Miss Elizabeth Bennet of Longbourn? Lizzy, please meet Mr. Fitzwilliam Darcy of Pemberley, Derbyshire."

Darcy started when Charlotte began to speak, and the young lady hid her smile at his reaction. Obviously, Darcy had been so focused on Elizabeth that he had not even noticed she was there!

Darcy bowed. "Thank you Miss Lucas. Miss Bennet, it is a pleasure to meet you."

"I am pleased to meet you as well, Mr. Darcy." Elizabeth dropped a curtsy. *So **this** is Fitzwilliam Darcy, about whom I have heard so much!*

"Miss Bennet, will you permit me to apologize for something I believe you overheard a few minutes ago? Had I known to which lady my friend was referring, I surely would have chosen a different subject to deter his efforts, for I would not have been able to utter words which are so far from being true." He shifted from foot to foot. *Incredible! I have not said that much in a ballroom in my entire life! I managed to compliment her, as well, did I not?*

"Yes, I did hear your conversation, sir, though not intentionally. Your apology is accepted, Mr. Darcy." Elizabeth's face lit up with a brilliant smile.

Darcy's eyes opened wider. *How does she manage to become more beautiful every moment I look upon her?* Just then, he noticed the music for the next dance beginning and before he knew what he was about, he had spoken, "Will you do me the honour of dancing the next with me, Miss Bennet?"

Her smile widened, "Yes, I would be happy to, Mr. Darcy. Excuse us, Charlotte." When their hands met, they both stopped as if stunned for a moment before Charlotte cleared her throat, bringing the couple back to reality.

Elizabeth felt very strange—but pleasantly so. There was a sort of tingling warmth beginning where he touched her gloved hand which slowly spread throughout her being. She wondered if everyone in Meryton could hear her heart beating.

As they walked away, Charlotte found herself hiding her smile as she thought, *Ah, Lizzy, he is already in love with you! Well done!*

Their dance had been extraordinary. At first, the warmth that enveloped Elizabeth's body and soul every time he touched her hand along with the look in his eyes whenever he caught hers in his gaze were all that occupied her mind. All around them were forgotten; it seemed as if they two were in the assembly hall dancing alone.

Jane was partnered by one of the Lucas boys and the movement of the dance had brought Jane in their direction. As she passed close by, Jane's voice startled Elizabeth from her enchantment as she whispered, "Lizzy, it is being spoken of…" she hesitated as the dance took her away from Elizabeth for a moment, "It is unlike you not to converse with your dance partner, and your doing such is attracting attention." Jane smiled a knowing smile and then whispered in an even lower tone on her next pass, "Mr. Darcy *is* very handsome!" Elizabeth blushed, but understood the implications of her beloved sister's whispered warning.

Elizabeth returned her attention to her partner. "Mr. Darcy, we must have some conversation. It would seem quite odd for us to be entirely silent for half an hour together."

Her statement would give him the opportunity to introduce a topic of great interest to him. The healthy glow of her skin affirmed that Elizabeth enjoyed spending time out of doors, and he hoped to glean information on the haunts that she preferred so that perhaps during his daily rides he would come across her again, as he had two weeks prior. "Since my arrival in the neighbourhood, I have enjoyed exploring the countryside surrounding Netherfield by horseback. Having visited Oakham Mount, and being quite pleased with the beauty I have come across there," he paused as his eyes twinkled with secret delight at the double-meaning of his words—that only *he* would understand, "I was wondering… can you recommend other sights in this vicinity that should not be missed, Miss Bennet?"

"Being a great walker and quite fond of nature, I have found many places worthy of notice—Oakham Mount being among my favourites. I find it would be difficult to direct you to most of them, especially since you are unfamiliar with the area. For instance, if I told you to take the path by Johnson's cedar northward and follow Conroy's creek until you come across the split beech, you probably could not make any sense of it!" Elizabeth's amused look turned to one of bafflement as she tried to think of a way to give him directions to some of her favourite places.

"I, too, am fond of nature. Perhaps we can arrange for a riding party and you can introduce to us the finer vistas of the area?" Darcy suggested.

"Oh—I am sorry, Mr. Darcy, but I do not ride." Elizabeth blushed. She could not ride sidesaddle and she had heard enough criticism from her mother on how improper it was for a lady to "ride like a man" that she never wished to expose herself to such censure again!

Darcy remembered how much time he had spent with Georgiana teaching her how to ride and before he knew what he was saying, he had blurted out, "I can teach you." His colour rose when he realized how improper the offer had been. "I was only thinking… I taught my sister…" he stuttered.

There was no trace of reproach upon Elizabeth's countenance, putting him once again at ease. "I thank you, sir, but I must decline. Though a walking party might be arranged, I doubt there are many who would enjoy walking out over the distances required for the group to see most of the places I have in mind — especially this time of year. There are a few closer to Netherfield that I could lead the way to… *if* we could find a few who are interested in what most would consider a long walk. Charlotte perhaps, and my sister Jane might be willing, but I cannot think of anyone else who would agree to the scheme. Do you know if a long walk would appeal to any of your party?"

Darcy was ecstatic that she had not taken offence to the slip born of his impulsive eagerness to spend time with her and had suggested an alternative instead. "I do believe Bingley would agree to go, though I do not think Mr. Hurst would enjoy a walk if it does not involve shooting. I am uncertain about Bingley's sisters."

The music ended and the dancers bowed to their partners. Darcy escorted Elizabeth to where Charlotte Lucas was still standing. "Perhaps this evening we can arrange an outing for a day in the near future." Elizabeth smiled brightly at Darcy, and then turned to Charlotte. "Charlotte?

Would you have an interest in accompanying a group of us on a tour of my favourite walks in the area surrounding Netherfield?"

"It sounds delightful! You *will* be kind to those of us who are not accustomed to the extended marches you enjoy, will you not, Lizzy? I believe I have not yet fully recovered from the one I accompanied you on last spring." Charlotte laughed.

Charlotte's brother John, two years younger than Elizabeth, escorted Jane from the dance and they joined the group. Both were introduced to Darcy.

After being introduced to Miss Bennet, Darcy was secretly relieved at no longer having to remember to say "Miss Bennet" when referring to Elizabeth, though he would much prefer having the right to call her "Elizabeth" instead of the socially correct "Miss Elizabeth" for a younger sister.

Bingley seemed to appear from nowhere, his eyes not leaving Jane's blushing countenance except when he was introduced to those yet unknown to him. The subject of the walking party was renewed and all agreed to attend except John Lucas, who would soon be returning to school. Upon Bingley's suggestion, since the weather had been unusually warm for that time of year, the plan was amended to include a stop along the way for a picnic.

Jane said, "It is kind of you to acquaint the Bingleys and Mr. Darcy with the hidden beauties on the grounds of Netherfield, Lizzy. There are many that you alone would know about. I am delighted to be included in the scheme. Will you take us to see the grove that Mr. Smythe planted? It would be interesting to see how it has progressed since I have seen it last."

"Mr. Smythe? Is he a neighbour to whom we have not yet been introduced?" Bingley inquired.

Charlotte replied, "Mr. Smythe was the former tenant at Netherfield, Mr. Bingley, though he had given up the lease two years past." Charlotte's eyes darted to Jane causing her to blush deeply, revealing to Darcy that there was most likely a bit of history there.

Just then, Caroline Bingley and Louisa Hurst *happened* to be passing by the group. "Mr. Darcy!" Caroline called out while carefully eyeing the ladies surrounding him for potential rivals. Seeming to decide that she was superior to all assembled, the lady raised her chin and looked down her nose at the others. "Louisa and I had given up on your returning to our party and have come in search of you." Caroline latched on to the gentleman's arm, quite obviously staking her claim. Elizabeth did not miss the look of annoyance which momentarily crossed Darcy's features before he regained control.

Elizabeth's eyes expressed a touch of amusement mixed with understanding and sympathy as Darcy's once again locked with hers.

How does she do that to the rhythm of my heart with only a glance? he thought.

Caroline continued, "Charles, did I hear you invite guests to Netherfield without soliciting my opinion beforehand? A *picnic*—this late in the year? Really, Brother! What *were* you thinking?" Caroline almost whined.

With some difficulty, Bingley tore his attention away from Jane. "Caroline! Louisa! I am happy you have joined us. May I introduce you to our new neighbours?" He then performed the necessary introductions. "We are to host a walking party to explore the area surrounding Netherfield. I had expanded the plan to include a picnic just now, due to the warm weather of late. When the date arrives, if the weather is too cool, we could arrange to have the meal at Netherfield. Do you not agree that it is a splendid scheme?"

Not at all satisfied with her brother's reply, Caroline's indignation was evident as she addressed her next question to Darcy. "How on earth did such a plan come into being?"

Darcy replied, "During our dance, Miss Elizabeth graciously offered to lead a walking party to introduce us to the beauties surrounding Netherfield."

"Miss Eliza!" Caroline noticed Elizabeth flinch a little. "How... *interesting* for you to make such an offer." The scowl Caroline wore, and her accompanying tone of voice, insinuated that Elizabeth had improper motives. In the same moment, Caroline tightened her grip on Darcy's arm, moving so that her form was firmly pressed against his side.

Darcy's eyes widened briefly and he stepped away from her slightly, extending his arm further away from him so that she could not repeat the action.

One of Elizabeth's eyebrows rose as her back straightened and her chin jutted out just a bit—it was all so subtle, but Darcy was struck with the impression that she was instinctively readying herself for battle in response to the accusation that Caroline had implied. In the next moment, Darcy was relieved when he saw amusement return to her eyes.

How intriguing! Darcy thought, *Studying Elizabeth's elusive responses could become a captivating occupation.*

Caroline began to speak again, addressing her brother but directing her gaze at Elizabeth, "Charles, it is very generous of you to indulge Miss Eliza in her *plans*, but I am not fond of long walks."

Something that Darcy could not quite identify flitted across Elizabeth's features as she responded, "I have been thinking… Miss Bingley, I would limit our tour to an informal trail that I have walked many times very close to Netherfield. There are hidden beauties nearby, and I do believe that *anyone* would enjoy seeing them. Perhaps afterwards we all would enjoy a carriage ride to Oakham Mount and have our picnic there? The view is lovely, as I am certain Mr. Darcy will attest to." She looked to Bingley for approval of the plan, being careful *not* to direct her gaze directly at Darcy while Caroline Bingley was scrutinizing her every move.

Always thinking like an estate owner, Darcy added, "It would be an improvement to the grounds, Bingley, to fashion a more permanent path through a series of interesting locales."

"Yes, I think it a very agreeable plan, Miss Elizabeth! I do hope you *all* will be able to attend." Bingley replied with a pointed look at Jane. "We will send a note around to Longbourn and Lucas Lodge once we have set the date, will we not, Caroline?"

Elizabeth had not thought it possible for Caroline to raise her chin any higher, but somehow she managed to accomplish it, and then she moved her head in such a way that it could have been understood any way that the others chose. Elizabeth met Charlotte's gaze and almost burst out laughing when she saw that her good friend was struggling to suppress a smile—indicating that she, too, had recognized that movement as similar to one that her sister Lydia used when placating their mother whenever she had absolutely no intention of committing herself to whatever had just been suggested by the matron.

John Lucas held claim to Elizabeth's next set, and so when the music began again, he led his partner to the floor. She was more than happy to leave Miss Bingley's presence, but found herself distracted away from her current partner by remembrances of the former set.

A few minutes into the dance, which Caroline could not help but notice that Darcy had spent watching Elizabeth—and ignoring herself—the lady made several remarks that led Darcy to offer to fetch her some punch. Darcy was happy for any opportunity to remove his arm from her tight, almost painful, grip, leaving Caroline and Louisa standing alone.

Having little to do this evening but agree with her sister as she rambled on with her complaints, Louisa had been observing her siblings' new neighbours. That Miss Bennet and Miss Elizabeth were different from the company she and Caroline usually kept was obvious, but in Louisa's opinion, they differed in a way that made her look forward to knowing them better. It would be a refreshing change to spend time with ladies that were well mannered but *not* artificial and stiff, as were most associations that Caroline chose for them. Louisa felt that with *these* ladies, she would not always have to fear duplicity in their motives and she could actually see them as becoming friends. Noticing Elizabeth's reaction to Caroline calling her "Eliza," she did not wish her sister to insult the lady by calling her by a name she did not like.

"Caroline, I think you should be told… judging by her reaction, I do not believe that Miss Elizabeth is fond of being called 'Eliza.'"

"Yes, dear sister, I *did* notice." Caroline snickered.

Louisa recognized the look in her sister's eyes and sighed with genuine disappointment. Knowing Caroline as well as she did, she should have been forewarned that Darcy's request to dance with Miss Elizabeth would have such disastrous results as these—Caroline had declared "war" on Miss Elizabeth Bennet.

Whenever Elizabeth was dancing, she could feel Darcy's eyes upon her. On several occasions she had embarrassed herself—any time her eyes met his, she was unable to follow even the simplest of dance steps and would falter momentarily. She was sure he would think of her as clumsy!

Shortly after each set, Darcy appeared at her side. Discovering that they shared many of the same interests, the two found much to discuss, such as literature, plays, and music. Their opinions were not always in accordance, which made for some interesting discussions.

Amazing himself, Darcy was pleasantly comfortable when speaking with Elizabeth, even more so than he was with Bingley—much like the easy way he could speak with his cousin Richard. He decided that it was time to broach a much different topic. "Miss Elizabeth, it has come to my attention that earlier this evening I had unintentionally insulted your mother, and I should like to apologize to her."

Elizabeth blushed prettily and smiled. "I am afraid there was no way I could avoid hearing of it, sir." At his blush, Elizabeth became thoughtful for a moment. Tilting her head a little to the side, she continued, "Mr. Darcy, I am not certain how to word this tactfully, so I choose to speak honestly instead. My mother is often… *distracted* by the fact that our estate is entailed away from the female line and she has no sons. She is convinced that when my father passes on, she—and her daughters, of course—will be turned out of Longbourn to 'starve in the hedgerows.' Therefore, in the interest of her family's welfare, my mother's main aim in life has been for at least one of her daughters to marry a gentleman who is… there is no way of putting it delicately, sir… well-off financially." Elizabeth hesitated, once again attempting to form her thoughts into more civil words. "Mama is not truly mercenary in every sense of the word, sir; I do not believe she would wish her daughters to be *unhappily* married to a man that she does not think pleasant in some way." Her eyebrow arched before saying, "Your unintentional insult may have provided protection for you against any designs that were forming in her mind."

Darcy was surprised, exhilarated, and amused by her honesty, and these emotions shone from his eyes. "Miss Elizabeth, please tell me—do I understand you correctly? Are you suggesting that I should *not* apologize to Mrs. Bennet?"

Elizabeth's brilliant smile left Darcy momentarily dazed. "Mr. Darcy, allow me to convey my point in another way. If a gentleman understood the nuances of society specific to this part of Hertfordshire, then he would certainly wish to allow the situation to remain unchanged for the time being and apologize at a later date. The reason being that Mama is one of Meryton's leading ladies, as well as one of Hertfordshire's leading gossips. By following this course, he would find himself well protected from *all* the marriage-minded ladies in the area as they do not wish to be…" she struggled once more to find the most discreet phrasing, "… to be the next *subject* of the local gossip by aligning themselves with a gentleman of whom my mother held a less than favorable opinion. I would think that a gentleman in this position would find that his stay in Hertfordshire would be a great deal more pleasant if he were not being chased all over the countryside by young ladies of marriageable age… and he could be almost entirely assured that all this would most likely come about by simply *delaying* his apology." At the end of her speech, her eyebrows rose up high, an enchantingly impish grin was displayed across her lips, and the light in her eyes danced with such alluring mischievousness that Darcy almost kissed her.

After taking a moment to gain control over this impulse, Darcy was struck with such an overwhelming sense of mirth that he could not hold back his laughter.

Not being able to stop herself, Elizabeth joined in—more than relieved that Darcy had not been offended by her impertinence. Seeing his handsome face graced with such a smile as *this*, and hearing his rich laughter resonate throughout the room, her heart beat accelerated, almost matching its pounding whenever he had touched her hand while dancing. She had never been so affected by any other man and felt herself in great danger of falling in love with him. Elizabeth knew it to be an impossible situation, and yet she could not help herself.

Darcy's mind was engaged similarly, although *he* was already certain he had fallen for Elizabeth. As a direct result of the light dancing in her eyes, several moments passed before Darcy recovered his senses enough to see anything else, but then his smile faded away when a flash of bright orange silk caught his eye.

Recollecting that the end of the evening was drawing near and he had not yet discharged his duty of a dance with his hostess, Darcy knew that no matter how reluctant he might be to part with this charming lady, he must. After all, it was expected of him.

~%~

~Longbourn Estate, Hertfordshire

That night Elizabeth and Jane spoke of the gentlemen who had caught their interest.

"I was pleased to meet your Mr. Darcy, Lizzy. He does seem shy, as we had heard of him, but when he was conversing with you alone, I noticed that he was more animated."

"Jane, he is not *my* Mr. Darcy! He is a kind gentleman and that is all."

"Well, Charlotte seems to think he *is* your Mr. Darcy, and so do I. He shows good taste in falling instantly in love with you!"

"At times, Charlotte has an excellent imagination, Jane, and I am certain that is all it is! But I did detect a very marked partiality in *your* Mr. Bingley." Elizabeth laughed.

Jane blushed. "Lizzy! He is not my Mr. Bingley, though I did enjoy his company greatly. He is just what a young man ought to be…" said she, lost in reflection momentarily.

"He is also very handsome," replied Elizabeth, "Just as he should be."

"I was very much flattered by his asking me to dance a second time. I did not expect such a compliment," Jane stated seriously.

"I did for you. He certainly is very agreeable. I give you leave to like him; you have liked many a stupider person."

"Dear Lizzy!"

"You are prone to approve of people too easily, Jane. You never see a fault in anybody. I have never heard you speak ill of a human being in my life."

"I always speak what I think."

Elizabeth smiled and thought, *Yes, I know you do, dear Jane. You are so sweet and good, and you think all others are like you. I do hope you do not become injured one day as a result of being so naive!*

"There is something we need to speak of, Jane. Neither of us wishes to advertise to the neighbourhood just *who* all our friends are in Town, and Papa insists that we do not. But, do you think it is necessary to tell our new friends since they frequent London… Mr. Darcy especially?"

"Similar thoughts occurred to me several times since we met him, but I do not know what to do."

"Really? I did not believe it possible that you thought of something other than Mr. Bingley's smiles this evening," Elizabeth teased.

"Lizzy! Do be serious!"

"Yes, serious thought is required just now. I am quite confused about what the best course of action might be. I feel almost guilty keeping this information from Mr. Darcy, but then again, I am uncomfortable to think that *telling* him would seem as though we are attempting to use our friendships with others to gain an advantage of some kind! Also, our friends have been attempting to introduce us to Mr. Darcy for years with certain… *hopeful expectations* as to the outcome of that introduction. No matter how many times I have explained to them that I would not wish to be the cause of all that happened to Mr. Hainsworth being repeated, they seem persistent on this point. If I admit to Mr. Darcy that I know them, I must write to our friend informing her of the introduction, and I am certain that she would answer immediately with many questions that I am not prepared to answer… or at least *not* to her satisfaction. I am almost resolved not to speak of this to anyone at this time—but I would like your opinion, Jane."

"Lizzy, you continue to take too much upon yourself when it comes to what happened with Mr. Hainsworth! I believe the gossips would not have been at all severe on him if they had known that *you* were the lady he had such a marked interest in, but you do make valid points for not mentioning any of it to the parties involved. There is no sense in disappointing the hopes of our friends when we do not know what the outcome will be, and we have discussed many times our reasons for not wishing our neighbours to know of our friendships with certain members of London society. Besides, I know that Father would not like it if we exposed our connexions. When all is taken into account, I think the sensible choice *at this time* is to refrain from discussing it with anyone." Jane stifled a yawn after her speech.

"Thank you, Jane. I am glad we spoke of this before retiring for it would have weighed heavily on my mind and prevented me from any hope of slumber if we had not. But now, I think we must go to sleep. Mama will be very angry with me if I do not let you get your beauty rest since she is absolutely convinced that Mr. Bingley will call on the morrow!"

Jane blushed and smiled prettily as she said, "Lizzy!"

After Jane fell asleep, Elizabeth could not quiet her mind from thinking of Darcy. Her heart swelled thinking of the attentions he paid to her tonight.

He was intelligent, caring, attentive, and able to carry on interesting discourse on a variety of subjects. Their sense of humour was similar—though his seemed on display only when they were speaking alone. She had to admit that he was much quieter when others approached, but she knew instinctively that it was due to his being shy.

Darcy was just the sort of man she could fall in love with.

No! I will not allow my thoughts to stray in that direction! His attentions meant nothing more than that he was feeling remorse for insulting me, and was bored with the company of Mr. Bingley's sisters. I refuse to have any expectations; he is too highly placed in society to be interested in that way. I, of all people, know what trouble it would cause for him, ***and*** *for Miss Darcy. Mr. Darcy is too sensible a man to entertain the idea. I must limit myself to enjoying the time spent with such a superior friend—and that is all!*

~Netherfield Park

Caroline Bingley was vexed.

All evening, with increasing dissatisfaction she had watched Darcy paying his attentions to Miss Eliza Bennet. At all previous balls, Darcy had always danced with Caroline and Louisa, rarely with another friend's sister, perhaps a relative, but never anybody else. She knew her dance with him was something he felt was an obligation to her brother, but someday that would change—she only required *time* to persuade him.

The way it stood, circumstances were at least partially satisfying to Caroline in that Darcy would discharge his requisite duties at the beginning of the evening. As the evening wore on, the other ladies in attendance would eventually come to realize that while she had had the opportunity to partner the most handsome and eligible bachelor at the ball, they would *not* have that honour. To her, it was a most enjoyable pastime to witness their jealousy build over the course of the evening—with the added bonus of the other ladies usually being of higher rank than she!

Tonight, she had not expected to have the same degree of gratification since there were no high ranking ladies in attendance, but she had anticipated satisfaction to a lesser extent when she would gain the envy of these country bumpkins by the sophisticated style and grace displayed when Darcy danced with a truly worthy partner of the *ton*—her.

But tonight, Darcy had been busy watching, speaking to, and dancing with Eliza Bennet and had made absolutely no effort to hide that he was reluctant to leave her side, even if his expression was obvious only to those who knew him well. He had the audacity to ask Caroline to dance at the *end* of the evening, almost as if it were an afterthought, ruining any chance of pleasure she could have taken from watching the disappointed hopes of all the country misses who should have been drooling over the prospect of his requesting their hand.

What strange creatures some of these country ladies were! She saw some of them with genuine smiles on their faces while watching Darcy and Eliza dance, as well as her brother and Jane Bennet, instead of the usual resentfulness she had become accustomed to seeing on the faces of ladies of the *ton*. Had they no intuitive sense of self preservation, no true awareness of the harsh realities of life? These ladies would never survive in London!

Caroline spoke with Louisa before leaving the assembly. Both had noticed that their brother was interested in the eldest Bennet daughter, and Caroline felt this was a distressing prospect based on what they had discerned of the Bennet's fortune and connexions this evening—though it worked in Caroline's favor when it came to Darcy.

In the past, Charles had a series of harmless flirtations, most with ladies of whom she had approved, but she wished to make certain this one *remained* harmless. The sisters had not recalled ever before seeing Darcy act in the manner he did tonight, and so his behaviour was even more alarming than their brother's.

Caroline devised a plan of action, which Louisa agreed to follow. They would repeat what they had heard about all the families they had met that night, with particular attention paid to detailing the drawbacks of being connected to the Bennet family. Both gentlemen were certain to see the error of their ways once all was brought to light.

As the Netherfield party returned home and retired to the drawing room, Mr. Hurst drank down a full glass of brandy and then fell asleep immediately thereafter on a sofa upon which must have found it agreeable to doze since he did it so often. Once the remainder of the party seated themselves comfortably, Caroline led the attack.

Caroline began with a similar critique of the general population as she had at the ball. Darcy crossed the room to the brandy decanter and sighed as he poured himself a glass—civility required he stay in the drawing room for at least a short while, but he did not think he could listen to these odious remarks *once again* without a little something to brace himself.

When the ladies' observations became limited to the Bennet family, both Bingley and Darcy paid closer attention. Longbourn estate garnered an annual income of two thousand a year. The daughters had a dowry of only one thousand each! What they could discover about their connexions was limited: Mrs. Bennet's father had been a tradesman, her sister was married to an attorney who practiced in Meryton, and her brother was a tradesman in London, living in Cheapside.

Bingley stated, "Caroline, if the Bennets had tradesmen uncles to fill all Cheapside, I would not find them any less agreeable."

"But do you not see that their connexions and fortune materially damage their chances of marrying well, Charles?" Caroline countered. "Jane Bennet is pretty, sweet, and well mannered, I will admit. But her mother is vulgar and mercenary! She never stopped speaking of your income all evening! Excepting of course Mary Bennet who is a prosaic bluestocking, her sisters are all bordering on wanton in their behaviour." She and Louisa laughed, as Caroline proceeded to criticize Elizabeth's appearance, one feature at a time.

While Caroline paused to take a breath, Darcy suddenly stood and walked to the window in an attempt to refrain from commenting. At a look from Caroline, Louisa took advantage of the opportunity to agree with everything her sister had said, if only to avoid Caroline's disapproval later.

Caroline began once more. "I am certain we all recognize the wanton impropriety of Eliza Bennet suggesting that she take Mr. Darcy on a tour of the woods surrounding Netherfield! Do be careful, Mr. Darcy; I think she is attempting to entrap you—though I believe you are in no need of my warning since you had converted the invitation to a group outing yourself!"

Though he could not understand her views, Caroline was entitled to her own opinion about Elizabeth's beauty, but hurling such insulting and potentially *damaging* comments at the lady—enough to ruin her reputation—was quite another matter and would not be tolerated for a moment.

Seething with anger he could no longer contain, Darcy boomed, "Miss Bingley! I will have you know that the outing was *not* Miss Elizabeth's idea at all. It was after *my* request that Miss Elizabeth agreed to a tour, and *she* was the one who made it clearly understood it would be a group event. There was nothing but the *most proper* behaviour displayed by Miss Elizabeth during the entire evening!

"Excuse me, Bingley, I have heard quite enough of this slander; I shall retire directly." With that, Darcy stormed from the room without taking leave of anyone else.

In his rooms, after he had calmed himself, Darcy let go of strict propriety. He kicked off his boots, stripped down to his lawn shirt and breeches, and slipped into his robe and slippers. Pouring himself a brandy, Darcy took his book to the comfortable chair next to the fireplace and sat down to read for a while. But his mind could not comprehend the words on the page; his thoughts continually wandering to Elizabeth as he sipped his brandy and stared into the fire.

Some of her family's behaviour at the assembly was not pleasant, but it could be something he could overlook, he was sure. Whoever has a family where all members are perfect may cast the first stone, but *he* surely would not have that right! He saw Elizabeth was embarrassed by much of her mother's and younger sisters' behaviour throughout the evening and that spoke well of her personal standards.

Tonight, when he was near her, he was not as nervous as usual about being among so many people. As long as she was by his side, he was able to have a few—though admittedly limited—conversations with others. Her discourse was absorbing, and he had forgotten all else. During the time he had spent in her company, not for one moment was he bored.

Elizabeth did not once agree with him just to agree, which set her apart from every other lady of marriageable age whose acquaintance he had made. Darcy chuckled when he thought about the time he tested what was once known as the "Agreement Theory." Just after Darcy had turned twenty-one, his cousin Richard had not believed him when he observed that he could get any unmarried woman in the room to agree with anything he said, so he set out to prove it. He had planted his "opinion" on a certain subject with five single ladies of the *ton* at a dinner they both attended. Though the opinion was not at all fashionable, all five ladies agreed with him completely.

Over the next two weeks, Richard and Darcy encountered the same five ladies during a number of gatherings. Richard remained close by to listen to the conversations as Darcy voiced the exact opposite opinion of what he had previously. Every one of the five ladies agreed wholeheartedly with his new opinion, their phrases unvarying from when they had agreed to the original, but opposite, view. If any of the ladies noticed Darcy's attitude had changed, not one of them had commented on it.

Richard attempted to duplicate the results himself, with no success. Darcy explained by stating Richard was a second son and not to inherit, therefore the ladies did not feel the same need to agree. He felt if a married man had done the same as Richard, the results would be similar. Only the eligible "catch" would reap the unsettling effect as did Darcy.

How refreshing, then, that Elizabeth was nothing like any woman he had ever met!

He hoped that once he acquired more information about Elizabeth's situation, his obvious course of action might change, but from what he knew now, he could not pursue a relationship with the lady past friendship.

Darcy tried to push these thoughts from his mind, but time and time again, his mind returned to Elizabeth. He promised himself that, for *her* sake, he must not display a decided preference in company again. He did not want to raise her hopes, nor did he wish to disappoint Elizabeth—ever.

Since he knew that sleep would be elusive this night, he sat down and gathered supplies to write a letter. As always when he was away from her, he would correspond with his sister often during his stay with Bingley. He told Georgiana about the house, his housemates, and the neighbours they had met at the assembly. If he wrote more about Elizabeth than of anyone else, it was not intentional.

Wednesday, October 16, 1811

~Longbourn Estate

Over his morning meal, Mr. Bennet heard much talk about the assembly held the previous night, and of his new neighbours. He had met Bingley when he did his duty and visited shortly after his arrival at Netherfield, but Bingley's house guest was not present at that time. Now he wished he would have at least learned the man's name so he would have been better prepared this morning when he heard the news that Fitzwilliam Darcy was in the neighbourhood.

Mr. Bennet knew of Darcy's reputation through well-connected friends in London. Lizzy was especially close to Robert and Adelaide, and since both ladies had similar interests, they continued to correspond frequently—even playing games of chess through the post.

He had first met them through Mrs. Bennet's brother and his wife, Edward and Madeline Gardiner, when Jane had just turned sixteen and Lizzy was fourteen years of age. Since he had felt his two daughters still too young to travel alone with only a servant as chaperone, Mr. Bennet had taken it upon himself to deliver them to London for an extended visit with their aunt and uncle, remaining there for a few days before returning to Longbourn alone. Upon arrival, Mr. Bennet learned that the new friends of the Gardiners, Robert and Adelaide, had generously included their houseguests in an invitation to dine at their fine home the following evening.

Edward Gardiner was a sensible, gentleman-like man by nature as well as education. Madeline Gardiner was an amiable, intelligent, and elegant woman. Their characters could not help but recommend them to any individual with sense, no matter what their rank in society. Regardless of Edward's occupation as a tradesman, the Gardiners were often invited to dine with people of many varied social statuses. It was obvious that *some* invitations were extended only due to a perceived need to impress others, and they felt confident that by associating with the Gardiners, they would achieve this end since the Gardiners were acquainted with several members of higher society—a circumstance that Mr. Bennet found rather amusing. And then there were those who, like Robert and Adelaide, truly had good taste and *enjoyed* the company of the Gardiners.

Upon making their acquaintance and finding them to be surprisingly worthy of the time and effort of continuing such, Mr. Bennet had decided that he and his daughters should keep the association to themselves once they returned home. If told, his wife would do nothing but gossip about having such connexions, and when the time came for her daughters to be out in society, he knew she would exert an inordinate amount of pressure on Jane and Lizzy to marry within the first circle to which they had been introduced by Robert and Adelaide.

As time wore on, Fanny Bennet's behaviour, even without this knowledge, proved his fears. Short of confining her to the house without permitting visitors, he did not see a way to stop her from acting in a covetous manner, and he wished to confine her behaviour to Hertfordshire whenever he could. If she discovered the acquaintance at that stage, Mr. Bennet knew that his wife would demand to accompany the girls to Town, and would press Adelaide to seek husbands for her five daughters, in turn, while sobbing about how he would one day leave them to starve in the hedgerows if Adelaide did not assist them.

He certainly did not want his daughters to be known as fortune hunters and social climbers! He was proud that their characters were exactly the opposite.

Since he had become quite close to Robert and Adelaide himself over the years and trusted their judgment, Mr. Bennet also trusted their opinions on the young men of the *ton* who took an interest in his daughters while spending time in company at their home.

While hc thought they might be a little prejudiced in favor of Darcy, he *did* have faith in their overall opinion of him. He had heard quite a bit about Darcy through the years—most every word good—and much of it before the idea of matching him with Lizzy came into Adelaide's thoughts. Adelaide also had the annoying habit of asking unconcerned individuals their opinion of the young man whenever conversation allowed it, within his and Lizzy's presence, obviously to prove Darcy's worthiness. From all reports, the gentleman was considered an honourable young man who had already accomplished much—a man to be admired and respected.

Ever since Lizzy had come "out" and Adelaide had become convinced that Lizzy and Darcy were formed for each other, Mr. Bennet and Robert had shared much amusement on the subject. It had been to the disadvantage of Adelaide's plans that her scheming was so obvious to the people who knew her well. Robert also shared his knowledge that Darcy was, by then, thoroughly well-versed at avoiding matchmaking schemes. Mr. Bennet also had to laugh when Adelaide admitted to never telling Darcy Lizzy's name so that he would not be frightened off if he met her by chance!

And so, Lizzy and Darcy had never met until last night. No matter the amount of effort that Adelaide had expended trying to convince him to attend a function that Lizzy had also been attending, he had not appeared. More than likely, her enthusiasm had tipped the young man off about the scheme!

Now that his daughter had finally met the man, Mr. Bennet was curious to see if there was any truth to Adelaide's prediction that Lizzy and Darcy would be well-matched.

~%~

~Netherfield Park

Over the next few weeks, the party from Netherfield and the Bennet family were often in company together. Autumn had moved in quickly, and the unusually warm weather seemed to be a thing of the past. It was now either colder than comfortable for an outside gathering, or it rained. While not cold enough to keep Elizabeth or the gentlemen from enjoying the countryside, the other ladies of the proposed party were not willing to brave the weather, and Caroline had every excuse keeping her from setting a date for their excursion. As Caroline privately congratulated herself on her escape, the remainder of the group voiced their disappointment.

Concerning the outing's assumed demise, Darcy was torn between a sense of being preserved from, and despair upon the loss of, spending time with Elizabeth among her favourite places. He often reminded himself that his duty was to his family, not to himself, and thus tried to maintain *The Mask* in order to keep his distance from Elizabeth, attempting to restrict his admiration to simply watching her from a distance at every gathering.

Though observing Elizabeth was very enjoyable, he could feel a sensation radiating from her at all times, pulling him and threatening to overthrow his willpower. He therefore spent each gathering teetering between two courses of action. At first it was very difficult, and his resolve to stay away from her would only last a few minutes—but with practice, he was able to keep *The Mask* in place longer and longer.

It was for *her* he did this, he repeated to himself. If he took into account his own feelings alone, he would spend every moment possible in Elizabeth's company.

In his play, "As You Like It," the Bard had written, "All the world's a stage, and all the men and women merely players", but Darcy soon learned that Elizabeth's countenance itself was a stage all her own on which she displayed an enthralling performance. The intricacies of her unique character were perpetually unfolding. This particular production was, to him, captivating and enchanting.

Her thoughts and feelings were expressed through infinitesimal changes that one would only notice with constant study: the angle at which she held her shoulders and head, the tension in the muscles of her neck, how she moved her hands, the changes in the pressure that she applied to her lips, the twitching of the corners of her mouth, the slight movement of her cheeks, the height and angles of her brows, the depth of the crease that at times appeared on her forehead, and, of course, the many different degrees of flashes, sparkles, and fire that danced in her eyes.

In the time he had been privileged to spend graced with her presence, even if only from across a room, Darcy felt he had succeeded in identifying the combination of barely discernible adjustments that made up amusement, frustration, respect, disgust, friendship, and familial love. After spending many covert hours on this undertaking, Darcy longed to spend a lifetime learning every combination that could play out upon her countenance—categorizing each reaction, and interpreting what she was truly thinking and feeling when propriety did not allow her to express herself otherwise. He especially ached to see what heavenly combination would make up *passion* on the "stage" that was Elizabeth's beautiful face.

It was coincidence and *not* by design, of course, that as each evening wore on, the distance between Elizabeth and Darcy slowly diminished. It was pure civility and *not* preference, by any means, that a little while later, one could observe Elizabeth and Darcy sitting in a quiet corner and sharing a private conversation.

It was also completely by chance that Darcy often came upon Elizabeth while he was out riding. It was his right, after all, to allow his horse to take him wherever *it* liked. It was a coincidence, surely, that whenever the almost agonizing ache to see Elizabeth would grow to be too difficult for him bear that it would be the same day that his horse would prefer to take him to Oakham Mount.

~Longbourn Estate

Elizabeth was confused. Darcy had unexpectedly become a part of her everyday life. Though she would not see him for days at a time, she thought of him almost constantly, and his behaviour in company was becoming most puzzling.

She understood he was more than a little shy around most people until he knew them well. At the assembly, Elizabeth had seen that his demeanor took on a friendly turn soon after their misunderstanding had been cleared up. For her part, she had been comfortable immediately afterwards; she quickly came to feel almost as if she had always known him.

Elizabeth knew she could not expect what her heart hoped for, but she did suppose that they could be friends. She was disappointed when his manner did not always seem friendly. Although she had noticed a pattern to his behaviour, she could not make any sense of it.

At every gathering, Darcy would begin by acting in an aloof manner toward her, uttering the barest of civilities in his greeting, and often he seemed to avoid greeting her at all. He then headed toward the side of the room farthest away from her and mirrored her movements so as to remain as far away as possible. After several minutes, his eyes would begin to follow her every move. Then, he would slowly make his way across the room until he was before her. She would greet him, and he would turn to her with an expression that tended to convey that her words were a much needed remedy to a long standing ailment. The remainder of the evening would be spent in pleasant conversation between themselves or with others, and they would not part until the carriages arrived. Throughout the night, the only time he spoke to anyone outside his party was during the moments he stood beside her—and he smiled only when in private conversation with her.

Then there were the accidental meetings at Oakham Mount. They were the strangest of all! A few times he would just ride away after wishing her a good morning. Other times, he would walk with her part way to Longbourn, and they would converse on a diverse range of topics.

Elizabeth was not the only one to notice this behaviour. She was a bit surprised when Charlotte brought up the subject. Though Charlotte could have no way of knowing about Oakham Mount, and Elizabeth was not inclined to volunteer that information, they had all been in company together at most public occasions.

"What do you think of the odd behaviour that Mr. Darcy has displayed toward you, Lizzy?" Charlotte began, eager to discover whether Elizabeth's conclusions concurred with her own.

"You noticed it, too, then? I thought I was imagining it! I cannot make him out at all, Charlotte! It is all so strange."

Ah, I should have known she is too modest to see it as I do, Charlotte thought, and then said, "No, you are not imagining it. Lizzy… I feel I must say this. I think Mr. Darcy is in love with you but is fighting this inclination for some reason of his own. Though he starts out each evening by denying himself your company, he cannot keep away from you for long!"

"No, Charlotte! That cannot be so. Mr. Darcy is a member of the first circles of society; he could no more have an attachment to me than he could to a scullery maid! Well, perhaps that is an extreme example, but I am certain you understand my meaning. My mother has often pointed out that I am nothing to my sisters, and I know that if he can withstand *their* beauty, he certainly can elude mine! We have many of the same interests; I can easily understand his selection of my company over the options offered by his own party. So you see, Charlotte, Mr. Darcy's interest in me is *friendship*, and that is all. But assuming we are correct in our theory that he is struggling with something, I do tend to wonder why he feels he could not be friends with a gentleman's daughter."

"I can see I will not turn your mind about Mr. Darcy being in love with you—but mark my words, Lizzy, he is. Do you not see the way he looks at you? I know the matrons have not seen it, or at least have not recognized it for what it is, since your impending marriage to the gentleman is not already spread about the village, but *I* have seen it and believe me when I say it is *not* merely friendship that is shining from his eyes as they follow you around the room!" Elizabeth blushed at this statement as Charlotte continued.

"Though, now that you mention it, part of your reasoning may be sound, Lizzy. It *could* be the differences in your stations in life which is keeping him from declaring his affections. The expectations placed upon him from his social circle must be great, indeed."

Elizabeth thought on this for several minutes before answering.

"I could believe that Mr. Darcy's behaviour is an attempt to shield me from gossip that may arise in the community if he pays particular attention to me. Also, though I know it *is* limited to friendship, he might not know that I *do* understand this. He could be trying to save me from my own expectations as well. Though, being an intelligent man, when at a gathering he becomes bored with the usual civilities, he naturally drifts toward me to start a more interesting conversation!"

A triumphant grin spread across Elizabeth's face at her analysis. "There, I have explained it! That is much more likely the answer! I will make certain he knows that I do understand when at your house tomorrow night. Afterwards, he will no longer worry about *my* expectations being for anything more than friendship!"

"Lizzy, take care! I believe your aim in this declaration is to convince yourself more than to convince me or Mr. Darcy. I do not think…"

Elizabeth interrupted, "No, Charlotte! I am confident that you are wrong about the direction of Mr. Darcy's feelings for me. I am certain this is the correct way to proceed and I will hear no more on the matter." And with that, Elizabeth began speaking of another subject.

Friday, November 8, 1811

~Lucas Lodge, Hertfordshire

The principal families from the neighbourhood were all in attendance at Lucas Lodge and, so far, the time had passed according to Darcy's previously established pattern.

Elizabeth had noticed Darcy hovering nearby as she spoke to Colonel Forster and decided to include him in her conversation with Charlotte. "Did not you think, Mr. Darcy, that I expressed myself uncommonly well just now, when I was teasing Colonel Forster to hold a ball?"

Oh, how he loved the mirth twinkling from her eyes! He could not but want her to continue looking at him in this manner, and so replied, "With great energy—but it is a subject that always makes a lady energetic."

Elizabeth smiled slightly and arched her brow. "You are severe on us."

"It will be her turn soon to be teased." Charlotte was enjoying their exchange but was required to shorten it due to a signal from her mother. "I am going to open the instrument, Lizzy, and you know what follows."

"You are a very strange creature by way of a friend—always wanting me to play and sing before anybody and everybody! If my vanity had taken a musical turn, you would have been invaluable, but as it is, I would really rather not sit down before those who must be in the habit of hearing the very best performers."

Heavens, no! Do not have her **sing**. *Please, Miss Lucas, ask her to play, but not sing! You know not what her voice does to me!* Darcy thought frantically.

Charlotte knew well what she was doing for she had seen Darcy's expression whenever Elizabeth played and sang, and she persevered. Elizabeth finally relented.

Darcy felt it necessary to move as far away from the pianoforte as possible to find a seat. He thought that situating himself behind most of the other people would make the expected changes in his countenance when he heard Elizabeth sing less likely to be noticed. He purposely chose a seat where she would not see him, but he could watch her. What Darcy did not realize was that Charlotte was observing him, a slight smile playing at the edges of her lips.

Darcy was so entranced by the performance, and the performer, that he did not notice when Caroline Bingley took a seat just behind him. The lady leaned forward in her seat and whispered in his ear, "I believe I can guess the subject of your reverie."

He was startled at finding Caroline so close to him, as well as by her choice of words, momentarily wondering if she could have noticed the alteration in the fit of his trousers. Without thinking, he re-crossed his legs in the other direction. The idea of exactly *what* her attention may have been focused on to be able to voice such an observation disgusted him completely! This thought and the feel of her breath on his neck made him shudder, quelling any amorous feelings in which he may have been indulging before this encounter began. Darcy leaned away from her lips as he replied in a low voice, "I would imagine not!"

"You are considering how insupportable it would be to pass many evenings in this manner—in such society; and indeed I am quite of your opinion. I was never more annoyed! The insipidity and yet the noise, the nothingness and yet the self-importance of all these people! What I would not give to hear your strictures of them!"

Darcy relaxed a little and almost laughed as he thought, *Hearing this as the subject of your thoughts—again—is a relief for once, after what I was imagining! How ironic that you are describing your own self to perfection, Miss Bingley, and in fact I do not think you would enjoy hearing my remarks upon the subject.* The audacity of interrupting Elizabeth's performance with this petty and abusive commentary was far too much for him to hold his tongue, and so he answered, "Your conjecture is totally in error, I assure you. My mind was more agreeably engaged. I have been meditating on the very great pleasure which a pair of fine eyes in the face of a pretty woman can bestow."

Caroline's eyelashes fluttered; she smiled coyly and looked quite pleased with herself. "And may I ask what lady had the credit of inspiring such reflections?"

"Miss Elizabeth Bennet."

An unbecoming expression of shock crossed Caroline's face. "Miss Elizabeth Bennet! I am all astonishment."

To Darcy's great relief, after this remark, the lady left him in peace. He quickly forgot the incident as he once again allowed Elizabeth's performance to envelop him.

When her second song was done, Elizabeth stepped aside for her sister, Mary, who was persuaded to play some Scottish airs so that those of the company who were so inclined could dance. The company began to move from their seats to make room.

In order to further her plan to assure Darcy of her "disinterest" before the night was through, Elizabeth decided that she must hasten along his usual pattern of behaviour and moved towards him.

When he saw Elizabeth approaching while looking directly at him, Darcy's breath came more quickly. The scene was unfolding just as he had dreamt after he had last heard her sing… though he knew what had happened next in the dream could *not* happen—not in company, at any rate. His colour heightened a bit at the thought, and he attempted to counter it by thinking of Caroline whispering in his ear once again—a recollection which could cool even the most heated of blood.

By the time she was before him, Darcy had managed to avoid a most embarrassing predicament from arising once again, though her beautiful smile and sparkling eyes, combined with what she said next, began to stir his ardor once more. "May I speak with you alone, Mr. Darcy?"

OH! The same words she spoke in the dream! No, it could not be! His body betrayed him as he blushed deeply.

At his mortified expression, Elizabeth jumped to the wrong conclusion and struggled to keep her manner teasing while saying, "Mr. Darcy, I am not a dangerous female about to compromise your honour! I meant only to find a quiet corner as I have something of import to discuss with you and do not wish to be overheard or interrupted."

His blush only deepened at the thought of how inappropriate his imaginings had been. The embarrassment of Elizabeth actually guessing what he had interpreted as her meaning was overwhelming. *What must she think of me?*

Elizabeth was unsure of what to do next. She had thought her teasing would make him relax, as it had always seemed to do in the past, but this time it did not. He appeared to be even more uncomfortable than before—and now she felt herself begin to colour as well. She had been jesting, but perhaps… did he really think she would throw herself at him if they were left alone? Could his opinion of her be as dismal as that?

Now even more determined than ever to make her point, Elizabeth took a deep breath and decided to change tactics. Glancing to see if anyone was close enough to hear, she found no evidence of it, and then, with an arched brow and a slight smile to temper her next words, she spoke just above a whisper. "Well, then, perhaps we should speak here instead, since I am so likely to corrupt you?"

When she received no answer, the smile fell from her face, and before she lost her resolve, she began.

"Mr. Darcy, in all seriousness, I have been told there is at least one person in the neighbourhood that has expectations of… of *more* than what can ever exist between us. I assure you that this person is trusted by me to be discreet and would never spread this conjecture further than bringing it to my attention.

"I have since corrected this assumption, but as a result of its disclosure, it occurred to me that perhaps *you* might suspect that *I* have expectations similar in nature. To be candid, this is the only explanation I can surmise for your change in behaviour toward me.

"If this be the case, I feel I should take this opportunity to reassure you that I do *not* suffer from any such delusion, sir. The expectation of our acquaintance progressing past friendship does not exist in my mind. Please allow me to ask for your forgiveness if any of my actions or words have caused you to think otherwise. I *do* understand how the world works, Mr. Darcy.

"I value our friendship highly, sir, and have looked forward to continuing on in a friendly manner… but if that friendship makes you uncomfortable in any way, please know that I do not wish to become a source of distress to you, Mr. Darcy. I would much rather not be the cause of any further suffering, nor do I wish you to feel forced to maintain our acquaintance if it has become unpleasant to you.

"I ask you the favor of thinking upon this. I will allow your future behaviour to guide my own. Thank you for listening, sir. Good night." Elizabeth curtsied, turned and walked away before a shocked Darcy could recover enough to say anything, or even bow in reply.

Darcy had a sudden, urgent need for the solitude of the balcony. Blinking into the darkness, he tried to process what Elizabeth had just said. Feeling as if he had been punched in the gut several times, he could not breathe past the lump in his throat.

Had she rejected him? No! He had offered nothing to reject. She had made it clear she did not wish for, but did expect his rejection of her friendship, not the other way around.

She was asking for forgiveness? For heaven's sake, why? Should he ever find the need to blame her for being so perfect for him, he would forgive her readily.

Could he have heard her correctly? Did she say that she expected their friendship was causing him distress and suffering? The only distress or suffering he had experienced was in *denying* himself her company, certainly not from spending time with her!

Did she really think that he considered their acquaintance unpleasant? It had never been anything but pleasant… so pleasant that he never wanted to leave her side.

What a selfish being he was! Caught up in his own struggle between duty and the longings of his heart, he had never taken into account what *she* must be feeling, how *she* must be interpreting his odd behaviour. The dilemma he was facing did not stem from within her, it was due to his obligations—and yet she was blaming herself.

But she had rejected him in a way, had she not, by saying that she did not expect anything more than a friendship between them? Was this her way of telling him she could never love him?

No, that was not what she had said.

Did that mean that if he declared himself, she would accept him?

Darcy's mind was a whirlwind of pain, indecision, self-censure, and hope.

A movement nearby attracted his attention. The door to the next balcony opened, and a figure emerged, walking out to the garden. He was sure he would recognize that figure anywhere, under any conditions, day or night. It was *his Elizabeth.* He could tell by her quick movements that she was anxious and upset. Darcy closed his eyes momentarily as he censured himself. One of the last things he had ever wanted to do was to cause her any discomfort or pain.

I need to make a decision soon and act correctly upon it. The thought shocked him. Had he not already decided he would never be able to be with her, no matter his feelings?

He ached to go to her, pull her into his arms, and comfort her—to kiss the tears from her cheeks and replace all of her sorrow with a passion opposite in nature—but even a small portion of such behaviour would cause her confusion and distress.

If he could offer nothing else, at least he would make certain that she was safe walking through the gardens alone while she settled her emotions.

After walking away from Darcy, Elizabeth tried to go about the usual business of a social gathering, but found she could not. At the end of her soliloquy, she had realized Charlotte was correct, but not in the way her friend thought. It was true; Elizabeth had been trying to convince *herself* more than Charlotte when saying that Darcy and she could not be anything more than friends. Elizabeth had no doubt that he felt nothing but friendship for her and that all the things she had said to him were most likely true, and yet once she had given him the option of ending their friendship, she felt a great, aching loss at the prospect. It was then that she had recognized that she was in love with Darcy, but also that he could never return her affection.

Which would be better, or less painful, for her? To avoid him, to cast off his friendship? Or would she do better to encourage a friendship with the man she loved but could never have?

To be involved in his life in some way must be better than to be deprived of his company forever! But then she would have to bear witness when he married, as she was certain he would since an heir was required.

Would it be worse to see him marry out of convenience, as so many at his level of society did, or to watch him fall in love? If he married for love, would it be too painful for her to bear? Or would it be more painful to watch him enter into a marriage devoid of love, knowing that he would never find true happiness?

If they remained friends, would *she* ever be able to move on? But even if they spent the rest of their lives apart, would she ever fall in love with another?

Elizabeth had always maintained that she would marry only for the deepest love. Since she knew finding true love to be a rare event and very unlikely to occur to her, she had resigned herself to the idea of becoming an old maid, content with the prospect of being a good aunt to her sisters' children. Many times Elizabeth had said these words to Jane as if she was jesting, but the sentiment was deeply felt.

She brushed at a strange feeling on her face and became aware that she was crying. She reached into her pocket for her handkerchief and became angry at her weakness as she wiped away the tears. *I must accept the way things are! Tears are of no use, and I will waste no more energy on them. I have left the decision about our friendship up to Mr. Darcy and will accept whatever he decides.*

Hearing a burst of applause from inside as the gathered company showed their appreciation to Mary for her efforts on the pianoforte, Elizabeth knew she would have to return to the party. Elizabeth swiped at the last of her tears, took a few deep, calming breaths, and turned back to the house. Any further reflection on this subject would have to wait.

As she did, she noticed some movement in the shadows by the house. She knew it was *him*—she could feel his eyes upon her. She ignored his presence since he obviously did not want her to know he was there. Elizabeth wondered how long he had been observing her and if he had watched her in the garden. Somehow she knew it to be so.

If he did care about her, why had he not come to comfort her?

The last bit of hope that Charlotte had been correct about his feelings for her, which she just now became aware that she had been holding in her heart all this time, was cleared away by this thought. Elizabeth straightened her back, raised her chin, took another deep breath, and walked through the balcony door, hoping any evidence of her sorrow had been left behind.

Outside show is a poor substitute for inner worth
--Aesop (Greek author 620 BC – 560 BC)

Monday, November 11, 1811

~Netherfield Park

The day following the party at Lucas Lodge, an invitation arrived from Colonel Forster of the militia for the gentlemen of Netherfield to dine with his officers. The day of the event, Caroline realized that they would be quite bored without the gentlemen present, so the ladies discussed inviting Miss Jane Bennet to dinner as entertainment. To deter their brother's interest in the lady, Caroline conspired with her sister to pepper *dear* Jane with questions to further illuminate her want of connexions, and report their findings to the gentlemen upon their return.

"After all," Caroline stated, "everyone loves to talk about themselves!"

Thinking her plan a good one, Caroline wrote a note to Miss Bennet extending the invitation, and received a note accepting it.

As the gentlemen readied to depart for their engagement, Caroline and Louisa met them in the hall to see them off.

"What have you ladies planned for today?" A touch of fear entered Bingley's eyes, "I do hope you are not planning to redecorate the drawing room *again*!"

Ignoring her brother's remark and the clear evidence that Mr. Darcy was suppressing a smile, Caroline responded, "It will be lonely here with only the two of us; therefore, we have invited a guest to join us for dinner, Charles." She had purposely not told him earlier in the day for she was afraid he would not go out if he knew Jane Bennet was coming to Netherfield. She wanted to pry information from Jane about her family, *not* to spend another evening watching him moon over his latest obsession!

After all of her complaints, Darcy was curious about whom Caroline Bingley could possibly wish to invite to dine. "Who is to be your guest, Miss Bingley?"

"One would think that it is obvious, Mr. Darcy! There is only one lady in the neighbourhood that we would wish to get to know any better. It is Miss Jane Bennet, of course."

Bingley froze amidst donning his coat. By the look on Bingley's face, Darcy half expected him to cancel their engagement with Colonel Forster, even at such short notice as this. "Ja… Miss Bennet… coming here? To Netherfield? To dine?" In his tone, the words "without me?" could almost be heard.

"As I said, Charles," Caroline replied with a sly smile.

Bingley blinked a few times before he returned to the task of dressing suitably for the rain that was expected. Assuming his sisters were interested in getting to know his lady love without the distraction of the gentlemen, a smile spread across his features. "What a wonderful idea!"

Just then, the carriage was heard and the gentlemen took their leave, Bingley displaying a grin from ear to ear, Darcy suspicious of what Caroline was up to, and Mr. Hurst anticipating the food, drink, and talk of sport and war to be had with the officers of the regiment.

About three quarters of an hour later, after it had begun to rain heavily, the ladies of Netherfield began to expect to receive a note from Longbourn putting off their little party for another day. Therefore, they were not surprised a few minutes later when the doorbell rang. What caused them to become a bit curious was when they heard a few dainty sneezes coming from the direction of the hall.

Their surprise *was* great, however, when a dripping, sneezing, shivering, and obviously mortified Jane Bennet was announced. The ladies of Netherfield stood, mouths agape in shock momentarily before their good breeding took over. Dear Jane was ushered upstairs to a guest room to be fussed over. A blazing fire was ordered and Louisa, closer to Jane's size than Caroline, lent her some clothing until hers could be cleaned and dried. To Jane's face, her hostesses' manners displayed nothing but polite concern, but whenever Jane's back was turned, Caroline's countenance showed her utter exasperation with the entire situation.

While Louisa's maid toweled and brushed Jane's hair, Caroline asked with a voice oozing with affection, "Now that you are more comfortable,

I must satisfy my curiosity, poor, dear Jane. How did you come to be out in the rain?"

Blushing, Jane said, "I received your invitation to dine. Was I in error as to which day I was to come?"

"The invitation *was* for today, but when the skies darkened, we were no longer expecting you to come—and especially not on horseback! Did your father not allow you to use his carriage?"

"My mother said the carriage horses were needed on the farm today, and so I came on Nellie." Jane's colour deepened, and she kept her eyes on the rug and thought of what else her mother had said—that the rain would make it necessary for Jane to stay overnight, and, consequently, she would see Bingley. "It was not raining when I left Longbourn. When the sky darkened, I did think I could make the trip before the rain began. By the time it started to rain, I was closer to Netherfield than to Longbourn." Jane was thoughtful for a moment before continuing, "I apologize, Miss Bingley; I had not thought of the inconvenience it would cause upon my arrival. I should have turned back."

"Dear Jane! There is no need to apologize, for it is perfectly understandable! Many small estates cannot afford to keep horses for the carriage and others for the farm. Why was Nellie not on the farm as well?" When Jane was not looking, Caroline shot Louisa an amused look.

"Nellie is now too old to be of use on the farm, Miss Bingley."

Nodding, Caroline stated, "Now that you are in a dry gown, you should have a hot cup of tea before dinner. Let us remove to the drawing room."

Jane was soon seated near the fire in the drawing room with a blanket over her lap, another around her shoulders, and hot tea in her cup. Caroline had just begun to ask about Mrs. Bennet's family in order to expose her connexions when dear Jane suddenly became weak and fainted. A servant was sent for salts, and Jane was roused, but Louisa became more concerned when she discovered that Jane was quite feverish. After a servant carried her to a guest room, they sent for the apothecary.

After all the "good hostess" orders were made for the staff to care for their unexpected guest, the Netherfield ladies returned to the drawing room, for neither of them had the nerves for the sick room. Caroline instantly began to criticize the Bennets for inconveniencing her by sending Jane in the rain and then moved on to ridiculing them for not having the funds to keep two sets of horses. She did not notice that Louisa was no longer agreeing with her and was now looking upon her sister with disgust.

After Caroline could think of nothing more to say about the Bennets, the ladies were left with their time completely unengaged. When Caroline's whining about being bored became too much for Louisa to listen to any longer, she suggested they take turns playing the pianoforte.

~%~

The chime from the hall clock echoed through the halls.

"Mrs. Robinson..." Netherfield's butler approached the housekeeper. "It is almost time for the master and his friends to arrive home." He hesitated. "Do you know Miss Bennet?"

"Yes, Mr. Brown, I've lived here all my life. I've known the Bennet girls nearly since they were born. I also stood in for Longbourn's housekeeper for three months last year when Mrs. Hill's mother was ill."

"Since I am from London and have only just seen Miss Bennet as she entered the house today, being familiar with the lady, perhaps it would be better for *you* to explain the day's happenings to the master when he returns?"

Mrs. Robinson nodded. "I agree."

"Mrs. Robinson... just between us two... I would like to inquire about your orders to the staff regarding Miss Bennet."

Mrs. Robinson smiled. "I know the servants originally from Town are surprised at our reaction to Miss Bennet's illness, but Miss Bennet and her sister Miss Elizabeth are favourites of all the working families near Meryton. These two treat everyone right, no matter their station. Any family in need can depend upon their charitable natures. All the children love 'em, and all their parents are grateful for 'em." She hesitated. "You've been hearing stories told below stairs?"

At Mr. Brown's nod, she continued, "There are quite a few tales about their goodness, but my personal favourites are accounts of Miss Lizzy's capers when she was a lass." She laughed softly. "The girls are different from each other, but both are kind. Miss Bennet, considerate as she is, has even *apologized* to the maids that are tending to her, afraid that she's interrupting their work! Can you imagine?" Her smile widened. "Better get used to it, Mr. Brown. If there's something we can do to make Miss Bennet a little more comfortable, we will."

Mr. Brown turned up his nose. "Why would Miss Bennet ride here in the rain?"

Mrs. Robinson frowned at the implication, though being familiar with Mrs. Bennet's "quirks," she could see Mr. Brown's point even more clearly than he did. Being an intelligent woman, Mrs. Robinson had her suspicions that Miss Bennet was more than likely sent on horseback on purpose by her mother with the specific hope that it would rain.

She also knew that Miss Bennet's personality differed drastically from her mother's. The good daughter she was, she would never think of disobeying a parent's orders.

Her loyalty was to her master, whom she liked very much, but Mrs. Robinson would not dare betray Miss Bennet by exposing Mrs. Bennet's probable motivations for what had occurred this day. She decided that while she would not lie to the master, she would not tell all of what she knew to be probable.

"I'm sure Miss Bennet had her reasons." The housekeeper raised her chin. "Don't you worry, Mr. Brown. Depend upon it—Miss Bennet is a true lady in every sense of the word!"

~%~

Upon the master's entering the house, Mrs. Robinson voiced a brief account of the unusual circumstances which occurred while the gentlemen had been dining out.

Mr. Bingley insisted on being repeatedly assured that Miss Bennet had nothing more than a trifling cold and was being well cared for.

A little more than two hours later, Mrs. Robinson smiled to herself when Mr. Bingley asked, for the tenth time, how Miss Bennet fared. She finally confided in him that the staff was quite fond of Miss Jane Bennet, and he could be confident that they would show her every attention possible. This seemed to calm him a little; Mr. Bingley now made inquiries on the hour instead of every quarter.

Tuesday, November 12, 1811

~Longbourn Estate

The next morning, a note arrived from Jane saying she was "very unwell," and that Mr. Jones the apothecary had been called in to see her. This worried Elizabeth a great deal since she knew that Jane usually minimized her own symptoms of illness, and she could not be comfortable without seeing Jane as soon as could be arranged. As the carriage was not to be had, she declared her intention to walk to Netherfield. After some discussion, she was on her way, accompanying her two youngest sisters on their walk to Meryton.

After parting with Kitty and Lydia at the village, Elizabeth continued on to Netherfield alone, deep in thought. She almost feared seeing Darcy for the first time since her speech. How would he react to her presence there? Had he decided to continue as friends, or would he rather not count her among his acquaintance at all?

As she neared her destination, Elizabeth examined the state of her clothing.

"You will not be fit to be seen after walking three miles, considering all that rain yesterday!" her mother had argued before she had left home, hoping to convince Elizabeth not to make the journey to Netherfield. Mrs. Bennet could not have been more correct!

With her mother's words in mind, Elizabeth went around to the service entrance so that she would not embarrass Jane by being presented in such a state. After being greeted by many among the staff, a young maid by the name of Maggie showed Elizabeth to Jane's chamber while Mrs. Robinson notified Mr. Bingley of his guest's arrival.

The ladies of Netherfield visited the invalid and her sister soon after breaking their fast. Later in the day, Caroline pointedly stated to the gentlemen, "Eliza Bennet *walked* three miles to see a sister who has only a trifling cold! Her skirts were at least six inches deep in mud! She looked positively wild. Did she not, Louisa?"

Louisa nodded.

Bingley could not understand why his sisters were so put out. "It is obvious to me that Miss Elizabeth knew she was not fit to be seen since she did not ask to be announced. You have just told me that when asked to join us at luncheon, she declined, requesting a tray be sent up so that she could help Miss Bennet take some nourishment. In my opinion, this proves she had no more in mind with her visit than a pleasing affection and concern for the wellbeing of her sister."

Caroline glowered at her brother, and then turned to their guest. "Surely *you* do not share my brother's opinion, Mr. Darcy?"

Darcy replied, "Her behaviour displays a willingness to inconvenience herself for the comfort of others."

Caroline's eyes narrowed. "I cannot understand your forgiveness of the spectacle Miss Eliza has made of herself today! Would you like to see your sister, dearest Georgiana, expose herself in such a way, Mr. Darcy?"

Darcy hesitated, knowing his answer might anger Caroline, but he decided to reply fully regardless of her expected reaction. "Would I enjoy learning that my sister had walked three miles alone, ending her trek with her skirts six inches deep in mud? No. But I am convinced that Georgiana would suffer through almost anything if she suspected that my health was in any danger, and I would do the same for her sake without hesitation."

Caroline's eyes flashed with vexation and Louisa could see that her sister was seriously displeased with the turn of the conversation. Louisa knew what would be coming next and before Caroline could respond with something that could only insult everyone in the room, she placed her hand on her sister's arm to stop her. "Caroline, did you not say that you wished to ascertain whether your guests have any further needs?"

Caroline turned her head quickly towards her sister, giving her a sharp look. After seeing the warning in Louisa's eyes, she huffed, and nodded. With a quick curtsy, she left the room, Louisa following closely behind her.

Upon their arrival above stairs, the ladies found that Elizabeth was taking leave of her sister.

Noticing that Jane's fever was rising and seeing how unsettled she was at the thought of Elizabeth's leaving, Louisa asked, "Caroline, may I speak with you for a moment, please?" and led her into the hall. Once the door was closed, Louisa continued, "After seeing Jane's distress… might it be better for Jane if Miss Elizabeth stayed, Caroline?"

Caroline's eyes opened wide, "I am shocked that you would even suggest I have *Eliza Bennet* stay under *my* roof!"

Louisa felt having her sister with her was important for Jane's welfare and decided it was worth inciting Caroline's ire—but she wished to keep it to a minimum. Remembering a phrase that an acquaintance had once used when speaking of Darcy's mother, and how Caroline had decided that she would need to be generally spoken of in a similar manner in order to win her prize, Louisa said, "Dearest sister, that your skills as a hostess are *fine* is often mentioned amongst our acquaintance… but is it not the mark of a *superior* hostess to put aside her own discomfort for the benefits of her guests—especially one who has fallen ill?"

Caroline paused, and Louisa could see by her expression that her inner battle was intense. Eventually, the wish to be thought of as a *superior* hostess won out, though Louisa doubted that Caroline would have acted in a similar manner if she had not been bent on impressing Darcy with her worthiness to become his wife. The ladies returned to Jane's bedchamber, and Elizabeth was invited to stay for the remainder of *dear Jane's* illness.

Elizabeth was even less comfortable about the idea of her staying at Netherfield than was her hostess, but after seeing the relief on Jane's face at the request, she agreed. Her clothing was sent for and arrived just in time for her to change for dinner.

The smaller the mind the greater the conceit.
--Aesop (Greek author 620 BC – 560 BC)

~ Netherfield Park

Caroline Bingley was vexed.

Hearing loud grunts emanating from a small chamber that the mistress used to write her letters was of no concern to those under her employ; it served only as an alert that a great amount of work would be required soon in order to recover any degree of order in the room. They were all aware that the mistress was usually upset about something, and that it was best to avoid her during these times lest the staff suffer harm from the bric-a-brac that did not survive her frustration.

At this moment and despite her frequent irritation over this particular topic, Caroline was displeased about the evening's seating arrangement for dinner—precisely *where* would be the best place for *Eliza Bennet* at dinner in relation to Darcy? That was an extremely difficult, and potentially life-altering, decision to make.

She always thought of her as "Eliza," mostly due to the satisfaction of picturing her initial visible reaction betraying her feelings concerning being addressed in that manner. Elizabeth obviously despised the name, and consequently, Caroline used it as often as possible, though Elizabeth's reaction was now better concealed.

Thinking on this subject was satisfying in its own way, but offered no solution to her current predicament: with six at dinner, there were only two places to seat the chit.

The first was to place Elizabeth across the table from Darcy, but then he would stare at her in that disgusting manner he had become so fond of. Seeing that look on his face—directed not at herself, but at a low-born rival—made her nauseated, and she would not abide it! Especially not at her own table!

Caroline did not envy Elizabeth the way Darcy looked at her. Louisa had explained to her to what end those looks could lead, and based on Louisa's reaction to her time spent alone with her husband, it must be horribly degrading. She realized that if she could make Darcy look at *herself* that way, it would give her a certain power over him which would be helpful in achieving her goal—but once they were married she would make absolutely certain those looks did not continue past bearing an heir! *And* she would be sure to bear the heir as soon as possible!

In order for that to happen at all, she had to keep the gentleman from looking at Elizabeth that way now*!*

If she sat Elizabeth next to Darcy, they could speak easily to each other, and Caroline would be ignored for most of the meal. She could not move Louisa, as she was needed to help direct his attention toward Caroline.

But this created another vexation in the seating arrangement as husbands and wives did *not* sit *next* to one another when dining in the first circles… not that Elizabeth would notice the breach—but certainly Darcy would!

"Oh! What complex problems I must solve!" Caroline whined aloud. She grabbed the nearest breakable object and threw it at the hearth, watching it scatter into hundreds of pieces with a feeling of release. It was a shame that it had been the bric-a-brac that Louisa had made such a fuss over giving her.

Louisa should know better! Bric-a-brac has such an unfortunate history of accidents in our household. She smirked.

Weighing the options for several minutes, Caroline decided that forcing her way into a conversation was preferable to watching Darcy moon for an extended length of time, and so she would seat Elizabeth next to him for the remainder of the Bennets' stay. Louisa would be only too happy to assist, as she always was in any of Caroline's schemes.

Louisa lives to be of service to me!

She stood looking out the window, fantasizing about the conversations she would have with her future husband… and planning how to exclude the intruder from joining in.

What a relief Caroline felt as she ran her fingers over the beautifully designed place cards, written in her own elegant hand, on the finest paper available in this backward part of the country, and made her way to the dining room. With a genuine smile, she imagined what fun it would be to address even finer place cards and invitations with the names of dukes, earls, viscounts, and barons once she was married! She would brook no opposition to her dreams—she *would* become Mrs. Caroline Darcy, mistress of Pemberley of Derbyshire and Darcy House of London!

After all the cards were perfectly placed on the table, Caroline realized that she was tired from the immense mental exertion of the past hour and decided to rest before dressing for dinner. What beautiful gowns she would wear once she was Mrs. Darcy! Only the finest silk, satin, and lace would do for one of her anticipated station in society.

In the hallway, Caroline admonished a maid, Sarah, on how the staff must cease placing bric-a-brac too close to the edge of the mantle since even the slightest draft in her study caused them to fall and shatter. She informed Sarah that she would begin deducting pay from all of the servants to compensate for the cost of the broken pieces if the oversight continued.

Sarah took the reprimand with grace, an apology, and a low curtsy as she always did, and was off to clean the mistress's study, knowing very well that all who worked at Netherfield would prefer no decorative items be in that room at all, but the mistress insisted on their presence.

Caroline congratulated herself on her wonderful idea. Now she could replace any damaged bric-a-brac from the funds set aside to pay the servants and save her pin money for more important things.

The thrill of being in control of this house and those who served in it was truly lovely indeed. She could not wait until she was in control of such a grand estate as Pemberley and its multitude of servants—and a much higher monthly allowance!

~*~*~*~*~*~*~*~*~*~*~*~

Elizabeth was truly in a bind. For the sake of civility, she knew she must join the rest of the party for dinner, but she did not want to seem as if she were throwing herself in Darcy's way either. He probably already thought poorly of her for coming to Netherfield at all, let alone agreeing to stay overnight. She told herself she would avoid conversing with him, or even looking at him, unless he addressed her first. This would be a test to see what Darcy's decision about their last conversation had been.

Would he talk to her? Did he wish to continue their friendship? Would he ignore her presence aside from civilities? Elizabeth was nervous as she descended the stairs to the dining parlor.

She was seated to the left of Mr. Bingley, across from Mr. Hurst, and surprisingly, next to Darcy, who was on Miss Bingley's right. Mrs. Hurst sat to the left of Miss Bingley, across from Darcy.

It was a strange seating arrangement; Elizabeth had expected Miss Bingley to seat her as far from Darcy as possible, but during the meal Elizabeth could see why it was set up this way. Mrs. Hurst and Miss Bingley talked almost constantly to Darcy, keeping him from looking in her direction long enough to say anything to her at all. It seemed to be by design, and it was quite amusing. While one ate, the other kept Darcy busy with insipid conversation, and then they switched roles. Mr. Bingley was never at a loss for making amiable conversation, and he kept Elizabeth engaged, though she was certain he was not aware of the ladies' plan. Mr. Hurst simply ate and drank, both in large quantities.

She was watching Darcy out of the corner of her eye. The poor gentleman had a difficult time consuming any of his dinner while attempting to remain polite. At the beginning of the meal, Elizabeth could tell he saw through the sisters' plan as well. He shot her a few amused glances, which made her heart lurch at the same time as it caused her almost to begin laughing out loud. If she saw a bit of an apology or longing in his eye, she felt safer to dismiss it as wishful thinking. These exchanged glances with Elizabeth increased the sisters' demands for conversation with him. After a while, Elizabeth could tell by the way his muscles of his jaw were tensing that he was becoming extremely annoyed. She struggled to think of something to do to calm him.

While Miss Bingley took a breath, Elizabeth quickly turned her head toward Darcy and said with a teasing sparkle in her eye, "Mr. Darcy, are you not enjoying the partridge? You have not touched your plate, sir. Perhaps Miss Bingley's fine cook could prepare you something more to your liking?"

Darcy opened his mouth to answer. When Mr. Bingley broke in, he closed his eyes briefly in frustration. "I happen to know Darcy greatly enjoys partridge, Miss Elizabeth. It is not *dislike* that is preventing my friend from partaking; it is Darcy's good breeding! Louisa, Caroline! Please allow him to eat his meal, and give the rest of us a chance to enjoy Darcy's conversation. I have been waiting for an opportunity to say something to him through almost two courses!" Bingley went on into a long discourse about the hunting they had enjoyed earlier that day.

Elizabeth hid her smile behind her napkin when she saw hunger take precedence over conversation and propriety as Darcy began to eat without regard for anyone's speeches. She could see the corners of his mouth turn up slightly as he noticed her action.

When Bingley finished his speech, Darcy spoke up, purposely including Elizabeth. "Miss Elizabeth, when you have been in London, have you been to the theatre or the opera?" he turned to her with a mischievous gleam in his eye, which filled her with curiosity. She knew as well as he did that they had discussed this previously, and she could not help but think, *What is he up to?*

Alas, Elizabeth would not find out.

Caroline's plan was that if Elizabeth broke into the conversation, they would begin to ask her about her relations. The sisters felt that to hear how unsuitable her family was from Elizabeth's own lips would condemn both Bennet ladies irreparably in the eyes of the gentlemen.

Louisa interrupted, "Miss Elizabeth, you have been to London? Where did you stay?"

"My aunt and uncle live in London, Mrs. Hurst. I have been invited to visit with them quite often through the years."

"And where in London do your *relatives* live, Miss Eliza?" Caroline asked.

"My mother's brother and his family live on Gracechurch Street, Miss Bingley."

"That is in Cheapside, is it not?"

"It is near Cheapside, Miss Bingley. My uncle's warehouse is located nearby, and therefore it is convenient for him."

"Oh… is your uncle in trade then?" Louisa feigned a surprised look that would not fool a child of five.

Elizabeth used her napkin again to hide her smile before answering, "That is correct, Mrs. Hurst. My uncle owns an import/export business as well as a bookshop."

Darcy looked as if he was about to ask something when Caroline interrupted again, "Miss Eliza, does your mother have any other siblings?"

"You may have met my mother's sister, Mrs. Philips, as she resides in Meryton with her husband. Mr. Philips is an attorney, Miss Bingley."

Louisa went on with the show, "Hmmm. And your father? Does he have any siblings?"

"No, Mrs. Hurst, none living."

Dinner was over and Elizabeth was tired of being peppered with questions about her faulty connexions. She knew exactly what the sisters were up to. They were trying to show Darcy just where in society Elizabeth was placed in relation to his own standing. Did they not think her intelligent enough to understand how society worked and that she could not possibly have expectations of him past friendship? Elizabeth excused herself to check on her sister.

~Darcy House, London

The honourable Colonel Richard Fitzwilliam was stationed in London, for the moment, with the Dragoons Light Calvary. Though only the *second* son of the Earl of Matlock, his good looks, amiable manners, and witty humour made him popular with the ladies. He was not considered an eligible marriage prospect, which suited Richard quite well, but he certainly knew how to entertain. He was a tall man, almost as tall as his cousin Darcy, with black hair and deep blue eyes—a trademark of the Fitzwilliam family—which usually danced with mirth.

Richard often stayed at Darcy House when he came to Town so that he could spend some time with Georgie and Darce, as Richard called them. If an ulterior motive for staying with the Darcys was a wish to be out from under the ever watchful and critical eyes of his parents, his cousins did not mind. Staying at Darcy House provided all the luxuries of "home," without his parents' constant examination of his actions.

Richard was currently enjoying the company of his beloved cousin Georgiana. A tall, slim girl of sixteen, she had a classic beauty in the features of her face and a fine figure. Being shy had not dimmed her responsiveness to those closest to her, as Richard was. Her Fitzwilliam-blue eyes shone with intelligence and affection.

Georgiana and Richard were just finishing breaking their fast when a letter from Darcy arrived from Hertfordshire. As he was interested in how his cousin was faring, Georgiana read him the letter. Georgiana was quite amused, and Richard found it interesting, to hear so many references to Miss Elizabeth Bennet coming from a man who rarely looked at a woman but to find a blemish. It became intriguing, in fact, when Georgiana went on to tell him about how Miss Bennet was mentioned, and quite highly praised, in *all* his prior letters from Netherfield as well. After noticing Richard's interest, Georgiana hurried up to her room to retrieve all of the letters from her letter box and returned to read the relevant parts to Richard.

Richard was unsure about what to think. Having Darcy write *anything* positive about a lady was a novelty, but to have him write *to his sister* of a lady he had met possessing so many favorable qualities was—alarming! Could any lady possibly be as wonderful as his cousin implied this one was? Since Darcy had little experience with women he did not find repulsive, would he confuse a strong attraction or a passing infatuation with love?

Being wary of the woman's intentions, he wanted to meet the one who had inspired this change in his cousin. Though Richard was not a target for mercenary ladies, he had seen enough of "the chase" through watching the tactics of these young ladies with which his elder brother, the future Earl of Matlock, Darcy, and their wealthy friends had to deal on a daily basis. Richard did not believe Darcy would fall for any of their duplicity after his years of experience in dodging such schemes, but one never knew. The more he thought about it, the more anxious he became to meet Miss Elizabeth Bennet personally and determine whether Darcy was being taken in… before it was too late!

~Netherfield Park

When dinner was done, Elizabeth returned to Jane's chamber to check on her. Finding her sleeping peacefully, she dawdled for a while. Though she did not wish to return to the party below, she knew civility required her to make a short appearance in the drawing room.

The group was involved in a game of loo when she arrived, allowing her the blessed option of reading a book as opposed to participating in any conversation with the other ladies.

Caroline was intent on complimenting Darcy, as usual. She spoke of the wonders of Pemberley and of its unparalleled library. She then moved on to voluminous praise of Miss Darcy and her many accomplishments. Bingley remarked on how all young ladies were so accomplished.

"*All* young ladies accomplished! My dear Charles, whatever do you mean?" Caroline asked with surprise.

"Yes, I am sure I never heard a young lady spoken of for the first time without being informed that she was very accomplished."

"Your statement has too much truth. The word is applied to many a woman who deserves it not. I cannot boast of knowing more than half a dozen in the whole range of my acquaintance that are really accomplished," Darcy stated.

"Nor I, I am sure," said Caroline, confident in the fact that *she,* at least, numbered among the privileged six.

"You must comprehend a great deal in your idea of an accomplished woman," observed Elizabeth.

Darcy started a bit when he heard *her* voice. "Yes, I do comprehend a great deal in it." His heart quickened in anticipation of the verbal duel he hoped lay ahead. He endeavored to hide his disappointment when he heard Caroline's voice next, listing all which she would include when assessing a lady's level of accomplishment.

Darcy thought of the particular importance of *liveliness* and *integrity,* which had been left off of Caroline's list, but knew he could not voice this opinion. He simply added, "And to all this she must yet add something more substantial, in the improvement of her mind by extensive reading," with a nod to Elizabeth's book.

Elizabeth noticed the slight twitch at the corners of his lips, and she felt the release of the tension that had built between them. A sparkle entered her eye as she said, "I am no longer surprised at your knowing only six accomplished women. I rather wonder now at your knowing *any.*"

Darcy's heart warmed at seeing her expression change, but wondered, *Does she not recognize herself? No, she is too modest.* Aloud he said, "Are you so severe upon your own sex as to doubt the possibility of all this?"

"*I* never saw such a woman. *I* never saw such capacity, taste, application, and elegance, as has been described, united," Elizabeth said.

Yes, modesty must be added to the list, my Elizabeth, and genuineness, Darcy thought with a slight smile directed at her. *You are the model of perfection in my eyes and in my heart.*

Caroline and Louisa both cried out against the injustice of her implied doubt and were protesting that they knew *many* women who answered this description when Mr. Hurst called them to order, with bitter complaints of their inattention to what was going forward in their game. All conversation ceased.

Elizabeth went to check on her sister and found her unwell enough to necessitate her immediate return above stairs. Upon returning to tell the others of Jane's condition, and that she would need to stay with her sister, Bingley offered to call Mr. Jones immediately, but Elizabeth did not think her sister's condition warranted the apothecary, agreeing to call him in the morning if Jane was not any better.

They all bid her good night, and improved health to her sister. Elizabeth noticed something not easily identified, but pleasing, in Darcy's eyes as he said his *adieus*. With a little smile directed at Darcy, Elizabeth left and returned to Jane.

~%~

Jane was uncomfortable for the first part of the night, and Elizabeth spent the time applying damp cloths to Jane's forehead, wiping down her arms and face to help cool her fever… and thinking of Darcy.

It was nice to have a return of some of the friendliness they had experienced at the beginning of their acquaintance. She had missed his conversation terribly since their last talk at Lucas Lodge. Would they ever return to the previous level of ease, or would it be only short bursts interspersed with almost unbearable tension like tonight? What was the meaning of that look in his eyes as she said goodnight?

Oh, stop it Lizzy! There is no use in worrying about it. The future will tell itself. I cannot spend my time thinking on this subject any longer. I will put him out of my mind unless I am in his presence! And yet, images of Darcy crept back into her thoughts every time she pushed them away.

Jane's fever lessened about halfway through the night, and she fell into a more peaceful sleep. Elizabeth did not want to leave her sister, so she undressed and climbed into bed with Jane, wearing only her chemise.

Elizabeth's presence in the same house was overwhelming to Darcy. Much like before, any time she was in the same room, he would immediately forget his plan of distancing himself from his feelings for her. Her radiant smile caused his heart to skip a beat. When she turned her head just so, a particular curve to her neck set off a reaction within him that made it absolutely essential for him to prevent himself from rushing across the room, for he would surely begin to caress her porcelain skin to ascertain whether it was as silky as it was in his dreams. A distinct twinkle in her eye—often displayed just prior to her making an impertinent remark—made his breath catch in his chest. When she arched her brow in just the right way, it triggered his heart to quicken. The trace of scent that would trail behind her as she passed by always left his senses reeling. The musical quality of her laughter sent a pleasant shiver down his spine. He was relieved that the other ladies had not asked her to play and sing for he would surely have been lost! Darcy had to hold himself in strict control at all times because the impulse to act on his feelings was gaining strength with every minute she was near.

There was no doubt that Caroline Bingley had noticed his attraction for Elizabeth since her barbs directed toward the lovely lady were obviously intensifying. Whenever she was not present, Caroline's criticisms of Elizabeth were bordering on brutal. He wanted to put an end forcefully to Caroline's incessant chattering, but it was not his place, so he held his tongue, seething internally. Bingley seemed too distracted thinking about Jane's having fallen ill to notice most of what was going on around him.

When Elizabeth was not present, the best Darcy could do to gain control over his temper was to leave any room in which Caroline resided. While literally hiding from Caroline, he tended to gravitate toward places where he had spent time with Elizabeth, or at least spent time pleasantly observing her from afar. In doing so, he felt great relief in being somehow closer to the essence of *her*, and he often found his thoughts wandering to what she might be doing just then. Darcy recognized this was not the wisest thing to do, but he was unable to stop himself.

Wednesday, November 13, 1811

As was his habit since her ailment had begun, Bingley often sent a maid to bring him word of Jane's condition. For the past two nights before retiring, he had left orders for a maid to check on Jane's progress first thing in the morning and notify his valet so he would be informed of her current state immediately upon waking.

Therefore, Maggie's first duty this day would be to check on Jane. When entering the room, Maggie smiled tenderly at the picture of Elizabeth snuggled up near her sister, knowing how close they were. She hesitated to disturb either of the ladies, especially since she knew Elizabeth had gained little rest since arriving, but then noticed several items that needed her attention. She moved around the room as quietly as possible, tidied up a bit, and refreshed the water in the pitcher and basin. Maggie felt Jane's forehead and smiled again when she detected that her fever was lower. As she was turning to leave, Elizabeth's book slid from the bed.

Elizabeth awoke to the sound of the book hitting the wooden floor and was a little confused about where she was. Upon seeing Jane, she remembered that she was at Netherfield. The gentle light of daybreak came through the window, and she noticed Maggie standing near the doorway with some dirty linens.

"Miss Lizzy! I'm sorry, ma'am! I didn't mean to wake you!" Maggie apologized quietly while bobbing a curtsy.

"Good morning, Maggie! I did sleep for a few hours, thank you," whispered Elizabeth. She checked Jane's temperature and was satisfied to find her cooler than the night before. "Maggie, would your duties permit you to stay with Miss Bennet for a little while this morning? Since my sister seems to be a little better, I would like to freshen up and take a short walk. I will not venture far from the house in case I am needed." Fresh air always helped clear her mind and Elizabeth felt in desperate need of it.

Maggie blushed a bit when she told Elizabeth she had to report back to Bingley's valet about Jane's condition first, and then she would return directly. Elizabeth smiled at the reference to Bingley's concern over Jane's health.

She dressed hurriedly in Jane's robe, gathered up the clothes from the previous night and did not bother to put her hair up… after all why go through all that trouble just to walk one door down? Jane being taller than she, the robe was too long, but to avoid tripping, she held it up. What were the chances of meeting anyone in the hall at *this* time of the morning?

Elizabeth slipped from the room, quickly entering her own bedchamber door. She did not realize Darcy had just been leaving his room nearby.

As had been Darcy's routine since coming to Netherfield, he awoke early for a ride. He enjoyed watching the day begin as he cleared his head of the previous night's dreams with a gallop around the grounds of the park. His valet, Hughes, had helped him to dress quickly. Ordering his bath for an hour hence, he left the room.

Darcy halted when he heard the door to Jane's chamber open and saw Elizabeth exit, her hair down and her attire consisting of what seemed to be only a thin robe that left the shapely lower part of her legs exposed.

He had imagined and dreamt of her with her hair down and in similar—though more elegant—attire numerous times, but all of that was nothing compared to the reality before him. She was an absolute vision with her dark curls tumbling around her shoulders and down her back, the early morning light filtering through the windows in the hall picking up auburn highlights, and each lock moving in an orchestrated harmony as her bare feet padded across the floor. The thin robe she was wearing did little to conceal the soft curves beneath.

If the sight before him were ever caught by an artist, it would be praised as a masterpiece and admired throughout eternity.

As Elizabeth withdrew through the door to her own chamber, he exhaled the breath which had caught in his throat when she had appeared. The impulse to follow her through that door was so intense he could hardly stop himself. He had taken two or three steps in that direction before realizing what he was about, and he froze in the middle of the hallway.

What would she think of him if he marched into her bedchamber? She would despise him forever! He could not—*would not*—do this!

Taking stock of his physical state, he knew he was not fit to be seen in public, and forced himself to turn back to his own room. The pulling sensation he usually felt when Elizabeth was near had been magnified at the moment, attempting to draw him back out that door and down the hall. He quickly crossed the room back to his door and locked it… to delay himself long enough to *think* should this impulse overtake his reason. He needed to keep busy, so he decided to take a bath. Darcy stepped into his dressing room, beginning to pace when he realized that Hughes had gone.

Hughes returned a few minutes later. Surprised to find his master had returned so quickly, at first he thought Darcy had forgotten something… but upon seeing the master's agitated state, he did not know *what* to think.

"Hughes, I have decided to forego the ride and take a bath *now*."

"Mr. Darcy, I apologize. I have only now returned from the kitchen where I had ordered the water for your bath for *later*, as you had requested, sir. I diverted the hot water that is available now to Miss Elizabeth Bennet's maid instead. The staff has orders from Miss Bingley to heed your requests before hers, sir. I can have the water redirected to your bath if you prefer." Hughes knew it was a mistake to mention that Miss Elizabeth was preparing to bathe when he noticed the expression on his master's face. *Ah, so* ***she*** *is the reason for his erratic behaviour of late!*

Darcy's back stiffened. *God help me! Why did he have to tell me that Elizabeth is taking a bath right now?* The images this information conjured up in his mind were far too much for him to handle without losing what little composure he had regained during his pacing. Resorting to something that had worked for him in the past he thought, *He said Miss Bingley is taking a bath, Miss Bingley!*

"I do not wish for hot water, Hughes, get me a *cold* bath… now… GO!" he boomed as the intensity of his pacing increased. *If only I was at Pemberley, I would jump in the lake!*

Hughes left the room wondering how the kitchen staff would react when he requested a cold bath for Mr. Darcy.

~Netherfield Park

When she returned from her walk, Elizabeth met her mother and sisters, as well as Mr. Jones, in the entrance hall of the manor house. It was obvious to Elizabeth that the apothecary was not happy when the matron decided that the entire gaggle of Bennet ladies would attend the examination.

Jane was taking a final sip of broth as the party arrived at her door. Pleased to find that Jane's fever had lessened, Mr. Jones announced that, while he did not feel she was in any danger, she was still too ill to be moved. Since the tension at Netherfield was almost unbearably high, it was disheartening to Elizabeth that they could not return home, but she would do what was beneficial for Jane; therefore, she did her best to conceal her disappointment.

Mrs. Bennet did nothing to hide the delight she experienced at hearing that Jane must remain at Bingley's house. Jane and Elizabeth blushed that their mother would speak of such a subject in front of the apothecary, but since Mr. Jones understood the personalities of the family quite well after taking care of them for so many years, he wisely acted as if he did not hear. The Bennet ladies visited for a while, and then left Jane to rest while they waited on the ladies of the house.

As they were shown into the morning room, Elizabeth found it amusing to see Mr. Hurst slip out the door without taking his leave of anybody.

Bingley greeted his guests. "I do hope you have not found Miss Bennet worse than you expected, Mrs. Bennet."

"Indeed I have, sir. She is a great deal too ill to be moved. We must trespass a little longer on your kindness."

Obviously unsettled, Bingley replied, "I am certain that my sister would not allow Miss Bennet's removal until she is *fully* recovered."

"You may depend upon it, Madam," said Caroline with cold civility.

Mrs. Bennet was profuse in her thanks for their hospitality for Jane's sake and then went on to enumerate Jane's good qualities, saying, "I often tell my other girls they are nothing to her! Why, just two years past, Mr. Smythe, who was leasing Netherfield at the time—a kind gentleman of four thousand a year—said that she was the most beautiful lady he had ever seen. He even wrote some verses on her, and very pretty they were."

There was an awkward pause while Elizabeth blushed furiously. That her mother would say such things in company was beyond even *her* ability to forgive. She tried to think of something to say, but was speechless. As she replayed the visit in her mind later in the day, it would be difficult for Elizabeth to judge which of her mother and younger sisters' pronouncements was the most inappropriate.

Elizabeth's eyes opened wide as her mother began to speak again, afraid of what she might say next.

"I must apologize for saddling you with Lizzy as well. You are too good! I do hope Lizzy is not giving you any trouble by carrying on in a wild manner as she does at home!"

Lydia and Kitty both giggled loudly at her statement, and Caroline smiled at this direct insult to Elizabeth from her own mother.

Elizabeth's blush deepened. Daring to glance at Darcy, she saw him staring at her mother in wide-eyed disbelief.

Bingley allowed a touch of discomfort to show as he replied, "Miss Elizabeth is the *perfect* house guest, madam; I assure you. It would be a pleasure to have her company at Netherfield for any length of time."

It was difficult to say whether or not Mrs. Bennet heard Bingley's answer for she immediately followed it up by saying, "You have a sweet room here, Mr. Bingley. I do not know a place in the country that is equal to Netherfield. You will not think of quitting in a hurry, I hope, though you have but a short lease."

Grateful for the change in subject and anxious to keep it from returning to the former, Bingley quickly replied without any thought, "I tend to act hurriedly, and if I should decide to return to London, I would probably be off very soon after I had made up my mind. But at the moment, I have no intention of leaving the neighbourhood."

"It is exactly what I had thought of you," said Elizabeth.

"Had you?" asked Bingley, turning toward her.

"Oh yes! I understand you perfectly."

Bingley laughed a little and said, "I wish I could take this for a compliment, but to be revealed so effortlessly is distressing."

Mrs. Bennet, afraid her daughter had insulted Jane's suitor, interrupted the conversation. "Lizzy! Remember where you are and do not begin to run on in an insolent manner!"

Darcy became angered at Mrs. Bennet's slanderous remarks about *his Elizabeth.* He knew if he spoke up at that point, what he said would not be fit for feminine ears, so Darcy turned away from the company and walked to the window in an attempt to reign in his temper. After what happened at the assembly, he did not want to insult her mother once more. He could feel Elizabeth's eyes following him and was hoping his behaviour was not causing her more pain, but he knew he would not be able to control his anger otherwise. Clasping his hands behind his back was his reminder to himself to resist the impulse of escorting her away from anyone who might hurt her. *Oh, Elizabeth! Not only do you have to endure Caroline Bingley's unwarranted abuse but now you have to abide this behaviour from your own family!*

"It does not necessarily follow that a deep, intricate character is more or less respected than one such as yours, Mr. Bingley." Elizabeth clarified her opinion.

Bingley said, "I did not know before that you were a studier of character. It must be an amusing study."

"Yes, I do enjoy it."

Having calmed a little at the sound of her voice, Darcy moved toward the rest of the party and joined the conversation—partly wishing to put Elizabeth at ease and partly desiring to show the others that he was *not* in agreement that her behaviour was disrespectful. "Living in the country must limit the opportunity for this activity. Is not the society confined and unvarying?"

He was rewarded with a small smile and a slight tilt of her head as Elizabeth answered, "But people themselves alter so much that there is something new to be observed in them forever."

"Yes, indeed!" cried Mrs. Bennet loudly, startling everyone in the room. Offended by his manner of mentioning a country neighbourhood, she did not hide her anger at Darcy while saying, "The country is a vast deal pleasanter than Town, is it not, Mr. Bingley?"

"I enjoy both. The country and Town each have their advantages and I find myself happy in either." Bingley replied, a bit anxious as to what unexpected meaning Mrs. Bennet might read into his own words as she had been doing with Darcy's.

"*You* have an agreeable nature, Mr. Bingley, and would find something to value wherever you go. But *that* gentleman," pointing at Darcy, "seems to think the country is nothing at all!"

Darcy returned to the window and closed his eyes for a moment while taking a deep breath, thinking, *I have managed to insult her mother once again after all!*

Elizabeth blushed and said, "Indeed, Mama, you quite misunderstood Mr. Darcy's intentions. He only meant there are not as many people here as there are in London."

"I believe there are few neighbourhoods larger than Meryton. After all, we dine with four and twenty families!"

Caroline stifled a laugh as Louisa was blushing slightly for Elizabeth's sake and attempting to school her features. If anyone understood how it felt to be in company while a relative made insulting and embarrassing remarks, it was Louisa. Though her sister's comments were usually *implied* insults rather than the outright ones hurled by Mrs. Bennet, Caroline's were usually more biting.

Elizabeth's mind moved rapidly in an attempt to find something to distract her mother. "Has Charlotte been to visit at Longbourn since I have been away, Mama?"

Mrs. Bennet's annoyance with Darcy could still be heard in her voice when she replied, "Yes, she called yesterday with her father. What an agreeable man Sir William is. So much the man of fashion; so genteel and so easy! *That* is my idea of good breeding; and those persons who fancy themselves so important that their company is not worthy of hearing their voices quite mistake the matter." She said looking directly at Darcy.

Elizabeth quickly asked, "Did they dine with you?"

"No, Charlotte and Maria would go home." After a few moments of silence she continued, "The Lucases are very good girls, but it is a pity they are not at all handsome."

"Miss Lucas seems a very pleasant young woman," said Bingley.

Mrs. Bennet saw the opportunity to call attention to Jane's superiority once again. "Oh dear, yes—but you must own she is very plain. Lady Lucas herself has often said so, and envied me Jane's beauty."

Lydia and Kitty, who had been whispering and giggling since they had arrived, now giggled loud enough for the whole party to turn in their direction. Since she had their attention, Lydia felt it was only right that she should speak. "Mr. Bingley, you have promised to give a ball. It would be a great scandal if you should not keep your word!"

"I am perfectly ready to host a ball when Miss Bennet is recovered so that she might attend."

While grateful for the interruption of her mother's insulting remarks directed at Darcy, Elizabeth was not happy with Lydia's impropriety and was dreading what her sisters might say or do next.

Lydia and Kitty both jumped up off of the sofa, giggling and clapping their hands. Lydia exclaimed, "Oh yes! It would be much better to wait. By that time Captain Carter would be at Meryton again, and I *so* wanted to dance with him!"

Darcy, who had turned toward the company during Lydia's speech so as not to insult anyone by appearing to ignore them, could not understand how Mrs. Bennet could belittle Elizabeth for behaving well and *not* censure her younger daughters when their behaviour was such as this? He noticed Elizabeth was in an even higher state of agitation than before and wished he could comfort her. *Can the two eldest actually be* ***related*** *to these silly girls?*

In an almost constant state of mortification since her mother and sisters had arrived, Elizabeth tried unsuccessfully to change the subject once more by asking whether or not she had received the letter she was expecting from her aunt in London; however, once the subject of balls and dancing had been introduced, nothing would distract them.

Bingley was as kind as ever, though Elizabeth had seen him blush a few times during the visit. Darcy had held himself rigidly throughout, and she had seen a look of anger in his eyes the few times she had dared to glance at him. Caroline did not even attempt to hide her shock or disgust at some of the Bennet family's statements. After the most recent outburst from her sisters, even Louisa could no longer hold her countenance, and her features displayed similar emotions to her sister's.

Elizabeth's family did not notice any of this and would not be dissuaded.

Oh Mama, do you not see what you are doing? Please silence your tongue and those of my sisters! Elizabeth thought. *If they had set out on purpose to mortify Jane and me, they could not have done a better job.*

Elizabeth was relieved to say goodbye to her mother and younger sisters, after which she immediately escaped to Jane's room. She decided not to tell Jane about the humiliation she had suffered during the visit, sharing only Bingley's kind manner and how there was talk of a ball after Jane was completely recovered.

As Jane fell asleep, Elizabeth wondered what was being said of the visit downstairs… especially what Darcy was thinking about her family's behaviour.

Darcy could not blame Elizabeth for escaping above stairs to check on her sister after her family had gone. How he wanted to follow her and offer her comfort! One thing he knew was that *he* did not wish to listen to Caroline review every detail of the visit, so he escaped to Bingley's study with the excuse of a pressing need to write a letter to his steward.

Once there, he stood by the window contemplating the fact that if ever he pursued Elizabeth, these women would become his family as well. He understood that Elizabeth's fortitude stemmed from her love for them, but *he* did not love them. Could he possibly tolerate them?

~ London

While at the office of his General, Richard overheard an assignment being issued for correspondence to be delivered to a Colonel Forster of the militia stationed near Meryton, Hertfordshire. Richard thought this occurrence to be a happy coincidence since he knew Bingley's residence was near that village. He immediately volunteered for the assignment and was granted permission for a fortnight of leave time there to visit family.

Georgiana grinned and clapped her hands excitedly when she heard of Richard's plan; she looked forward to hearing her cousin's opinion of Miss Elizabeth Bennet, thinking that perhaps *he* might be a more objective observer than her brother could be since it seemed William was besotted with the lady in question. Richard retired early, telling Georgiana of his plan to be off at sunrise, and promising to write as soon as he had any news.

~ Netherfield Park

Jane was still feverish, but much less so. Her throat was painfully sore, and she found speaking difficult, so she had been spending most of the day alternating between napping and listening to Elizabeth read. Elizabeth saw to it that Jane took some broth and tea, though the exertion seemed to take its toll on her as she fell asleep while Elizabeth was out of the room changing for dinner.

Caroline had again decided that their evening's entertainment would consist of keeping Darcy as occupied as possible so that he did not have a chance to speak to Elizabeth.

Elizabeth was much relieved the conversation at dinner had not turned to her relations and connexions as it had the day before. Following dinner, Elizabeth went to check on Jane, who was still sleeping soundly, and then joined the others in the drawing room. Mr. Hurst and Bingley were engaged in a game of piquet, while Louisa observed the game. Darcy sat at a writing desk composing a letter to his sister as Caroline hovered over him.

He certainly does write to his sister often; they must be quite close. She seemed to be such a sweet girl. I am happy that he is such an attentive brother. Elizabeth thought.

Caroline seemed to be doing her best to test the limits of Darcy's patience by interrupting, asking him to send messages to Miss Darcy on her behalf, and commenting on his handwriting.

She must think she is flirting, but he is obviously annoyed by her attentions. Will she never learn to read his expressions? Elizabeth wondered, her eyes dancing with amusement.

"How delighted Miss Darcy will be to receive another letter from you!"

Darcy made no answer.

"You write very quickly."

"Actually, I do not."

"You write a great number of letters, Mr. Darcy! I should not like to do the same!"

"Then it is advantageous that it is *I* who must write them." Darcy glanced at Elizabeth and saw the sparkle in her eyes as she looked upon the scene. Without planning to, he began to move his eyes to meet Elizabeth's as he made *each* of his responses to Caroline.

"Will you tell your sister that I look forward to seeing her again?"

"I have already told her so once, by your desire." Understanding what he was about, Elizabeth could barely keep her countenance. Darcy was obviously in a teasing mood. She adjusted her book and turned her head toward it, moving her eyes only when he spoke, hoping no one would discover their silent exchange. After each of Darcy's rebukes of Caroline, Elizabeth would attempt to read to distract herself from her repressed smiles before they got away from her, but she could not attend the words on the page—spending the time in anticipation of *his* next words instead.

"Tell your sister I am delighted to hear of her improvement on the harp."

"Miss Bingley, I must ask to include your message in my next letter. At present I have not the room."

Even from across the room, Darcy could almost see his own thoughts in Elizabeth's eyes, *Perhaps she should write her own letter?*

"I shall tell her myself in January. But do you always write such charmingly long letters to *dear, sweet* Georgiana, Mr. Darcy?"

Darcy had to restrain his laughter, and as he glanced at Elizabeth, seeing the way she pressed her lips together to suppress her smile was of little assistance to his struggle. "They are generally long, but whether always charming, it is not for me to determine."

"A person who can compose a lengthy missive with ease will always do it well."

Bingley laughed. "Darcy does not write with ease, Caroline! He studies too much for words of four syllables."

Darcy smiled. "My style of writing is very different from yours."

"Oh!" cried Caroline, "Charles leaves out half his words and blots the rest."

"My ideas flow so rapidly that I have not time to express them—which means my letters sometimes convey no ideas at all to my correspondents." Bingley addressed this comment to Elizabeth, the only person in the room who had never seen his letters.

Elizabeth joined in with a smile. "Your humility, Mr. Bingley, must disarm reproof."

Darcy could not resist challenging her on that point. "Is it humility or merely the appearance of it? It could be considered a disguised pretension."

Bingley raised his eyebrows before he said, "And which of the two do you proclaim my statement to be?"

"An indirect boast; for you are in truth proud of your defects in writing. The power of doing anything with quickness is always much prized by the possessor and often without any attention to the imperfection of the performance. When you told Mrs. Bennet this morning that you tend to act hurriedly, and if you should decide to return to London, you would probably be off very soon after you had made up your mind, you meant it to be a compliment to yourself—and yet what is there so very estimable in a haste which must leave very necessary business undone and can be of no real advantage to yourself or anyone else?"

Bingley cried, "Upon my honour, I believe what I said to be true!"

"I daresay you believe it, but if as you were mounting your horse a friend were to say, 'Bingley you had better stay till next week,' you would probably do it—and at another word you might stay a month."

Elizabeth had heard enough to answer to the challenge she had seen in Darcy's eyes earlier. "You have only exposed that he is an even better friend than he stated himself."

Bingley chuckled, "I am afraid you are giving what Darcy said a meaning which he did not anticipate, for he would certainly think better of me if this occurred and I were to refuse and ride off as fast as I could."

"According to the circumstances as stated, you must remember that the friend who asked Bingley to stay has not given any reason for him to do so." Darcy answered looking only at Elizabeth.

"To agree to change one's plans in order to satisfy his friend's desire holds no value to you?"

"To yield to another's desire without giving the surrounding situation any consideration is not a tribute to one's intellect."

Elizabeth stood and moved closer to Darcy, her brow arched in that way which could drive him to distraction. "It appears to me, Mr. Darcy, that you do not place any worth on the power of friendship and affection. A regard for the friend making the request would often make one readily yield to a solicitation, without expecting the need to be talked into it. I am not speaking of Mr. Bingley. But in ordinary cases between friends where one of them is desired by the other to change a resolution of no very great importance, should you think ill of that person for complying with the desire, without waiting to be argued into it?"

Darcy relished the opportunity to debate any point with Elizabeth for she had impressed him by proving to be one of the most worthy adversaries with whom he had been in contest so far. But this particular subject struck him deeply. Had Elizabeth realized what he already had privately discerned earlier in the conversation—that *she* had only to request something of *him* and he would more than likely agree to it without question? No, he could see in her eyes that there was no double meaning in her words; she was too modest for the idea that she had any power over him to even enter her mind!

He stood and took a step closer to her before answering, "Will it not be advisable before we proceed on this subject to arrange with rather more precision the degree of importance which is to apply to this request, as well as the degree of intimacy existing between the parties?"

Bingley interrupted their discourse, "By all means let us hear all the particulars, not forgetting their comparative height and size, for that will have more weight in the argument, Miss Elizabeth, than you may be aware of. I assure you that if Darcy were not such a great tall fellow in comparison with myself I should not pay him half so much deference. I declare I do not know a more awful object than Darcy on particular occasions and in particular places—at his own house especially and of a Sunday evening when he has nothing to do."

Darcy smiled slightly, but it did not reach his eyes. Elizabeth thought she could perceive that he was rather offended.

Darcy replied, "I see your design, Bingley; you dislike conflict and want to silence this debate."

"Perhaps I do. I should like it much better if you would continue your debate only when I am not present."

Elizabeth exchanged a glance with Darcy. It was a feeling of relief to both to be speaking easily again.

Elizabeth said, "Perhaps we should both see to our sisters, Mr. Darcy."

Darcy bowed to her and returned to the writing desk to do just that, hoping Elizabeth understood he was yielding to his friend's wish by ending their debate—even though a discussion of the reasons behind the decision *had* been necessary.

Elizabeth took her leave, saying she had been away from her sister for too long.

Darcy excused himself for the night shortly after she left, not trusting his thoughts to refrain from showing on his face.

Thursday, November 14, 1811

The next morning, Caroline commanded Darcy and Louisa to attend her on a walk about the grounds. After they had returned to the house, the party joined Bingley and Mr. Hurst in the sitting room for tea. A few minutes later, to everyone's surprise, Colonel Richard Fitzwilliam was announced.

A bewildered Darcy crossed the room and met Richard with a hearty handshake and a heartfelt grin. "Richard! What are you doing in Hertfordshire?"

"Thank you for making me feel so welcome, Darce!" Richard teased.

As Bingley approached the two, Richard extended his hand in greeting his host. "Since sudden but brief military business has brought me to the area, I decided to take you up on the offer extended when I last saw you in London, Bingley. You did say to come for a visit anytime! If it is inconvenient to your household, I could stay at the inn at Meryton."

With his usual good humour, Bingley replied, "Fitzwilliam, I am glad to see you! What nonsense you speak! It is never inconvenient to welcome a good friend to my home! How long can you stay?"

"Thank you! It is good to see you as well. My cousin's recent letters to Georgiana have piqued my interest in meeting your new neighbours myself, Bingley. My General seems to think I am in need of some diversion; therefore, I have been granted a fortnight's leave of absence. Though, I would not wish to disrupt your *plans*." He glanced sideways at Darcy, whose eyes widened a bit in response to the speech.

"Your company would be agreeable for as long as you manage it. I hope you will be able to attend the ball we are planning when Miss Bennet has recovered." Remembering Richard did not know the Bennets, Bingley went on, "Oh, we are short two of our party this afternoon, as poor Miss Bennet is ill and her sister, Miss Elizabeth, is above stairs nursing her. They are staying with us until Miss Bennet is well enough to remove to her home nearby at Longbourn." Turning to the rest of the party, Bingley continued, "You may remember my sister, Miss Caroline Bingley, my brother, Mr. Alexander Hurst, and my sister, Mrs. Louisa Hurst."

Richard shot Darcy a pointed look at the information that Miss Elizabeth Bennet was actually staying under the same roof! As they knew each other so well, Darcy could not but understand the true nature of Richard's visit once he recognized the meaning of that look, and he was more than a little disturbed.

Darcy knew that the moment they were left alone, Richard would pounce upon him to gather information about Elizabeth. He had had no idea that Richard would be in London, or any reason to suspect that Georgiana would read his letters to him out loud. Darcy wracked his memory in the attempt to recall what he had written about Elizabeth, but obviously it had been enough to make his cousin, and perhaps his sister, suspicious. He could well imagine the two of them conspiring to find a way to deliver Richard to Netherfield. Darcy would also wager that if there had been a legitimate excuse, Georgiana would have come along.

Perhaps the inevitable meeting with Richard would be helpful for him to sort through his feelings, but he needed some time to think of what he would reveal to his cousin. Or was that too much to hope for?

~*~*~*~*~*~*~*~*~*~*~*~

When she joined everyone in the dining room, Elizabeth was introduced to the new arrival, and she soon found herself seated between the cousins.

Richard's easy manners soon found him engaged in pleasant conversation with Elizabeth, while Darcy seethed with jealousy. It seemed the more uncomfortable he felt, the more Richard would flirt with her. He could not help but feel that the smiles she directed toward Richard were supposed to be *his!* There were many instances when he was torn between the impulse to flog Richard or to take hold of Elizabeth and carry her far away from him. Scotland would serve. But *this* was absolutely maddening!

So far during the meal, in order to keep his temper under regulation so he would not verbally attack Richard, Darcy had remained silent. He now had to find a way to join in Richard's conversation with Elizabeth, to have her look at *him*, smile at *him*! He felt as if he would burst with rage if she smiled at Richard once again.

Caroline was livid. Now Darcy *and* Richard were paying a great deal of attention to Elizabeth—and both were ignoring her. No matter how she tried this evening, she could not engage Darcy in conversation; he was far too busy watching his cousin and Elizabeth converse. This was not to be borne! She thought the way to remedy this would be to point out to the newly arrived guest, and remind Darcy, of course, just what a worthless country hoyden Elizabeth Bennet really was. Connexions in trade indeed! "Miss Eliza, you had shared with us recently that your uncle in London owns an import/export business, am I correct?"

"Yes he does, and he has owned a bookshop for the past fifteen years as well."

Darcy saw that here was the perfect opportunity to gain Elizabeth's attention. "Pray, what is the name of your uncle's bookshop?" He meant to ask this the last time it was brought up since he was familiar with many booksellers in London, but had been interrupted.

"Gardiner's Books, sir."

Darcy's surprise was displayed on his face. "Miss Elizabeth, your uncle is Mr. Edward Gardiner?"

Elizabeth smiled at him, providing a very much needed balm to his heart. "Yes, he is my mother's brother. Do you know my uncle, Mr. Darcy?"

Darcy's eyes widened a bit in surprise. *Mrs. Bennet's brother? The personalities of these siblings could not be more opposite!*

Elizabeth understood exactly what that look meant, and her smile changed a bit to one of understanding as amusement danced in her eyes; she had thought the very same thing many times.

"Aye, he does, as do I, Miss Bennet!" the Colonel said with a smile, while Darcy glared in his direction.

Darcy stepped in before his cousin could say another word. "I have been frequenting Mr. Gardiner's shop for years; my father would take me there as a young man whenever we were in London, as did my uncle with Colonel Fitzwilliam. In size, it is smaller than most booksellers, but looks can be deceiving. What a treasure is housed inside! He has one of the best shops in London for a person who is interested in collecting as well as in buying new editions and everything in between. Mr. Gardiner's talent in finding impossible-to-find editions is invaluable!"

With a wide smile, Darcy shifted his gaze and continued, "Bingley, you met Mr. and Mrs. Gardiner at my home the week before we came to Hertfordshire. His was the shop I showed you the following day." He looked back to Elizabeth. "We chose several books to begin Bingley's collection, Miss Elizabeth. They are here in the library at Netherfield."

Caroline looked as if she had eaten something sour.

"I must agree with my cousin on everything he has said. I have spent many happy hours browsing your uncle's store," Colonel Fitzwilliam stated.

"In conversation with Mr. Gardiner, as well," Darcy agreed.

Caroline could no longer hold her tongue. "Excuse me! Mr. Darcy! You entertained a *tradesman* at your *home*?!" she asked, her disgust in clear view.

Darcy tried to hide his smile. Bingley's fortune was made in trade by his father and grandfather, though his sisters conveniently forgot that fact whenever possible. "Mr. Gardiner is a *friend*, Miss Bingley. I had the great pleasure of meeting Mrs. Gardiner as well when they honoured my sister and me with their acceptance of our dinner invitation. It was a nice surprise to find that Mrs. Gardiner grew up in Lambton, not five miles from Pemberley. Georgiana enjoyed discussing the area with Mrs. Gardiner. My sister and Mrs. Gardiner have exchanged several visits since I have been in Hertfordshire."

Bingley was beaming. "Yes, I cannot agree with you more, Darcy; it certainly was an honour to meet Mr. and Mrs. Gardiner. What a delightful couple! Mrs. Gardiner certainly did much to ease Miss Darcy's shy nature. I have never seen her so animated! Of course, Darcy's knowledge of bookshops is much greater than mine, but even I was impressed with Mr. Gardiner's shop."

At the mention of Darcy's sister, Louisa knew Caroline would normally say something complimentary about Georgiana in order to ingratiate herself with him, but she also knew that if Caroline uttered a word at this moment, she would not be able to stop herself from saying something much different. Caroline had already insulted Darcy by criticizing his taste in dinner guests, and in Louisa's opinion it would be best if she remained quiet for the time being. Under the table, Louisa put her hand on her sister's arm hoping to still her tongue.

Elizabeth's eyes betrayed how happy she was to hear such praise of her favourite aunt and uncle. "Gentlemen, you might continue on all evening in this vein and not compliment my aunt and uncle highly enough, in my opinion! They are wonderful people. I had no idea you all knew each other." Turning to Caroline, she said, "Miss Bingley, my aunt and uncle are often invited to dine with their customers, as are Jane and I when we are staying with them."

This conversation was not going at all as Caroline had intended! Instead of bringing the Bennets' faults to the forefront, it had initiated a more intimate degree of conversation between Elizabeth and the gentlemen—and they continued to completely ignore *her!* Caroline did not even attempt to hide her displeasure and rose to signal it was time for the ladies to separate from the gentlemen.

Though the gentlemen would have been happy to forego the custom this particular evening as was common in the country, they did not feel they could do so without causing insult. In fact, when in company with Caroline, Bingley and Darcy were usually the ones to *insist* upon the separation. Caroline assumed it was because, being so highly placed in society, Darcy was used to more formal dining and so she attempted to impress him with her "Town hostess" abilities by agreeing without complaint. The truth of the matter was that after spending all of dinner listening to Caroline's generally insipid remarks in addition to Louisa's concurrence of all her sister's opinions, by the time their repast was done the gentlemen *required* some time away—and a bit of brandy to brace themselves before more of the same began in the drawing room. Had they not separated tonight, it might be too obvious that it was due to the gentlemen's finding the company more pleasant than usual.

Elizabeth took the opportunity to escape above stairs to check on Jane. If she felt well enough, Jane would return with her to the drawing room for a visit.

Elizabeth entered Jane's bedchamber and closed the door firmly behind her. Jane could tell something had unnerved her sister by the way she was moving. "Lizzy, what is it?"

"Jane! Colonel Richard Fitzwilliam is here!"

Jane's shocked "Oh!" was all that was heard for several minutes as both ladies were lost in thought.

Elizabeth said, "Perhaps it was not a wise decision to remain quiet about the subject of our London connexions after all? It will seem odd if we brought it up now, though, would it not? Oh! I should have told Mr. Darcy sooner! Telling one person would have been much preferable to telling the entire group."

"What do you think Mama will do when she finds out, Lizzy?" The two knew exactly what would happen; it did not need to be said aloud—the very thing their father had been avoiding by ordering them not to mention it these past years—though now they would be chastised endlessly for not telling her sooner. She would crow to the entire neighbourhood about her daughters' connexions and insist upon accompanying them to London very soon to make certain they *caught* affluent husbands.

"At least we have avoided it for a few years, Jane," Elizabeth said, her disturbed thoughts obviously displayed on her face, "But really—*must* we expose the connexion now? After Mr. Darcy and Colonel Fitzwilliam's current visit is done, we may never see them again in Hertfordshire. We may see them only in Town, or perhaps never. If we do, we can then confess… and nobody here will need to know. Additionally, Papa is unprepared..."

Jane's furrowed her brow before saying, "It is true, Papa would be made quite unhappy if we exposed the acquaintance. But Lizzy, we must speak to him about it when we go home. We may have avoided overly exciting Mama up until now, but we cannot do so forever. If nothing else, I believe the next time we visit in London, upon our return we should be honest with Mama about whom we visited while there."

"Yes, I agree, Jane. Also, if the acquaintance does come up in conversation tonight, we shall not lie about it."

With that, Elizabeth helped Jane downstairs.

The most virtuous are those who content themselves with being virtuous without seeking to appear so.
--Plato (Greek philosopher 427 BC - 347 BC)

~Netherfield Park

Because he had spilled gravy on his cravat during dinner, Richard retreated to his chamber to change it. When his valet, Hanson, immediately appeared with a fresh cravat, Richard was surprised. "Why did I not have to request this, Hanson? Have you been spending time chasing the kitchen maids again?" he quipped. Richard knew that one of the best ways to discover information was to speak to staff members and the local inhabitants of a neighbourhood; consequently, he had sent Hanson to learn what he could about Miss Elizabeth Bennet, her sister, Jane, and their family.

Hanson had been one of Richard's finest officers as well as his right-hand man until he was wounded in battle and relieved from duty. Since the man had nowhere to go—returning to work as a farmhand would have been out of the question considering his injury—Richard hired Hanson and was training him to be his valet. The Dragoons Light Calvary division Richard commanded specialized in reconnaissance, and Hanson's talents in rooting out facts were almost as fine as Richard's. Hanson was able to get nearly anyone to supply him with the information he desired—most of the time without alerting the person to the fact that he had given anything away at all. Since becoming Richard's valet, his most essential task continued to be gathering intelligence for Richard's investigations, personal as well as professional.

Hanson began his report as he assisted with his master's cravat. "I was in the kitchen when a footm'n come to tell me that you'd need it, sir. They're an able group.

"This afternoon, I was at the tavern talkin' t' the locals, and I spent the rest of the day in the kitchen speakin' with the staff, sir. I've a good report for ye. 'Tis true that I've never 'eard anything like it, not even at Matlock. The locals think well of these two Bennet ladies. Even Bingley's staff come outta London agree to it.

"The locals call 'em angels o' mercy and the best o' ladies. They're more partial to 'em than the new mistress, though they like the new master well enough. The staff 'as went to a 'eap o' trouble to make sure Miss Bennet and Miss Lizzy—beggin' your pardon, but I've 'eard 'er called 'Miss Lizzy' all day—Miss Elizabeth, are comf'table durin' their visit.

"I 'eard it more'n once that, other than a Mr. Smythe takin' the place for a few months 'bout two years ago, Netherfield's been settin' empty for years before Mr. Bingley came. These two ladies couldn't leave the tenants without anyone lookin' after 'em. They took care o' the sick and 'elped 'em find jobs when they've been without. Even since the new mistress of Netherfield 'as been 'ere—well, it's said she's been known t' talk plain about 'er poor opinion of 'avin' t' mix with the tenants—these two Bennets 'aven't forsaken 'em.

"My understandin' is that their mother isn't looked up to by the locals; she isn't cruel like… *a certain lady* who's new to the area, but she's demandin' in 'er own right. Nobody's agreed over whether *she* is mercenary or just worried that the six ladies will end up starvin' in the 'edgerows when the old gentlem'n 'as seen his last days on account o' Longbourn is entailed, sir. The youngest two girls are wild, an' their mother sees nothin' wrong wit' it. The middle girl is a blue-stocking an' goes 'round doin' nothin' but quotin' sermons all day an' night. Everybody says that they'd never guess these two an' the father is related to the rest, but I've been told that they *look* like each other in one way or another." Hanson raised both his eyebrows and nodded deeply to emphasize his last point.

"Mr. Bennet is a clever gentlem'n an' the two oldest are 'is favourites, 'specially Miss Elizabeth. 'e's also kind to the Netherfield tenants. Mr. Bingley can thank the Bennets for findin' Netherfield in such fine o' shape as 'e did, 'cause 'e kept an eye out an' went after the owner when things needed fixin'.

"I 'ave a good report 'bout the specific worry you 'ad, too, sir. The two oldest, they've both turned down proposals from rich men. From what I 'eard, the missus. doesn't know about it, but the gentlem'n does. Miss Bennet refused Mr. Smythe, an' 'e quit the estate directly. Miss Elizabeth refused a gentlem'n 'bout the same time, but seems like it was in Town an' they don't know 'is name—just that she would've been mighty well-off if she 'ad accepted. No matter 'ow many I talked to, nobody disagreed wit' any of this." Hanson completed his report.

"Do you think they were bribed to give a favorable account?" Richard asked.

Hanson raised his brow a bit for the slightest moment as, after all he had heard, he had come to feel a bit protective of the Bennet ladies, but then he schooled his features. "No, sir, I don't think so. I'll tell ye', though, that the first couple reports made me suspicious o' the same. But I've talked to too many today for it not t' be true. Any time I mentioned their names, people smiled. A few times I even went as far as insinuatin' I believed somthin' insultin' to see what 'appened. I was 'ollered at more than once, an' one of the footm'n—the really big one, sir—would've prob'ly knocked me down if the 'ousekeeper 'adn't put a stop to it!" Hanson laughed and winked. "They always give the best info'mation when they're angry! The 'ousekeeper said that everybody is mighty fond of the ladies an' I shouldn't talk o' 'em like that no more. After everything I 'eard o' 'em, the Bennet ladies almost won *me* over!"

Richard laughed, for he knew that Hanson was not one to be easily impressed or to exaggerate. "Thank you, Hanson. Excellent work, as usual. Keep me informed if there are any changes in opinion. You certainly have given me much to think about. I will be in the drawing room, and then I am planning to play billiards if I can round up a game, so you do not need to wait up for me. I will fend for myself tonight. Good night, Hanson."

"G'night, Colonel." Hanson replied as he left Richard to his thoughts.

Richard was very confused. He had rushed to Hertfordshire expecting it to be necessary to rescue his cousin from the clutches of a wickedly unethical charlatan who had somehow discovered an unanticipated ploy that Darcy had fallen for. He was not at all prepared to meet with an intelligent, witty, graceful, well-bred beauty with a sly sense of humour who did not seem to have a mercenary bone in her body. In fact, Richard had been so impressed with her that he would have thought of her for himself *if* she had not been absolutely perfect for his cousin—and if she had had some sort of dowry, of course.

As for Darcy, from the way he looked at Miss Elizabeth, Richard knew this was *no* infatuation—he was in love. A part of Richard had been actually looking forward to arriving to find him the moon-eyed, fawning lover, jumping to satisfy the lady's every whim, but he had met with the opposite. If it were not for that one conversation during dinner about her uncle's bookshop, the two would not have spoken at all. It was as if he were avoiding her!

Darcy should be courting and flirting with such a fine lady! Why on earth was he keeping his distance?

Richard thought that maybe Darcy needed a bit of a push to get him headed in the right direction and set out to make his plan of attack.

After being held "prisoner" in her room by her illness for days, Jane's spirits were low. Elizabeth hoped the company of a certain gentleman would cheer her gentle sister. Seeing that Jane was well enough to visit for a short while, Elizabeth helped her to the drawing room.

Elizabeth could not help but smile when Bingley began to fuss over Jane the moment she entered the room. He escorted her ever so carefully to the chair nearest to the fire, made certain that she was not being assaulted by any drafts, and fretted until both Jane and Elizabeth assured him that Jane's shawl and blanket were situated flawlessly. Bingley also saw to it that Jane's tea was perfectly prepared before pulling his own chair a bit closer than propriety normally allowed—after all, it would be a great risk indeed if he allowed her to strain her voice and do further damage to her throat while conversing with him.

Seeing that Jane was in good hands, and wishing to allow the couple some private conversation, Elizabeth crossed the room to find an occupation. She noticed that Mr. Hurst was already sprawled out on the sofa, sleeping soundly, and Louisa was entertaining herself with her jewelry. Caroline was making a slight effort to appear as though she were reading the second volume of the title Darcy was perusing, though she seemed more concerned with fidgeting, sighing, and staring at Darcy than she was with perusing her book. Colonel Fitzwilliam was not present.

Elizabeth browsed the pile of books on a table and was delighted to find a collection that she had begun to read in the past but had been unable to complete. She selected the second volume.

Colonel Fitzwilliam walked in and raised his eyebrows in surprise when he noticed the book in her hands. With a smile he said, "Miss Elizabeth! Why does it not surprise me that you read Latin? Tell me, which of Plato's dialogues has caught your attention this evening?"

Darcy's head snapped up as his attention became riveted on the pair.

Elizabeth smiled, "Yes, I do, Colonel. I am reading the *Republic* at the moment. My father owns a different interpretation, but I prefer this one as I feel that Serranus has made an excellent translation from the Greek into Latin. Years ago I had borrowed it from my uncle's store, but as I was reading volume two, he sold it directly out of my hands as I recall! I never did have the opportunity to finish the *Republic*, and missed out on reading this translation of the *Laws*, the *Epinomis,* and the entirety of volume three of the collection."

As he stood and began to walk toward her, the grin that spread across Darcy's face was breathtaking. "I must apologize, Miss Elizabeth, for suspending your pleasure for all this time. I remember Mr. Gardiner having to delay my purchase and have the collection delivered the following day since the second volume was missing from the shelf. He did mention his niece was reading it at home. You may borrow the entire collection now, if you would like." He motioned to the table where the first and third volume lay.

A light shone from Elizabeth's eyes as her glance moved to Colonel Fitzwilliam and returned to Darcy. "I thank you, Mr. Darcy. Since your family appears intent on interrupting my reading of the *Republic* each time I begin, it seems a proper compensation." She looked more closely at the bookmark in her hand—a white ribbon with "ECB" embroidered in the corner. With a delighted smile she continued, "So this *is* my ribbon that you are using as a bookmark! I had left it in the book by mistake." She pointed to the initials as Elizabeth handed it to Darcy.

Darcy looked flustered. "Miss Elizabeth, had I noticed the embroidery on the bookmark I would have returned it to Mr. Gardiner. It is now returned to its rightful owner." He tried to hide his reluctance as he handed it to her. Darcy knew it was irrational, but now that he knew it was Elizabeth's ribbon it meant a great deal to him—it seemed to bind them together in some way since she had placed it in his book years ago.

Darcy realized that before he had met Elizabeth, he would have laughed at another man had he spoke of a similar dilemma, but his reluctance to part with the only physical reminder he might ever have of the woman he loved was almost overwhelming.

"Nonsense, Mr. Darcy, it is only a ribbon, one I had missed only for a day until it could be replaced. It would be a shame to separate the two who have travelled from London to Pemberley and now to Netherfield together like old friends." After saying this, she blushed, thinking, *That was such a silly thing to say!*

Darcy's eyes caught Elizabeth's and neither could look away. His heart filled with an emotion that he did not understand, and he could only reply, "Thank you, Miss Elizabeth."

Caroline was vexed that Elizabeth was monopolizing the attention of both the eligible men in the house—*again*. Her tone of disapproval filled the room, breaking the enchantment. "Miss Eliza, why would your governess teach you Latin? It is widely known that French and Italian are the *accepted* languages for ladies, not Latin."

It took her a moment to recover her wits after the confusing intensity of the look she had shared with Darcy. Turning her attention to Caroline, Elizabeth replied, "Miss Bingley, I must apologize. There must be something lacking in my manner of communication, for I distinctly remember answering similar queries on three previous occasions. Since there is still some confusion on your part, I shall attempt to enlighten you again. My family has never employed a governess."

Caroline smirked, "Well! It is perhaps a country tradition to choose not to educate one's children, but proper young ladies are educated in respectable subjects by a governess and later go to school or have several masters attend them."

"My mother taught us the basics, Miss Bingley, and then those of us who had the desire to learn more, did so. None of us were ever discouraged from learning—quite the contrary, I assure you. We did have a teacher from Meryton for the French and Italian languages. I showed more of an interest in philosophy, science, languages, and mathematics than my sisters; therefore, my father continued my education in those areas. Jane and I both had an interest in literature and history. It was my father who taught me Latin. I am afraid my talent for learning languages did not extend to Greek, which is why I require a *translation* of Plato." Elizabeth laughed.

"These country ways are most confusing to those of us used to the ways of proper society, Miss Eliza. To be teaching a lady subjects which are normally meant only for gentlemen is most irregular and might even be considered scandalous by those who move among the higher circles of the *ton*! Next, I am certain you will tell me that you play *chess*!" Caroline sneered.

Darcy was about to speak, but Colonel Fitzwilliam interrupted, afraid that the rage he could see burning from Darcy's eyes would tempt him to say something rather inappropriate. "Miss Bingley, I am very glad that you should bring up this subject since Georgiana has been tutored in the very same *scandalous* studies that Miss Elizabeth has mentioned! Imagine my surprise upon hearing just now that she will never be referred to as a proper young lady! I wonder... since it is obvious that both my cousin and I, as her guardians, have erred in the hiring of masters for Georgiana, would you be so kind as to advise us further on the matter?"

"Colonel, I would not..." Caroline choked on her words.

"But perhaps it would be better if I inform my mother, the Countess of Matlock, of this *faux pas*? I do think she would be interested in your kind words of caution since she happens to approve her niece's course of study and personally chooses the masters that will work with Georgiana before Darcy and I implement anything in regards to her education.

"Hmmm... the longer I think on the matter... perhaps we had better not. Mother also plays chess, has studied Latin extensively, and has a rare talent for mathematics. I expect that at this point in her life, it is a little late to apprise her that she could never be thought of as a *proper* and *respectable* lady. Are you of the same opinion, Miss Bingley?"

At the sight of Caroline's pale countenance and gaping mouth, Richard felt it would be only polite to divert the room's attention away from her. *That is correct, Miss Bingley, you managed to insult half the people in this room with your tirade born of jealousy.*

Richard turned to Elizabeth and continued smoothly, "Miss Elizabeth, Georgiana did not take to Greek very easily, either. I do remember Darce here having a difficult time with it as well!"

Elizabeth had found it a challenge to suppress her laughter during Richard's admonishment of Caroline. She knew instinctively that if she had met Darcy's eyes during Richard's speech, there would have been no hope of keeping either of them from falling into fit of laughter, so she had kept her mind busy studying the pattern in the carpet instead. After a couple of deep breaths, she was able to school her features well enough to look at Richard with only the hint of a smile and reply, "It is interesting to know that there is something Mr. Darcy does not do well, sir. According to some accounts, Mr. Darcy *has* no faults."

She looked at Darcy and could see his amusement at her statement in his eyes.

Colonel Fitzwilliam chuckled. "Darce has no faults? Did *he* tell you that? I could name several without its being necessary to consider the matter for even a moment…"

Darcy interrupted, "I think that will do well enough for now, thank you, Richard. I certainly would never mislead Miss Elizabeth in such a way as to pass myself off as a man without fault."

Elizabeth's lips twitched once more until she looked across the room and noticed Jane's countenance. "Gentlemen, this has been a *most* interesting conversation, but I see my sister is becoming fatigued, though she would never admit it for fear of interrupting our agreeable discourse. Will you please excuse us for the evening? I must return her to her room to rest. Good night, Colonel, Mr. Darcy." Elizabeth stood and curtsied. The two gentlemen bowed and bid the Bennet ladies a good night, extending their best wishes to Jane for a speedy recovery. Bingley offered his arm as support to Miss Bennet and escorted the sisters above stairs.

Darcy watched Elizabeth go. *I cannot help but love her.*

Richard saw his chance to get Darce alone and asked him for a game of billiards. Darcy declined and bid good night to the remainder of the party, knowing full well that Richard wanted to talk to him about Elizabeth... but he was not yet ready.

Richard saw that his cousin was avoiding him and allowed him this one reprieve—but resolved that tomorrow *would* be different.

As Darcy entered his chamber, his mind turned to the dinner conversation regarding Mr. Gardiner and his bookshop.

The most agreeable memories he had of time spent with his father after his mother's death were when they attended the book sellers in London. There was one bookshop that his father was especially keen upon visiting, and this feeling was shared by his son. He had watched his father become friends with the new owner of the bookshop—Mr. Edward Gardiner. Mr. Gardiner was a man of intelligence and good breeding, and while both of the Darcys were uncomfortable among most company, Mr. Gardiner had an extraordinary talent for putting them both at ease.

To this day, Darcy continued to favor his shop above all others and had spent much time there through the years with Mr. Gardiner. He had often thought to invite Mr. Gardiner to his club or his home; however, though Darcy was proud to call Mr. Gardiner "friend", tradesman or not, he feared it would be inappropriate for him to do so and did not want to cause gossip for his sister's sake. It was only recently that he discovered that Mr. and Mrs. Gardiner were frequently invited to dine at other gentlemen's houses, and Darcy had immediately extended an invitation for them to dine at Darcy House.

It was truly a pleasure to have them as his guests! At the time he was shocked at the thought since he could not remember ever feeling this way when dining with people who were not certain members of his own family or close friends, like Bingley.

It did not surprise him to hear that Elizabeth and Miss Bennet had spent a great deal of time in London at their uncle's house. The Gardiners being Elizabeth's uncle and aunt finally made things clearer about how that side of the family had influenced Elizabeth and Miss Bennet.

~*~*~*~*~*~*~*~*~*~*~*~*~

Once alone, Elizabeth noticed Jane avoided looking her in the eye. Elizabeth was able to catch her gaze while helping Jane undress, and Elizabeth smiled. "Your Mr. Bingley was excessively attentive tonight, Jane."

A little smile appeared on Jane's lips, but disappeared almost as quickly. "He is not *my* Mr. Bingley, Lizzy. He was a perfect host tonight, was he not? He is all that a young gentleman should be." Then with an amused grin she continued, "But I am surprised you noticed Mr. Bingley's manners at all considering the attention you received from the other gentlemen in attendance. What was the subject of your discourse?"

"Were you so distracted that you did not hear what the remainder of the room was speaking of?" Elizabeth asked while she held the bed coverings open for Jane, and then she sat on the coverlet.

Jane blushed. "Lizzy!"

"We were discussing reading Plato…or rather *not* reading Plato."

Jane looked confused and Elizabeth laughed. "Oh Jane, both gentlemen are entertaining but I see no future with either of them. They are of the first circle after all."

Jane could see a marked sadness in her younger sister's eyes. She had noticed Elizabeth's preference for Darcy, but she also knew that Elizabeth was not yet ready to admit it—not even to herself.

Elizabeth interrupted her thoughts. "You must rest now, my dearest Jane. Though mama might not mind us staying here an extra few days, I do not think it is wise to put your health at any further risk in order to achieve such a thing! Sleep well, sweet Jane."

Jane smiled up at her sister as she laid back amid her pillows. As Elizabeth pulled the covers up to her chin, Jane answered, "Good night, Lizzy."

Friday, November 15, 1811

~Netherfield Park

Darcy awakened after a usual course of dreaming, an act that always began in ecstasy and ended in torment.

From the first day he had met her, he usually spent entire nights in conversation with Elizabeth, reveling in her smiles directed solely at him, enjoying Elizabeth's laughter in response to something he said, sitting next to Elizabeth as she was comfortably nestled in the library at the London house or Pemberley, listening to Elizabeth play and sing to him, becoming entranced with Elizabeth's responses as she attended plays and operas, watching Elizabeth walk toward him in his homes, feeling Elizabeth's hand on his arm while walking on the paths of Pemberley, seeing Elizabeth's reactions to his favourite hideaways on their grounds, observing Elizabeth interact with their children, and—the part that he looked forward to most of all—experiencing the *activities* that would take place to bring those children into existence. Last night he could add assisting Elizabeth to bathe to the list of events that took place in his dreams. Darcy smiled at the memory that, for the moment, seemed so real.

Upon waking, Darcy felt as he had every morning since he first saw her—as if he had been torn away from a little bit of heaven. Disoriented as usual, he reached for Elizabeth so that he could move toward her and gather her in his embrace. The surprise he felt at finding his bed cold and empty sent a jolt through him. He opened his eyes and stared at the pillow that in his dreams had been covered with a rich mane of curls framing her beautiful, smiling face—but now it was more than obvious that it had truly been vacant. After a few moments, the realization of its having been only a dream came crashing over him, and as he pulled the pillow to hold it tightly against his chest, his heart plunged into despair.

As it did several times a day, the war between Darcy's heart and mind began anew.

Why? Why could he not simply surrender to his feelings for Elizabeth and look forward to what he was certain would be a future filled with the love and mutual respect that he had in his dreams?

A strong sense of inherent obligation pulled at his conscience, and the ache within his heart doubled in intensity. It told him that he *must* abandon his own desires—renounce his love and yield to the expectations of society and family—for the sake of his sister's future.

Darcy admitted to himself that the exquisite torture of loving Elizabeth had increased tenfold since she had been staying at Netherfield. Delight and misery, elation and agony were combined into every moment of his waking life. On one hand, he relished the opportunity to be near her so often, but on the other, it was especially difficult because her presence fixed his longings for her at the forefront of his mind.

He had hoped more than believed that these times went unnoticed by the others, as he would immediately walk to the window with a sudden, intense interest in the landscape or bury his face in a book and feign reading, seizing any opportunity to recover his equanimity. Though, judging from the way that Caroline treated Elizabeth, Darcy admitted to himself that he most likely had not succeeded in hiding his interest.

Yes, he loved her and he knew he always would… but he would never be able to be with her. He was confident that he would soon recover once he was away from her, but for now—until he would leave Hertfordshire—he would hoard his memories of time spent with Elizabeth.

Darcy knew he could not avoid Richard forever, so he consented when Richard asked him to go for a ride. Usually, he enjoyed his kinsman's conversation, but not today. His cousin was unrelentingly enumerating Elizabeth's charms. During their ride across the grounds of Netherfield, Richard brought up the subject of Elizabeth one time too many, and Darcy lost control.

"Enough!" Darcy roared as he reigned in his horse. Richard slowed down and came alongside him. "What are your intentions toward Miss Elizabeth, Richard?"

Richard bit back a smile. "Intentions?" He shrugged. "I suppose they are somewhat honourable."

Darcy's colour rose in anger. "Richard, you have been informed several times that Miss Elizabeth does not have any dowry to speak of. As a second son, you have almost nothing to live on other than your officer's salary. Since your tastes run higher than your income, you cannot afford to marry without consideration of the lady's fortune. Though your marked attentions to Miss Elizabeth cannot but show your good taste in *choice* of objects on whom to dispose them, you must know that you cannot marry her. Am I correct?"

Richard continued with great effort to hide his amusement at his plan's success. "Of course, you are correct! You know my situation as well as I."

Darcy dismounted and approached Richard's horse. "If this be the case, please explain to me how your intentions towards Miss Elizabeth could possibly be *somewhat honourable*? Luring her into a *somewhat honourable* attachment when there is absolutely no hope of a future will only cause her pain. I will not allow it to continue. Elizabeth is not the type of female some men might use as a diversion; she is most assuredly a lady in every sense of the word! You will abandon this game you are playing now, or else you will have to deal with *me*!"

Richard noticed the use of Miss Elizabeth's Christian name, but Darcy did not. *Finally! He is almost ready,* he thought, *I need to push just a little further, and hope that I do not get a black eye in the process.* With a chuckle Richard replied aloud, "Shall it be pistols at dawn, then?"

Richard dismounted as Darcy's colour rose again. "I full well know that you do not wish to duel, and neither do I. I am not in jest, Richard! Please, will you desist in this infuriating teasing for the remainder of this conversation?"

With a slight bow of his head, Richard raised his brows and chose his words carefully. "What is Miss Elizabeth to you, Darce? Why are you so concerned with how I treat a woman whom you so obviously deem unworthy of your notice?"

"Unworthy of my… This is not about me, Richard; this is about *your* behaviour toward Miss Elizabeth!"

"Well, Darce, you are in such a quiet mood when we have been in company with Miss Elizabeth, unless, of course, we are talking of books, that anyone can see you do not think highly of her. I did not think you would care what my intentions were, honourable or not."

"I am through with your attempts to turn the subject, Richard! Answer me! Are your intentions in any way dis honourable?"

*Oh, I **am** going to get a black eye!* Richard stood up straighter. "I ask again, Darcy, what difference that should make to you?"

Darcy was absolutely livid with Richard's evasiveness and what it implied. "Leave her be, Richard. She is a *lady* and, as a gentleman, it is my duty to protect her in any way I see necessary!"

Ah, ha! He is ready now! Richard laughed. "Duty? Ha! Oh, why do you not just say it, Darce? Or can you not admit to yourself that you are in love with her?"

Darcy stumbled back a step.

"Others may not see it, but do you honestly think that *I* cannot? I, who knows you better than I do my own brother? You are in love with Miss Elizabeth! There, I have said it for you! What do you think I have been doing since I arrived? Trying to get you to act! I have no intentions toward Miss Elizabeth past those of friendship, and I think she is quite intelligent enough to understand this. If it will make you feel better I will make *certain* she does when the next opportunity presents itself." Darcy visibly relaxed before Richard continued, thumping the back of his hand on Darcy's chest accusingly. "But you—you have spent most of the time in company with Miss Elizabeth ignoring her. From your treatment of her, I doubt she is able to discern that you feel anything but indifference toward her!"

Darcy then informed Richard of all the reasons he had for *not* pursuing Elizabeth, leaving out the most important—his promise to his mother that he would marry well. He then told him about the conversation between Elizabeth and him concerning their friendship.

"Good show, if your goal was to completely confuse her, Darce."

The gentlemen grumbled to themselves as they remounted their horses and steered them onto a path through the woods. Through the grove of trees they spied a group of children trying to fly a kite to no avail. The gentlemen dismounted and began to make their way over to the children to show them how to use the kite when they noticed a lady headed in the children's direction. They stopped and watched the exchange to judge whether or not their assistance was needed.

~*~*~*~*~*~*~*~*~*~*~*~*~

Elizabeth was walking the grounds of Netherfield, mulling over all that had occurred since her arrival. She came upon a group of the servants' and tenants' children trying to fly a kite just outside the bounds of the Netherfield's park.

"Miss Lizzy! Miss Lizzy has come! Will you help us?" The children all squealed with glee to see their favourite playmate.

"Hello, children! It is good to see you all! How are you faring on this beautiful day?" Elizabeth curtsied to the group as they approximated bows and curtsies themselves.

"We are well, thank you, Miss Lizzy," the eldest boy, Jimmy, replied. "Did you come to play?"

"I am sorry, Jimmy, but I cannot stay long. Miss Jane is ill and staying at Netherfield, and I must return to tend to her. But what is this I see, a kite? Are you having trouble with it?"

"Yes, ma'am. Helen's father made us this kite, but we haven't been able to get it to work. Do *you* know how to fly a kite, Miss Lizzy?" Jimmy gave her an eager look.

"Why, it is a good thing that I happened along just now, for I am known as the "queen of kites" across all of Hertfordshire these few years past! Helen's father also taught me how to fly, and even *make,* my own kite years ago. And I am especially good at getting kites down from trees." She laughed with the children since *everyone* knew that she was fond of climbing trees. "Let us see what I can show you now before I must return to the house."

Elizabeth spent a few minutes showing the older boys the basics of how to fly the kite and gave them the responsibility of teaching the younger children. She reminded all the children of their promise not to tell anyone of her running, slipped off her shoes, hiked her skirts up a bit, and ran with the kite through the field until it was flying high above. Elizabeth handed off the kite to Jimmy. While the older children each took a turn with the kite, Elizabeth lifted up each younger child and twirled them around.

As she was saying her goodbyes, little Lucy, a girl of about five years, began to cry. Elizabeth embraced Lucy to comfort her. "Oh! Lucy, what is the matter?"

Jimmy answered for her, "Lucy's afraid the ogress queen will try to cook and eat you and Miss Jane, like in the story you read to us last week, Miss Lizzy."

Elizabeth remembered reading them Charles Perrault's *Sleeping Beauty*, but was still confused as to why they thought that she and Jane would be eaten by such a person. "The ogress queen?" When Elizabeth realized they were referring to Miss Bingley, she could not help but laugh out loud before checking her mirth. "Do you not think *I* could defend Miss Jane and myself from an ogress queen?"

The children all shook their heads in the negative. Jimmy said, "Miss Lizzy, we know you'd be able to defeat all sorts of evil creatures, but from what we've seen of Miss Bing… I mean the ogress queen, she seems too vicious."

Elizabeth ignored the slip of tongue. "Children, I can assure you there is no ogress queen at Netherfield. Miss Jane and I are quite safe there. And, if an ogress queen or any other dangerous creature *were* to appear, there are three brave and good knights to protect us. We shall be in no danger, I promise you. Do you believe me?"

They all nodded yes. Elizabeth dried off Lucy's tears and gave her a kiss on the cheek, resulting in a smile on the little girl's face. "Now children, I must return to the house. No more talk of ogress queens, agreed? That was just a tale." She curtsied to the children, and they bowed and curtsied in return. "Will you walk with me as I return?"

"We cannot, Miss Lizzy. Miss Bingley has told our parents that we cannot go any closer to the house than this field. Those in the house cannot see or hear us when we play here. Last time we went too close to the house… well… *that* was the day we thought there was an ogress queen living at Netherfield. We won't go near it again!"

Elizabeth sighed and then bid them goodbye before turning back toward the house.

~%~

"We should not have eavesdropped." Darcy said, though he was glad they did. His heart was deeply touched by Elizabeth's kindness toward the children.

"Well, we did begin with the best of intentions. It probably would have been better to make our presence known after a while, but the picture of Miss Elizabeth interacting with the children was too charming to interrupt. If we had moved off, they might have seen us. She will be a wonderful mother some day. Being able to interact so nicely with the tenants and their children is a good asset for the mistress of an estate of any size, as well." Richard openly smirked at Darcy.

Darcy changed the subject. "Miss Bingley, does, at times, remind me of an ogress queen!"

The two had a good laugh as they continued their return to Netherfield.

The following day, Jane was feeling much better and was able to come down for luncheon. Earlier, as Jane was concerned about the imposition they might be causing for the family by staying any longer and Elizabeth was more than happy to get away from Miss Bingley, the ladies had sent a note to Longbourn asking when the carriage could be sent for them. The answer stated that the horses would be needed on the farm for the next few days and their carriage could not be sent until Tuesday. Both ladies knew that their father had probably not been consulted in this plan, and they would be unable to convince their mother to send the carriage sooner. They decided that at luncheon, Jane would ask Mr. Bingley for the loan of his carriage.

When the subject was broached, Mr. Bingley insisted they return to Longbourn after luncheon the following day and, after a bit of convincing, the Bennet ladies agreed to his plan. He was just announcing that it was settled when his sister interrupted.

Caroline Bingley by that time had quite enough of Elizabeth's attracting all of Darcy's attention. "Charles, do not be so inconsiderate. Miss Bennet and Miss Eliza must be anxious to return to their family. Of course the carriage will be ordered *immediately,* and the ladies will return to Longbourn as soon as they can be ready to depart." She walked from the room to make the arrangements.

The gentlemen, and even Louisa, sat silently, aghast by Caroline's rude contradiction of her brother's wishes and their guests' approval of the plan, but there was not much to be done about it short of running after her to cancel the order for the carriage.

Mr. Bingley was first to recover. "Ah, yes… well. So it shall be. We will be sad to see you go."

Elizabeth could not help but think that at least one inhabitant of Netherfield would *not* be saddened by the loss of their company.

The Bennets returned above stairs immediately after luncheon to pack. As soon as their trunks were ready, they bid farewell to the residents.

Thanks were given and received graciously, and many smiles were exchanged, though Caroline Bingley's was the only truly happy smile among them, which changed into a sneer as soon as she thought no one was looking. Little did she realize that there were two who did see.

Richard held Darcy back and whispered, "The children may have had the right of it—she is an ogress after all!"

Saturday, November 16, 1811

~Longbourn Estate

The day following Jane and Elizabeth's return to Longbourn was as uneventful as a day at Longbourn could be. Jane rested, and Elizabeth did a great deal of walking with the intention of clearing her head of Darcy, though it seemed to have the opposite effect. The two also discussed bits of nothing with their other sisters, but distinctly avoided speaking to each other about the gentlemen they had left at Netherfield. Mrs. Bennet was having fits of nerves about Elizabeth "allowing" Jane to come home without securing Bingley. Mrs. Bennet, Lydia, and Kitty were interested in hearing of Colonel Fitzwilliam, and Mrs. Bennet did not hesitate to voice her disappointment in hearing that he was only the *second* son of an earl.

At dinner, Mr. Bennet had some news. Their cousin who would inherit Longbourn upon Mr. Bennet's demise, was coming for a visit the following day. Mr. Bennet privately informed Elizabeth that he was looking forward to hours of amusement for them both once the man arrived, since the letter he had received from the young clergyman proved to be quite pompous and self-important. To prove his point, he read the letter aloud, and Elizabeth could not help but agree with her father's assessment of it.

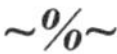

Sunday, November 17, 1811

The following day, Mr. Collins arrived at four o'clock, the exact time specified in his letter—so exact that Elizabeth and Mr. Bennet wondered if he had stopped somewhere on the way to arrive promptly.

A short, greasy man, Mr. Collins's style of expression was silly, his manner was bordering on the absurd, and he seemed to have an endless supply of inane chatter about his patroness, Lady Catherine de Bourgh, and her daughter Miss Anne de Bourgh. The only other subject of reverence was the de Bourgh estate, Rosings Park. He examined Longbourn minutely, and while he complimented Mrs. Bennet as he went from room to room, the *way* he looked at the contents in each caused some to feel that he was cataloging it all as his own future property.

His beady eyes examined every feature of the girls' figures minutely as well, returning several times to the two eldest, which induced a distinct feeling in both of being soiled by his gaze.

After they retired, Jane and Elizabeth discussed wearing much lace around their necklines while Mr. Collins was in residence and making certain that their bedroom door was locked any time either of them was within. It was unfortunate they did not think of locking the bedchamber door when they were *not* within.

~%~

Monday, November 18, 1811

The next afternoon, a cold shiver ran down her spine as Elizabeth opened the door to her room. "Mr. Collins! *What* are you doing in my bedchamber, sir?" she asked quite loudly. Elizabeth remained in the hall where she could be observed. Her younger sisters' bedchamber door had opened just prior to her exclamation, and it made her feel safer that she was not alone. She did *not* wish anyone to misunderstand the situation and think that she had been in her bedchamber alone with the man!

Lydia and Kitty came rushing out into the hallway, covering their snickers with both hands.

"Oh, uh… I seem to have lost my way, Cousin Elizabeth," he sniveled as he stepped forward, unaware that by doing so he was only *half* concealing what his hands were holding. He dropped one of Elizabeth's undergarments back into a drawer and closed it.

Elizabeth had lost all patience and almost all sense of civility. She blurted out, "*Why* were you in my dresser drawer if you were merely lost, Mr. Collins?"

He had no answer but left the room begging forgiveness and bowing so low she thought he would fall over. As he came out into the hall still bowing, both Lydia and Kitty could no longer hold back their giggles. Mr. Collins practically slithered down the hallway to the stairs in escape of the scene.

Elizabeth turned to her sisters and gathered them into their room. She said firmly, "I suggest you both keep your door locked at all times while Mr. Collins remains at Longbourn! I beg of you Kitty, Lydia," she pleaded, her hands pressed together as if in prayer, "please, do not say one word of this to anyone. I will warn Mary and Jane, but *please* do not tell mama or papa, or anyone else. I will *not* be forced to marry Mr. Collins! I swear nothing happened between us other than that I opened the door and saw him there!"

Though they thought it was ever so funny, they certainly could sympathize with why Elizabeth would not want to marry Mr. Collins! Both girls promised they would limit any discussion of the event between themselves in the privacy of their room.

Elizabeth turned quickly, walked into her room, and closed the door behind her—turning the key firmly in the lock. Leaning against the door, she closed her eyes and took several deep breaths. Her eyes flew open, and, as she tried to keep herself from retching, she opened the drawer and took the undergarment that had been in Mr. Collins's hand, throwing it into the fire that she was thankful was still burning. Though her next inclination was to gather every stitch of Jane's and her clothing to have it washed, Elizabeth refrained from doing so since it would create a great deal of work for Longbourn's limited staff. Elizabeth was so angry that her eyes filled with tears and she threw herself onto the bed. So as not to disturb anyone, she directed her sobs into her pillow.

A few minutes later, there was a knock on the door. She let Jane in, quickly closed and locked the door behind her, and fell into her sister's arms, her tears soaking her elder sister's dress within moments.

Jane had never seen Elizabeth this way. Moving Elizabeth to the bed, she whispered soothing phrases until she calmed before asking her what troubled her. A shivering Elizabeth told her all that had occurred.

Jane, who with her trusting nature could not think ill of anybody, insisted there must be some sort of mistake, though she did admit it seemed strange that Mr. Collins could get lost in such a small house.

"Jane, why would he have been going through our dresser drawers if he were lost?"

When pressed, Jane could not come up with anything, and so finally she did concede they had better lock the door at all times.

At dinner, Jane told the family that Elizabeth was indisposed and would have a tray in her room.

Tuesday, November 19, 1811

The next day, when Elizabeth returned from her early morning ramble, Mr. Collins and Mrs. Bennet were in the drawing room chatting while the rest of the family was breaking their fast.

The acoustics of Longbourn afforded anyone who was in the front hall to be able to hear voices in the drawing room if the door was left open slightly and the rest of the house was quiet enough. As Mrs. Hill assisted her in removing her outerwear, she could hear her mother telling Mr. Collins that the family was expecting Bingley to make an offer to Jane. Elizabeth smiled. *"Oh mama!"* she thought and rolled her eyes at Hill, who smiled in understanding.

When Elizabeth heard the next, she froze. Her mother told Mr. Collins, "Now, with Lizzy there are no prior attachments!"

"Yes! Yes, I would be delighted to marry my cousin Elizabeth! I am resolved."

Elizabeth stood staring at the drawing room door, eyes wide open in shock, listening to her mother's next words.

"Oh how wonderful! It is settled, then! You will marry Lizzy!"

Mrs. Hill became worried when she saw the colour draining from Elizabeth's face and watched her begin to sway. Not wishing the rest of the family to see her, the housekeeper led Elizabeth into the kitchen. Once she was seated, she handed young lady a cup of tea along with one of her favourite muffins and would not allow her to leave until she finished both.

Elizabeth dutifully followed instructions as she was too overwhelmed to argue. Slowly, she recovered her senses and looked worriedly at Mrs.

Hill, who reassured her. "The master would never force you to marry where you did not wish to, Miss Lizzy!"

Since Elizabeth and Mrs. Hill had a special bond between them, she took comfort in what was said. She felt that Mrs. Hill was right, though she did not know what would have happened if she had been compromised by the man. She would do everything in her power to avoid being alone with Mr. Collins… ever!

At breakfast, it was decided that the ladies of the house would take a walk into Meryton to visit their Aunt Philips. Mrs. Bennet suggested that Mr. Collins accompany them, and the gentleman prattled on interminably about how honoured he was to be offered the invitation. Though none of the girls wished him to come along, they knew very well that he would not waver in his intent.

Before they departed, Elizabeth had no time to tell Jane what she had overheard, but she had begged Jane with her eyes not to leave her.

Though she had thought long about what had passed the day before, Jane could come to no other conclusion than that Mr. Collins was *not* an honourable man. Whatever it was that was currently clouding the eyes of her favourite sister concerned her further, and Jane vowed to make this walk as comfortable as possible for Elizabeth. Since the happenings of the previous day, she became much more aware of *way* he looked at Elizabeth than she had before—and it began to frighten her.

On their walk, Elizabeth was able to avoid taking Mr. Collins's arm by pretending she did not notice his offer, but he did remain by Elizabeth's elbow. Jane attempted to place herself between them, but Mr. Collins continually thwarted her efforts. Her only success at distracting him from her sister was by asking questions concerning Lady Catherine and Rosings Park. With Mr. Collins's tendency to rattle on and his need to catch his breath often due to being unused to walking, this scheme took up most of the trek into Meryton.

As they entered Meryton, the two youngest Bennet sisters were obviously scouting the village for the red coats of the regimental uniforms worn by the officers of the Militia which was stationed nearby. They soon found candidates and scurried toward them with the excuse of wishing to see a new bonnet in the shop window that the officers were standing by. The elder sisters and Mr. Collins followed at a more leisurely pace, with Jane's and Elizabeth's thoughts centering on finding a way to check their younger sisters' exuberance.

The two officers were Mr. Denny and Mr. Saunderson, who were accompanied by another gentleman that the Bennets had never met. The young man was tall and very handsome, with dark wavy hair, a pleasing smile, and dark eyes—which were taking in Lydia's generous form a bit too eagerly, Elizabeth noted.

As Jane, Elizabeth, and Mr. Collins approached, much to her sister's embarrassment, Lydia suggested loudly, "Mr. Wickham, you are very handsome, but you would certainly look much better in regimentals."

As he was introduced, they soon learned that Mr. Wickham was soon to be Lieutenant Wickham and would be wearing a red coat after all.

The gentlemen were then all introduced to the ladies' cousin, Mr. Collins, which was the moment that Elizabeth noticed something very odd about the way Mr. Collins and Mr. Wickham interacted—a silent conversation occurring in their eyes and body movements that showed more than a small amount of prior knowledge of each other.

During the introduction, Mr. Collins moved uncomfortably close to Elizabeth. She tensed and felt a need to move away, but Mr. Collins took hold of her arm in an almost possessive way, preventing her escape. Mr. Wickham, though his manner of speaking was pleasing, unnerved Elizabeth with his leers at her person which, though not quite as obvious as Mr. Collins's had been, were even more disturbing in their intensity. As the two men spoke, Mr. Wickham drifted closer until she was trapped between them; she could not move without her body brushing against one or the other.

The entire situation was alarming. She tried to back away from the pair, but every time she moved to do so, they adjusted their positions, and one or the other would graze against her. Therefore she halted any movement and stood perfectly still. Almost overwhelmed with a need to cry out, she stifled it instead, her instincts telling her that doing so under the present circumstances would end badly. Elizabeth glanced at Jane to see if she had noticed, but Jane's attention was turned down the street toward a group of gentlemen approaching on horseback.

Elizabeth was too frightened to think of anything except her own situation. Her eyes darted between the men as they spoke to one another about frivolous topics, causing the feeling of panic within her to rise further.

If someone does not notice how close they are standing to me, it will appear as if nothing at all untoward is occurring! What is this game they are playing, and why must it involve me?

Suddenly another figure was in front of her. Startled, with a sharp gasp, she stumbled backwards into a wall of flesh. Elizabeth was surrounded!

~Meryton Village

Elizabeth was aware of hands grasping her upper arms, pulling her backwards—away from the three men before her. The hands were gentle, and there was a familiar energy associated with the touch that made her feel safe. Instinctively, she pressed her back more firmly against the safe wall behind her, and the energy enveloped her almost as if it were a soothing embrace. Instinctively, she knew that all would be well as a result. Her state of disquiet was still too high to recognize the voice connected to this energy as it boomed with venom, "Wickham!"

All colour drained from Mr. Wickham's face, and as he turned to leave, a hand came down to grasp Mr. Wickham's shoulder, putting a stop to his retreat. Elizabeth assumed the hand must be gripping tightly because Mr. Wickham winced, and then she could see fear rising in his eyes. At last, she felt able to look at the other man standing across from her and recognized Colonel Fitzwilliam. Though he smiled, at this close range it could be seen for what it was—forced as a show for any neighbours that might be watching this exchange. The colonel's expression of menace directed at Mr. Wickham was totally unfamiliar to her, and she was glad of it. "You were not going to leave our merry party, were you, *old friend*? The fun has not yet begun!"

Wickham's anxious mien quickly gave way to an obviously well-practiced mask of ease as he answered with a chuckle, "Of course not! It is a pleasure to see you again, Richard… William," and he tipped his hat at them both. Mr. Collins inched away from the group.

Elizabeth was still pressed against the soothing "wall," which she now knew to be Darcy. The urge to turn around, bury her face in his coat, and beg him to embrace her and never let her go was almost overwhelming, but she was able to resist.

Mr. Wickham smirked wickedly as his eyes moved repeatedly from

Elizabeth to Darcy and back again. She gasped.

She felt a vibration against her back, and heard a low, menacing sound which was nearly a growl. It was then that she realized Darcy had begun to move her away from the other men. Her legs were trembling violently and would barely obey her commands, but somehow she managed to move them. Darcy reversed their positions, putting himself between her and those who had been causing her discomfort, supporting her gently as they progressed.

The further she was led away from the group of men, the more relieved she became, and she was beginning to take in more of her surroundings. She noticed Bingley had moved into Darcy's position after he and Elizabeth had moved away, hopefully preventing either Mr. Collins or Mr. Wickham from bolting. Jane, now only a few steps to her right, was wearing a horrified expression. Mary seemed almost as frightened as their eldest sister. It was disappointing, but not surprising to Elizabeth, that both Lydia and Kitty were giggling.

Once his grip began to ease to a light touch, Elizabeth realized that Darcy was testing to see if her legs would support her weight. He continued to urge her toward Jane, and whispered something near her ear.

Confused and surprised, she turned her head to look at him. *How did he know?*

Darcy indicated to Jane and Mary that he would need to transfer his charge into their care, and then returned his gaze to Elizabeth. His eyes were full of a tenderness that warmed her to the core. Too quickly, in her opinion, he turned away and rejoined the party from which he had rescued her.

The excessive feeling of loss she experienced at no longer having Darcy near threatened to take her breath away. Instinctively, she reached out to him, but he was already out of reach. She was mortified that Jane and Mary had witnessed her act in such a way.

Jane and Mary supported Elizabeth while Jane motioned toward the shop window nearby, calling Kitty and Lydia's attention to the bonnet they had used as an excuse to cross the street.

Where have Mr. Denny and Mr. Saunderson gone? Elizabeth wondered. *Will they harm my 'knights'?*

Trying desperately to keep her knees locked so that she would remain standing, Elizabeth became more aware of her sisters' behaviour.

Distinguishing that their little group would do better away from the controversy, Jane led the group of ladies into the bookshop, where she also knew Elizabeth could find a seat. Finding a book of poetry to place on Elizabeth's lap, Jane suggested that Mary browse so that they might avoid suspicion. She then handed the latest copy of "The Lady's Magazine" to Kitty and Lydia, hoping it would distract them from discussing recent events while in public.

The bookshop owner well knew the Bennet ladies. Jane could tell that Mr. Hall recognized that something was amiss and shot him a pleading look. He came closer and asked, "May I be of assistance? Perhaps some water for Miss Lizzy?"

Elizabeth, now recovered enough to use her voice, cleared her throat and said quietly, "Yes, I thank you, Mr. Hall. I am feeling a little unwell, but I am sure it will pass. I hope you do not mind if I sit for a few moments. Just being in a room full of books will certainly restore my health quickly."

"Of course, Miss Lizzy! How often does an old codger like me have the pleasure of the company of so many lovely young ladies all at once? Excuse me a moment, please." he said gently as he moved into another room to fetch a glass of water and give the ladies a few moments of privacy.

Jane spoke softly to Elizabeth, "Oh, Lizzy! Are you well?"

"I will be after resting a few minutes; thank you, Jane."

"I knew not what to do! It all happened so quickly. I was happy to see the gentlemen moving in our direction!" As Mr. Hall reappeared with Elizabeth's water, Jane whispered, "We shall speak of this again later."

Distractedly, Elizabeth thanked Mr. Hall for the water, but her thoughts were with her friends outside. Imaginings of what might be occurring were running unchecked through her mind.

Jane could see Elizabeth's eyes fixed on the door and noticed her colour was dwindling once again. The elder sister said a silent prayer that all would end without violence.

Bingley had decided that the following Tuesday, the 26th of November, would be the date for the ball at Netherfield. Bingley held back the Bennets' invitation, wishing to deliver that one personally. Both of his friends heartily agreed to the visit, and they set off as soon as could be after breaking their fast.

While riding through the village of Meryton, both Richard and Darcy spotted Wickham at the same time and exchanged a knowing look. When they looked back, they noticed Elizabeth was being harassed by Wickham and another man. She seemed to be frightened, unsuccessfully attempting to back away from them, because of the determination of both men to detain her. Dismounting before their horses had come to a complete stop, they hurried to her aid; Darcy went directly to Elizabeth, and Richard took up the position opposite Darcy.

As he was walking over, Darcy could see that Elizabeth was even more terrified than he had originally thought. His rage only grew when he realized that Elizabeth was in such a state of agitation that she could not recognize Richard, starting when he appeared before her. Moving away from the newest threat, she stumbled backwards, coming to rest with her back firmly against his chest. Though grateful that his presence did not alarm her further, he was momentarily surprised that she did not move away from him as well.

Darcy's first instinct was to wrap his arms securely around Elizabeth and assure her that she would be safe, but such behaviour was unacceptable. He especially did not want Wickham to notice that he had any feelings for Elizabeth as Darcy feared what the results of his having that knowledge would be.

His heart ached for Elizabeth as he felt her trembling against him so forcefully that he was unsure she would be able to hold her own weight much longer.

"Wickham!" Darcy's voice boomed.

Wickham looked as if he would run off, but Richard acted quickly.

Filled with an anger he could barely contain at crossing paths with the scoundrel once again, Richard brought his hand down hard on Wickham's shoulder, gripping it tightly. "You were not going to leave our merry party, were you *old friend*? The fun has not yet begun!" Richard said, plastering a false grin across his features to distract any onlookers of the true nature of the meeting.

Wickham's panic-stricken expression quickly transformed to the sickly-sweet mask that both Darcy and Richard recognized so well. "Of course not! It is a pleasure to see you again, Richard…William." He tipped his hat at them.

Darcy's attention was caught by Mr. Collins as he tried to distance himself from the group. The man stopped at a venomous look from both Darcy and Richard.

When Darcy heard Elizabeth gasp, his gaze returned to Wickham to find him eyeing her with undisguised lust. If his first concern had not been supporting Elizabeth, Darcy was not sure whether or not he could have stopped himself from strangling the rogue right then and there, without a moment of hesitation! Incensed almost to the point of frenzy, he could not even form words but made a warning noise that came out almost as a snarl.

The sensation of Elizabeth pressed against him and her scent filling the air brought his errand into focus—he must get her to safety. He shifted, placing himself between the woman who held his heart and Wickham, gently moving her toward her sisters.

With a glance at Bingley, his friend moved into the place which Darcy had previously occupied. Bingley, usually the amiable, mild mannered gentleman, took on a stance that warned the men that he was not to be underestimated.

Darcy did not wish to allow Elizabeth out of his direct protection, but he knew he had to do so. Loosening his grip on her arms, he was relieved that she was able to stand under her own power.

Darcy leaned toward her ear and took a deep breath, filling himself with her calming fragrance, and then whispered, "Your knights will protect you from the ogres, my queen." She looked up at him with confusion in her eyes. Their lips were so close that he was sorely tempted to lean in the inch or so it would have taken to kiss all of her fears away—but he checked himself.

*I **will** keep you from harm, my Elizabeth!* Darcy thought before reluctantly handing her over to her sisters' care.

As he returned to the group of men, he saw that Jane was leading her sisters into a nearby shop. A touch of relief came over him knowing that they would not witness what might follow.

It seemed that not much had been said while he was gone. Three of the four men were staring at each other with angry expressions, and the stranger seemed frightened. Richard began, "Why do we not take this… *discussion* to a less public place, gentlemen?"

Up until that point, seeing Wickham had been wrong to accost Elizabeth, Mr. Denny and Mr. Saunderson had kept their distance from the confrontation, but at this statement, the two intervened. Mr. Denny said, "Excuse me, gentlemen, but Mr. Wickham has just today joined the militia. We cannot allow you to take him away for a *discussion,* as you call it. If you have a problem with Mr. Wickham, I suggest you speak to Colonel Forster."

"I may not be in uniform at the moment, but I am Colonel Richard Fitzwilliam of the Dragoons. Have no doubt, I *will* be speaking to Colonel Forster about Mr. Wickham, and soon, but for now I will take responsibility for Mr. Wickham's absence. Return to camp and notify Colonel Forster of the situation." Richard said the last with the authority of a man used to giving orders.

Every British soldier knew the name of Colonel Richard Fitzwilliam and had heard about the war hero's actions. Both men, visibly impressed by the man with whom they were in company, saluted to their superior officer and followed his orders without further delay.

Bingley led the group to a cluster of trees behind the shops, far enough away from the village to have a discussion without being overheard.

"First of all, who are *you* and why were you harassing Miss Elizabeth?" Richard asked Mr. Collins.

"Sir, I am Reverend William Collins, and I have been so fortunate as to be distinguished by the patronage of the Right honourable Lady Catherine de Bourgh, daughter of the Earl of Matlock, widow of Sir Lewis de Bourgh, whose bounty and beneficence has preferred me to the valuable rectory of the parish of Rosings Park. I was escorting my betrothed to the village of Meryton." Mr. Collins bowed repeatedly throughout the whole of his speech.

All three gentlemen's eyes widened. Darcy opened his mouth to speak, but Richard put his hand on Darcy's arm to quiet him. "Mr. Collins, we were speaking of why you were harassing Miss Elizabeth, not asking for a recital of my aunt's virtues. Which of the Bennet ladies is your betrothed?"

"Lady Catherine de Bourgh is your *aunt*, sir? Oh! To be in the presence of the nephew of my most gracious patroness! I am humbled by your attention! I am pleased to inform you that only a few days ago Lady Catherine was in the best of health, as was her daughter, the charming and amiable Miss Anne de Bourgh. What affability and condescension I have experienced from Lady Catherine…"

As Wickham rolled his eyes, Richard interrupted again, "Mr. Collins! Please! You are not answering my questions. Let us begin again. Which Bennet lady is your betrothed?"

"I do apologize, dear sir, I have been carried away by the wondrous nature of my…"

"MR. COLLINS!"

"Miss Elizabeth Bennet," Mr. Collins answered simply.

Darcy could not stop himself from exclaiming, "WHAT?"

Confused, Mr. Collins answered, "Miss Elizabeth Bennet, sir. I am here in Hertfordshire at the urging of my esteemed patroness Lady Catherine de Bourgh to choose a wife from among my cousins in compensation for inheriting Longbourn in the future when the unfortunate death of Mr. Bennet shall occur. Lady Catherine has advised me to choose with discretion a genteel lady who will know her place and obey me. In my opinion, this describes Miss Elizabeth. Mrs. Bennet and I have discussed the matter and agreed that my cousin Elizabeth will become my wife."

"And what does Mr. Bennet have to say to this?" Darcy could barely spit out the words without retching.

"I have not spoken to Mr. Bennet as of yet, sir, but I flatter myself that he will agree. Indeed, why would he deny my suit? I am next in line to inherit the estate and live in respectable and easy circumstances in a comfortable home at Hunsford; my wife will have the honour of the condescension, notice and kindness of the noble Lady Catherine de Bourgh. They could not expect a better match for their daughter."

Darcy's ire was so high that his face was red, and he was clenching his fists so tightly his knuckles had turned white. Richard thought to change the subject since he noticed Wickham was more than a little interested in Darcy's reaction.

"And so, since you believe her to be your betrothed, you feel this gives you and your friends the right to harass her in the middle of Meryton Village?" Richard asked.

"Esteemed sirs, I do not believe her to be my betrothed, she *is* my betrothed, and I was not harassing Miss Elizabeth, I was escorting her. I had only just been introduced to Mr. Wickham and his colleagues when Mr. Wickham moved closer to Miss Elizabeth than propriety allows. I was defending Miss Elizabeth's honour, sirs." None of the Netherfield gentlemen were satisfied with this explanation, but they all concurred with a look that this was probably the best they would get out of the buffoon.

"Wickham, what excuse do *you* have? Why are you here?"

"I have the great honour of having purchased a commission in His Majesty's Militia, Richard. I was only being friendly with my new acquaintances; if I stood too closely, I apologize. I meant no offence to the lady." Wickham did not try to hide his smirk and threw a pointed look at Darcy.

"So you say that you two have never met each other before today?" Richard was suspicious. Their actions were not those of two men unacquainted with each other, no matter what words they used.

"That is correct," Wickham replied.

"Wickham, you will stay far away from *anyone* named Bennet in the future, or I will not be responsible for what happens to you," Darcy said with his booming "Master of Pemberley" voice. "I will *not* be cleaning up any messes for you here—and I will be watching for mischief. Do I make myself clear?"

Before Wickham could answer, Richard chimed in. "You *will* behave yourself in a gentleman-like manner at all times while in Hertfordshire—and at all other times while you are in the militia. Be warned, the military does not take disgracing the uniform lightly. This is your chance to make a new start for yourself, Wickham… and believe me when I say it is your *last* chance." Richard added with a murderous gleam in his eye, and then said under his breath but loud enough for everyone to hear, "I would have been more than happy to run you through the last time we met. I give you fair warning—I will not hesitate again if you misbehave."

Wickham replied with a sarcastic grin, "Of course, gentlemen!"

Turning, Richard said with same expression, "Mr. Collins, as the parson of our aunt, you will conduct yourself in a gentleman-like manner at all times as well. Do you understand?"

"Did you say '*our* aunt'? Are you to say I am in the company of more than one of Lady Catherine de Bourgh's nephews? Oh, I am truly honoured…"

"MR. COLLINS!"

"Gentlemen, I would never wish to disgrace the honourable name of my noble patrone…"

"Mr. Collins, answer the question! Do you understand?"

"Yes, sir! I do understand, sir."

"Thank you. Wickham, you will return to camp and report for duty immediately. Collins, we will join you in escorting the ladies to Longbourn."

Richard spoke to Darcy and Bingley as they made their way back into the village, waiting until the other two were out of hearing range, "I do not know what else we are going to get out of these two. They are lying about knowing each other in my opinion, but I cannot see how to force them admit to it without applying the more… *vigorous* means of extracting information that I have found useful on military missions. I would not think of using those methods here—though I must say that I would enjoy using those techniques on Wickham."

Richard's expression was almost wistful, and then he shook his head as if to empty his mind of the thought. "We cannot do much on the basis of their standing too close to Miss Elizabeth unless we wish to damage her reputation in the process. I will talk to Colonel Forster and warn him about Wickham's past disreputable behaviour. I do hope Forster heeds my warnings; we know how believable Wickham makes himself."

"I have never been as tempted to resort to physical violence as I have been for the past half hour with both of those men. Can Miss Elizabeth actually be *engaged* to that… that… Collins?" Darcy looked as if he were about to be sick.

"By all reports, Mr. Bennet is an intelligent man who loves his daughters, especially Miss Bennet and Miss Elizabeth. Miss Elizabeth is his favourite daughter. I have reason to be certain that he, unlike some fathers, would not force her into a marriage without its being her wish, no matter how beneficial it would be to her family," Richard said.

"Just where have you heard this?" Bingley asked.

"I have my sources," Richard said with a sly smile.

"Yes, Bingley, have you not learned by now that Richard has spies everywhere?" Darcy's face was beginning to show less tension.

Chapter 16

Entering the bookshop, Darcy's eyes sought out Elizabeth's. Since she looked relieved to see him, he proceeded directly to her side. Bingley joined Jane, who was paying Mr. Hall for their purchases. Richard remained very close to Mr. Collins in case the man decided to make an attempt to get near Elizabeth again. He did not wish to find out how Darcy would react in such a case.

Darcy noticed Elizabeth's colour was returning, "Are you feeling any better, Miss Elizabeth?"

"Yes, thank you, Mr. Darcy, I do. Will you be joining us for tea at Longbourn, sir?" she said aloud while communicating with her eyes that she wished to speak to him on the walk.

"We had every intention of escorting your party to Longbourn, madam, and I am certain that I speak for the others when I accept your invitation for tea. Actually, we were on our way to Longbourn when we came across you earlier." Darcy reprimanded himself. *Ah, maybe I should not have mentioned what happened earlier.*

Bingley chimed in, back to his usual amiable self, "Yes, we were at that. Our intention was to deliver an invitation to the ball that will be given at Netherfield next Tuesday. I do hope you all will be able to attend."

Elizabeth smiled toward Mr. Hall. "Thank you so much, Mr. Hall, for your hospitality and the use of your chair while I rested. We shall see you again soon, I am sure."

As the group left the bookshop, Richard excused himself. "I thank you for the kind invitation, ladies, but I need to speak with Colonel Forster as soon as possible. I will, most likely, meet you all at Longbourn, but if the meeting goes long, I will go directly to Netherfield when I am finished."

Everyone bid Richard a good day in case they should not see him for tea.

Darcy extended his arm to Elizabeth, and they walked from the shop together. When Mr. Collins came near, Elizabeth tightened her grip on Darcy's arm and paled a little.

How is she going to be able to live in the same house with this man for several days more? Darcy worried. *Maybe I should speak to Mr. Bennet about what happened today?*

Jane noticed Elizabeth's reaction as well and called out to Mr. Collins to explain a passage that Mary had read in the Bible the previous day but could not understand. No matter what else he was, his occupation was a clergyman, and so he should help anyone engaged in theological inquiry.

Bingley and Jane shared a look that said neither wanted to leave Mary alone with Mr. Collins, so they slowed down to keep them company while Mr. Collins and Mary talked of the Bible passage. Elizabeth and Darcy continued walking at the same pace while Lydia and Kitty walked ahead.

Elizabeth made sure everyone was out of hearing before she spoke. "Will you tell me what happened while we were in the bookshop, Mr. Darcy?"

Darcy was surprised at the question. "Nothing untoward, Miss Elizabeth. There is not much we can do other than warn the men, at least without bringing you unwanted attention from the neighbourhood. They have both been cautioned, and my cousin is speaking to Colonel Forster to explain to him about Wickham's past instances of… *reproachful* behaviour."

He paused and looked at her intently. "Might you allow me to speak to your father about what happened today, Miss Elizabeth? Mr. Wickham is not a man to be trusted, especially around young ladies, as I am sure you have surmised. I should like to think he will heed our warnings, but past experience has taught me not to trust him to do so. I will tell you he has been told that this is his last chance to redeem himself. I do hope he takes the opportunity that he has been given.

"I also would like to tell your father about today because… I think your father should know that Mr. Collins needs to be watched closely while staying in his house with his daughters." Darcy said this last part quickly. He did not say what he was thinking—that he feared for her safety.

Elizabeth looked at him thoughtfully. "You might be proposing the better option."

"Better option? What do you mean?"

Elizabeth became visibly upset, causing Darcy to become apprehensive of what she might say in response.

"If you tell my father about what occurred in the village, he might be on his guard. I hesitate to explain further…" She was silent for a minute or two and then seemed decided. "I have told only my sisters about this, Mr. Darcy, but I do trust you.

"My sisters and I have felt there is a need to lock our bedchamber doors since Mr. Collins has been in residence. I do not want my parents to know about what happened yesterday because I do not want to be forced into marriage with that disgusting, ridiculous man!"

From the look of alarm on Darcy's face, she knew she had gone too far not to explain further. "I have not been compromised, sir, but some might think I was, and I do not want there to be *any* misunderstandings. I found him in my bedchamber… I am not sure how to word this… closely examining some... clothing from my dresser drawer." Elizabeth turned bright crimson and Darcy immediately understood just what type of clothing Mr. Collins had handled. "I remained in the hallway and called for my sisters' attention so that there would be witnesses, and then ordered him out of the room. My sisters all have seen… they all understand what a repulsive man he is and have promised not to mention a word of this to anyone, sir. Even Kitty and Lydia have not spread this as gossip, and I must say that is a first!" Elizabeth tried to laugh at the last comment, but found she could not.

"May I ask... what excuse did he give for being in your chamber?" Darcy asked carefully, trying not to become angry.

"He claimed he was lost! Really! It is practically impossible that someone should become lost in a house such as Longbourn.

"We all had already been keeping our doors bolted when within our rooms… due to certain… *indications* that it might be necessary. Since yesterday's incident, we have been locking our doors at *all* times. Mrs. Hill has a key that she keeps on her person so the maids can clean, but she has been asked to lock the doors at all other times. He cannot gain access again. I did not explain to Mrs. Hill *why* we would be locking the doors, though I know for a fact that she is trustworthy. Actually, she gave me the impression of being rather relieved when I told her this, which makes me suspicious that something else, about which I know nothing, has happened with the staff. I have wondered if he had been found in our rooms another time by the maids… or worse. Oh! I do not wish to dwell upon the thought!

"I *would* feel more comfortable if my father was aware of Mr. Collins having less than gentleman-like manners. That is what I meant when I said that telling him about today's events would be the better option."

Darcy was expending an enormous amount of effort in controlling his temper lest he turn around and throttle the man walking behind him, but it was required that he raise *The Mask* to accomplish this task. "Forgive me for asking, but can you trust the staff at Longbourn not to speak about the need to lock the doors to other servants in the area?"

Elizabeth was disappointed to hear an icy tone enter Darcy's voice and to see the stone-faced expression fall over his face—one that she recognized only because she had seen him use it with others. *I should not have told him! Has he lost all respect for me?*

Elizabeth's vision became cloudy as her eyes filled with tears. She could not answer without beginning to cry; therefore, she remained silent and looked off toward the landscape so that he could not see her expression.

"Miss Elizabeth?" Still she remained silent, but she wiped at her face with her glove. His heart squeezed painfully. *I have upset her enough to make her cry? Was it the question or...?*

Not wanting to take any chances, Darcy placed his free hand over hers and said, "Miss Elizabeth, I am having a difficult time controlling my anger at Mr. Collins at the moment, especially hearing this after what has just occurred in Meryton. I am sorry if I have insulted you with my tone of voice. If it was the question which has upset you, please know that most servants gossip among themselves. The news is easily spread to the gentry. I only wished to be certain that you were safe from being the subject of such slander."

She took a few deep breaths and recovered enough to smile a little. "I thank you, sir, for being so honest. It has helped. I am not quite myself and am a bit emotional after this morning! It has been even more eventful than you already know, in fact. To answer your question, the Longbourn staff is loyal to the family and not prone to gossip. They have been with us for many years—some since before I was born. Mrs. Hill is like a second mother to Jane and me. There is no risk of gossip…" she cocked her head to the side. "No, that is not entirely true… I should say no risk of *negative* gossip. I have often heard Charlotte, oh—Miss Lucas, say she has overheard her staff speaking of how our staff tends to praise certain members of our family. Some would call that gossip, but I think it is more pride than anything else." Elizabeth smiled again.

"Something you mentioned earlier made me think there is something else that needs to be discussed before we reach Longbourn, Miss Elizabeth. You said you did not wish to marry Mr. Collins. I – I should tell you that while we were at Meryton, Mr. Collins mentioned that he is betrothed to you." Darcy braced himself for her answer.

Elizabeth closed her eyes and sighed. "Oh dear. I guess I was wrong, sir; you do know *just* what an eventful this morning has been after all! Mrs. Hill and I overheard him talking to my mother before our morning meal. My mother happily agreed to 'save us from the hedgerows after Mr. Bennet's death,' but Mr. Collins has *not* yet petitioned my father, or me, about the matter.

"I can tell you exactly what will happen, though my initial reaction was not as rational as it is now. I will most certainly refuse him, and then my mother will ask my father to force me to marry Mr. Collins to save the family." She noticed Mr. Darcy shudder.

"But you see, sir, my father has a wish for his daughters to respect and love their marriage partners—something of which my mother has no understanding. I suspect he has learned from… how shall I say it… *experience* that this would be preferable when compared to a marriage of convenience. I do think if he believed me to be compromised by Mr. Collins that he *would* force me to marry him rather than ruin the entire family's reputation, but not otherwise. Though this morning when I overheard their conversation, I do admit to being upset, after consideration of the subject during the walk to Meryton, I have no fears… as long as my father does not hear about that other incident we spoke of earlier. The likelihood that he would misunderstand what happened is slim, but I would rather not depend upon probability." She finished her speech just as Longbourn came into sight.

"That is good to hear, Miss Elizabeth. Be assured I will *not* tell your father of the incident you have relayed to me a few minutes ago, only the one which I witnessed myself earlier today."

"Thank you, Mr. Darcy. I do appreciate everything you have done, and plan to do, on my behalf. You are a good friend, sir." Elizabeth said with a brilliant smile, as they approached the front door. *I have not lost his friendship after all!*

Darcy tried to keep a pleasant expression on his face, but he felt a sudden turmoil within himself. *'A good friend?' I do not* ***want*** *her to think of me in that way!*

~A bedroom somewhere near Meryton

When George Wickham departed from his encounter with William and Richard, he headed directly to see Colonel Forster to "explain" his relationship to the two men. The only way that Wickham could be more pleased by the outcome of the meeting with his superior officer would be if he could be there in person to see Richard's face when Colonel Forster rejected all that Richard would tell him! But, he would not take such a chance.

After this meeting, he went directly to his *appointment* with a tempting barmaid that he had met at the tavern the night before. All through this encounter, his mind was not on the barmaid but upon the lady he had met earlier today. Taking time to rest afterward, Wickham's thoughts wandered over his life and how he came to be here in Meryton.

Wickham had no scruples about how he got what he wanted, and he wanted anything he could get. His earliest adventures consisted of abusing a neighbourhood until his gambling debts, creditors, or indulgences with the female members of the locality necessitated an escape either from the local authorities ready to put him in prison, or an angry father with a pitchfork about to force him to marry his daughter—depending only on which indiscretion was discovered first.

There had been several duel challenges along the way, which he enjoyed immensely, for he would be expected to adhere to the engagement as any honourable man would. Smiling at the thought that he was *not* an honourable man, he remembered the many occasions on which he had escaped the area well before the appointed time. It greatly amused him to know there had been at least three people waiting for him at each of the specified dueling sites while he was already on his way to another location envisioning his next ploy.

Due to his polished charm, Wickham made friends easily. People of both genders flocked to him in droves and would believe almost anything he said. Sometimes he amazed even himself at the bold lies he could tell without being doubted. With a talent for instinctively knowing what most people wanted him to be, he would change his façade into whatever they wished to see. His confidence in this ability made him a bit careless at times, especially when he had been drinking, but he always made a plan of escape that could be carried out at a moment's notice.

In fact, planning his escape was the first thing he did upon arriving in a new area. Depending upon his mood, he chose some areas on the basis of a simple escape, but he also rather enjoyed the challenge of planning one in a less convenient situation.

While the escape was usually his first priority, during the planning he would determine his targets—for instance the scrumptious barmaid who was, at the moment, chattering away about some silly subject to which he need not pay any attention other than to nod every now and then. It was a requirement for there to be at least a couple of pretty and buxom, yet stupid and flirty, women for him to charm, plus one who would be "the challenge."

It mattered not to him what station in society they were from; in fact, the more women who were of the lower classes, the better he liked it. He knew servants, barmaids, and daughters of small shop owners would be overlooked by the upper classes in the neighbourhood, and their guardians would not have the funds to search for him for long, if at all.

The "challenge" was usually a gentleman's daughter who would normally not look twice at the son of a country steward; an intelligent or independent lady was ideal. He liked his women spirited, and he loved to violate that spirit usually first with his charms, and then later with his person. The lady was always willing, eventually.

The independent lady was the most amusing for the latter purpose, since they usually put up the most resistance. The gentleman's daughters who were intelligent were the most difficult to subvert since, even if they were conquered physically, their minds might continue to resist.

Once in a while he could convince a less intelligent woman to run away to Gretna Green and charm her into living with him for a while, all the time promising he would marry her *at some point…* until he became frustrated with her stupidity or became short on funds, and he would move on, leaving her to find her own way from that time forward.

Wickham had spent years in this manner, but only *after* being betrayed by his childhood friend, Fitzwilliam Darcy, whom he had grown up alongside.

Before his untimely death about five years past, Mr. George Darcy, Wickham's godfather and benefactor, had completely funded his debaucheries. Wickham had spent years testing the limits of what Mr. Darcy would continue to finance and then lied to Mr. Darcy to obtain funds for the rest of his habits. With his easy manners and ability to charm almost anyone, especially Mr. Darcy since Wickham knew the old man so well, it had been all too easy to do.

William, Mr. Darcy's son, was different from his father in many ways and would not provide funds as had his father, and so Wickham was forced to fend for himself after the original bequest had been run through. He was thankful he had the cleverness of mind to succeed in doing so, but was left with a feeling of bitter malevolence towards William for making it necessary. His father had treated them as if they were brothers, and so should he!

On occasion, he would endeavor to marry a lady with a fortune. He had tried this scheme a few times, but either the father, uncle, or brother had discovered his true character and had forbidden the match. The closest he had gotten to actual marriage, ironically, was to William's sister, Georgiana. A naive fifteen-year-old, Georgiana Darcy had known Wickham all of her life, but mainly her memories were of the few occasions they had spent together at Pemberley when he had used his talents to entertain the daughter in order to recommend himself to her father.

This past summer, Wickham had met Georgiana at Ramsgate by chance when he was involved in some local *business* for his new benefactor. He had easily discerned that Georgiana was conveniently unaware of William's opinion of himself. After all, what brother would tell his young sister of the activities in which William had witnessed Wickham's involvement while they had been at Cambridge together?

By happy coincidence, he knew Georgiana's companion quite well from past *business* dealings. Mrs. Younge became a willing assistant to his undertaking—at a price of course. Wickham was not surprised that William had hired this woman, for he knew part of her expertise lay in concealing past indiscretions. They had spent much time together in the past, learning quite a bit from the other's experience… in many different subjects.

Oh, it would have been a triumph indeed to have eloped with Georgiana Darcy! Wickham would have obtained all the fortune he could have needed whilst gratifying this consuming preoccupation to revenge himself on William all in one fell swoop! Unfortunately, it all ended in nothing as William thwarted the plan only one day before they were to leave for Gretna Green, once again fueling the fire of Wickham's almost physical need for revenge against the gentleman.

Wickham continued to have connexions with the Darcy family, though the Darcys were unaware of this fact. Within this past year, Lady Catherine de Bourgh, the sister of the late Mrs. Darcy, had become his new benefactress. He did not like taking orders from the old witch, but he did bear it since it benefitted him so greatly at this time. She paid him well for doing what he loved to do best… skirting his way around the law and society's rules. He loved the intrigue associated with the business in which she had him involved and the thrill of the risks it entailed.

Lady Catherine did not disapprove of his debaucheries as long as they did not interfere with his duties, though she always required that his actions come to pass in a place and time of *her* choosing. The most difficult of her rules to follow was her insistence that he had to be certain he duped any gentleman's daughters according to the old witch's timetable and not his own. If she wanted him in a specific town or village for a certain period of time, he was not permitted to change that plan. Soon he learned how to pace himself and discovered that the extended anticipation was even more exciting.

Recently, the old lady had sent him to a new village under the guise of a militiaman, paying for his commission herself through disguised channels. She had a plan for expanding her enterprise into this area, and she wanted him to keep watch on another of her *workers*, Mr. Collins.

The way Collins worshipped the lady, which made Wickham physically ill whenever he was witness to it, *had* to be the reason she had hired such a ridiculous man. Though she was oppressively egotistical towards him, he willingly fed her needs with his groveling. She was tyrannical and he was her obedient servant. She even forced him to be ordained and become her parson to keep him close by!

Collins's weaknesses were of the flesh, and he usually liked the same type of woman Wickham did. Collins was not really as stupid as he seemed to be, at least when it came to women. As soon as Wickham would abandon a girl, Collins had learned to act as if he felt sympathy for her, taking up right where Wickham had left off! Being of the clergy, once everyone else had turned away from the ruined girl, she would be in a vulnerable state and trust him, and eventually Collins would follow Wickham's example of escape. These situations were acceptable to Wickham since he had already had his fill—*first*!

This time, Wickham thought the old witch had gone too far, but Collins was still following her orders, so who was he to complain? She was forcing Collins to *marry* someone so that she could gain permanent access to the geographic area in which the lady's family resided.

When Wickham saw the lady Collins had chosen, even from afar he knew instantly by the look in her eyes that she was his *ultimate* challenge. He had heard about her from the townspeople, but he could tell much more by being in her presence. Not only was she proper and spirited, she oozed intelligence *and* independence from every pore of the luscious, yet innocent, body of a gentleman's daughter. It was unfortunate she did not have a fortune or she would have been his ideal marriage partner! After being in her presence only for a minute, he knew that *this* woman would be the masterpiece of his existence up to this point.

As he had stood there being introduced to her family and Collins, he began devising his plan. Until she was made Mrs. Collins, he would make the old lady happy and limit himself to flirting. He was absolutely certain that after she married Collins she would quickly tire of the boring, greasy, stupid man that would be her husband and gravitate toward one who was handsome, charming, and intelligent—himself. Then, once she had, he would enjoy her whenever he came to Rosings. He would hold off on dampening her spirit for a while, of that he was certain…the anticipation of *that* day would be reward enough.

But then…oh! Before long he had found out she truly *was* the ultimate prize! Once the gentlemen had arrived at the scene, it was plain for Wickham to see that William Darcy was *in love* with the country miss whom Collins was about to marry! The cold-hearted, severely moral, ever proper William actually had within him the ability to love!

His plan changed a bit after he realized this. He would not only do his best to encourage the marriage between Collins and Elizabeth Bennet in order to satisfy Lady Catherine's demands, but by doing so, he would break the heart of the man he despised more than any other!

The situation was beyond perfect! How could he pass on a chance to guarantee Lady Catherine's continued gratitude, have a source of recurrent pleasure in this delicious woman, dupe Collins repeatedly, *and* revenge himself on Darcy! *This* conquest would be considerably sweet indeed!

He laughed out loud at the prospect. When the barmaid made an inquiry as to why he was laughing, he hungrily took in the full length of her with his gaze, smiled rakishly, and said, "Time to have another go at it, my dear!"

~Longbourn Estate

After their return from Meryton, the group reconvened in the hallway, where all outerwear was handed over to the overwhelmed Mrs. Hill and Emily. Mrs. Hill whispered a warning to Jane that Mrs. Bennet had been in a high state of anxiety all day. Jane requested tea to be sent in for their guests, and almost everyone headed for the drawing room. Elizabeth made a gesture to Darcy indicating he should remain in the hall.

During the confusion of removing coats, hats, and gloves, Elizabeth slipped away to her father's study to inform him of Darcy's wish to speak to him.

Mr. Bennet's eyebrows rose as high as they could. Elizabeth began to laugh. "No, Papa, it is not what you think; Mr. Darcy and I are just good friends, though part of what he needs to say *is* about me. He wishes to speak to you about something that occurred while we were in Meryton this morning. Do you wish me to stay, or would you like to speak to Mr. Darcy alone?"

Mr. Bennet debated this internally. Being an astute observer, he had noticed that Darcy was much more comfortable talking to *anyone* with Elizabeth nearby; she seemed to bring out the best in him. But from the way Elizabeth was acting, he thought Darcy might need to say things which should not be said with a lady in the room—which alarmed him greatly. "With which alternative would you be more comfortable, my Lizzy?"

"I am not sure."

"Well then, since Mr. Darcy is most familiar with what he would like to say, let us allow him to make the choice, shall we? Call him in."

Elizabeth went to the door and waved Darcy into the study, not wishing her mother or Mr. Collins to be aware of this conversation. The gentlemen greeted each other and Mr. Bennet began, "Mr. Darcy, Lizzy tells me you wish to speak to me about something that occurred in Meryton today. Should Lizzy be present for this discussion, or should she rejoin our other guests?"

Darcy's gaze turned to Elizabeth, requesting her opinion on the matter, and she gave him a sign that she had decided she would like to stay, so he answered, "I do think Miss Elizabeth can stay, sir. She knows more than I about what happened before I came upon the scene, and I would like for her to hear the remainder."

Mrs. Hill had seen the two enter the study and had discreetly made up a second, smaller tea tray. The staff at Longbourn might not gossip, but that did not mean they did not *hear* the gossip from the neighbourhood. She had a feeling that those three would be in the study for quite a while and would require refreshments.

Mrs. Hill knocked on the door to the study and entered. Elizabeth smiled at her, motioned to the table nearby, and thanked the housekeeper. The two women exchanged a look that told Elizabeth all she needed to know.

Elizabeth asked, "Mrs. Hill? What is being said?" Mrs. Hill glanced at Darcy, and Elizabeth continued, "It is all right; you may speak freely."

"Well, Miss, Emily's boy, he was running an errand to the village and came back only jus' now. He heard some talk that upset him and came to tell me. 'Tis being said that *something* happened this morning in Meryton involving you, Miss, but nobody knows what. I'm afraid the gossips will begin to make things up, ma'am."

"Thank you, Hill." Mr. Bennet was clearly dismissing her, and Mrs. Hill left with a curtsy.

When the door closed, Elizabeth turned to the gentlemen and said, "Oh! I thought it happened quickly enough that nobody would notice." Her colour was beginning to fade, and Darcy was afraid she would react as she had earlier. Elizabeth surprised him when she began to prepare tea for the gentlemen instead. Commonplace actions always helped her to steady herself.

Mr. Bennet did not miss the expression of concern on Darcy's face. *Exceedingly interesting, Mr. Darcy!*

"Well then, I guess you had better tell me what happened before any of the gossips come from Meryton to see my wife! She is already excited about one subject today, which I am attempting to contain within the house by not allowing her the use of the carriage, but her sister is sure to come eventually." He looked at Elizabeth pointedly.

Elizabeth blushed, "Yes, Papa, unfortunately Mr. Darcy, Mr. Bingley, and Colonel Fitzwilliam already know about that subject as you could not limit Mr. Collins's access to the public as well, sir. Many things happened in Meryton." She quickly turned her head to Mr. Darcy. "Oh, did Mr. Wickham hear it, too?"

Darcy nodded.

"Who is Mr. Wickham?"

"Papa, I think I had better start explaining since I know what happened before Mr. Darcy and the other gentlemen arrived. As you know, my sisters, Mr. Collins, and I walked into Meryton. After we arrived, Kitty and Lydia began to talk to Mr. Denny and Mr. Saunderson who were with a man we had not seen before. Mr. Wickham was introduced, as he has only just joined the militia and will be in the area for some time.

"Then some odd things began to happen which made me… uncomfortable. I was standing nearest to Mr. Wickham when he was introduced to Mr. Collins—and upon seeing him, Mr. Collins attached himself to my side. The two men exchanged looks which told of them knowing each other well, but their spoken words were as if they were making each other's acquaintance for the first time." Mr. Bennet noticed that she had refrained from using the word "gentlemen" when referring to Mr. Wickham and Mr. Collins.

"I can tell there is much more to this than you have said. Go on, child."

"The two men… Papa, I am not sure how to describe it. It was as if they were silently fighting for possession… over *me*. They both moved in close to me… I was frightened…" Elizabeth was becoming too upset to speak.

Darcy continued for her. "That is when we arrived, Mr. Bennet. Bingley, Colonel Fitzwilliam, and I recognized a situation developing and immediately went to Miss Elizabeth's aid. Miss Elizabeth is correct; there was a struggle between them, and they stood close enough to her that she could not escape.

"I understand part of the reason for this since Mr. Collins later explained that he is under the impression… that Mrs. Bennet gave *her* permission… well, sir, he says that he is betrothed to Miss Elizabeth." Darcy said the last part slowly to see Mr. Bennet's reaction, while keeping part of his attention on Elizabeth throughout.

Mr. Bennet bolted up straight in his chair. "Mr. Darcy, my wife has been going on about Mr. Collins wanting to marry Elizabeth all morning, but are you saying she told Mr. Collins that he has *permission* to marry her?" He raised his voice during the last few words.

"This is what Mr. Collins asserts; yes, sir."

Mr. Bennet was furious at his wife and Mr. Collins, but he knew this story was not over. He took a few deep breaths, removed his glasses, and pinched the bridge of his nose to stem the headache he felt coming on. "Please continue."

"Mr. Bennet, it does explain why Mr. Collins was acting 'possessive,' as Miss Elizabeth calls it, but it does not explain why Mr. Collins is hiding his knowledge of Wickham, nor does it explain Wickham's actions. I must warn you about this man, sir.

"But first you should understand that my cousin, Colonel Richard Fitzwilliam, felt the same way as Miss Elizabeth does. These two men know each other and were making it seem as if they do not. There is more going on here than any of us understands, and I do mean *both* men are hiding something. I mention Colonel Fitzwilliam because he is well-known in the military for extracting information from those who are unwilling to give it. He can tell much from how people move, the manner in which they speak, and even from what they do *not* say. He is known as an expert in this area, sir. My cousin would be impressed by your coming to the same conclusion as he, Miss Elizabeth." Darcy smiled slightly at Elizabeth before returning his attention to her father.

"I should tell you both more about George Wickham. Colonel Fitzwilliam remained in Meryton to have a talk with Colonel Forster, but I would like to warn the shopkeepers and other gentlemen in the area about him as well, sir. Wickham is not to be trusted to extend credit to at the shops, and he is a cheat at gambling. He will not pay debts, and should not be at all trusted… let us just say that he should not be trusted with being near ladies of *any* station, sir." He glanced apologetically at Elizabeth.

"I have known Wickham all my life, as has Colonel Fitzwilliam. He was the son of my father's steward and was brought up nearly alongside me.

My father was good to him and sent him to school, including Cambridge. He fooled my father up until his dying day, sir, but I lived with the man at Cambridge—he could not hide his true nature from me. He is an evil man, though he has an amazing talent to charm almost anyone into believing that he is an angel instead. He makes friends easily, but he does not retain friendships for long. His true colours always show through, though usually too late for many of those who have trusted him.

"My cousin and I have recognized his ways, and have tried to help the people he has injured—those we know about at least. We know not exactly why, but the people he hurts are usually too afraid to lodge complaints with the authorities, sir. There have been those who have begged us not to report what happened to them, all in fear of Wickham! Unfortunately, he is also good at covering his tracks. Even Colonel Fitzwilliam cannot find him… usually.

"That he was unaware of our presence in the neighbourhood when we approached was clear, but unusual for him. Wickham should bolt now that he knows we are here, but if he stays… let us just say that would be a matter for great concern.

"That Mr. Collins knows him, but will not admit to it, is an even graver issue, in my opinion. Additionally, Mr. Collins's behaviour toward Miss Elizabeth was not appropriate in any way, even if the man believes he is betrothed to the lady. I must say I do not trust him. I can be more specific if you would like, sir, about what I have observed in the short time I have seen him, but I would ask Miss Elizabeth to leave the room first." Darcy blushed considerably, as did Elizabeth. As an afterthought, Darcy added, "Since Mr. Collins is your cousin, I mean no disrespect to you, sir, but after speaking to him, I wonder at my Aunt Catherine's offering your cousin the living at her estate. Perhaps if he did not have such a sought-after position, he would not be so confident in his behaviour."

"Lady Catherine de Bourgh is your aunt, Mr. Darcy?" Elizabeth asked.

Darcy nodded.

Mr. Bennet had become increasingly concerned all through Darcy's speech and more than curious about his protective feelings toward Elizabeth. "I am glad you have come to me with all this. I think I should be the one to warn the shopkeepers and neighbours in the area about Mr. Wickham's behaviour since I am the principal landowner in the area.

"Lizzy, I would ask you a question. Is there anything else you would like to tell me about Mr. Collins behaviour? Perhaps you would explain why all the girls' bedrooms are locked today? And why none of my daughters are allowing any of the others to be alone with Mr. Collins? Or mayhap you can tell me why the servants' wing has been locked since yesterday morning as well?"

Elizabeth's eyes widened at the information about the servants' wing being locked, and she noticed that the news made Darcy's back stiffen. She only said, "Sir, we are not comfortable with Mr. Collins in the house."

Mr. Bennet was thoughtful for a few moments. *Intriguing! Darcy reacted only to the fact that the servants' quarters are being locked, not to the girls' rooms. I am glad I brought it up in front of him. What did she tell Darcy that she does not feel she can tell me? And why does she trust him so? Do they have feelings for each other?*

"You have both given me much to think about. At present, though I think I should, I *cannot* tell Mr. Collins to leave Longbourn based on what you and the servants are willing to tell me. I have no way to account for it without causing more gossip, considering what Mrs. Bennet has led him to believe about Lizzy." At Elizabeth's worried expression he got up, walked around the desk and placed his hand on his daughter's shoulder. "Do not worry, child, I will not give my permission for him to marry you. You know me better than that, do you not?" Elizabeth smiled at her father, and then Mr. Bennet continued, "I will have a talk with Mr. Collins and set him to rights about the proper behaviour expected from a guest of Longbourn… and about your mother's scheming as well.

"After which, I will tell my wife that there was a slight misunderstanding in Meryton this morning which has been resolved by the gentlemen involved, and that it turned out to be nothing of consequence. That should clear up the gossip."

Darcy was confused. "How will telling this to Mrs. Bennet clear up gossip, sir?"

Mr. Bennet laughed. "Ah, I see you do not know my wife and sister-in-law well, Mr. Darcy! The pair of them are the most effective of all gossips in Hertfordshire. She will have *our version* of the story out there in no time at all as I will send for the carriage and she will be off to see her sister just after hearing it! All *will* be well, my Lizzy!"

"I do hope so, Papa," she said as she stood and kissed his cheek.

"Mr. Bennet, shall I stay? Did you wish for me to explain Mr. Collins's behaviour in more detail?" Darcy asked.

"No, Mr. Darcy, by the blush on both your faces when you brought it up, I can well imagine what kind of behaviour he has displayed. I actually prefer *not* to hear the details of it in reference to my daughter… as I am sure you would not if it were your sister, Mr. Darcy. But you can be assured that I will not allow it to continue." He rubbed his hand over his face. "Enjoy your tea with Mr. Bingley and my other daughters. I need some time alone before I send for Mr. Collins."

~*~*~*~*~*~*~*~*~*~*~*~*~

Elizabeth noticed Darcy's sudden withdrawal within himself as they joined the others in the drawing room. She could see he was deep in thought, and she wondered which subject that they had discussed with her father could have prompted an expression such as *this* to be displayed upon his face.

She could not have imagined what he *was* thinking. The relationship between Elizabeth and her father, and their easy way of conversing, had touched Darcy deeply… but it also made him uncomfortable on many levels.

Not only did seeing their rapport cause him to miss the close relationship he had had with his mother in his boyhood, but it also reminded him of the loss of a similar bond he had had with his own father before his mother died. It was almost as if both of his parents died that day, for in the years following her death, he could only watch as his father became a stranger to him and slowly grew closer to Wickham.

There was another reason for this discomfort, though he did not want to admit it to himself. That she had confided in him about the events of the previous day made his heart sing with pleasure—*he* wanted to be the man that Elizabeth was closest to, the one that she relied on for protection.

He knew these feelings were irrational, and he should rejoice for Elizabeth and her father's special connexion. Part of his consciousness did! But he could not help himself from envying what Elizabeth had with her father—that which he had been forced to relinquish with his own parents—nor from being a bit jealous that he would never be as close to Elizabeth as he wished to be.

Envy and jealousy were two emotions that could only shame him, and he had to rein them in.

Darcy did not react to anything around him until Mr. Collins approached Elizabeth, and then, since her father was not present, he stepped into the protective role that he had earlier longed to be allowed to take, moving between them. Guiding Elizabeth to a sofa which was large enough for only two, he sat beside her.

Mrs. Bennet attempted to persuade Darcy to move, clearly indicating that the space beside Elizabeth was Mr. Collins's rightful place, but Darcy acted as if he did not hear her. He did not trust himself to speak civilly to Mrs. Bennet just now—or to Mr. Collins for that matter.

After a while, Mr. Collins was called into Mr. Bennet's study. With a knowing glance at Elizabeth, Darcy began a discussion of Shakespeare's plays to distract her attention from what only they two understood was occurring in the study. After raised, but muffled, voices were heard from that direction, a door was slammed, and Mr. Collins's mumblings were made out as he ascended the stairs to his bedchamber, after which the sound of a second door slamming could be heard from above.

Elizabeth whispered to Darcy, "I think it would be wise for you all to depart before my mother hears the news, sir. I would rather you gentlemen *not* be witness to what I expect to be rather violent reproaches of me!"

Not feeling comfortable leaving her to endure what she described, he asked, "Miss Elizabeth, if it would be of any help, I would be willing to tell her what I witnessed."

Elizabeth smiled, knowing her mother would not be in the state of mind to understand anything Darcy had to say once she was told the match would never take place. "I thank you, Mr. Darcy, you are kind, but I do not think it will be necessary."

Darcy signaled to Bingley that it was time to go, and the two took their leave. Jane mentioned its being a shame that Colonel Fitzwilliam could not finish his business in time to join them. She, Elizabeth, Darcy, and Bingley, not wishing to speak of it aloud, exchanged looks all wondering what was taking Colonel Fitzwilliam so long.

Mr. Bennet poured himself a glass of port and thought for a while. Why did his wife have to be so silly and nonsensical? Why on earth did she feel she had the right to give consent for Mr. Collins to marry Lizzy? That Mr. Collins believed her without asking him was another mystery. Could it be possible that Mr. Collins was as ridiculous as Mrs. Bennet? Could Mr. Collins not see the revulsion Lizzy exhibited toward him every time they were together in a room?

Telling him that he would not be granted permission to marry Lizzy was going to be difficult based on what he had heard so far. He decided not to single out Lizzy in his reprimands of how he had behaved towards his daughters.

After a while, Mr. Bennet rang for Mrs. Hill, surprising her since he rarely did so. Mrs. Hill rushed in immediately. That she was thinking something must be terribly wrong was evident on her features, and Mr. Bennet could not help but chuckle before requesting that she send in Mr. Collins. Perhaps that bit of entertainment was just what he required to get through the next few minutes.

At Collins's knock on the door, Mr. Bennet bid him to enter and motioned to one of the chairs in front of his desk. Mr. Collins took it while displaying a wide grin, obviously anticipating that the upcoming conversation would be to his liking.

Mr. Bennet stood directly in front of Mr. Collins. Clasping his hands behind his back and looking down at the man, he said in a voice deep with all the authority that he could muster, "Mr. Collins, I understand you have *not* been behaving as a gentleman towards my daughters. I myself saw the way you looked at them when you first arrived, but it seemed that you were attempting to control yourself better after that first day. It has now come to my attention that you have been making the effort only within my presence, and that you have been displaying even less proper behaviour in public.

"You will behave in a manner which is expected from a guest at Longbourn, sir, or you will be expelled from the premises and prohibited from being in the company of my family ever again. You will treat my daughters, and all other ladies, with the utmost degree of respect and propriety."

Mr. Collins displayed a shocked expression. He was expecting Mr. Bennet to welcome him into the immediate family as fiancé to Miss Elizabeth, not *this*! He opened his mouth to speak but Mr. Bennet held up his hand to quiet him and continued in a booming voice which he used but rarely.

"I am not finished speaking, Mr. Collins. You *will* hear me out! I understand from my wife's ranting all morning that you wish to marry my daughter, Elizabeth. I have also heard from other sources that you have actually been *telling* people that you are already engaged to be married to her!

"I wish to make it perfectly clear that you do NOT have my permission to marry her. You have never even requested permission. I do not wish to cause you any disappointment, but I do wish to make certain you understand that you will never gain permission to marry any of my daughters, Mr. Collins.

"I will further add that you have greatly affronted me by assuming that you had permission to marry my daughter after a conversation with my wife. As long as I am alive, *I* am the master of this estate and the head of this family, and it would do you good to remember that fact, Mr. Collins! I am highly insulted that you have completely disregarded my authority.

"I do not want to hear further of any of these issues—not one word, sir. If I hear of any wrongful behaviour from you again, I will have my men take you and your things off my property and you will not be welcome back here again until after I am dead. As to an engagement, there will be *none.* I do not want to hear the subject even hinted at again!

"Now you may answer me in a one word reply, sir. Do you understand everything I have said to you?"

Mr. Collins replied, "Mr. Bennet, you do not understand. My offer…"

Mr. Bennet boomed even louder than before, "MR. COLLINS! I said I will accept a *one word* reply… you may say 'yes' or 'no'; do you understand all that I have said during this interview?"

Mr. Collins cowered and said meekly, "Yes."

"Good. Mr. Collins, do you *agree* to follow the rules I have set out during this interview? One word reply, sir." He held up one finger.

"Yes," he almost whispered.

"Good. I am satisfied. You may go."

"I must leave Longbourn?"

"You will leave Longbourn when your allotted visit is up, unless you do not follow the rules I have set forth, but *for now,* you must leave my room!"

"Yes, thank you, Mr. Bennet."

Mr. Bennet let out a great sigh when Mr. Collins slammed the door behind him. He poured himself a glass of port, drank it down quickly, and then poured another. He felt as if he had aged ten years in the past hour. Knowing he must next speak to his wife, he decided he needed a few quiet moments alone to prepare himself for the next round. He rubbed his face with both hands.

I will have to be even more firm with Mrs. Bennet than I was with Mr. Collins. I see I should have done this many years ago with her. I cannot believe she went so far as to give her permission without consulting me. I must address the gossip problem.

Standing by the window, he nursed his drink while thinking back on his life and his regrets. He could not regret marrying Fanny since his daughters, especially Jane and his Lizzy, were a product of that marriage, but he *did* regret not having taken as heavy a hand as he should have.

This event proved that his wife's deportment was beyond what he had ever thought possible, and he knew it was his fault for not seeing it sooner. He should have checked Fanny's behaviour from the beginning and should have helped guide the younger daughters as well. He did not think there was any hope for Lydia though he would now try, and he decided to do more with Mary and Kitty to help form their characters into those of young ladies more like their older sisters. He could no longer leave them to their mother's exclusive care.

He was glad his eldest two girls turned out to be the sensible ladies that they were, which was remarkable since they had been under her guidance the longest. He was happy they were both determined to look beyond a beautiful veneer when searching for a marriage partner… unlike the man he had been at their age. Mr. Bennet was well aware of the marriage proposals the girls had refused, though they all agreed it was best not to mention them to their mother.

Even *he* was impressed that Lizzy had possessed the integrity not to have been influenced by the wealth and rank of a grandson of a member of the peerage. She had refused him because she could neither respect nor care for the man—his wealth mattered not to her. She had always remained true to her values and, he hoped, would have a happy life as a result.

He wondered if Darcy was the man for her. In a few brief unguarded moments over the past months, Mr. Bennet had seen love in Darcy's eyes when he looked at Lizzy. The shyness he had heard so much about was obvious to him, though the rest of the neighbourhood saw it as arrogance. They did not see how Lizzy affected his behaviour for the better for some reason, and he thought that odd—yet most people did not study others as he did.

Lizzy was good for Darcy! He would be a truly great man with Lizzy by his side.

Was Darcy good for Lizzy? That was the question Mr. Bennet would need to answer for himself before Darcy came to him. He saw Darcy resisting his affections for Lizzy as well, and knew there was something Darcy needed to resolve first… though today he seemed closer to making a decision than he had been in the past.

But there are more immediate matters with which to deal.

Mr. Bennet drank down the last of the port from his glass, and then rang again for Mrs. Hill.

~*~*~*~*~*~*~*~*~*~*~*~*~

Mr. Collins went straight to his bedroom after the interview with Mr. Bennet and began pacing while wringing his hands.

Oh, what am I to do? Lady Catherine ordered me to marry Miss Elizabeth! Oh! I sent the express to her this morning after speaking to Mrs. Bennet saying we were betrothed! She will be extremely angry with me!

He did not want to admit his failure, but he knew what he had to do—send an express letter to Lady Catherine. He sat down at the small table and took an extraordinarily long time in preparing his writing materials.

What to say? How will she react? Oh, how did this happen?

He thought it best to begin and be done quickly:

> *My dearest noble patroness, Lady Catherine de Bourgh,*
>
> *I regret to inform you that I am <u>not</u> engaged to be married to Miss Elizabeth Bennet as her father has refused his permission for me to marry any of his daughters.*
>
> *Please advise me as to what to do next.*
>
> *Your faithful servant,*
>
> *William Collins*

~Militia Headquarters, Meryton

Colonel Richard Fitzwilliam waited in the outer office of Colonel Forster. The two gentlemen had renewed their acquaintance when Richard delivered the correspondence from his general a few days prior. Forster had been surprised that a celebrated war hero was delivering messages, but the confusion was cleared up once Richard explained that he was on his way to take leave in the area to spend some time with family.

Feeling it was an honour to gain his attention, Forster did not keep him waiting long. What he was not prepared for was the information Richard was passing along. He explained that his new recruit, Wickham, was not a man to be trusted and he requested permission to go into more detail for the purpose of warning Forster against him.

Forster had heard about an altercation between the men earlier that day when Denny and Saunderson had been to see him prior to Richard's visit, and then Wickham had reported to him immediately upon his return to camp. Wickham seemed a pleasant fellow and had already gained many of the men's friendly attentions with his open manners.

Though Forster was not a stupid man, he was not of as strong an understanding as some might think his position would require. The fact was, though he might not be as capable as others who might have held his position, his connexions in the world kept his place. He did not have the talent for seeing beyond the obvious as Richard did, nor of seeing hidden motives, and so the conflicting stories were confusing to him.

Based on his reputation, Forster had no reason to doubt Richard's information either. He recognized that while the man's connexions might have been better than his own and instrumental in gaining *his* position, the man had distinguished himself many times on the battlefield and behind the lines as well. He was one of the few who had *earned* the right to be called "Colonel" and "hero."

"I will hear you out, Colonel Fitzwilliam, but I must tell you that Wickham has made quite a good impression on me and all of my men, for that matter. What information would you like to pass on, sir?"

Wickham got to him already! Richard sighed and shook his head.

"Colonel Forster, Wickham has a talent for making himself seem all that is pleasant and charming and useful, but underneath it all he is one of the basest creatures I have ever met… and I have met many in my time. You cannot be cautious enough with him, sir.

"He is not only a rake of the worst kind, but he becomes cruel to the women he lures in once he has established himself with them, leaving a trail of ruined women—gentry among them—and fatherless children behind him. He will rob your men blind cheating at gambling, and when his luck runs dry, his gambling debts will never be paid. The local shops, and especially the tavern, should not allow him to run up lines of credit, for they will lose it all. He is the type of man who bleeds a village dry and then escapes.

"Colonel Forster, please, for the sake of your men, and for the community you are here to serve, you must keep a close watch on the man."

"Do you have any proof of these claims?"

"Those he leaves in his wake—from Cambridge to Cumberland, from Kellington to Cornwall, and quite a few places in between—*must* have been threatened somehow since most will not testify against him. Those few who have had the courage to testify against him do so too late; the man has made escape an art and there has been no trace of him by the time he has been reported. It is suspicious that some of those who have come forward have met with unfortunate '*accidents,*' but there is no proof tying Wickham to any of them."

Forster examined Richard closely. "Are you sure this is not a personal quest for vengeance, Colonel?"

Insulted, Richard raised his voice, "What do you mean, sir?"

"Wickham has told me about your shared background and of his dealings with Mr. Darcy. He reported here upon returning to camp just a few minutes ago to let me know that you, or possibly both of you, would come to see me soon and would try to blacken his character. He did admit to some indiscretions in the past, but I doubt there are many men among the ranks of the military who had not engaged in *some* folly as a youth. You say you cannot prove any of the more serious charges you profess him to be guilty of and yet expect me to believe you and blindly lay restrictions upon a man who has not shown any evidence of misdeeds to me personally.

"This I cannot do. Because of your reputation in the military, I will keep a watchful eye on him as a favor to you. But I can do no more than that at this time, Colonel Fitzwilliam.

"And Colonel… I will not stand for any of my men being harassed, even by a distinguished officer as you. This is not a military assignment you are on, sir; this sounds personal to me."

Richard was furious, and he made no effort to hide it. "Thank you for your time, Colonel Forster. I see that you will have to learn for yourself about the rascal. I just hope it is not a lesson too hard learned." He stomped out of the room.

Too angry to be of good company to the ladies during a tea at Longbourn, he headed straight back to Netherfield… hoping Caroline Bingley stayed far away from him once he arrived.

~Longbourn Estate

Mrs. Bennet passed through the door to the study and began chattering immediately about a match between Mr. Collins and Lizzy.

Mr. Bennet had absolutely no patience remaining and began, "Mrs. Bennet…"

Mrs. Bennet continued prattling without paying the slightest bit of attention to her husband.

In his most authoritative voice he interrupted, "MRS. BENNET! You *will* sit down, cease this mindless blather, and listen closely to what I have to say. NOW!"

Wide-eyed, she did as she was told, folding her hands in her lap. A few moments passed before she came to the conclusion that she should be insulted and began again, "Mr. Bennet, you should not speak to me that way. You must think of my nerves…"

"Quiet, woman! You *will* listen and not interrupt again. Do you understand, Mrs. Bennet?" he boomed even louder. *God help me, they are both worse than children!*

She nodded with a sour expression.

"Mrs. Bennet, I wish to be perfectly clear with you. You do *not* have the right to give permission to any man to marry one of my daughters. I am the head of this family and the only person who has that honour. From this moment on, you will not give so much as the slightest *hint* to any suitor who may call upon any of my daughters that they have even a remote chance of approval or disapproval should they ask for permission to marry one of them. Is this clear, Mrs. Bennet?"

She could tell by his colouring that he was quite serious. "But…"

"No 'buts,' Mrs. Bennet! You have insulted me in a most terrible manner by giving Mr. Collins *your* permission to marry my daughter. What were you thinking, madam? Do you have absolutely no respect for me as head of this family? Must I cut back your pin money to prove that I am the one in charge, Mrs. Bennet?"

She looked absolutely horrified. Take her pin money away? It could not be! She realized she had gone too far this time.

"I had no intention of allowing that ridiculous man to even *think* of marrying any of our daughters, and yet you told him he could and he went off informing others! Thankfully, Mr. Collins is an obviously absurd man, and it is just possible that those who heard his story did not believe it. Regardless of whether they did or not, I will NOT allow Elizabeth, or any of my daughters, to marry Mr. Collins."

"But Mr. Bennet, if Mr. Collins told others in Meryton today, there will be a scandal, will there not? You must see that Elizabeth… you must *make* her marry him!"

"No, Mrs. Bennet, I do not see it. If there is a scandal, well, madam, this was your doing and you will be the one to *undo* it.

"There happens to have been a difficulty regarding this matter in Meryton this morning, and you will fix it. You love to gossip, and now it is time to use it for your daughters' benefit. Say there was a misunderstanding between the gentlemen which has now been cleared up, and that is all. If anyone begins to say it was anything else, you will laugh at them and tell them it is nonsense. Use your talent for gossip, Mrs. Bennet, to save all your daughters' reputations, or you WILL be thrown out in the hedgerows when I am gone, for no worthy gentlemen will ever ask for any of their hands.

"I hope we have an understanding, madam. If you do not do what I say, you lose your pin money—completely. Mrs. Hill will take care of the household funds."

"But, Mr. Collins…"

"Once Mr. Collins leaves this house when his visit is up, he will not be welcomed back for another visit. Do you understand all that I have said, Mrs. Bennet?"

Angrily, she replied, "You do not have to treat me as a child, Mr. Bennet; of course I understand what you have said."

"It seems I *do* need to treat you like a child, madam, for you act like one and the only way I can get you to behave is to take away your privileges as punishment–*just* like a child. I will continue to treat you like a child until you begin to behave as an adult, Mrs. Bennet."

Mr. Bennet paused and took several deep breaths. In a much calmer voice, he continued, "Now, I have already had the carriage brought around. You will go to your sister's home directly and begin to work on undoing your mistake by saying *only* what I told you to. One word more or less and you will not be receiving pin money this coming month. Good day, madam." He motioned toward the door.

Mrs. Bennet did as she was told.

~Netherfield Park

Darcy and Bingley found Richard pacing in Bingley's study. It was obvious that the meeting with Colonel Forster had not progressed well. Richard was enraged.

As soon as the door was closed behind them, Richard began, "That conniving little *bastard*! What on earth could Wickham have told Forster that would make him think he cannot trust my word? What could completely *erase* my reputation throughout the military?"

The two gentlemen were absolutely shocked.

"Perhaps I should go speak to him…" Darcy began.

"No! No, you cannot speak to him. Wickham has tarnished your reputation as well! Forster would not trust you any more than he would trust me—perhaps less!"

Bingley offered, "If *I* went to talk to him…"

"Bingley, since you have no personal knowledge of Wickham other than what happened this morning, he would think Darcy and I influenced you, or *intimidated* you, depending on what Wickham told him, to say what we wished you to say. And none of us want the details of what happened this morning to become public knowledge or Miss Elizabeth's reputation might be damaged."

The three were thoughtful for a few minutes then Bingley asked, "Is Forster an imbecile or is Wickham *that* good at conniving?"

Darcy replied with a disgusted look on his face, "Wickham is *that* proficient at what he does, Bingley." He sighed. "We must keep a watch over our own, and hope that Mr. Bennet can convince the shopkeepers and other gentlemen in the area to keep watch over theirs. I can only hope now that Wickham knows we are here, it will prod him to move on and soon. Maybe one of us could follow him whenever he is in the village?"

"Ah! Believe it or not, Forster already warned me that we should not *harass* Wickham!"

"Yes… yes, I can believe it, Richard," Darcy said as he poured three glasses of brandy. "I know Wickham too well to doubt it."

~Rosings Park, Kent

Upon receiving Mr. Collins's express, Lady Catherine went into a rampage so intense that her staff could not understand what she was saying and was afraid for her health… or in some cases, to say that the staff was hopeful for her final demise would be a more accurate portrayal of their feelings.

When she finally had calmed down enough to write, she sent an express to Collins telling him to get himself and Wickham to her cottage near the village of Epping the following day before noon.

After sending off the express, Lady Catherine went to her study and began to pace as she tended to do at times of upset. She thought over the situation in great agitation and began to make new plans.

She had known Collins for a few years. He was a complete fool, but he literally worshipped her. Completely certain that he would do anything she asked of him, she had financed his education so that he could take orders and become her parson… after her last parson so conveniently died when he suddenly began to question her authority. She wanted Collins close to feed her pride, and she especially wanted a parson without a *conscience* that she could control completely since he was to be so closely involved in her pursuits.

Collins was ordered to get married as a ruse to make him look more legitimate as a vicar. She was also looking ahead. Longbourn would be a good acquisition in the perfect location and *legal*. She could not keep on buying up land all over England without raising conjecture from her steward, her solicitor, her nephew, and her brother, who all kept watch over her accounts.

If Collins would marry one of the daughters, he would have good reason to make trips there on a regular basis other than just to check up on his future inheritance… which would look too suspicious for a clergyman.

She did not like to attract undue attention to her endeavors.

Now that buffoon Collins had done something so serious as to get the father to prevent him from marrying *any* of his daughters? Had he exposed himself as the degenerate he was? Maybe she should have insisted he take a female along and install her at the nearby inn? Once he was married, she cared not what he did with his wife, but he was ordered to behave himself for now. Though, if it had been something so drastic as she had originally suspected, he probably would have been expelled from Longbourn by now—or worse! And then she would have had to go through the irritating task of finding someone to replace him.

There was only one man standing in her way of possession of Longbourn, and that was Mr. Bennet. She had tried the path of least resistance… now they would have to take a more hazardous course. Mr. Bennet had to die, and then Collins would inherit.

Wickham would know what to do; he always had before.

Between Longbourn and the last of her planned acquisitions, she would be set up for most of England. She already had her property in Somerset, Wales, Worcestershire, Norfolk, the north of York, Scotland, and Ireland–some inherited and others recently purchased. Once her daughter, Anne, married her cousin Fitzwilliam Darcy, the next phase of her scheme would be ready to proceed.

Pemberley… it should have been hers years ago! Her sister cheated her out of it by stealing George Darcy from her. She would make certain Darcy married Anne soon, and then it would finally be hers.

She smiled at how easy it was to manipulate the good, proper, honourable, and dutiful Fitzwilliam Darcy. She had been setting this up for years, beginning immediately following her sister's demise. When his wife died, Fitzwilliam's father had practically abandoned him, and so he had turned to her with any questions he had, which fit perfectly into her plans! As he had grown older, she had allowed him some time to sow his oats—though she did not think he actually *did* that sort of thing—but *now* it was time. She anticipated no problems with informing him that he needed to accept the responsibilities of adulthood, carry out his *duty* to the family, and marry his cousin.

She laughed at how George Darcy had been so foolish in trusting Wickham. She had always had a soft spot for Wickham because he was so devious and of good use to her in any of her endeavors. He was trustworthy as long as she kept him paid well, and his contacts in the shadier parts of England were invaluable. He had some intelligence, unlike that fool Collins, though not as much as Wickham would like to believe he had, but enough for her to buy him the commission in the militia so that he could keep a watchful eye on Collins on this assignment.

It sounded as if they had *both* failed so far, though they both could still be of use to gain the results she wanted. They had better not fail again, but in case they did, she would devise an additional plan to give Collins an excuse to go to the same area for "visits."

Wednesday, November 20, 1811

~Netherfield Park

When Richard walked into Bingley's study, an upset Darcy sat behind the desk, running his hand through his hair while reading a letter. He knew that Darcy had received an express not long ago, and Richard was concerned at his expression now. He asked if something was wrong with Georgiana.

"No, this is not about Georgie, Richard. Perhaps you might be of assistance if I can trouble you for your opinion on a matter of business? I have quite a lot to speak of."

"Of course, Darce!" Though relieved that the letter had not been about his young cousin, Richard continued to feel concern about the look on Darcy's face. He sat across the desk and made himself comfortable, settling in for a long discussion.

"I have received some disturbing news… I am unsure how to begin. I suppose I should start from the first time I heard of this matter.

"Years ago, when my father went over all of our properties and business with me, he told me of some unused property in India which he thought to be worthless. I did not understand why he would purchase land so far away and questioned him about it. He told me that Sir Lewis had talked to both of our fathers about buying this land as an investment since he had adjoining land and wished to buy more, but did not have available assets at the time to do so. The intent was that Sir Lewis would eventually buy the land from our fathers. Sir Lewis had been quite insistent, and the land was relatively inexpensive, so my father had invested in it to keep some peace with Sir Lewis and Lady Catherine. The earl did not buy the land. Sir Lewis passed on shortly thereafter, and my father felt strange disposing of it so soon and kept the land in his memory. He also informed me that though he most likely would not, that *I* should feel free to sell it at any time in the future.

"About four years ago, I spoke to your father about this same land, asking his advice. He advised me to sell it since he had it investigated at the time Sir Lewis had spoken to him and had been informed that it was not of much worth, which is the reason he did not buy it. He did not wish for Sir Lewis to waste money repurchasing it from him at some later date. Other concerns took precedence at the time, and I left the land to itself.

"Recently, I have been thinking about selling the land in India and investing in something locally. I contacted my solicitor, Mr. Thompson, to see if he had any contacts in India to look into the current situation of the land and see if there was any reason to continue holding it. Thompson had a cousin, Mr. Clark, who owns an investigation agency in India and has worked for Thompson when it was necessary. While checking on Clark's reputation with my own investigator, I found that the two had worked together in the past. Indeed, Mr. White gave Clark the highest recommendation and felt that he was the best investigator in India. A plan was put in motion to gather information. I thought this would be a simple matter and expected the business to be concluded as quickly as it could when corresponding over such distances." He shook his head. "I was quite mistaken!" Darcy closed his eyes for a moment and sighed before going on.

"Clark *has* since proved to be invaluable, as predicted. A few months ago I received a letter from Clark stating that there is a mining operation on my land, and he asked whether I had authorized it. Of course, I had not and was certain my father never did in his lifetime, so without delay, permission was sent to investigate further into this illegal mining operation on the land in question." Darcy walked over to the brandy and poured two glasses, handing one to Richard and taking a long gulp from the other. Darcy crossed to the window and stared out at nothing.

"Today I have received another report from Clark." He gestured toward the letter on the desk. “It states that there is much more amiss at the mine than simply illegal extraction of saltpetre. There is a shroud of secrecy surrounding the mine, understandable since it is illegal, and so Clark had sent four men into the mine posing as workers. It seemed no unknown Englishman could get in at all, so the men he used for this job were natives, experienced investigators well trained by Clark himself, and, consequently, Clark originally was not worried about them. The first two were able to pass along several messages, but then the communications ended abruptly. At first Clark thought his men were caught passing on messages and were being punished, so another two men were sent in to find the first two. There were no traces of the first two men, and after reporting back to Clark twice, the second set of men also disappeared. His professional opinion was that all four men were found out and killed.”

Richard reacted with shock. Darcy, visibly upset, said, “Yes, I agree!”

He stopped speaking to empty his glass and poured another, and then turned to Richard to continue, “Clark reported what little information his men had passed on to him and informed me that he would not be sending any additional men into the mine. He will continue to investigate as much as is possible from the outside and will also look into the operations of the company’s business in India.

“The information Clark’s men had managed to pass on was this: while the workers were local natives, the mine is run by the British-owned Bradstowe Company. They were mining saltpetre in large quantities, and the workers were being horribly mistreated.

“There are a few even more mysterious facts associated with the information that Clark has been able to gather. The mine on my land extends under the property that Sir Lewis had owned, which is now owned by our cousin Anne. It seems to have been the first part of the mine excavated, as that part has been emptied of minerals and the mine extended into my land is more recently dug, though connected to the old. There are no surface buildings on the de Bourgh land, but there is evidence of a previous entrance which was blocked years ago. In local government records, a mining operation is recorded as being opened and then *closed* while Sir Lewis was alive, but there is no information at all about the current operation.

“There is something else which confuses me exceedingly, and perhaps you might be able to shed some light on the matter, Richard. I mentioned earlier that *both* our fathers had told me that your father did *not* buy the land Sir Lewis requested him to purchase. Well, the newest part of the mine also extends onto land supposedly owned by the earl!"

Richard got up and began to pace. *What the devil is going on in India?*

"The only information they had about the Bradstowe Company's operations outside the mine was that they also own ships which are being used to transport the saltpetre brought up from the mine, along with the usual native products we see in the shops here in England. The strangest thing of all is that the saltpetre seems to be stored in *hidden* compartments while the other goods are stored on the flooring above them. At first, Clark's operatives thought the reasoning behind this was to be able to transport a greater number of goods, but hiding the saltpetre does not seem to be dependent on how many local goods are being shipped. Two of the ships were not half full of local goods, yet the saltpetre was stored in the hidden compartments. In fact, one of those two ships was carrying only enough local goods to *cover* the hidden compartments' multiple hatch doors!

Darcy stopped Richard's pacing with a hand on his shoulder and said, "Richard? Why would they hide saltpetre? It makes no sense. If anything, the saltpetre should be on top, not the other goods! *Those* are the goods which are being shipped illegally!"

Richard thought for several minutes before answering, "I know saltpetre is necessary to produce gunpowder, among other things. With the war on the continent and the many naval battles recently, there is a great demand for gunpowder in England. But from what I understand, saltpetre is in abundant supply from English mines in India, among other locations, and the price of saltpetre is not high in England. It is shipped directly to England on a regular basis openly. There is no reason to hide it."

Darcy rubbed his hand over his face. "Why were four men *killed* over this, Richard?" and then to himself he thought, ***I** sent these men in!*

Richard just shook his head.

Darcy sighed deeply. "Unbelievable as it may seem, there is more to be told! Another oddity is that the destinations of all of the Bradstowe Company's ships are closely guarded. The dock master and dock workers are all so secretive that even a substantial bribe could not persuade them to speak. There was no way for Clark's men to gain access to the maps, ships' logs, or any other papers aboard without being detected. All such paperwork was *carried by the captain* of each ship in a satchel and it almost never left his side. The few occasions the captain was not in possession of the satchel, his first mate was. There is no paperwork filed on land about these shipments. Clark will be following up on some leads in this quarter as well as a few others.

"Richard, I do not understand… if the ships are going to England, why the secrecy? Where are these ships going if not to England?"

The two men both were silent for a few minutes, staring out the window.

Darcy spoke again, "I want to talk to my uncle again, since I was told by Clark that the mine extends onto land that is listed in his name. There is need to confirm that I understood him correctly during our conversation when he stated that he did not buy the land himself. Then, if your father agrees, I will authorize Clark to investigate this aspect of the situation further as well as all the others. Could it be that I misunderstood? Perhaps your father said he *did* buy the land?

"I also want to make sure the earl has not authorized this mining operation. Could it have been an oversight that resulted in my not being notified? I know I am not receiving profits from the mines, or any communications from the Bradstowe Company. I do not think the earl has any knowledge of this, since I am certain he would not have allowed an oversight of this magnitude, and that he would not be involved in anything this illegitimate.

"But if my uncle *has* authorized the mining under some great misunderstanding, then he needs to know how the Bradstowe Company is treating its employees, for I am sure he would not agree to the detestable treatment that Clark detailed in his letters."

Richard shook his head again and said, "Darce, I know my father is kept well-informed of all his properties and reviews the books with his solicitor frequently. He would have noticed by now that no checks were being cut to you with profits. Could my father have an employee cheating him by showing in the ledgers that there are monies being sent to you while in fact they are being diverted elsewhere? But if he knows about this mining operation, then why has he never brought up the subject with you since you have not? Surely he would have discussed this with you it if he thought was a joint venture."

The two puzzled this out for several more minutes before Richard continued, "No, I do not believe Father knows anything about this.

Father keeps my brother thoroughly informed on all his inheritance so that when the inevitable happens, the viscount will be able to take over his duties immediately, just as you did when your father died. Father sits with me twice a year as well, for if, God forbid, something were to happen to both the earl and the viscount, I would inherit—and Father believes in always being prepared.

"In all the times we have conferred, I have never once heard of any interests in India, let alone owning and operating a mine there. I am also certain that my brother would have spoken to me of it if he had known about it, as he does with all the other holdings that he will eventually inherit."

The two discussed the subject for a while longer but came to no new conclusions, and ended only with more questions. They were both concerned, especially about the deaths and mistreatment of the workers.

Darcy finally decided he would make out an express immediately to White, his investigator in London, sending him in search of information on the Bradstowe Company in England while Clark handled the same in India. Meanwhile, the day after Bingley's ball, Darcy and Richard planned to leave for London to speak to the earl and White in person.

They both silently hoped Wickham was out of the area by then.

Darcy walked out of the study, only one thought repeating in his mind. *It is **my** fault these people are dead!* He had to escape, had to be alone! He rushed toward his chambers and literally bumped into Caroline as he turned a corner. In no mood for her antics, he excused himself, mumbled that he was going for a ride, and then took the stairs two at a time to change into his riding clothes.

A sudden, overwhelming need to see Elizabeth came over him, but he thought better of riding to Longbourn in this state. What would he say when he got there? Darcy could not deal with Mrs. Bennet and the silly younger sisters at this moment.

He rode to Oakham Mount instead, where he had first seen her and had met her numerous times, where her presence was most strongly felt by him when she was not with him. Darcy stood where she had stood his first day in Hertfordshire and looked down upon the view that spread before him. It truly was beautiful; he could see why she so enjoyed this place. How he needed her right now… her *essence* was not enough. He could not think of anyone else in the world he wished to talk to.

The guilt of the suffering of the miners and all of the lives lost at the mine suddenly became overwhelming. He sat on a fallen tree log, and one tear was soon followed by another. Once he had let loose the control that had been firmly in place since his mother had died, he could not stop *all* of the emotions that he had repressed for years from surfacing.

Every heart sings a song, incomplete, until another heart whispers back.
--Plato (Greek Philosopher 427 BC - 347 BC)

~Oakham Mount, on the border between Netherfield Park and Longbourn Estate

Elizabeth had to escape! The constant screeching and bitter words from her mother about the failed attempt to match her with Mr. Collins, mixed with reminders about "the hedgerows," was unbearable. After confirming that her sisters did not wish to accompany her, and with a word to Mrs. Hill of where she was heading, Elizabeth slipped away from her mother's notice and set off to Oakham Mount.

As she climbed the hill, she heard a strange noise. At first she could not identify it, but then as she got closer she realized it was the sound of someone crying. She almost turned back to give the person some privacy, but then realized she should make certain there was no one injured and in need of assistance. Elizabeth walked up the hill as quietly as she could. If no one was hurt she did not wish to cause any embarrassment by making them aware that she had witnessed a private moment. When she saw who it was, Elizabeth's heart ached, and she could not turn away. Her instincts guided her actions; she was pulled toward him. Elizabeth gently placed both her hands on his, which were covering his face. He gasped and suddenly stopped crying, but he did not move.

There was no way he could mistake the distinctive feelings associated with Elizabeth's touch. A sense of shame consumed him as his Aunt Catherine's words from years ago rang out in his memory. That Elizabeth should have found him displaying such weakness! Darcy refused to look at her, remaining on the log with his elbows on his knees and face in his hands.

Her hands gently caressed his and a sense of being at *home* came over him. He could not help himself... he was completely under her control; he would allow her anything. He turned his hands into hers, and she held them tightly.

Afraid of losing her respect, he fought the draw of her eyes, terrified that he would find disgust there similar to what he had seen when his aunt had found him crying upon his mother's death. However, he could not resist for long—he had to face facts and *know* what she thought of him.

Darcy raised his head to meet the eyes that he loved so dearly, and his breath caught. Her expression was filled with compassion mixed with something for which he had no words, and it touched him to the core. As if she were absorbing his pain, tears were gliding down her face; one fell on his cheek mixing with his own, another on his lip. As if by reflex, his tongue darted out to catch it before it rolled away.

Tasting her tears, taking part of her within him—was so personal an act, he was almost completely overwhelmed. The future that he hungered for, it was all there within his reach; he could see it whenever he looked into Elizabeth's eyes.

As her hands gently brushed the tears from his face, Darcy closed his eyes forcing more to escape. He leaned into her touch. *Elizabeth is the answer to every question. Elizabeth is life, love, and happiness. Elizabeth is perfection itself! Yet, I cannot be with her! Please God, help me to understand what Mother had told me all those years ago... what I am to do? I feel as though I cannot breathe without Elizabeth!*

Elizabeth saw his suffering increase and intuitively leaned forward, taking him into her embrace. Darcy buried his face in her waist, wrapped his arms around her, and pulled her closer.

She ran her fingers through his hair with one hand and gently caressed his shoulders with the other. Tears welled up in his eyes for all that he had found which would be denied, for the ache of longing for Elizabeth that he knew would stay with him for eternity, even if he never saw her again.

Elizabeth pulled him even closer.

It was as if her ministrations opened a floodgate within him, releasing all of the sorrow he had repressed over the years. Taking him completely off guard, he became consumed by the grief he had felt for his parents' deaths, for the failure to keep the promises made to his mother, and for his sister's suffering in the past summer. All of the tears that had been denied for so many years filled his soul to overflowing and found release through his *Elizabeth!*

Elizabeth could not help but weep with him. Her love increased to a deluge, and she felt lost in it. She would have given him *anything* of herself just now... anything and everything to ease his pain. As she stroked his hair and upper back, soon she felt him beginning to calm.

Abruptly, Darcy pulled away quickly with a deep gasp of surprise at his lack of self-restraint, eyes closed tightly. "What have I done?" he croaked out as he wiped all remnants of tears from his face.

What must she think of me for acting so? I will lose her good opinion forever!

He could feel the heat of her near him and the almost magnetic pull her soul always had upon his own. Darcy stood and walked a few steps away, needing to put some distance between them, afraid he would do much more than embrace her if given the chance in this weakened state. His gaze swept the landscape as if he were looking for strength there.

Finally recovering enough to use his voice he turned and their eyes met momentarily, but he looked away. "I cannot apologize enough for my actions, Miss Elizabeth." He turned away and continued angrily, "I denounced Collins and Wickham for their treatment of you, and then I act *much worse*! Please forgive me!"

Elizabeth did not know what to do. She wanted to say just how much she *approved* of his behaviour, but she knew she could not. Holding him in her arms, sharing such deep emotions—in her opinion, there had been nothing wrong about it. It had been the most *correct* moment she had ever experienced!

But she could never have him that way; he could never love her as she loved him. They were friends, and friends comfort each other. Holding a friend who is crying is an everyday occurrence. It *was* unusual that the friends should not be of the same gender, but the *concept* was acceptable—to her anyway.

She walked around in front of him and waited for him to look into her eyes. "Mr. Darcy, I am not offended, but I will accept your apology if it makes you feel better. I know that you are a gentleman and I trust you completely, sir. I am not afraid of you."

Darcy swallowed hard and searched her eyes. She truly was *not* afraid of him. She had no idea what his longings could lead him to do if he lost control; she thought of him only as a friend.

It was absolutely necessary to him to prove himself worthy of her trust, and Darcy promised her silently that he would double his efforts to control himself in the future. He could not risk her good opinion! It would kill him if she ever thought badly of him, he was certain of it.

She took his hand, led him to the large boulder that she usually sat upon when coming to this place, and motioned for him to sit beside her. He was amazed at the strength of her trust in him. He sat next to her, a proper distance between them, and sighed.

Elizabeth waited quietly for Darcy to decide whether to speak to her about what was bothering him, and he knew it. Though he longed to tell her all that was in his heart, he did not feel it was proper to do so—but he *could* tell her about India.

Darcy stood and began to pace before her. "I inherited land in India, which I had ignored until recently. I hired an investigator to see whether it was worth retaining. It was discovered that a mine—which I did *not* authorize—is being operated on the land. Posing as workers, four of the investigator's men were sent in to shed some light on what exactly was happening there."

His voice cracked at the last of this speech, and he took a moment to collect himself. Darcy could no longer look to see her reaction, but he continued to speak, "The men *I* sent in there were able to pass along some information... before they were *murdered*." He heard a gasp and out of the corner of his eye, he saw Elizabeth's hand move to cover her mouth. "Their information told of those operating the mine mistreating the workers badly. Men are dying every day from being overworked and underfed. On *my* land! I might as well be killing them myself!" he exclaimed.

He saw Elizabeth shake her head, but he spoke again before she could interrupt him. "I know not how long this has been going on, nor how many people have died because of my inattention. I know not who the people operating this mine are.

"The only true information we have is that they are mining saltpetre, which is readily available to be mined all over India and other parts of the world as well. It makes no sense! Why are people being *killed* over saltpetre?" The anger in his voice had built until he said the last with such force that he was almost shouting.

Waiting to make certain that he was finished, Elizabeth stood before beginning. "Let me see if I understand the situation correctly. Your father passed on, and you inherited an estate which provides the livelihoods of hundreds of families here in England. As a young man, just as you reached the age of majority, you were suddenly fully responsible for this great estate, property in London… are there others?" At his nod she continued, "In addition to other properties, all of which provide the livelihood of countless *other* families, you took on the serious responsibility of raising your young sister.

"Any one of these would have been difficult for most people to take on *individually*, yet you did so all at once and at a time of great distress—upon your father's death.

"Sir, by all accounts that I have heard—and I do *not* mean Miss Bingley." She almost smiled. "You do not know of some of my more excellent sources…" At his questioning look she said, "Mr. Darcy, every lady must have her secrets!" Treating him to a saucy grin, she went on to say, "You, sir, have done quite an exemplary job of it *all*."

She held up her hand to stop him as he opened his mouth to protest his alleged competence.

Elizabeth continued, "There was also some land, half a world away, to which your father paid little attention while he was alive, and of which you had absolutely no reason to believe was anything but abandoned, with *nobody* depending upon it for anything at all.

"And now, sir, you are chastising yourself because some contemptible men have used that land—illegally, I might add—while you were exceedingly busy managing a *tremendous* amount of responsibility suddenly laid upon your shoulders right here in England.

"Have I summarized the situation in which you now find yourself correctly, Mr. Darcy?"

He blinked a few times and searched for something to say, but was having trouble finding his voice, both uncomfortable at hearing her praises of him and thrilled that she thought so highly of him. She was right! Not about how he did so well with it all, for *he* knew how many mistakes he had made along the way, but she was correct about the numerous responsibilities which he had taken on at his father's death. At length he said, "But the land in India is my responsibility…"

She nodded and raised both eyebrows. "Yes, and I suppose it would have been *much* more prudent had you abandoned all of your responsibilities here in England—including your sister—and boarded a ship bound for India to check on the seemingly deserted and insignificant bit of land there?

"Have you thought about just how long you would have had to be absent from England to do so? How much time does it take to travel to India, sir? Six months, I believe? And how long would it have taken to travel by land once you arrived at an Indian port?"

Elizabeth hesitated to allow her words to truly be understood. "If you had gone, would you have prepared yourself to deal with these degenerates who are on your land, or would you have suffered a similar fate to those who did go there more recently—who presumably were well-trained to expect the worst since they were working for an investigator, unlike yourself if you had gone alone. What do you expect would have happened if you had? Can you tell me that you would not have been killed, leaving your sister alone in the world?"

She paused again for a few moments. "Mr. Darcy, can you not see that you made the only *responsible* choice?"

Darcy began pacing anew. *Elizabeth has made some good points. What else could I have done?* Aloud he said, "I could have made inquiries sooner..." He did not sound convincing, even to himself.

She tilted her head, raised both eyebrows even higher and crossed her arms across her chest.

Darcy smiled a little. "Yes, I do suppose you are right, Miss Elizabeth."

She displayed a brilliant smile that warmed his soul. "Of course I am, Mr. Darcy! I am glad you have come to see reason, sir."

Darcy almost whispered, "I must thank you, Miss Elizabeth, for helping me to see more clearly."

Elizabeth instinctively knew that this was not the only reason he had been so upset, but he was not able to voice his other concerns. She hoped that someday he would share all of his burdens with her, but she knew this hope was in vain. At that thought, with a touch of sadness in her voice, she replied softly, "I am glad to have been of assistance, sir." She then frowned a bit. "But I am afraid I must make my way back to Longbourn, Mr. Darcy, before my family forms a search party to come after me."

He looked up to the position of the sun and was surprised to see that they must have been there quite a while. "To show my thanks for your voice of reason in this matter, I would be honoured to escort you home, madam." He bowed.

"I do believe I will accept, sir." She curtsied, and off they went in the direction of Longbourn, Mr. Darcy's horse trailing behind them.

After walking a few minutes in silence, Darcy said, "I have been thinking, Miss Elizabeth. You should not be walking alone with Collins and Wickham in the area. But I know you enjoy your morning walks… would you allow me to meet you in the morning to escort you on your walk when the weather permits?"

Elizabeth was a bit taken back by this offer, but it did make sense. "Mr. Darcy, your concern is sound, I believe. I am surprised I did not think of the danger sooner, but it was probably a prejudice in favor of my morning rambles which prevented it from entering my head." She laughed. "I do believe your suggestion is a good one, but I would not want you to meet me at the house for it might… no, I must admit it *would* give my mother the wrong idea, sir. I will show you where I will meet you as we get closer to Longbourn. Agreed?"

"Yes, agreed." He expected to have a need to argue his point and was happy to see she was being reasonable instead. He then asked her if she had been reading the Plato that he had loaned her, and their discussion went on from there.

~A cottage in the forest near Epping, Essex County

The meeting at the cottage near the village of Epping took place at noon; Lady Catherine spent about three quarters of an hour ranting about the disruption of her former plan. She mostly blamed Collins, but she found enough faults to cover Wickham with her venom as well, for he had been sent to watch over Collins. Collins spent the entire time bowing to her ladyship, while Wickham sat in a lackadaisical pose, rolling his eyes and sighing whenever she was not looking in his direction. After her rage was spent, Lady Catherine revealed part of her new plan to both men.

"Who is the next likely candidate for a wife for you, Collins? I want it to be the daughter of a landowner in the area so that you have good reason to visit frequently to carry out our pursuits," Lady Catherine said.

Collins stopped bowing and stood wide-eyed in shock. He had not thought of this option and did not consider any other woman in the area able to meet *his* criteria of a wife. "Your consideration is most generous, Lady Catherine, but I do not know of any other suitable ladies in the area. I would suggest…"

Wickham cut him off, "Of course there is, Collins! Why, Charlotte Lucas would be perfect for your plan, Lady Catherine! She would make a charming parson's wife."

Collins stuttered out, "But Miss Lucas is… is not…"

Lady Catherine was interested. "Wickham, tell me more."

"Charlotte Lucas is the eldest daughter of Sir William Lucas, who happens to own the land *next to* Longbourn. She is on the shelf, and therefore has little chance of finding a marriage partner at her age. She strikes me as an intelligent lady who does not wish to be a burden on her parents or her brothers, and she would probably settle for a marriage of convenience with this… disgusting toad." His lips twisted with a sneer at the end of his speech.

"Oh… no! Lady Catherine, I beg of you, she is not the sort of woman I would want to…"

With her most authoritative voice, Lady Catherine announced, "It is settled! You will make an offer to Miss Lucas as soon as possible. Having a connexion with the property adjoining Longbourn will be beneficial for our purposes. If Wickham thinks she would make a proper parson's wife, better yet. Parsons should be married to set an example for the community. Now you go wait outside; I need to speak to Wickham alone."

Wickham's eyebrows rose slightly, but he slipped his "disinterested" mask into place, attempting to hide his anticipation. He knew that when the old witch wanted to speak alone, a very interesting assignment was about to begin.

Collins made his final twenty or thirty bows and several sickly-sweet compliments while backing out of the room. In a way, Wickham was glad the sycophant was present so that the old witch's need for groveling could be satisfied without inconveniencing himself.

Wickham was secretly terrified to tell Lady Catherine about Darcy's attachment, but he knew that he must. After Collins was gone, he began, "It seems that your favourite nephew 'the always good and pious Darcy' is about to greatly disappoint you as well, your ladyship."

"What does Darcy have to do with any of this, Wickham?" Her eyes narrowed. "What are you up to?"

"So you are unaware that he is in Meryton, just as Collins and I were before we happened upon him there? He is visiting his friend Bingley, who is leasing an estate neighbouring Longbourn. It was quite a surprise to me to meet with both Darcy and Richard Fitzwilliam in the village. It would be much simpler for me to leave the area. Having them there might create certain *difficulties* for me, but ones I would be willing to endure for an increase in wages." Wickham displayed a dazzling smile.

She knew having him there was necessary to accomplish what she wanted and so she agreed—after some haggling. "Now, why do you say Darcy is about to disappoint me?"

"I have known him a long time, Lady Catherine, and I have never seen him besotted with any woman in my life. From what I can see he is *in love* with Miss Elizabeth Bennet."

Lady Catherine's eyes flew open wide. Seeing Wickham's reaction of stifled mirth, she rearranged her features into a sterner countenance. "He would not do this to me! Not after all the years I have spent stressing the importance of his duty to marry my daughter Anne! He will *not* offer for the same creature that I had *barely* approved of for Collins to marry! He is a Darcy and a Fitzwilliam, and he would never disgrace those noble lines in this manner! What means has she used to lure him in?"

"Let us just say that she is *my* type in looks, and from what I hear, she has intelligence to match Darcy's, as well as a sense of humour to outdo Fitzwilliam." Wickham found he was enjoying this when he saw the old witch's face redden.

"*Your* type in looks! That is the key. She has drawn him in with her arts and allurements! I know of her connexions and fortune well; she has none! Her father is a country squire and her mother is nobody—a daughter of a *tradesman*." She almost spit out the last word, her nose wrinkling in distaste. "The shades of Pemberley will not be thus polluted! I am ashamed of my nephew for being taken in by this country chit! She will not ruin all my plans for Anne and for Pemberley, in addition to the operation! This will not be borne!

"He will come to his senses, I am sure. He will use her, possibly set her up on the side… yes. After Anne bears the heir to Pemberley, he will not need to bother her in that manner again. Darcy can go off and have his way with that *wench* instead. I am sure that is his plan. He could never *marry* Elizabeth Bennet." She nodded, appearing to feel much better after reaching this conclusion. Lady Catherine continued, "Now, let us speak of Mr. Bennet. Do you still have some of those powders that you used on the old parson who defied me?"

Wickham's look changed to one of even more interest. "Yes, I do have enough for one more use. You must be warned that I will never have another opportunity to obtain any additional concoction like this one. The man who made it up for me is now in prison."

"You will use the last of the powders on Mr. Bennet. He has angered me beyond all consideration to have disrupted my plans–in more than one way! To have conceived a daughter to tempt Darcy is unforgivable in itself, but then to forbid Collins to marry any of his daughters! He must be punished for defying my will! And so will all his daughters and wife when he dies, because Collins will turn them out of the house immediately!" She nodded again, displaying an evil smile. "Mr. Bennet will take the powders and fall ill for a few days, growing weaker and weaker until he dies, just like the old parson did. I will have Longbourn soon."

"Then why have Collins marry?"

"I want to be sure of his having connexions in this area!" Her eyes tightened. "I will not take another chance in case you fail me again! It is only a matter of time before Collins commits some disgusting act to get sent away from Longbourn, and I want him engaged before he does so. He must be married as soon as possible!" she screamed, and then added, "But Wickham, be ready to *ruin* Elizabeth Bennet at a word from me! You must wait until I tell you to… Do you hear me, Wickham? You must wait! I want her available for Darcy to have his way with her if he so desires."

Wickham licked his lips. "I would be *most* gratified to carry out this order when it is time! It is always a pleasure doing business with you, Lady Catherine!"

Thursday, November 21, 1811

~In the woods between Longbourn and Meryton

The next morning, Elizabeth met Darcy at the appointed spot at sunrise. He had taken a Netherfield horse this morning and let it loose when he arrived at their meeting place, knowing it would find its way back to the stables there.

"Good morning, Miss Elizabeth. What a surprise to meet you along this path." His eyes twinkled.

She smiled the brilliant smile that always caused his heart to lurch. "Good morning, Mr. Darcy. I have brought along breakfast. I always do when I go to the place I am about to show you."

Darcy took the basket from her, and they began to walk.

She wanted to show him her favourite spot about halfway between Longbourn and Meryton. Since she had been there many times and had never come across another person, nor had she ever brought anyone else there, she thought of it as her own. She ventured there only when she wanted to be alone for a length of time.

Elizabeth did not tell Mr. Darcy how special this place was for her, but felt a need for him to see it. In the future, when he was gone and happily married to another, and she was a spinster acting as governess to her nieces and nephews, she would always have the memory of sharing her favourite place with *him*.

The wet summer followed by a dry, warm autumn had lengthened the season for the leaves to remain on the trees. They walked beneath mostly beech trees still bearing much of their foliage, but the ground was carpeted with yellow and orange as well. It was a misty morning, and where the sun made its way through the trees, the haze made the beams of light visible. The effect was lovely.

After the sun had burned off the haze, Darcy could hear the unmistakable sound of a stream nearby. Elizabeth led him towards it. As they walked through a break in some tall bushes, he was delighted by an array of colourful plants in a small clearing with a wide stream running through it. The clearing was surrounded by the same bushes they had just passed through and there were more striking yellow-orange beech trees like the ones they had been walking under most of the way there. A sweet chestnut tree grew just across the stream from where they stood, its reddish-orange leaves making it stand out against the brilliant yellow-green foliage of the black poplars behind it. Several different kinds of bushes bearing berries coaxed the birds to feast in the place.

The shore on their side of the stream was sandy, and off to the right of the entrance they had come through was a flat boulder, large enough for several people to be able to sit upon. Someone, and he could guess who, had arranged flat rocks across the stream as stepping stones. The opposite side of the stream bordered a larger grassy area beyond the shore which was covered with light yellow and purple autumn crocuses and blue love-in-a-mist flowers.

The entire scene was enchanting, and he could imagine how it would look in the full bloom of spring, carpeted with bluebells, snowdrops and early crocuses; he envisioned it in summer covered with lavender and the now bare rose bushes blanketed in flowers.

On the opposite side of the stream, one of the beech trees had been split by lightning and part of the trunk was hanging over the grassy area making an arch low enough to the ground that even Elizabeth might have to duck down to pass under. Darcy could imagine Elizabeth sitting on it, inspecting her private world… and he smiled.

Elizabeth stood silently, watching the emotions play across his face as he surveyed her special place. She could see she was right to think that he would be as pleased with it as she was. He turned to her with the most brilliant smile she had ever seen from him, and she could not help but match it with one of her own. She took the blanket out of the basket and spread it over the boulder, and then sat upon it setting the basket down next to her.

Darcy took a seat on the other side of the basket as she unpacked its bounty. He was afraid to speak as the moment seemed to call for silence. This was too perfect; he felt as if this were all a dream, and he did not wish to wake up, ever. He kept reminding himself she was *not* his wife; he could not pull her into his embrace or touch her or kiss her or—no, he would not even think about *that,* as he was absolutely certain of what would have happened next if it had been a dream.

Elizabeth finally broke the silence, and when he did not wake up, Darcy was no longer afraid to speak.

They shared her breakfast and discussed many subjects, speaking of their sisters, music, plays they had seen, operas they had attended, and museums they had visited. They found they had many of the same tastes, and those upon which they disagreed always began an interesting conversation or debate. Elizabeth asked questions about Eton and Cambridge and how he had met Bingley. Darcy inquired about how she had found the place, and she told him of happening across it one day adding that whenever she found a flower or plant that she enjoyed, she would bring seeds or a cutting to her special place to plant. They shared many smiles and laughs, and both inwardly acknowledged to themselves that the morning had been perfect. All too soon it was time for Elizabeth to return to Longbourn.

~%~

Time alone reveals the just man; but you might discern a bad man in a single day
--Sophocles (Greek poet 496 BC – 406 BC)

Elizabeth and Darcy had been walking in companionable silence when they heard two men speaking. Both of the voices sounded familiar to Elizabeth, and Darcy would have recognized Wickham's voice anywhere. Darcy put his finger to his lips indicating that Elizabeth should be quiet, and they began to move away from the voices, not wanting to eavesdrop.

They both froze when they heard Wickham say the name "Bennet" in the same phrase as the word "plan." A shared look confirmed that they were in agreement—they should listen to what the two men had to say about her family. Though Darcy was tempted to motion for her to go ahead since he knew of Wickham's tendency to use vulgar language when in the company of other men, he was afraid that if she moved they might be discovered, and he did not want her to be alone in the woods anywhere near Wickham.

Wickham was laughing. "Denny, what is the problem? It is a good deal of money just to put some powders in Mr. Bennet's tea!"

Still in hiding, Darcy noticed Elizabeth was becoming pale, and he placed his arm around her waist, pulling her closer to him to steady her.

Denny said, "Why can you not do this yourself, Wickham? I do not feel comfortable doing it. If it is ever found out, it could mean my commission… or worse."

"You forget, Denny, Mr. Bennet does not like me because of the lies those bastards, Darcy and Fitzwilliam, told to set him against me. He will not even allow me on the grounds of Longbourn. You, on the other hand, are often invited for tea by Mrs. Bennet," Wickham reminded him.

"I will not even think about this until you tell me what the powders are for and why you wish for Mr. Bennet to take them."

"If I tell you, you must first promise to keep this between us, Denny. No matter what happens, you cannot tell a soul!"

When Denny promised, Wickham went on, "Miss Elizabeth and I are in love and wish to run away together to Gretna Green…"

On the other side of the bushes, Elizabeth's eyes flew open wide, and

Darcy could feel her take a deep breath. Afraid she would say something; he pulled her even closer to him and quickly placed his hand over her mouth. They had to learn what Wickham had planned!

Suddenly realizing he was touching her mouth made Darcy's heart pause, and he slowly moved his hand away, brushing his fingers against her lips. What a strange combination of emotions was coursing through him in this situation!

Wickham was still speaking. "The problem is, Mr. Bennet discovered that we have been meeting clandestinely whenever she goes on her 'solitary' walks. Now her father is keeping her in the house under lock and key! I need to give Mr. Bennet this strong sleeping powder that I obtained from an apothecary friend of mine in London. It will make him sleep for a full day, maybe longer, and my darling Lizzy will be able to sneak away and meet me. We can be well on our way to Scotland before Mr. Bennet even knows she is missing. The day or so that he sleeps will give us enough of distance ahead of anyone coming after us, that by the time they do catch up, we will already be married. Is that not a wonderful plan?"

Elizabeth's knees were weak, and she was leaning into Darcy now for additional support. She could not believe what she was hearing. Wickham was an amazingly skilled liar! If he had not been speaking of her, he could have easily convinced her that he told the truth!

Denny obviously was taking this seriously. "Well, congratulations, Wickham! I did not think a lady could catch you, but Miss Elizabeth is not just any lady. Your plan sounds reasonable, but what if someone *does* follow you before Mr. Bennet wakes up?"

"By the time they catch up to us, we will have spent an entire night together alone." The men both laughed, Darcy's every muscle tensed, and Elizabeth began to tremble. "Mr. Bennet, of course, would not allow *all* his daughters' reputations be ruined by forbidding us to marry at that point, so we would have to get married, *with* Mr. Bennet's reluctant consent." Wickham said.

Wickham had to raise the payment twice, and Denny still was not happy about tricking Mr. Bennet… but as long as nobody would find out it was his doing and nobody would be harmed in the end, Denny agreed that he would do it.

Wickham warned him, "I am told the powders will not dissolve in cool liquid; it must be hot such as tea or coffee."

"As a matter of fact, I am on my way there now, and I am sure Mrs. Bennet, the ever dutiful hostess, will call for tea as soon as I arrive. Do you want me to do it today?"

"Yes, today is perfect! I can meet my beautiful Lizzy after they have all gone to bed tonight, and we shall be off for Scotland. You will have my eternal gratitude for doing this, Denny; you know not how much she means to me."

Denny took the powders as Wickham said, "You must be careful with them because I do not have any more. All of our happiness rests on your shoulders... and that small vial of powders. I am depending on you, my good friend."

Denny promised he would be careful and the two laughed at some jokes about Wickham having a last roll in the hay with a barmaid while Denny did his duty with the tea. As they began to move away, Wickham stopped short and said to Denny, "Remember this is a secret, Denny! You must not mention the plans for the marriage to *anyone!* Really, Denny, you should never mention any of this to anyone at all, ever."

They shook hands on the deal and off they went, Denny to Longbourn, where he was meeting Saunderson, and Wickham to have a bit of fun and congratulate himself on choosing such a wonderfully gullible person like Denny to do the job for him.

~In the woods between Longbourn and Meryton

Elizabeth had not realized that by the time the two officers had gone, Darcy was holding her tightly enough that she was no longer supporting any of her own weight. Somehow she was in the position she had wanted to be in for what seemed like an eternity—in Mr. Darcy's arms being held so close to him that her entire body was pressed against him—and the irony of it was that with all she had just witnessed, she could not enjoy it! She felt ill indeed, but she did not want to move for fear that Denny and Wickham would hear her.

Meanwhile, Darcy was well aware of every word of the conversation as well as Elizabeth's physical condition, but he was too disgusted by what he was hearing and too worried about her to enjoy their closeness any more than she did. He saw her colour continue to drain and felt her trembling so violently that he knew her knees would fail her, so he had continued to tighten his embrace. Her hands came up to his chest and her colour changed again–but this time she was turning a sickly green. He tried to rub her back to calm her long enough to at least delay the inevitable until the men were far enough away not to hear her. She managed to wait long enough for them to be well out of hearing range, and then pushed away from Darcy, making it only as far as the first tree before her breakfast made a reappearance.

Darcy's mind was busy thinking of running after Denny and taking the vial of powders… but he could not leave Elizabeth! The two men went in opposite directions, there was no telling whether Wickham would come back this way in the near future if what he said about the barmaid was part of the ruse, and he had no idea where Collins was. He would not leave her.

After accepting a concerned Darcy's handkerchief and taking a moment to recover, Elizabeth said, "I am so sorry you had to witness the lies that so *easily* rolled off Wickham's tongue, and what they have done to me, sir. I am feeling much better, thank you, and my mind is turning again—since Wickham lied about everything else in that conversation, he must be lying about what the powders are as well. What could they be? Why would he want to hurt my father?"

"Please, do not be embarrassed, Miss Elizabeth; Wickham has often made me ill as well." She could hear anger in his voice, but she knew it was not directed at her.

Elizabeth's eyes widened when a horrible thought occurred to her. "If I am correct about Collins and Wickham concealing the fact that they know each other, could the powders be something that would make Collins's inheritance happen that much sooner?"

A deep feeling of dread came over Darcy, and he knew she could be right. "I hesitate to say this and frighten you further, but I feel I must. Wickham has made many people who had wanted to report him to the authorities *disappear* and made it all look like natural causes. Some were physical deaths, such as carriage accidents or trees falling, but perhaps *this* is how he managed some of the sudden and short illnesses which all led to death? It was possible that he could be in contact with a dishonest apothecary somewhere who would provide him with a lethal concoction for a price."

Elizabeth's eyes opened wide. "We need to start moving, Mr. Darcy. We must get to Longbourn!"

Elizabeth hiked up her skirts and began to run. Darcy could not help but smile a little as he started after her. She was a good runner, but Darcy had longer legs.

"Go, Mr. Darcy… Go ahead…" she said between breaths.

"I will not… leave you here… in the woods alone," he replied. It turned out Elizabeth was a bit more used to running than Darcy thought. His having to slow his pace for her in the beginning worked out well since he began to lose the lead—her endurance was better than his.

As they neared the immediate grounds of Longbourn, Elizabeth suddenly stopped. Darcy passed her, and then moved back toward her with a curious expression upon his face. She said, "We… cannot walk in… completely…out of breath!"

Both being in good health, their breathing became closer to normal fairly quickly, and the two began to walk at fast pace to the house. Elizabeth told him, "It is ironic that up until recently my father would stay in his study and not be present in the drawing room for visitors! Since our talk with him about Wickham and Mr. Collins, he has been much more attentive to spending time with the family when there are male visitors, especially when an officer is in the house. He cannot seem to belay my mother or sisters from inviting officers, but it is clear to everyone in the family that Wickham is not allowed on our grounds."

They arrived at the house quickly, and as they entered, Elizabeth asked Mrs. Hill, "Were there any visitors while I was out?"

"Mr. Denny and Mr. Saunderson are in the drawing room, Miss Lizzy. There were no other visitors."

"Has tea been served yet, Mrs. Hill?" she asked, attempting to keep the panic from her voice.

"Emily just brought it in as you entered the house, ma'am." Elizabeth wasted no time, opening the door to the drawing room immediately with Darcy on her heels.

There was not a moment to spare to warn Mr. Bennet. Denny was standing near the tea service while Saunderson was telling a joke. Both Elizabeth and Darcy saw Denny dump the vial into a cup while everyone else was distracted by Saunderson, and Denny insisted on bringing Mr. Bennet his tea. Darcy was about to step in, but Elizabeth walked across the room *accidentally* bumping into Denny's arm. Mr. Bennet's tea cup fell to the floor and shattered, spilling the contents all over the floorboards.

There was a flurry of activity as everyone moved forward offering napkins and cloths, but Elizabeth would not allow anyone to touch the liquid.

Darcy exclaimed forcefully, "I will clean it up!" and the entire room turned to stare at him with wide eyes... Mr. Darcy, clean up a spill?

Elizabeth smiled and stated calmly, "Mr. Darcy, you are our guest we cannot allow you to clean our floors! As I have forgotten to take off my gloves upon coming indoors, I will be the least likely to be cut by the sharp pieces of broken china." She began to wipe the floor with a napkin. When the tea soaked napkin was loaded with the china pieces, she took some water and another napkin, wiped the floorboards well, and then left the room.

Darcy was alarmed and was having trouble regulating his breath, *What if the tea soaked through her gloves?* He had already acted in a suspicious manner, and he could not think of any way of stopping her without making the entire room even more curious.

~%~

Mr. Bennet had been silently observing the pair since they walked in the room. First, why was Darcy here? He also noticed something was wrong… exceedingly wrong with them both. They were in such an agitated state, both seemed to be overheated, and their clothing and hair were in disarray. He was becoming concerned that Lizzy had been compromised, albeit with her own permission or she would not have brought him to Longbourn with her. That Lizzy still had her gloves on was observed by her father just before she knocked the cup out of Denny's hand, without a doubt *on purpose*. Darcy's reaction to Lizzy's cleaning up the mess was extremely disturbing. The look of panic in Darcy's eyes completely erased any notion of Lizzy being compromised by Darcy.

Why have these two conspired to keep me from my tea, and why is Mr. Darcy so worried that Lizzy touched it?

What Mr. Bennet observed next was just as confusing as what had preceded it.

~%~

While the rest of the room was in a state of agitation about the spilled tea and the broken cup, Denny was wearing a confused expression. He could not understand why Elizabeth had knocked the cup from his hand, and he was absolutely sure she did it on purpose! She *must* have been in on the plan… but if she had been, why had Wickham not told him to hand the vial of powders to Elizabeth so that *she* could give them to her father? Suddenly, Denny realized something was very wrong about the entire situation. Could Wickham have been lying?

Abruptly, Denny gasped, and all colour drained from his face. How could he have taken on this task without knowing exactly what those powders were? He was ashamed of his trust in a man he hardly knew and was relieved that Elizabeth had spilled the tea. Wickham had said these were the last of the powders, and Denny was glad they were gone.

Darcy was watching Denny as well. He walked across the room to Denny and whispered, "Do not trust Wickham, Mr. Denny. I can see you have just realized he is not what he appears to be, and I wish to confirm it for you. It is lucky for Mr. Bennet that his latest plan was not brought to fruition." Darcy stared into Denny's eyes for a tense moment and then walked into the hallway to find Elizabeth.

Darcy found Mrs. Hill and asked where Elizabeth had gone. Mrs. Hill had seen there was something wrong from the moment they had entered the house together. To say Darcy was concerned about Elizabeth at the moment would be an understatement, and Mrs. Hill had an intuitive feeling that her dear Miss Lizzy would want Darcy to find her. She led him through the kitchen and out the door to Elizabeth who was standing with her back to them; she then curtsied and returned to the house.

Elizabeth was trying to start a fire in the large pit that Mr. Hill used to burn trash, but her hands were shaking too severely to manage lighting the match. Another match was lit off to her left and shielded from the breeze. Elizabeth started; she was too deep in thought to have noticed when Darcy had walked up to her. After seeing who it was, she closed her eyes and took a deep breath, held the napkin containing the china cup over the burning match until it caught fire, and dropped it into the pit. After setting the other napkin afire, she threw that and her gloves into the fire as well.

Darcy pulled her away from the pit in the direction from which the wind was coming, and said, "Do not inhale the smoke, and you must wash your hands immediately, Miss Elizabeth. I am concerned. Please do not be upset, but I would like to stay as long as I can to make certain that you are well. Can you contrive a way of inviting me to dine here this evening?"

Elizabeth nodded and led him back into the kitchen where she laughed as he supervised the washing of her hands, telling her to use more soap and rinse again and again. He took the bowl away and emptied it into the yard, then asked for the bowl to be filled again and used his "Master of Pemberley" voice to direct Elizabeth to repeat the entire sequence after she protested the first time. Elizabeth bit her lip trying to contain her mirth.

The kitchen staff was curious about the way Darcy and Elizabeth were acting, but Mrs. Hill gave them a stern look, telling them to mind their own business.

By the time they returned to the drawing room, the officers had left. Darcy briefly considered going after them to attempt to recover the container the powders had been in, but he was fairly certain that after Denny's realization a few minutes ago, he would have disposed of it immediately.

Mrs. Bennet was screeching about Elizabeth's clumsiness in breaking her best china. Mr. Collins seemed distressed only when Mrs. Bennet mentioned that the cup was part of the *best* set of china, and now it was no longer complete. He postulated about the chance of procuring a matching piece and his state of upset increased when he heard that it was no longer available, but he was not disturbed enough to have been aware of Wickham's disrupted plan. Then soon after, Mr. Collins was back to his usual self. It was strange, and Darcy and Elizabeth exchanged a few looks communicating their thoughts to each other.

Mr. Bennet watched them watching Mr. Collins and was amused by the way that they informed each other of their thoughts without speaking to each other. *They do seem formed for each other, just as Adelaide has always insisted.*

Mr. Bennet was the one who invited Darcy to dine with them, wishing to watch him together with Elizabeth over a greater period of time. Darcy was more than appreciative of the invitation, and he sent a note to Netherfield informing them of his whereabouts for the evening, as well as sending for his horse.

Elizabeth was not having any ill effects from handling the powder-laden tea, but Darcy rarely took his eyes off her. He continued to shoot questioning looks in her direction, to which she responded with a little smile.

What would I do if she became ill? I know not what was in the tea to tell a doctor!

Darcy noticed that Mr. Bennet was watching him, and he decided to speak to Elizabeth about telling her father what had occurred.

After dinner, as the ladies began to move to the drawing room and the men to the study, Darcy signaled Elizabeth to stay behind.

"We need to tell your father what happened. He must be aware that someone might make another attempt on his life!" Darcy whispered.

"Yes, those were my thoughts exactly. Please ask for a word in private when he is ready to join us in the drawing room. "

"I will. There is one thing we did not discuss, and I am surprised it has not yet come up. No one has asked how I came to be here this afternoon! Shall I say we just happened across each other while walking or…?"

Elizabeth smiled. "Tell the truth to my father. Explain I did not want my mother to get the wrong idea; he will understand *that*!"

Her eyes were twinkling in a teasing way, and his mind went back to the way she had felt in his arms earlier today. The situation did not allow him to enjoy it at the time, but the memory of her body pressed against his would be ingrained in his mind forever… paired with now being so close to hear her whispers, drink in her scent, see that wonderful twinkle in her eye, close enough to almost taste the small, teasing smile upon her lips—he felt his control slipping. He swallowed loudly and stepped away from her.

She was confused by his expression and actions but only said, "If my father would like to speak to me as well, I would be happy to join you both."

At that point Mr. Bennet, who had been watching the exchange from the doorway but without being able to hear what was being said except for the last, cleared his throat and said, "Oh yes! I think it would be a grand idea for you *both* to come to my study right now. I will dismiss Mr. Collins first—join me in one minute." He left the room.

As they entered the study, Mr. Bennet was seated behind his desk in a reclined position with his hands laced together across his stomach. He watched the two sit in front of his desk and waited for them to begin.

Not knowing how much he had heard, Elizabeth made a quick decision to tell him the whole truth. "Papa, I am a stubborn person…" she hesitated, and Mr. Bennet smiled at her declaration. She went on to say, "After what happened the other day in Meryton, Mr. Darcy felt it was not prudent for me to be out walking alone, but I refused to discontinue my rambles. Yesterday we met quite by accident, and he walked me home. At that time we agreed to meet this morning at my usual time for a walk, and so we did."

Darcy was uncomfortable, for he knew he really should not have been out walking with a lady alone. He was afraid that Mr. Bennet would misunderstand his intentions... or perhaps he was afraid that the older gentleman would understand his wishes too well.

Elizabeth continued, "I am relieved that Mr. Darcy *had* insisted because something of a serious nature happened today. Papa, I know you noticed some odd happenings here this afternoon, and I was expecting your inquiries, as was Mr. Darcy. Mr. Darcy was about to address you about this alone, but I am glad to be here as well. Sir, we came across Mr. Wickham and Mr. Denny during our walk this morning…" she could not continue without some water to swallow the lump that was forming in her throat.

As Elizabeth drank some water, Darcy continued, "Mr. Bennet, we overheard Wickham and Denny planning to give you some sort of powders in your tea today during Denny's visit at Longbourn."

Mr. Bennet, now alarmed, sat up straight abruptly, placing his hands flat on his desk. "What?"

Darcy continued, "Wickham said they were sleeping powders and gave Denny a completely slanderous excuse to convince Denny to give them to you…" Darcy's countenance changed to one of anger, "involving Miss Elizabeth. Do you wish to hear Wickham's entire excuse, sir?"

"Yes, I believe I would. Lizzy?" He gave a pointed look to Elizabeth.

"He—he said... he said that…" Elizabeth trailed off.

Darcy began again, "Mr. Bennet, what we overheard was quite upsetting. Wickham told Denny that you had discovered that Miss Elizabeth and he were in love and meeting secretly. You had forbidden them to see each other, giving this as the reason he is not allowed on your property. He told Denny they planned to run off to Gretna Green to be married, but they needed you to sleep for a full day in order to get far enough ahead so that you could not stop them. Denny believed this ridiculous story and accepted payment to put the powders in your tea." Darcy was seething with anger by this point and had to stop to gain control over his emotions.

Elizabeth took up where he left off. "We were on the other side of a hedgerow, and Wickham and Denny did not know we overheard them, Papa. I was upset at first, and Mr. Darcy would not leave me in the woods alone with Wickham unaccounted for. By the time I was recovered enough, we knew we had to run all the way here, and we arrived just in time, too!"

Understandably, Mr. Bennet was visibly upset by the news. He walked over to the brandy and poured three glasses, then handed them out, giving one to Elizabeth as well. "This will calm you a bit, my dear. Please drink a little."

Elizabeth took a sip and wrinkled her nose, choking as it burned going down. "Are you sure this is supposed to *help*?"

Suddenly, Mr. Bennet turned white and grabbed the glass away from her. "Could he have put something in the brandy?"

"No, Mr. Bennet, not to worry! Wickham specified it had to go in something hot to dissolve. He also warned Denny to be careful with it since that was the last he had and doubted he could get more... thank God!"

Mr. Bennet closed his eyes and took a long breath. Handing the glass back to Elizabeth he said, "Then, yes, my dear, it will help."

"Papa, you do know that Wickham lied about *everything* in reference to me?" Mr. Bennet nodded and she continued, "Since that is the case, Mr. Darcy and I do not think it was a *sleeping* powder."

"That much I have already concluded, my Lizzy. But why would Wickham want to kill me?" A look of understanding crossed his face. "Lizzy and Colonel Fitzwilliam both witnessed behaviour that indicated Wickham knows Mr. Collins much better than they are allowing to be generally known. Could Collins wish to... *inherit* sooner rather than later?"

"We thought of that as well, Mr. Bennet, but we both observed Collins closely this afternoon. I am not sure how to word this, sir, but he does not seem *disappointed* that the plan was foiled. It is as if he did not know of the plan at all."

"Yes, Papa, Mr. Collins was upset that the set of our best china, which will someday be his, was no longer complete, but he seemed to have no knowledge that your *demise* had been checked."

"Then we are back to the same question. Why would Mr. Wickham want to kill me?"

"I do not know," Darcy said. "It *is* possible he wanted to hurt you because you trusted me instead of him, but I do not believe even Wickham is capable of doing something this serious for a reason as petty as that."

A thought occurred to Elizabeth. "Is it possible that there is something on Longbourn's property that Wickham wants to which he cannot gain access since you will not allow him to come to the house?"

"Other than farmland, a few cows, and sheep? We have nothing in the house of great value. No, I have not the slightest idea what could possibly attract such attention!" Mr. Bennet replied.

"I am afraid we may never find out, Mr. Bennet. I know Wickham pretty well and can say the only thing he *did* sound truthful about this morning was his saying there was no more of the powder that he gave to Denny. I do not believe you are in danger from poisoning at this point, sir. If I were you, I *would* check your carriage rigs and saddles fairly well from now on, and I suggest you not go out alone until he has left the area. Mr. Bennet, do you own a pistol?"

Mr. Bennet nodded.

"Then I suggest you begin to carry it, sir, whenever you go out."

"Yes, and keep a close watch on my tea at all times just in case," Mr. Bennet quipped.

"Can we not have Wickham and Denny arrested?" Elizabeth asked.

"We have no proof of any of this, and I doubt that either Wickham or Denny will confess to the authorities. If the cup had not been broken there might have been evidence…" Darcy saw the look on Elizabeth's face and was quick to say, "No! Miss Elizabeth, please do not misunderstand me or take any blame upon yourself. It *had* to be done the way it was done; there was no time for anything else. I was about to do something similar when you stepped in, and I must say I would have been much less discrete about it than you were. We did the best we could under the circumstances. I only meant if there had been *time* to recover the powders or the tea, we might have had proof. As it was, we have none and cannot bring charges against either man."

"If I had not been so weak and fallen ill after what we had heard…"

"I do not think there is a woman in England who could have done better than you did, Miss Elizabeth. After hearing what those blackguards said, most women would have been useless for at least a full day. You ran all the way to Longbourn and put an end to a plot to kill your father. Do not doubt your strength of character, madam. I will not allow it." The last two statements were made in the "Master of Pemberley" voice, which always made the corners of Elizabeth's lips twitch.

"Touché, Mr. Darcy," she said with a brilliant smile, referring to their discussion on Oakham Mount. He understood and returned it.

Mr. Bennet thought, *He will not allow herself to take responsibility, to take any guilt upon her. He is a good man... and very much in love with my Lizzy, unless I miss my guess. He is intelligent as well, as he can obviously see her worth. Can he get past the social barriers, though? I wonder just how much he knows about Lizzy's connexions. If Lizzy wants him to know, she will tell him... I must not interfere. She is in love with him as well. This is just what I wanted for her! But I do not believe either sees the other's true feelings. Do they even know the strength of their own?*

Mr. Bennet knew he had been forgotten and cleared his throat. "I will not ask what that last comment was about! I do agree with Mr. Darcy." He smiled at his daughter, then continued, "Before we join the others in the drawing room there is one more thing I must say. I do agree you should not be walking alone for the time being, Lizzy, but I do *not* think that it is proper for you to be walking unchaperoned with Mr. Darcy." Turning to Darcy, he said, "I know you are trustworthy, sir, but I do have to think of my daughter's reputation as well. You have my permission to escort Lizzy on walks, but one of her sisters must be present as well."

They all rose and began to move toward the door. Mr. Bennet had one last request before rejoining the others. "I certainly hope we will not be having such serious discussions as the last two every time we meet in my study. Perhaps next time we can play a round of chess, Mr. Darcy?"

"I would enjoy that, sir."

"And the winner will play Lizzy? She is quite the player after all..."

"Certainly, sir." Darcy smiled.

Elizabeth blushed quite deeply. "Papa, overestimating my talents will only disappoint Mr. Darcy who is used to playing the finest masters in London."

"My dear, I doubt it is possible that Mr. Darcy *could* be disappointed in your performance," Mr. Bennet replied, his words perfectly chosen to imply a different meaning to each of them. Elizabeth knew that she was a better chess player than most, but was too modest to admit to it. Darcy, on the other hand, suspected that Mr. Bennet was beginning to know his true feelings for Elizabeth.

The evening progressed much like any other, with the exception of Mr. Collins now having three people observing his actions. Before long, it was time for Darcy to take his leave, and Elizabeth disappeared upstairs for a moment to retrieve the book which she had borrowed from him.

She used this as an excuse to walk with him outside, since he could not possibly mount a horse holding such a large volume in his hand.

Darcy looked at the sky. Upon seeing dark clouds in the distance he said, "It seems we may miss our walk tomorrow."

Elizabeth frowned. "Aye, and I will be forced to listen to talk of lace and ribbons and dresses for Mr. Bingley's ball instead of watching you play chess with my father. But perhaps we can bore Mr. Collins enough with such talk that he will leave early, even if it *is* raining!"

She meant for her comment to amuse him, but his expression turned serious. "Miss Elizabeth, please do be careful around him. There is something about the man that makes me more uncomfortable every time I see him."

"I do understand your meaning, and I promise I will be careful. My sisters and I have agreed never to leave anyone alone with him. Worry not, my friend." She said the last with a smile.

Friend, he thought sadly, but aloud he said, "I hope you do not mind if I inform my cousin of today's events?"

"Not at all. I think he *should* know."

"Thank you. And… you are well, are you not? No ill effects from handling the tea?"

"None! I thank you for your concern, but I am perfectly well… or as well as one can be with a mind heavy with such worries as these."

Just to be in her presence made him feel more complete than he ever had in his life. He would have liked to stay all night there in the moonlight with *his* Elizabeth, but could think of no other reason to delay his departure. He mounted his horse.

Once mounted comfortably, Elizabeth handed him the book. "Thank you for the loan of the book, sir."

He looked at the book and noted with both pleasure and relief that her bookmark was still inside. "When I see you next, I will give you the third volume to peruse at your leisure."

She flashed him the brilliant smile that made his heart ache, and they bid each other goodnight. Elizabeth watched him ride away for as long as she could see him in the darkness, then whispered, "Good night, my love."

When they retired, Jane asked, “Lizzy, what happened today? I saw you join Father and Mr. Darcy in the study for a while after dinner. I had hoped…” she hesitated and gave Elizabeth a mischievous smile as Elizabeth coloured, “but you did not look as happy as I expected you would when you joined us afterward, so I dismissed it.”

Elizabeth knew that Jane would notice she was not in the drawing room, but she had not had time to think about what to tell her. Should she disclose all? Elizabeth decided to think on it and talk to her father before disclosing anything. “No, Jane, it was not what you were hoping for.” She continued the sentence to herself, *though I wish it were.* Elizabeth sighed and feigned a yawn. “Can we speak of it another time?”

Jane was not convinced by the yawn, but she would press no further. “Certainly, Lizzy. Good night.”

Friday, November 22, 1811

After a good sleep, Elizabeth awoke to the sound of pounding rain. It had begun during the night and looked as if it would continue all day. She would not be seeing Darcy this morning.

Mr. Collins surprised the entire family by keeping his dinner engagement with the Lucas family though it had been raining all day and the roads were sure to be in a horrid condition.

The following two days, though the weather continued to be inclement, he returned for a full-day visit with Sir William. It struck them as odd, but none lingered too long on the thought as all were relieved to be out of Mr. Collins’s company.

While her mother and sisters were busy changing ribbons on Jane's ball dress, Elizabeth slipped away to speak to her father.

"Papa, last night Jane asked why I had joined you and Mr. Darcy in your study, and somehow I managed to avoid her inquiry. You and I had not discussed whether Jane should be told about yesterday's happenings, and I wish to be prepared if she does ask again."

Mr. Bennet thought for a few minutes and said, "I do not think this is something that Jane needs to know. Additionally, it would do no good to tell her. I am certain that after fretting for a while, she would declare the whole as a mistake of some sort and dismiss it."

Elizabeth nodded. "If she asks again?"

"I will leave that to you, Lizzy. We did speak of playing chess, so if you were to say we were discussing that subject, it would not be a lie, and since Jane knows little about chess, she will most likely not inquire further." Mr. Bennet winked at Elizabeth and gestured to dismiss her.

Elizabeth attempted to keep herself occupied in helping to boost Jane's spirits, hiding her own depressed condition in the process. She knew that any *sane* individual would stay at home in such weather. They would not be receiving any visitors from Netherfield.

Yet, no matter how she tried to distract herself, Elizabeth found the separation from Darcy a torture. She could not seem to turn her mind from thinking about the way it felt to be held by him, and she longed for more—she hoped under much more pleasant circumstances. She spent quite a bit of time trying to puzzle out what emotion he had displayed before he moved away while they were alone in the dining room. Whatever it was, it made her heart race and her breath come faster every time she thought of it. She attempted to analyze the reason why he would not allow her to take any guilt upon herself. When he spoke of them as a unit, at the simple word "we," she felt a shiver of pleasure move down her spine. The conversations that they had shared over the past weeks were reviewed in her mind, their mutual interests and understandings showed how suitable they were for each other.

No, Lizzy! You must stop thinking in this way. You are friends, nothing more! she would chastise herself, and she would turn her thoughts to another subject… but it did not suffice for long.

~*~*~*~*~*~*~*~*~*~*~*~

~Netherfield Park

Darcy had gone to bed anticipating the pleasure of spending as much time as possible with Elizabeth before he had to leave for London immediately following the ball. Even if he did not look forward to enduring the behaviour of her younger sisters, the prospect of having them along on their morning walks gave him some measure of relief as well. He knew that their presence would help him to keep his longings for Elizabeth in check.

When he heard the sound of falling rain upon waking, his first reaction was one of deep distress and disappointment. After a few minutes of deliberation, he had convinced himself that it might actually be beneficial in regards to his sanity.

It seemed the more time he spent with Elizabeth during his waking hours, the less time he spent in his dreams simply spending time with her. His nightly slumber had become filled with visualizations that were much more physical in nature, and Darcy had been having an increasingly difficult time controlling his impulses while near Elizabeth in reality. There were several instances when he had almost taken her hand in his, and he had come very close to reaching out to caress the bloom of her cheek without thinking.

But that difficulty turned out to be nothing when compared to the pure torment of Elizabeth's being merely three miles away and his not being able to look upon her, talk with her, or hear her laughter. Often during that long, dreary day, he found himself pacing the library like a caged animal, glancing at each window every time he passed to see if the rain had yet receded.

Would increasing the distance between them by relocating to London make life without her pass more easily or would he become more wretched? He knew he would never be happy without her, but would the length of time that they were separated make contentment more or less difficult to attain?

At the end of the second day of rain, Darcy was sure he would go mad if he did not spend some time with Elizabeth. He paced his room, shaking his head. He had no reason to doubt that what he felt now would only become more intense once he removed himself to London.

Pausing by the window, he looked out in the direction of Longbourn and took a long, deep breath. Promise to his mother or not, living the remainder of his life in this way—without her—would be absolutely impossible. His heart could no longer be denied… he would ask for permission to court Elizabeth.

Relief and joy filled him to overflowing at these thoughts. It *must* be the correct choice if making this decision caused him to feel as if he had been under water for too long and had just broken the surface.

He would go to Longbourn tomorrow afternoon, rain or not. He would say that since everyone at Netherfield had been occupied with the preparations for the ball, he had been incessantly bored and had come to play chess with Mr. Bennet. Elizabeth had said that she wished to watch them play, and Mr. Bennet had suggested that whoever won the first match would become her opponent. Afterwards, he would ask for a moment alone to speak to Mr. Bennet to gain his consent to speak to *her* alone, with the intention of asking her to enter a state of courtship.

Darcy pictured Elizabeth leaning over the board to move her pieces and his heart raced. He was more than certain that if he were to play her, he would lose. He smiled as he wondered how he could possibly concentrate on the game. A morning dress might be much less of a distraction, preventing him from making a complete fool of himself, losing after only a few moves.

The afternoon scenario reappeared in his mind, and he smiled again, deciding he cared not if he lost *this* game. He would go later in the day, hoping the fact that it was not the proper time to visit would help convince the family that he was desperately bored at home and in need of occupation. The rewards were worth the risk of their thinking him a little odd.

Darcy laughed at himself. *Perhaps the distraction of a lady's neckline is the reason most men do not allow women to play chess! Hmmmm... billiards would be an even more pleasing game to play opposite Elizabeth... and it would be most satisfying to teach her to play.*

That night, someone other than Elizabeth crept into Darcy's dreams…

Darcy was at Pemberley. He walked up the front steps and entered. His mother, Lady Anne, was there to meet him. Overjoyed to see her, he rushed across the hall to embrace her, but she seemed furious and immediately pulled away from him. He did not remember her acting this way at any time in his life. She had always been firm but gentle when disciplining him, so the intense look of censure that she was directing at him was wounding—even frightening.

She took him by the hand and led him into her sitting room. Feeling as if he were six years old again, he dutifully sat in the chair she motioned to. His hands were trembling with an inexplicable fear of what his mother would say to him.

Her voice was so full of command that he did not recognize it. "A report of a most alarming nature has reached me just now, William, and I came at once. I was told that you are in all likelihood going to be united with a fortuneless country nobody's daughter whose only connexions are in trade! Has not my sister informed you of my wish for you to marry your cousin Anne?"

Darcy, wide eyed, could not speak past the tightness in his throat. He felt himself heading towards frenzy.

Lady Anne continued, "I am ashamed of you, William! Are you lost to every feeling of propriety? Have you no esteem for the memories of your father or me? Have you no respect for the promises you made just before my death? You have failed me twice now, will you fail me again?"

Darcy finally found a hoarse, gravelly voice, "Mother, I am in love with Elizabeth! I do not believe I can live without her in my life. Am I not permitted happiness?"

"Love... happiness?" A mirthless laugh that he was not familiar with echoed throughout the room. "These are inconsequential! Duty, honour, decorum, and prudence forbid this match, William! If you willfully act against the inclinations of all your family and friends, Elizabeth will be censured, slighted, and despised by everyone connected with you. This alliance will be a disgrace to Georgiana, and none of your names will ever be mentioned by anyone again! The match will make you three the contempt of the world. Both Elizabeth and Georgiana would grow to resent you, leaving all of you miserable, forever. If you insist upon having this girl in your life, then marry Anne and take her on the side."

Darcy was shocked. "Mother! How could you suggest such a thing? I would not dis honour Elizabeth. I would rather give her up forever."

"Then so be it, William. Let me be rightly understood. This match can never take place. Never!" His mother brought her fist down on the table next to her, making a horribly loud noise.

Darcy awoke with a start, sitting up immediately. His sheets were drenched with perspiration, his breathing was rapid, and his heart felt as if it were about to burst.

He jumped out of bed and tripped over the book that he had been reading as he fell asleep which must have slid off his bed—the very one that Elizabeth had borrowed and returned to him.

Lighting a candle, Darcy took it with him to the wash basin where he splashed water on his face. The mirror caught his attention, and he was forced to quickly look away from the agony of his tortured soul that reflected back at him.

What had he been thinking by deciding to court, and eventually marry, Elizabeth?

Of course his family would not accept as his wife the daughter of a country squire with an insignificant estate and connexions to! His aunt had told him time and time again that he was expected to marry within the first circle of society and obtain connexions with either a titled family or one of great wealth—preferably both.

But Elizabeth was the one woman for whom he felt something special, even from the first moment he laid eyes on her. He had always been able to behave as his true self when with her; a very rare occurrence indeed!

Did it really make a difference what was earned by her father's estate and that her relatives earned their living? For his own sake, he would have to answer no… not when the reward was so great. To be able to spend a lifetime with Elizabeth would be heaven on earth, but others would have an entirely different view.

Though he would not hesitate if it were only himself, he had his sister to consider. Every move he made affected her future greatly.

Walking over to the brandy decanter that Bingley had provided for his room, he brought it with him to his seat by the fire and poured himself a glass.

Why did the woman who seemed formed for him in every respect that mattered to *him* have to be an unacceptable choice according to *society*?

The last time he could remember even feeling content for any significant period of time was when his mother was alive—more than fifteen years ago. Since then, there were several short bursts that he had spent with Georgiana and Richard during which his memories were pleasant in nature, but these times did not seem to last more than a limited while.

While in Elizabeth's presence, he experienced joy at all times. The future he could envision with her was filled with *continuous* happy days and nights.

Darcy could no longer sit still; he began to pace before the fire.

His mother…

Darcy ground his teeth to repress the emotions welling up within his chest. He had failed his mother by not being able to take care of his father after her death. He had failed her by not looking after Georgiana well enough—what happened last summer at Ramsgate had proven that point.

The third promise was crucial. He must do as she asked or else fail her completely!

Before coming to Hertfordshire, there was no question that he would honour his promise, and he expected to have little difficulty in finding a mate who met with society's many expectations for his wife. It had seemed to be the easiest of the three to honour.

Once he had met Elizabeth, what his mother truly *meant* by "marry well" was of the utmost importance to him. He wished her words to mean something that no one else had voiced to date: choose your marriage partner well, someone that you can love and respect, someone who makes you happy.

Darcy stopped pacing and stared into the fire, finally admitting to himself what he had struggled not to since awakening.

The dream was the sign he had asked for in order to resolve his confusion!

The clock in the hall chimed, revealing to him that hours had passed since he had awoken from his dream.

Darcy closed his eyes and took several deep breaths, knowing that his original plan had been the correct course of action. He would return to London—without visiting Longbourn and without speaking of courtship.

Darcy collapsed into bed, hoping that he would dream of his angel, Elizabeth.

When making your choice in life, do not neglect to live.
--Samuel Johnson (English author, 1709-1784)

The next morning Richard sought out Darcy to discuss their plans of going to London. It was decided that they would leave the afternoon on the day following the ball and proceed directly to Darcy House to spend the evening with Georgiana. The next day, they would speak to the earl about the property in India, after which Darcy would arrange to have his solicitor and investigator meet with them all at Darcy House as soon as possible.

Richard then asked Darcy when he would be coming back to Netherfield.

Darcy answered without meeting Richard's eye, "I will not return for a long time, if ever."

Richard's eyes opened wide. "You will let her go then?"

"Of whom do you speak?" Darcy asked in an almost disinterested tone, seemingly absorbed in brushing a piece of lint from his jacket.

Richard was infuriated. "*Of whom do I speak?* Darcy! Are you daft, man?" Richard walked away and paced for a few moments, trying to calm himself before continuing, "I have learned lessons I hope most people will never have a reason to learn in the same manner as I did, though it might do them some good. When facing death, one realizes what is important in life—and what is not. Hang dowries and society's expectations!" he yelled. "You, sir, need to tone down that inflated 'Darcy pride' of yours and realize what your paramount concerns should be! You forget that I know Miss Elizabeth and can see how perfectly suited you are for each other! You would be a complete and utter fool to let her go without making her an offer. You should *beg* her to marry you if necessary!"

Darcy responded, "You do not know *all* of my reasons for yielding to the expectations of society, Richard. I refused to explain further." He turned his back to his cousin. *He can never understand the promise I made to Mother and why I must keep it!*

As he stormed from the room to prevent himself from slapping some sense into his cousin, Richard grumbled loudly enough for Darcy to hear, "Damned fool! A life filled with happiness is within his grasp and he throws it away for the sake of a handful of people who would not care one stitch about him if he had little fortune and his name was *Smith*!"

~Longbourn Estate

Though Mr. Collins spent a great deal of time at the Lucases' house, the Bennet family did see him over the three day period of rain. With time, Elizabeth was completely convinced that Mr. Collins had no idea about the plot against her father. It baffled her why Wickham had attempted this. Every explanation she could think of was too ridiculous to even think of bringing it to the attention of her father.

She also spent some time considering the reason Mr. Collins was spending so much time with the Lucases. Was it possible that he was interested in her good friend, Charlotte?

Charlotte was not of a romantic nature, though Elizabeth *did* think she was more romantic than she would admit. She had often claimed that she would be perfectly content in a marriage of convenience as long as the gentleman was respectable and had a comfortable income. Elizabeth thought Charlotte was a beautiful woman, but Charlotte had been told so many times that she was plain that she seemed to believe it. Elizabeth felt that her friend only needed more of a chance to get away from Hertfordshire, which was quite short of bachelors, to meet a man who would recognize her true worth.

Aunt Madeline Gardiner had invited Charlotte to London several times in the past, but for one reason or another it was not possible for Charlotte to come along when Elizabeth had visited. Now that she was older than the age at which most ladies married, Elizabeth was afraid that if Mr. Collins proposed, Charlotte would accept without hesitation. She had no found time alone with Charlotte to tell her of anything which had transpired with Mr. Collins since his arrival.

Elizabeth felt an urgent need to warn Charlotte before it was too late!

~*~*~*~*~*~*~*~*~*~*~

Tuesday, November 26, 1811

~Netherfield Park - The Ball

Darcy could scarcely believe that he was actually looking forward to a ball, but his eagerness was indisputable.

Earlier in the day, it had finally stopped raining, and his inclination bent towards rushing to Longbourn immediately after the sun had peeked out from behind the clouds. It helped that Caroline Bingley had been deeply involved with planning the ball and overseeing the final details of the decorations, so she had not had much time to be chasing after him for the past few days.

To keep himself from giving in to his longings, he had replayed the dream of his mother in his mind repeatedly, even going so far as writing down everything his mother had said. Whenever his chest began to ache unbearably, he would take out his mother's words and read them again and again. *"This match can never take place. Never!"* she had said, and he *told* himself he had finally accepted this fact.

In the future, when Bingley married Elizabeth's sister, as he was sure that he would, Darcy had already decided that he would not attend the wedding. He would also avoid the Bingleys any time Elizabeth was staying with them. If seeing her sister Jane pained him too greatly, he would have to make the drastic move of ending his friendship with Bingley.

He hoped that once married, Bingley would decide to buy a different estate, for he knew that he could never visit them at Netherfield so long as Elizabeth was but three miles away. *But perhaps after she has married and moved away, I could visit at Netherfield.* The thought caused his chest to tighten in immense pain. Even though he could not be with Elizabeth, but he did not think that he could bear to watch her someday fall in love and marry somebody else!

For a short time this afternoon, Darcy was tempted to stay above stairs all evening instead of attending the ball, questioning his ability to leave tomorrow if he spent time with her tonight. But how could he *not* take this last opportunity to see her, to hear her, to fill himself with her scent just *once* more? Elizabeth was everything!

But, I should keep my distance… I will listen and watch, but not speak to her. I will ***not*** *dance with her!*

~%~

Mrs. Bennet had made certain that Jane's gown was the best that could be found in Hertfordshire. Jane was attired in a cream silk gown with a fine crepe overlay slightly hinting at pink, covered with tiny pink embroidered roses. *The loveliest gown belongs to the loveliest lady present,* Elizabeth thought.

Elizabeth's gown was white muslin, adorned with red roses embroidered around the neckline, sleeves, and hem. It was simple yet elegant, and though she felt that she could never be as beautiful as Jane, she thought she looked well in it.

As she entered Netherfield, Elizabeth began searching the crowd for Darcy but did not see him anywhere. She had to smile when, upon the Bennet family's arrival, Bingley abandoned his duties as host, deserted the receiving line, and firmly established himself at Jane's side. Anyone seeing the couple together would know they were deeply in love. He made Jane so happy—how could Elizabeth not love him as a brother already?

Passing through the receiving line was an amusement in itself. Bingley's sisters were examining their guests' clothing with critical eyes. Caroline Bingley was barely civil to her, but that was not unexpected. Louisa surprised Elizabeth by extending more of an effort, but she had barely begun to speak before her sister's glare put a sudden halt to her sincere-sounding words of welcome.

They both greeted Jane warmly, but Elizabeth could tell that neither Jane nor Bingley saw the look of disdain that Caroline shot at Louisa after welcoming Jane to the ball.

Perhaps Jane was better off not knowing as she was too far influenced by the happiness of those around her. If she recognized that his sisters did not want her to marry their brother, would Jane refuse him? Elizabeth did not wish to dwell upon the question, for she suspected she would not like the answer. Yes, it was far better for Jane if her attention was too distracted by Bingley's eyes to notice his sisters.

Bingley offered Elizabeth his free arm, and escorted the ladies into the ballroom. It was then that she saw Darcy. Though she had suffered the three days without having seen him, she truly had not realized how much she had missed him until that moment. He was even more handsome than ever in his formal attire, but it was more the look in his eyes as he followed her entrance into the ballroom that took her breath away. Even at this distance she could see it, and it raised her hopes considerably. It was a look filled with passion and longing and… could she dare hope… love.

For a moment, all of Elizabeth's attempts at dismissing the prospects that Jane and Charlotte had voiced since the assembly failed. She could not but hope that he truly did love her when he looked at her like *that*!

~%~

Darcy thought he was prepared to see Elizabeth, but when she walked through the doors of the ballroom, he found that he was not. Elizabeth was always stunning, but this night she was absolutely spellbinding. He could not tear his gaze away from her.

He felt protective of her and could not but become her shadow throughout the evening. The other people in the room were mere obstacles between them, their bodies blocking his view of her, their voices drowning out the sound of her voice. To him they did not really exist; they were mere annoyances.

~%~

Elizabeth was confused and greatly disappointed when Darcy did not approach her. She had hoped they would dance the first set, but he did not request it, nor did he ask for any other. She could feel his eyes upon her, watching her every move, and yet still he did not come to her. She had not expected this behaviour from him again after all they had recently shared. Knowing that if she approached him it would feed the gossips' coffers, she refused to do so.

Charlotte Lucas's first set was with Mr. Collins. Absolutely intent upon warning Charlotte away from the man, suddenly she was not sure exactly how to go about it. Whilst she pondered her strategy, Elizabeth saw that they had stood up together *again*!

~%~

What Darcy felt while watching *his* Elizabeth dance with other men at the ball was absolutely unacceptable to him, but he found this feeling beyond his control—raging jealousy! He had never felt it at this intensity in the whole of his life! It was likely he would do something without thinking tonight with this emotion ruling him.

Though he was alarmed over what seemed to be her control of his every breath, he could not resist the magnetic pull of Elizabeth. No matter what his resolve had been before the ball began, Darcy felt he must dance with her, feel the touch of her hand, be the sole object of her attention, and receive her smiles, just once more before he left Elizabeth forever.

It would be beneficial for him to have a farewell dance to look back on. Yes, that would be acceptable.

~%~

Finally, Charlotte was standing alone across the dance floor, and Elizabeth headed toward her. After exchanging the usual civilities, Elizabeth asked with a teasing sparkle in her eye, "Did you enjoy dancing with Mr. Collins?"

Charlotte replied with a tone of admonishment, "Yes, I was pleased to dance with Mr. Collins, Lizzy."

Elizabeth doubted her friend was telling the truth for she had seen with her own eyes that Mr. Collins had little knowledge of dancing, had made wrong turns throughout, and had trod on poor Charlotte's feet at least three times. It should have been an embarrassment, not a pleasure. She and Charlotte were usually more honest with each other than this!

Elizabeth gave her friend a look of reproof which was met with Charlotte's responding in the same tone of voice as before, "Lizzy, I only ask for a comfortable home, and considering Mr. Collins's character, connexions, and situation in life, I am convinced that my chance of happiness with him is as fair as most people can boast on entering the marriage state."

Elizabeth's eyes widened. "Are you saying that Mr. Collins has made you an offer, Charlotte, and that you have accepted?"

"Oh… yes, Lizzy. We decided to keep it a secret until after the ball, but by the look you were giving me, I thought that you already knew!"

Elizabeth was speechless. It was too late! She had failed Charlotte.

Charlotte said, "I know you are surprised dearest Lizzy, but will you not wish me happiness?"

"Charlotte, there are some things you should know about Mr. Collins…"

"No, Lizzy, I do not wish to hear it. I believe happiness in marriage is entirely a matter of chance. It is better to know as little as possible of the defects of the person with whom you are to pass your life."

"Charlotte, you know that is not sound…"

"No, Lizzy! I thank you for your concern, but I will not hear you other than to wish me every chance of happiness."

Elizabeth knew not what to do next. "Charlotte, I *do* wish you to have every chance of happiness in life, which is why I feel you must listen to me. The betrothal has not yet been announced; you can put an end to it before…"

"Lizzy, please! I will not speak of this any further!" said Charlotte angrily before walking away.

Elizabeth thought of speaking to her father of the situation, but it seemed a hopeless case. What could she say to Charlotte? She had no proof of anything untoward that she could show her friend. He had acted as no gentleman should, but he had excuses for what he did that might be believed. She continued to wish to suppress the fact that he was found in her room, even to Charlotte, for she knew if Charlotte would cancel the engagement, she would need to tell Sir William all the reasons why, and then the news would be spread all over the county—and then *she* would be forced to marry Mr. Collins. Perhaps it was incredibly selfish, but Elizabeth did not want to make such a sacrifice, not even to save Charlotte from the same fate.

~%~

After a few dances, Darcy saw Elizabeth cross the dance floor to speak to Charlotte Lucas, and he recognized that Elizabeth was becoming upset during their conversation. Darcy's protective nature took precedence, and he could no longer restrain himself from going to her. When he neared, Charlotte seemed angry at Elizabeth, but they were still speaking civilly. He delayed any further approach to give them privacy in their conversation, feeling more comfortable being close by in case Elizabeth needed him, though what threat Charlotte could possibly be was beyond his ability to reason at the moment. Charlotte suddenly walked away, and Elizabeth seemed more upset than before.

Darcy advanced toward Elizabeth and asked, "Are you well, Miss Elizabeth?"

"Mr. Darcy!" she said with surprise, and she hesitated to answer. Elizabeth wished to speak to him and ask for his advice about Charlotte and Mr. Collins, but it seemed that he had been shunning her so far this evening. She did not want to bring this unfortunate circumstance into their conversation now that he was paying his attentions to her, not to mention that Charlotte had said it was a secret. They had shared too many negative experiences so far; she wanted to have more positive memories with Darcy to look back upon.

She continued, "Yes, I am well, sir. Charlotte and I had a disagreement about… a certain matter, but I am well."

"I am glad to hear it," he said softly, searching her eyes to gauge whether she would be receptive to a request for a dance at this moment. The distressed look in her eyes turned more toward the sparkle he had gotten to know and love, and so he requested the next. She accepted.

Chapter 26

Darcy led her to the dance floor, and it was as it had been at the assembly. The world ceased to exist with the exception of the two of them. The tingling warmth which spread through her every time they touched left her wanting much more. Her breath quickened when he looked at her *that* way again, the same way he had when she had entered the ballroom, and she wondered if he could hear the beating of her heart.

All of the thoughts of him that she had suppressed over the past few rainy days came upon her at once as they moved through the dance. His eyes caught hers, and she thought, *Do you know how I love you?* For a moment Elizabeth feared she had said the thought aloud because Darcy's expression changed… but it was one of such happiness that it took her breath away. It must have been an illusion, a wish, a hope, a dream, for as soon as it had appeared, it vanished. Her doubts returning, she was suddenly sure that if she had said it aloud, he would not have been happy to hear it.

She did not wish to think this way any longer if it was to raise false hopes within her, so she began to talk of her dance with Colonel Fitzwilliam. Elizabeth became concerned when Darcy's countenance changed to one of agitation.

~%~

Their shared dance was everything and nothing like Darcy had imagined, both at the same time. The thrill of her touch, even through their gloves, was magnificent—it penetrated his being to his very heart.

Darcy was at first confused by the emotion he saw in her eyes, but it raised in him a hope that she could somehow be interested in him as more than a friend. Just then, the words from the dream echoed through his mind, and all hope was crushed.

The feeling of jealousy that he had experienced earlier while watching her dance was increased twenty-fold when she mentioned something his cousin said to her during their dance, but then luxurious warmth spread throughout him when he realized she did not look at Richard as she did at him. She looked at *nobody* as she did at him!

Before Darcy knew what he was doing, he asked to sit with her for supper, and she accepted. Elizabeth's next partner came to claim her hand.

As she walked away from him on another man's arm, he felt a weight on his chest so heavy that he feared he would be unable to breathe.

This is how my life will be without her. I shall have nothing. Another man shall win her hand and her heart someday. What power is this that Elizabeth holds over me? That I should feel as if I cannot breathe... that my heart does not beat unless I am near her? ***Can*** *I stop loving her, wanting her, and needing her? Do I wish to stop?*

He was almost overtaken by an urge to follow Richard's advice and beg her to marry him right there in front of the entire neighbourhood.

But how could he live with himself if he did? Subjecting Elizabeth and Georgiana to the things he was warned of in the dream was intolerable. The thought that marriage to him would make both of the women that he held so dear miserable was unacceptable!

He could not do it.

The way she looked at me during the dance was a gift, but for Elizabeth's sake, I must leave and never return. It is distressing enough to know that she will be unhappy at losing our friendship, but if I leave now, that pain will fade in time. If she did learn to feel more for me, it would hurt her more deeply—as leaving now will hurt me. This way, she will forget I exist and go on with her life.

The ache in his chest increased to think that someday she would not remember him when as early as the first moment he saw her, he had known instantly that he would never stop thinking of her until he lived no more.

Perhaps it would be much better for her if she thought of me as less than a friend. Should I attempt to make her dislike me? Do something—say something unforgivable?

A feeling of panic enveloped him, *No! I cannot! I cannot! I would not survive knowing Elizabeth was alive in the world and thinking ill of me!*

Darcy spent the rest of the time before supper contemplating these thoughts while watching Elizabeth grace the ballroom, and her partner, with her presence.

There is, indeed, nothing that so much seduces reason from vigilance, as the thought of passing life with an amiable woman.
--Samuel Johnson (English author, 1709-1784)

Colonel Fitzwilliam had been doing his duty to his host and had engaged himself to dance with several unattached ladies of Hertfordshire successively. His next set was with Miss Charlotte Lucas, with whom he had been in company a few times and had spoken to only once. She was a pretty girl with a pleasing personality. Richard had stayed away from her purposely since every time her eyes met his he felt… peculiar, but he certainly could not dance with every other single lady in the room and then slight Miss Lucas! When he caught sight of her across the room, he could not understand why he heard people refer to her as plain. Tonight especially, she was beautiful. He walked up to her to claim his dance, and that peculiar feeling came over him, stronger than ever.

"It is a wonderful ball, is it not, Colonel Fitzwilliam?"

"Yes, it is, Miss Lucas. Were I as rich as Bingley, I would have at least four balls a year, I believe, one for every season."

"And being the son of an earl, are you not accustomed to attending many balls?" she said with the slightest hint of a playful smile.

"Aye, I am, but it is different when it is in one's own home. When my parents hold a ball, I take pleasure in watching the transformation from the familiar place that I have lived most of my life. It amazes me how the mistress of the house plans every last detail, and I do enjoy watching how the servants orchestrate it all from her plans. It could be compared to setting up a battle, but the weapons used are much prettier, and when the 'soldiers' fall, it is with a much more pleasant result! Though in the early morning light when everyone leaves the 'field,' the chaos left behind *is* similar!" They both laughed. "Having a small income as a colonel, I do not expect to see such a transformation for a ball again when I am no longer benefitting from my parents' generosity."

"Do not younger sons of earls usually marry ladies of large fortunes, sir?" Charlotte said teasingly.

"That is usually how it works, Miss Lucas." Suddenly Richard felt like a hypocrite. He had been telling Darce not to pay attention to dowries and society's expectations, yet he himself would.

Charlotte smiled knowingly and said, "Colonel, it is not common knowledge as of yet, but I am recently engaged to be married. I would like to assure you of having nothing to worry about from *my* expectations of a simple dance! No warnings are necessary."

Richard laughed, "That is good to know, Miss Lucas." He was confused by a strong feeling of disappointment which came over him as he continued, "May I wish you joy, madam?"

"I thank you, sir."

When the set was done, they found neither of them had a partner for the next. Richard fetched some refreshments and sat with Miss Lucas. The two talked through the next set, and he found himself quite attracted to the person, opinions, and sense of humour possessed by Miss Charlotte Lucas. The "peculiar feeling" continued to grow stronger until he realized that he was feeling a more particular regard for her than he had ever felt for any other woman before.

Richard turned thoughtful. *It is impossible for anything to happen between us. Darce said it best the other day: I live above my income. I cannot support a wife in the manner to which I am accustomed and to which she deserves.*

Though, with a woman such as this, I could well become used to living on my officer's salary, as long as Charlotte would be willing. Should I ask her?

Ask her! Am I mad? I have only spoken to her twice, and the first time we barely exchanged civilities. She said she is recently engaged, as well. Impossible!

However, her engagement is not yet announced...

I barely know her! Now, after only one hour of dance and conversation, I am ready to ask her to cast away her reputation, break an engagement, and court a man who can barely hope to support her? She would think me ready for the asylum!

There is no time, though; she said her engagement would be announced after the ball. I will have no time to get to know her better, no chance to court her before it is announced, and then I can never ask her.

She is ***engaged****! I should not even be thinking of her at all!*

Charlotte had been having a lovely time with Colonel Fitzwilliam, but then he suddenly became quiet, and she watched as turmoil erupted upon his features. "Are you well, sir?"

Startled out of his reverie by Charlotte's voice, he turned and said, "Oh, yes… yes, Miss Lucas, I am well." He took a deep breath to calm himself before continuing. "I have not asked you, madam, if I have met the man to whom you are betrothed."

"You do know him, sir; it is Mr. Collins."

"COLLINS! Not my aunt's parson?" Richard suddenly felt nauseated. *There must be another Mr. Collins! There must!*

Colonel Fitzwilliam's reaction almost frightened Charlotte. "Why, yes, sir, I believe he is quite grateful for your aunt's patronage."

Richard needed to think. He must stop this marriage. This wonderful woman could *not* marry that toad of a man. After treating Miss Elizabeth in such a way, who knows what he would do to a *wife*! He had to say something to change her mind, but he could barely compose a sentence. "You cannot be serious! I ask you to rethink this decision… the engagement is not yet public… I cannot allow you to… did not Miss Elizabeth talk to you about…"

A shocked expression came over Charlotte, and she interrupted him. "Colonel Fitzwilliam! Did Lizzy ask you to speak to me about this?"

"Miss Elizabeth?" Richard said, confused.

Charlotte was angry now and stood up. "Sir! You have barely made my acquaintance, and you will offer me advice on whom I am and am not to marry? It is presumptuous of you to think that you have any rights at all in regards to me! Good evening, Colonel Fitzwilliam!" Charlotte walked away.

"Good show, Richard!" he mumbled to himself, feeling quite awful. *She is absolutely correct. I am nothing to her. I cannot tell her whom to marry.*

Charlotte found a quiet place on a balcony to hide away with her tears and her thoughts. *Why am I so angry? Why will I not allow anyone to tell me what they think of Mr. Collins? Why is Lizzy saying the same sort of things as Colonel Fitzwilliam in regards to him? Is there truly something more I should know about Mr. Collins?*

Charlotte scowled. *Oh! But who else would ever offer for me? Colonel Fitzwilliam... if ever I were a romantic, I would have to say I had fallen in love with him at first sight. But I am not a romantic; a second son cannot marry me, nor would he ever be interested in someone like me.*

I have no alternative to Mr. Collins. I am already a burden on my family, which will only increase with time. I will have a life being completely dependent upon them and spend my time being passed between my brothers' houses, taking care of their children. My only option for independence would be to become a governess, and have little liberty in the process. With Mr. Collins, I could have a home and children of my own. My choice is clear!

Caroline Bingley was vexed and becoming increasingly so as the evening progressed. She had watched Darcy carefully, waiting for him to claim his dance with her. Though she knew that he never danced the first dance of any ball since that showed a decided preference to those assembled, Darcy, as her houseguest, should have requested the honour of one of her first few dances of the evening, and yet it was now supper, and he had yet to do so. Whenever she was not displaying her superior dancing abilities, Caroline would place herself near Darcy, hoping he would notice her and speak with her. But he spoke to no one. She fanned herself quite vigorously, but the movement did not attract his attention. Once, Caroline was so eagerly fanning herself that she needed to return above stairs to have her coiffure repaired.

Instead, much to her chagrin, Darcy spent the entire time completely consumed by watching, talking to, and dancing with Eliza Bennet! The way he looked at Eliza when she was *not* looking his way was even more sickening than when she had encroached upon Netherfield while her sister was ill!

Caroline had watched every move they made during their set, and she was extremely displeased with what she had witnessed passing between them. Now they were having supper together! Both ignored everyone and everything around them. The hoyden was practically throwing herself at him. She could see Eliza played the game well—she smiled, laughed, feigned interest in what he said, and barely took her eyes off him. And to her particular dismay, Darcy was acting the part of a besotted fool, almost exactly like her brother was acting with Eliza's sister, Jane.

Oh, had they never met the Bennets! Though Caroline was unhappy that she had not been able to spend much time displaying her charms to him during the planning of the ball, she was satisfied that Darcy had stayed to attend the ball and see the results of her efforts. She had proved without a doubt that she could plan an event in the elegant style required by the first circle.

It annoyed her excessively that Darcy had eyes only for Eliza while her family was displaying behaviour he would normally consider horridly inappropriate. He noticed none of it! If she had hired circus clowns to entertain her guests with their ridiculous performance, they could not have done a better job than the Bennet tribe. She half expected one of them to produce a piglet and have the other guests chase it.

Caroline would certainly make sure he heard all about every detail of their atrocious conduct when he was not as… distracted. Seeing his behaviour toward Eliza tonight, she was glad that Darcy would be leaving the following day for Town. Away in London, he would be no longer influenced by this vixen. She would also use the same points to convince her brother to follow Darcy to Town, and both gentlemen would then be out of range of those grasping Bennets!

Chapter 27

They spent supper quite pleasantly discussing many different subjects. Elizabeth loved the way that Darcy's dimples appeared when he smiled just so, the way his eyes captured hers, the sound of his rich voice, and the rumble of his resonant laughter. She loved the way his entire countenance lit up when he spoke of his sister or Pemberley. She loved looking at him, being with him, and listening to him. Paradise was being in his company.

At the end of supper, paradise came to an end when Darcy told her he was leaving for London to discuss the problems in India with his uncle, solicitor, and investigator.

Her heart dropped at the thought of his leaving for a few days, but it felt as if it had been torn from her chest when he said that he did not know if he would be coming back to Netherfield. The pain was almost unbearable.

Elizabeth was convinced that she understood what had happened. She had exposed her feelings to him unwittingly, and he was trying to tell her what she already knew—they could never be more than friends. He was a prince, and she was a peasant, and they could be nothing more than that. He was warning her that she would probably never see him again after tonight.

Yes, they were friends, but a single man and a single woman could not even correspond even if they were *only* friends. Elizabeth would never know what he did, thought, or felt about anything ever again. If they did ever meet in the future, she would be forced to see him married to a woman of beauty, accomplishment, wealth, and consequence. While he would forget she ever existed, she would think of him every day for the rest of her life.

When supper was over, he asked for the last dance of the ball. Elizabeth hesitated. It would be excruciating, but how could she not take this last chance to spend a few minutes with the man she loved? She accepted with a nod and excused herself. Elizabeth needed a few minutes alone before the dancing began again.

When it came time for the last set of the ball, Darcy approached Elizabeth, took her hand, and led her to the dance. They proceeded in silence, not a word was spoken between them. They stared into each other's eyes, passing too closely to each other, their hands lingering a little too long, brushing shoulders and arms. Both were memorizing by the warmth of every touch, every feature, every curve, every movement, every eyelash, and every dimple. Each thought they saw in the other's eyes what they wanted to see and allowed themselves to believe it, if only for a few minutes. They just wanted to enjoy a bit of fantasy that the other loved them—and would rather drown in the other's eyes than deal with reality which would surely come crashing down upon them eventually… when the music stopped.

Darcy could not leave her side after the dance. In the confusion of guests leaving for the evening, no one was paying attention to them, and it was as if they were alone in the partial darkness of a corner of the entry hall. His breath sped. He stood too near as he helped her with her cloak, brushing the skin of her neck with his fingers, moving his hands too close to her shoulders, his fingers barely grazing her skin; his hands lingered too long after the cloak was on. Part of him knew it was wrong to do so, but it felt so right to touch Elizabeth. When she did not object, when she *thanked* him, the look in her eyes and her quick breath made his mind fill with thoughts of her wanting his touch as much as he wanted hers. It was almost too much for him to resist leaning down to kiss the lips that had fascinated him so over the past months… but resist he did for at that moment he heard her mother's voice ringing out over the others. Their eyes met and he took half a step away from Elizabeth, but did not release her gaze until her mother neared.

The Bennet family met in the entry hall to wait for their carriage. Mrs. Bennet had somehow arranged for their family to be the last to depart. Bingley and Jane were standing a little apart from the group talking. Darcy and Elizabeth were off to the other side of the group.

Darcy took Elizabeth's gloved hands, pulled her a little further away from the others and looked into her eyes. *How can I live without gazing into these beautiful eyes every day for the rest of my life?* He took a deep breath filling his lungs with her scent as he bent down a little and whispered, "Elizabeth? Promise me you will not walk out alone after I leave for London? Not until Wickham and Collins leave the area."

He called her by her Christian name, and it was as if he had caressed her soul. She knew that this was the moment they would say goodbye, and she did not want him to leave. It was irrational, she knew, but part of her felt that if she did not look at him, she could keep him there by her side. Part of her mind was angry, but she realized it was her way of protecting herself… to keep from breaking down into tears in front of him at saying goodbye forever. She wanted to remain angry, not be lost in his eyes and overwhelmed by this agonizing love for him. She turned her eyes to the floor.

Her heart was shattering into a million tiny slivers. She would never see him again. Purposely, she would avoid him if he came to see Bingley once he and Jane married, as she was sure they would. Seeing him with another woman as his wife could not be endured.

When she did not answer, did not even look at him, Darcy begged, "Please, Elizabeth?" He waited for what seemed like an eternity but she would not answer him. "Please?"

The pleading tone of his voice forced her to look up. Once she was lost in his eyes she would have promised him anything. "Yes, I promise," Elizabeth whispered.

He swallowed hard to allow his voice to have a chance to move past the lump in his throat. "Thank you."

Darcy knew he should not, knew he had no right to do it, but he could not stop himself. He moved his body to block her from her family's view, slowly removed her gloves and kissed the back of her hands reverently, first one then the other.

At first, Elizabeth was too overwhelmed to react. She watched his lips touch her skin but never did she expect the power of the reaction within her body and soul when they did. When he turned her hands over and kissed each palm, she could not stop a gasp from escaping.

Darcy looked up from her hands, and the ache within him turned into absolute misery and despair. He watched her slowly lift her eyes. What he saw was what he had been longing to see for months… *passion* and *love* on the "stage" that was Elizabeth's lovely face. *Oh! She loves me! How I would rejoice if circumstances had been different! I have erred greatly. Please forgive me, Elizabeth! I cannot be so selfish as to marry you. I cannot be the cause of the life of the misery that my dream has predicted. I love you too much!*

The anguish she saw in his eyes was staggering, and she gasped again.

Darcy took a step back but did not release her hands or her eyes until the carriage could be heard outside. He offered his arm to escort her and she accepted, and then he handed her into the carriage.

As the carriage began to move, his mind screamed, *I will never see her again!* What was left within him was an oppressive pain. His heart no longer beat, it drummed. His lungs no longer breathed, they expanded with searing fire. His head pounded with the last words she had said, repeating over and over again: *"Goodbye, Mr. Darcy."* He could see it in her eyes when she looked back as the carriage began to move away; she knew… she knew they would never see each other again.

The remainder of the Netherfield party returned indoors, but Darcy remained outside. He stood watching the carriage and continued staring at the end of the drive after it had disappeared from his sight. His heart was urging him to run after her. He knew that he would do just that if he moved. But he could not… he could not do it! So he did not move at all.

"Elizabeth!" he whispered.

~%~

The permanent staff at Netherfield liked and respected Mr. Darcy. They had also seen the way he looked at Miss Lizzy and were hoping for a match between the two. Molly and Sarah had been cleaning the ballroom along with a group of servants who had been hired for the event. The girls could see Mr. Darcy standing outside every time they passed the windows and exchanged many worried looks between them. Something was wrong, but knowing their place, they were unsure what to do.

More than an hour later, Molly noticed Colonel Fitzwilliam walking about the house, seeming to be looking for something. She had a whispered conversation with Sarah, and the two agreed that Mr. Darcy's situation should be brought to the colonel's attention. They both doubted that Colonel Fitzwilliam would be angry, but they cared enough about Mr. Darcy to step out of their place even if it meant losing their positions.

Molly sought out Colonel Fitzwilliam and said, "Pardon me, sir, your attention is required in a delicate matter." Molly led him to the window, then curtsied and returned to her duties.

Richard stood at the window for a while watching Darcy stare at the empty road leading to Longbourn. He had thought that after what he saw happening at the ball tonight, Darcy must have changed his mind about Miss Elizabeth, but now it did not seem so. Why was Darcy being so stubborn about this? There had to be more to it than he would speak of to him! He would just have to wait and see.

Sighing deeply, he made his way outside, crossing the courtyard to Darcy's side. After seeing Darcy's condition, he knew he should not say a word. Very glad the others had already retired and the servants were all too busy cleaning after the ball to be in the hallways, Richard pulled his cousin into the house and led him to a chair in his bedchamber, and then closed the door behind him leaving his cousin to himself.

~*~*~*~*~*~*~*~*~*~*~*~*~

~Longbourn Estate

The ache within Elizabeth's soul increased to an almost unbearable magnitude as the carriage pulled away from Netherfield. She had closed her eyes against the tears threatening to release themselves, turning her head to lean her forehead on the wall of the carriage—away from any curious eyes.

It had been a monumental task to gain control over her emotions in the carriage, and even more difficult once they arrived at Longbourn. To hear her sisters chatter on about how much they had enjoyed the ball, and to have to listen to her mother chastise Jane for not securing Bingley tonight and then in the next breath, gush about how Jane had made such a conquest with Bingley was all too much for her frayed nerves.

She laughed a little to herself; she was beginning to think like her mother! That thought helped her to keep her countenance until she was alone in her room with Jane.

Once there, she had Jane to contend with. Normally, the hours after a ball were spent discussing all the events that had transpired during the evening, but Elizabeth did not think that she could manage that tonight. She did not want to worry Jane or to ruin Jane's memories of this evening, but how was she to hide *this* from her most beloved sister? With enormous effort, Elizabeth managed a small smile and said little while she listened to Jane talk of what Bingley had said and done during the evening. Elizabeth was counting on Jane's being too happy to notice that she was not behaving much like her usual self.

When, after what seemed like an eternity, Jane fell asleep, Elizabeth escaped to the only room she could think of where she would not be overheard—her father's study. She stood in the middle of the room for quite a while staring at the chair in which Darcy had sat both times that he was in this room, waiting for the tears to begin to fall… but they did not come.

She had built a wall around her emotions so well that she could not let it down even now that she *wanted* to release them. She could feel nothing. And this completely rational mind, devoid of all emotions, was allowing her to question things that she would never examine with her emotions in the way.

She wondered if this was how Darcy felt when he was in society. She had watched him put up *his* wall many times, and had watched it fall whenever she neared. Suddenly a stone cold face would appear animated when he looked at her. Why had he never put up his wall for her except for that one time on the walk back from Meryton? Was she special to him?

What were the emotions she saw in his eyes tonight? She thought she saw clearly into his soul a few times and thought she saw that he loved her.

Why would he leave if she was special to him, if he loved her? Was she just *wishing* to believe his rejection was based upon society's demands upon him? Or was there truly something terribly wrong with her that he could not see past? Was Caroline Bingley correct in her declarations that her accomplishments were too masculine in nature?

It must be that she would be an embarrassment to him if they were seen together outside the company of the people who already knew her.

When the emotional turmoil she had expected did not appear, Elizabeth went to bed. As she slipped into a deep sleep, she wondered how Darcy had learned to remove the wall when he no longer needed it… how he was able to *feel* again. She knew she would never be able to ask him.

Wednesday, November 27, 1811

The next morning, Elizabeth slept very late, and she awoke to find that the wall protecting her from her emotions was still in place. Moving through the day without emotions was difficult at first, but Elizabeth found that with practice, it became almost natural to feign a smile at appropriate times without much effort. She thought she managed well enough.

Not many in the family looked closely enough to notice, but her father and Jane were becoming concerned as the day progressed. Her eyes gave her away; they were dull and empty. The sparkle was gone.

To the great relief of Mr. Bennet, one bit of news was much talked of at breakfast. Kitty and Lydia had somehow discovered that Mr. Wickham had left Meryton, and it was assumed that he had deserted his new post in the Militia. Mr. Bennet expected some sort of reaction from his Lizzy—an expression showing that she took comfort in the news or a pointed look in his direction—but he received none.

Mr. Bennet remained with the family for part of the day instead of disappearing into his study as was his usual custom. Though the talk after this news had been relayed was of no interest to him, he wished to watch Elizabeth's reactions to it.

Mr. Collins had left early in the morning for Lucas Lodge and returned with Lady Lucas, Charlotte, and Maria for tea, as was their custom after a ball. It was announced that Charlotte and Mr. Collins were to marry.

Everyone wished Charlotte and Mr. Collins joy, but Jane was the only person in the room to offer her true feelings about the match. Jane could see that Charlotte was content, and so she would be happy for them. Elizabeth did not speak during the visit, giving Charlotte the impression Elizabeth was resentful about their discussion the previous evening. When tea was over, the Lucas ladies and Mr. Collins returned to Lucas

Lodge to plan the wedding.

The moment the front door closed, Mrs. Bennet's nerves surfaced. She was sure that Mr. Collins had been taken in and trusted that they would never be happy together. She also blamed Elizabeth that Charlotte would someday be taking her own place as mistress of Longbourn and would take great pleasure in throwing them all out to starve in the hedgerows the moment Mr. Bennet was dead. She swore that she would never speak to Elizabeth or Charlotte again.

The half hour which had passed since his wife's rants had begun had caused Mr. Bennet's degree of concern about his Lizzy to increase alarmingly. Usually at times like this, she was exchanging amused looks with him, sharing looks of fellowship with Jane, and making some soothing comments in an attempt to calm her mother. During her mother's most recent outburst, Elizabeth had steadfastly continued with her sewing without even once looking up. There had been absolutely no response from her about the outrageous betrothal.

Mr. Bennet saw Jane flash him a look of distress followed by a glance at Elizabeth. He nodded that he, too, had noticed her unusual behaviour.

What had happened to his Lizzy?

He thought he had an idea of the subject, but he was not certain what *exactly* had occurred. If this behaviour continued, he would need to find out. In the meantime, he had every intention of discussing this privately with Jane.

~On the road to London

The carriage ride to London was a silent one. Richard was sleeping, or at least feigning it, leaving Darcy to his own thoughts.

A sense of melancholy overcame Darcy. Life without his Elizabeth would be lonely indeed.

No, she was not *his* Elizabeth. He must stop thinking of her in that manner. That thought caused the loneliness to worsen; the last time he had felt a portion of this feeling was just after his mother's death.

He knew that he had grown up too soon because of these happenings. It was difficult enough for him to be away at school due to his shyness, but to be away from Georgiana and his father after promising that he would look after them had induced a great sense of guilt. He had returned because his father told him to, and he had felt the need not to fail his father's expectations. It had caused a great conflict within him.

After a while, he had become comfortable with a select few of the boys, but his need for approval from his father ruled over his need for camaraderie. While the other boys at Eton and Cambridge had been enjoying themselves, Darcy was studying, trying to make his father as proud of him as he could.

When his father became too ill to continue handling his daily business concerns, Darcy had been obliged to attempt to take over the responsibilities of the huge estate of Pemberley plus other smaller landholdings peppered throughout England, Scotland, Ireland, and India, though his father was available for advice and approval of major decisions. All the other young men of his acquaintance were taking tours of Europe and sowing their wild oats.

When his father died, he had then taken on full responsibility for the properties as well as the obligation of raising Georgiana, who was ten at the time. The only person he had become especially close to during all those years was his cousin Richard, with whom he shared guardianship of Georgiana, but since Richard was often away with his army regiment, most of the responsibility fell on Darcy. He would write to Richard to receive his approval or advice, but most of the time, he had needed answers immediately, and by the time he received Richard's answer, it was too late for advice. While Richard had been on the Continent, sometimes it took months to receive a reply. Richard never held any of it against him, even if he thoroughly disapproved of a certain action Darcy had decided to take. Richard understood the pressure Darcy was under better than anyone else.

Darcy had met Bingley at Cambridge, and they had become good friends soon after. It was surprising to most people, since their personalities seemed to be opposite, but when one looked at how close Darcy and Richard were, it was understandable. Richard was similar to Bingley in personality in many respects.

There were others with whom he had developed trust, but never true friendship. Georgiana was growing up fast, but still–he was more of a father to her than a brother, and definitely not her friend. It was easier when she was younger, as he often did not understand the changes that were taking place now that she was growing into a woman.

There had been a few ladies to whom he had been physically attracted—to whom others assumed had become more than mere acquaintances of his—but there was always some elusive quality missing. He never let them get too close to him. They were attracted to his position in life, not Darcy the man, and neither did he know the ladies nor could he truly see himself as being happy if they had married. He made an effort to convince himself that this was all he would ever be able to expect, but he could not bring himself to accept this as fact or to settle on any particular woman of his acquaintance as a potential wife.

He wanted the relationship his parents had enjoyed. He knew that while his mother was alive, they had been equals, and they had loved each other deeply.

Darcy always felt marriage in the *ton* was similar to animal breeding, but not as formally defined. Animals were bred to combine certain characteristics that were strong and positive in the line, such as gentleness of personality, strength in animals used for labour, speed in those groomed for occupations requiring it, or physical traits such as softer wool in sheep.

The upper classes of British society bred for a pedigree of names, titles, and wealth, not taking into account any specific personality traits in the lines. From what he had observed, the unfortunate result had been the creation of a mercenary class of people who thought nothing of those not in their own circle, and if one looked honestly, one would see that they cared but little for those *within* their own circle. As long as one could make an advantageous marriage for rank or wealth, one was accepted. Love and happiness were "just not done."

They talked of how important marriage was to them, but their wedding vows meant *nothing* to them. The whole of the *ton*, all those marriages of convenience, completely disregarded the reasons why marriages were supposed to take place!

He knew he would one day have to promise to love, comfort, and honour a woman so long as they both should live. How was he supposed to repeat these words to someone he married only for her name and wealth? How did people live in marriages of convenience knowing they lied, not only to themselves and their spouse, but to *God*? How did people live that kind of lie, day after day, with every breath they would take?

Was there not more to life than that?

*Yet, **this** is expected of me,* he thought.

He did not want Georgiana to live like that. He did not want her to marry for convenience or the sake of duty and honour. He wanted his precious sister to be happy in her choice.

To make this possible for Georgiana, *his* only option was never to see Elizabeth again.

His body and soul filled with a horrid painful ache. He was glad that Richard was asleep.

~Netherfield Park

Caroline met Charles and Louisa in the breakfast room.

"Charles, we must speak to you about something. After last night, you must understand that you cannot have serious designs on Jane Bennet! Jane is a sweet girl… but her family!"

Bingley barely looked up from his meal. "Of what are you speaking, Caroline? Her younger sisters are a bit lively, but I will be marrying Jane, not her sisters."

"Marriage? Are you considering marriage with Jane Bennet? Really, Charles, after last night one would think you could see the reason why that is impossible yourself. Did you not see her family's behaviour? Her youngest two sisters are wild and wanton. Her mother has no sense of decorum or propriety. Eliza spent the evening using her wiles trying to draw in poor Mr. Darcy. Mary Bennet exposed herself and all her family to ridicule with her display of her inferior talents on the pianoforte. Mr. Bennet was rude to his own daughter in front of the entire neighbourhood. This is the family you wish to ally yourself with? A lady whose highest connexions are having one uncle who is a country attorney and the other in *trade*? And Jane has a dowry of a mere one thousand pounds! The idea is absurd, Charles."

"Caroline, I am not sure that Charles has the same interest in this affair as do you. He is not concerned about connexions and fortune; he wishes only to be happy. It is plain to see he is in love with her." Louisa braced herself for the worst. "I wish my brother to be happy as well, Caroline."

Louisa's marriage was one of convenience and she was not happily married in any way. At night, she would sneak away from her husband's bed immediately after he fell asleep and would sit imagining what her life *could* have been like had she married for love… had she not listened to Caroline's persuasions to marry Mr. Hurst, and instead, waited for the man she did care for to offer for her. Mr. Campbell was not good enough for her sister because he was in trade, but Louisa had loved him with all her heart, and she thought he had loved her as well. She did not wish the same unhappy fate for her beloved brother.

If looks could kill, the glare Caroline directed at Louisa certainly would have.

Bingley had been too distracted by Jane to have noticed her family's behaviour, but it mattered not to him. He stood up and said with conviction, "Caroline! *We* are the first generation of Bingleys not in trade! I realize that you do not wish to remember this fact due to our father's desire for me to become a gentleman and for my sisters to marry gentlemen, but you *should* remember it in situations such as this. You cannot tell me I will not connect myself to tradesmen when our father, his father, and his grandfather were tradesmen! If you must look at it in this way, Jane is a gentleman's daughter, and I would be taking a step up socially by marrying her! Jane is perfectly acceptable in every way, *and* I love her! I have the greatest respect for Miss Elizabeth and Mr. Bennet as well. Mrs. Bennet and the youngest two are lively, yes. Mary Bennet might be a blue stocking and be a little too eager to please, but there is nothing wrong with that. I see no difficulties in connecting myself with the Bennet family. I *will* marry Jane… if she will have me, of course." Bingley braced himself for her answer, knowing his sister would not give up easily.

Caroline paused a few moments seeking a new direction in which to take the discussion in order to convince him. "Charles, you know that Jane is an obedient daughter and whether she likes you or not, she will listen to her greedy, mercenary mother and accept you."

Bingley's countenance turned to one of distress. "Caroline, are you suggesting that you think Jane does not care for me?"

Ah ha! I should have known! He has so little confidence in himself!

Caroline thought, and then said aloud with concern almost dripping from her voice, "Oh, Charles! I did not want to pain you by mentioning it earlier, but yes… yes, I do. You must agree it should be miserable to find out *after* you are married that she was only following her mother's orders, do you not?"

He sat down heavily, as if his legs would no longer hold his weight, and turned to his other sister. "Louisa, do you feel the same way?"

The downhearted expression on her brother's normally happy face pained Louisa greatly. She thought Jane would be *content* in a marriage with Charles whether she loved him or not—but did Jane love Charles? Would she be *happy*? She could not know.

Though Louisa was the elder sister, Caroline had the stronger character. Louisa had always followed where Caroline led, and rarely had she made her own decisions in the past—she had not developed this skill for Caroline always told her what to think of everybody and everything. Very much like her brother, Louisa disliked any sort of dispute. It had been easier to do what Caroline told her to do in order to avoid conflict, and she had rarely come across a situation important enough to her to be worth the discomfort of an argument with Caroline.

But Charles's happiness *was* important to her! If she had realized that Charles had such serious intentions about Jane Bennet, she might have put some effort into observing Jane's actions instead of believing Caroline's assertions that this was another of their brother's temporary infatuations, as so many had been in the past. Louisa was intelligent enough to suspect the possibility of Caroline's ability to lie when her own selfish plans were at risk. Perhaps it was time to stop following Caroline blindly—in *all* matters.

"Charles, I must say that I am unsure. Jane has a serene countenance; she wears a little smile much of the time and rarely shows any other emotion. It is difficult for me to tell you either way. I do wish you to be happy, brother, so please do not follow what anyone tells you blindly. What do *you* think?" Louisa answered honestly, knowing very well Caroline was going to voice her displeasure vehemently once they were alone.

It was several minutes before Bingley responded. "Well… I thought I was certain that Jane loved me, but Caroline could be correct. Is it possible I saw in Jane's eyes only what I *wished* to see? No matter how I have tried not to, I did hear Mrs. Bennet speak often of my income and that she expects me to offer for Jane. Jane is an obliging person—she wishes for others' happiness before her own. She is so good! Most of all, I do wish her happy, even if the man who could make her happy does not happen to be me." Bingley's throat became too tight to continue.

Caroline took the opportunity to pounce, her reply dripping with a sweetness Louisa could detect was not truly felt. "Yes, I do think dearest Jane deserves to live a happy life, Charles. You would be miserable if she was made unhappy by becoming your wife. I am certain if we return to London, it would be much less painful for you than to stay here where you would see her often. Please, Charles, I am *only* thinking of your happiness… and that of dear Jane, of course."

He sighed deeply. The look of anguish on his face made him appear ten years older. "If you think it would be best, Caroline. Louisa, are you open to returning to London?"

Louisa could only answer, "I am not opposed to it, Charles. I do not think Mr. Hurst would be against it now that he has had his share of shooting. But please be sure this is what *you* wish to do before making the decision to close Netherfield, Brother."

Bingley was thoughtful for many minutes as his sisters waited, one very impatiently. There were many sighs heard as a multitude of emotions crossed his face. His final thoughts before he answered were that he did not wish to have his Jane forced to marry him for mercenary reasons when she was so wonderful that she could surely find someone who *she* loved to marry instead. Even though he would never be happy without Jane, he could not allow his selfishness to destroy her happiness. At length he said, "It is settled, then. We will close up Netherfield and return to London. When do you think it would be possible to leave?"

Caroline's eyes were alive with victory. "Oh, I do believe we could be packed by tomorrow, and we could depart the morning after. Anything left behind can be sent to London by the housekeeper. Will you send an express to London, Louisa, and ready your house in Grosvenor Street? Can it be ready for us the day after tomorrow?"

"Yes. I will speak to Mr. Hurst about it directly." Louisa rose and left the room.

Bingley leaned his head on the back of the chair and closed his eyes. "Caroline, what should I do about taking leave of the neighbourhood? I do not think I could face Jane… Miss Bennet… just now. Or anyone else for that matter."

"Oh, I will write notes to all the main families of the area, Charles, explaining that sudden business has taken you to London, and since we will be spending Christmas in Scarborough, we have decided to stay in London for the season."

With his eyes still closed, Bingley said, "Whatever you think is best, Caroline."

Caroline smiled her evil smile. *Oh, this* ***is*** *best, Brother! You will not ruin my chances with Mr. Darcy by marrying Jane Bennet! You will forget her as soon as the next pretty face happens by—I do hope it is Miss Darcy this time. I will be in London and make myself quite accessible to Mr. Darcy until we must leave for Scarborough. Yes... this is definitely best.*

~Longbourn Estate

Later that day, Mr. Bennet discreetly called Jane into his study, not wishing for Elizabeth or the others to know. Jane knew why she had been summoned and sat in one of the chairs in front of his desk, waiting patiently for her father to begin.

"Jane, I know you were distracted and not paying close attention to all that occurred around you last evening." When Jane's expression changed to one of self-recrimination, he quickly added with a small smile, "Oh, I am not scolding you, my dear. But I had little else to do but watch the multitude of events unfold upon and around the dance floor. There are a few things you should know if we are to help your sister.

"I have noticed a pattern in Mr. Darcy's behaviour since he has come to Hertfordshire. He usually begins the evening avoiding being close to our Lizzy, but then, he has not been able to stay away from her and joins her before long.

"Last night, he stayed away longer than usual all the while watching her intently, but then followed the same pattern he always has. The only lady he danced with was Lizzy, and he did so twice. He also sat with her at supper. They seemed to enjoy their time together, but at the end of supper, she seemed upset. As we left Netherfield, they *both* were quite disturbed. I know not what caused this distress, but I do intend to find out now that Lizzy is acting as she is.

"I know you are as worried for her as I am, Jane. You can see the change in her, though your mother and sisters do not seem to have noticed, which to me is surprising since it is such a drastic change. She is unhappy and has withdrawn from us."

Mr. Bennet sighed and leaned forward onto his desk before continuing, "If Lizzy will confide in anyone, it will be you, Jane. I would like you to attempt carefully to discover just what is causing this melancholy Lizzy has fallen under."

He looked a bit uncomfortable. "I will try to say this as delicately as possible, but I must say that her behaviour this day alarms me, my dear. Though from all we have heard of him, it does not seem likely, I fear that Mr. Darcy may not have acted as a gentleman towards her, and this is something I would need to know. When she confides in you, if it is something I do need to know, no matter what you had to promise her in order to find out, you *must* tell me, Jane. Do you understand what I am saying? This is important."

Jane was shocked to think that Mr. Darcy might have behaved in a less than gentleman-like manner toward her sister, but she did understand why her father would need to know if it had happened. "Father, I do not believe Mr. Darcy capable of it, but if Lizzy even hints that something of this nature has happened, I will inform you. Sir, if Lizzy will not confide in me, what shall we then do?"

Mr. Bennet was thoughtful for a few minutes, and then answered, "If this behaviour persists and she will not confide in you, I will call her in here for an interview. I will order her to tell me what is wrong if I must. If she continues to refuse, I will go to London and speak directly with Mr. Darcy."

Jane gasped and covered her mouth with her hand. "You would do that, Father?"

"Yes, I would, Jane. Lizzy is too important to act carelessly. If she has been compromised…" He could not continue.

"Sir, I do not believe that that is the case, but I do understand."

Mr. Bennet came around the desk and stood in front of his daughter. "You are too good, Jane. Mr. Darcy is a gentleman, but he is also a man, a man very attracted to Lizzy. I cannot be too careful with my precious daughters." He leaned over and kissed her on the forehead. "Now run along. I have some work to finish, and I will see you at dinner. If there is any change in Lizzy's behaviour, please inform me."

Jane gave him a little smile. "I will, Father. I do think this is temporary; perhaps there was a misunderstanding and they quarreled? She will be feeling better soon, I am sure of it."

~Darcy House, London

When Richard and Darcy arrived at Darcy House in London, Richard quickly took Georgiana aside to speak to her while Darcy went to freshen up after greeting his sister. They had corresponded frequently while he had been at Netherfield, and he knew that Georgiana was excited about what she had heard concerning Miss Elizabeth Bennet.

Richard had spent the last part of the trip to London trying to think of what to say to Georgiana to prevent her speaking of Miss Elizabeth to her brother.

"Georgie, I would ask you not to mention Miss Elizabeth Bennet to your brother until I give you leave to," he began. "He is quite cross about having to leave her behind, and I do not think speaking of her will be helpful at all."

"Oh, Richard! I wanted to hear what William thinks of her! It might be helpful to relieve his mind if he were to speak of her," Georgiana said with a pout.

What should I reveal to her? Richard thought, and then aloud he said, "Georgie, trust me on this matter. Please? Promise me you will try your best not to speak of her unless your brother brings up the subject? If he does, I suggest you allow him to do the talking."

"Well, I will promise only if *you* will tell me more about her privately!"

"Yes… yes I will. But not today; traveling after a ball the previous evening is very tiring." Glad to make his escape before he said too much, Richard made his way toward his own room—attempting *not* to think about Charlotte Lucas.

Absence from whom we love is worse than death, and frustrates hope severer than despair.
--William Cowper (English poet 1731-1800)

Thursday, November 28, 1811

Keeping in mind the reason he had given Elizabeth for his return to London, Darcy wished to take care of the India business directly. Upon arriving at Darcy House, he had immediately written to his uncle to request an audience with him the following day about an important matter of business.

The next morning, he and Richard met with Richard's father. The earl confirmed that he did not purchase the land in India when Sir Lewis spoke to him nor had he done so at any other time, and he wished to know why his nephew was bringing up the subject once again. Darcy and Richard reiterated the entire story to Lord Matlock.

Lord Matlock was quite upset. Over brandy, the three attempted to sort out what could have happened, but they came to no conclusions. A plan was made for the three gentlemen to meet with Darcy's contacts regarding the matter in three days' time.

~Longbourn Estate

That afternoon, a letter was delivered from Netherfield for Jane. Expecting good news, such as an invitation to tea with Miss Bingley, Jane looked over the letter. She allowed a pained expression to pass across her face briefly before concealing it with some effort. Her mother prodded for information, insisting that Jane read it aloud, but Jane could manage only, "The letter is from Caroline Bingley. The whole party will leave Netherfield in the morning on their way to Town without any intention of coming back again."

Mrs. Bennet's nerves were affected greatly by the news. She was ill used by everyone. Jane should have done more—she wore her necklines too high and did not flutter her eyelashes as she had been told to do. If only Jane had listened to her! It was now absolutely certain they would be starving in the hedgerows before long! Her tirade went on for the rest of the day and throughout the evening. Elizabeth kept on with whatever employment she was engaged in and ignored her mother.

Even Jane's seemingly unending patience wore thin. Her mother's constant ranting, added to her own feelings about Mr. Bingley's leaving, was enough to fluster anyone, but her sister's lack of response to it all increased Jane's worry about Elizabeth's unnatural behaviour. Jane had to leave the room several times to regain control over her countenance.

Seeing this, Mrs. Hill pulled her into the kitchen where only the loudest of Mrs. Bennet's ravings could be heard. They shared a special cup of tea along with Jane's favourite biscuits and sat in complete silence.

Later that evening, when they retired to their own room, Jane went into more detail about the letter. "I do believe Caroline Bingley means to warn me, Lizzy. She says that she and her sister entertain the idea of her brother's being attached to Miss Darcy."

Elizabeth said, "Oh this is too much—not you, too, Jane." She hugged Jane. "You are much too good for anyone to treat in this manner." Elizabeth pulled away and looked into Jane's eyes while still holding her shoulders. "I have been thinking all day. Please understand, Jane, I do *not* accuse Mr. Bingley of being unkind, but I *can* believe it of his sisters, especially Miss Bingley. It is my opinion that they have convinced him to follow Mr. Darcy to London with the intent of Miss Bingley's continuing to pursue her beloved Pemberley and first-circle stature. She writes about Miss Darcy to dash your hopes, not as a warning, dear. She may act your friend in your immediate presence, but Jane, please believe me that Miss Bingley is *no* friend of yours. You must not believe what she says in this letter."

"Lizzy, I do not believe that Miss Bingley could be so unkind. She might be mistaken, seeing her wishes as if they were fact, but I do not think she would be purposely cruel." Jane hesitated, seeming to shy off the subject, and then looked as if she forced herself to continue, "What did you mean by saying 'Not you, too' Lizzy?" At Elizabeth's surprised look she said, "Please tell me, dearest? Please unburden yourself. I am concerned about you. Will you not ease my mind?"

Elizabeth was quiet and composed, not meeting Jane's eye. Jane was a patient person and would wait as long as it took for Elizabeth to make up her mind about what to say. After quite a while, Elizabeth answered, "Jane, Mr. Darcy made it clear that I will not be seeing him again."

"Dear, did something happen…" Jane coloured. "Is there any reason… did he make promises that he did not keep… or *do* something that was not entirely proper?"

"No, Jane, it is nothing like that," Elizabeth hesitated again, a bit shocked that Jane, of all people, would suggest such a thing. "I just… though I *knew* nothing could ever come of it, I foolishly allowed myself to come to care for Mr. Darcy a great deal. I do not think I can manage the feelings associated with knowing I will never see him again. At the moment I feel… numb. I will be well again, Jane, I promise. It just might take a little time…"

Jane was relieved at first that something terrible had not happened, but became more concerned as Elizabeth continued to speak. "Dearest Lizzy, I am sorry." She was thoughtful for a few minutes before continuing, "Maybe Mr. Bingley's coming to Netherfield was *not* such good luck after all."

Friday, November 29, 1811

Jane opened the door to her father's study following his bid to enter. When he saw Jane, Mr. Bennet's anxieties about Elizabeth increased to an almost palpable degree. It seemed that Jane had an answer. He motioned toward the chair.

Jane sat and worked up her courage to say what she must. "Father, you asked me to inform you when I had information about Lizzy. I do not wish to break her confidence, but I must tell you it is *not* what you thought. She has not been compromised in any way, sir."

Relief was evident upon his face and Jane smiled.

"Did she tell you more, Jane? I would like to know what is amiss."

"Yes, sir, she did, but again I do not wish to betray her confidence. Lizzy feels she needs some time to get past this, and I suggest we give her that time."

Mr. Bennet was silent for several minutes and then said, "We will give her some time, if you both feel it is necessary. But I cannot guarantee how long I can wait if this behaviour continues, Jane. Lizzy has me very worried, but I will make an attempt to be patient."

~Darcy House, London

Almost the moment Bingley arrived in London, he sent a servant with a note to Darcy stating that he had decided to return to Town well before visiting his family in Scarborough for the holiday, detailing the reasons behind this decision. Bingley asked Darcy to send word to the Hursts' house letting Bingley know when he was available, for he desperately needed to confer with him on an important matter. He was hopeful that Darcy's habit of close observation had provided him with an opinion on Jane's feelings that would negate his sisters' arguments.

Darcy had left directions with his housekeeper that any letters from Bingley were to be separated from the rest of his personal correspondence and placed in a drawer he rarely looked into. This had been deemed necessary after his first agonizing, sleepless night in London. As the sun rose above the horizon, he had finally given up his attempt at repose and began to think of what he could do to rid his mind of these constant musings centering on Elizabeth. He was fully expecting news that Bingley had become engaged to marry Jane Bennet, and he knew it would cause him significant pain to read of Bingley's happiness. He admitted to himself that it was excessively selfish of him, but he had every intention of ignoring all of Bingley's correspondence until he felt the distance and time away from Elizabeth had eased his pain enough to read this news without feeling further discomfort.

Therefore, Darcy did not see that Bingley's missive was from London, not Netherfield, and he never responded to Bingley's urgent plea to speak with him. There is no telling whether he would have read the letter had he known from where it was sent.

Monday, December 2, 1811

Lord Matlock, Darcy, and Richard all met at Darcy House on the appointed morning. Mr. Thompson, the solicitor and cousin of the investigator in India, and Mr. White, Darcy's investigator in England, arrived within a few minutes of each other and were shown into Darcy's study where the others were already assembled.

Both men had been in communication with each other since Darcy had received the last news from Mr. Clark in India. They had exerted themselves to find information about the Bradstowe Company in England, but were completely unsuccessful. White had two men working exclusively on the matter. No trace of the company, not even gossip, was found. They would continue their efforts, but it did not seem as if they would find any information on this side of the world. Neither Darcy nor Thompson had heard from Clark again as of yet.

The entire business was strange. How could there be an English-owned company having no records of doing business in England, nor of any of its ships docking at ports in England? There were also no warehouses under that name.

What was going on in India?

The five gentlemen drafted a letter to Clark, including authorization to look into any information he could find about the land held in Lord Matlock's name in addition to continuing his investigation into what was happening on Darcy's land.

The gentlemen discussed Clark's last letter and wondered what had been happening in India over the past months since it had been written. Darcy was disturbed by the conversation, and he prayed that Clark and the mine workers were safe.

A look of misery briefly crossed his face as Darcy's thoughts turned to Elizabeth and her words at Oakham Mount… and all else that had passed between them that day came flooding into his mind. Before he could fully lose control of his emotions and concentration, he raised *The Mask* in place once again.

Richard was the only one to see it, and he quietly asked Darcy if he was well. Darcy did not answer; he instead walked to the window to hide the expression of agony that he could no longer repress.

~Longbourn Estate

In some ways December passed as it usually did at Longbourn, with the ladies arranging Christmas decorations and planning for Christmas festivities, including Boxing Day preparations. With the Bingleys gone from the neighbourhood, Jane and Elizabeth decided to continue their usual holiday customs with the tenants of Netherfield as well as Longbourn and hoped the servants would be remembered by their master.

In other ways, the month passed much differently than in years gone by. Though Jane tried her best to behave normally, whenever she thought nobody was looking, occasionally a wave of dejection would overtake her countenance. Usually Elizabeth's attempts at comforting Jane would have been more effective, but Elizabeth was still far from being herself, and anything she said or did was not of much assistance—the difference in her behaviour only seemed to cause Jane to become more concerned for her sister's wellbeing.

Elizabeth wondered if she had made a mistake in confiding in Jane about Darcy, since that was more than likely adding to Jane's distress. Elizabeth spent much of the month reviewing her interactions with the gentleman in an attempt to break through the wall preventing her from feeling her emotions, but with no success.

Mr. Collins returned to his parish to prepare his home for the arrival of the soon-to-be Mrs. Collins. His leaving was a relief to the daughters of Mr. Bennet, *and* his staff.

Hints made by Mr. Collins that he should be invited to stay at Longbourn when he returned to the neighbourhood were ignored. Usually not one to hold grudges, Mr. Bennet continued to feel uneasy that his daughters and servants did not feel safe enough to unlock their doors while Mr. Collins was under the same roof.

Therefore, when Mr. Collins did return a fortnight later, he stayed at Lucas Lodge, not Longbourn. He accompanied the Lucas ladies every day to Longbourn, for it seemed that Lady Lucas could not make plans for her daughter's wedding without reviewing every detail with Mrs. Bennet first.

That Charlotte Lucas was to be married before any of her own daughters agitated Mrs. Bennet beyond all her prior states of nerves, and whenever Lady Lucas left Longbourn it was declared she was gloating without reserve—among many other things. Jane maintained that perhaps Lady Lucas recognized Mrs. Bennet's talents in planning important events and sought out her approval of the arrangements, which soothed her mother's upset ever so slightly.

As Christmas drew near, the news of the wedding plans slowed considerably, much to Mrs. Bennet's relief—and to all those who had to bear the consequences of her nerves.

A happier day dawned when Mrs. Bennet's brother, Mr. Gardiner, his wife, and their young family arrived at Longbourn two days before Christmas.

Mrs. Gardiner immediately detected a difference in both Jane and Elizabeth. She had been forewarned of the possibility of encountering a certain *something* in Elizabeth's behaviour upon her arrival by her friend, Adelaide, in London. The lady, who was a correspondent of Elizabeth's, had inquired of Mrs. Gardiner if there was a problem since Elizabeth's letters had stopped abruptly months ago.

The changes in Elizabeth were so dramatic that it worried Mrs. Gardiner a great deal. She spoke to her husband about it and found that he had noticed the same. They would normally speak to Jane about any concerns they had about Elizabeth, but Jane's disappointment with the loss of Mr. Bingley was all too often detailed for them by Mrs. Bennet, and even with every attempt to change the subject, Mrs. Bennet would not desist. They did not wish to distress Jane further.

Mr. Gardiner did mention the subject to Mr. Bennet, but it seemed Mr. Bennet knew little, or at least did not wish to disclose more. As Elizabeth seemed unwilling to speak to her aunt of her unhappiness, and no further information was forthcoming from the other family members, Mr. and Mrs. Gardiner were left to debate between themselves what could change such a naturally vivacious young lady as Elizabeth into this pale shell of her usual self. Additionally, Mrs. Gardiner had nothing to report in her letter to their mutual friend other than, "Lizzy does not seem well and is quite out of spirits at the present time."

Upon finding Elizabeth and Jane alone, Mrs. Gardiner suggested that they both return to London with them. Elizabeth quietly refused without detailing her reasons, but Jane accepted. Plans were made, and Jane accompanied the Gardiner family to London a few days after Christmas.

Where grief is fresh, any attempt to divert it only irritates.
--Samuel Johnson (English author, 1709-1784)

~Darcy House, London

When Darcy returned to London after the Netherfield ball, he had tried to convince himself that he was *not* in love with Elizabeth. It was an obsession, and obsessions could be overcome. He told himself that putting time and distance between them would end it—but was not surprised to find that it had not.

Darcy realized what he was doing, but he was determined. During the months of December and January and part-way into February, he went out into society almost constantly to keep busy and to search for a lady among the *ton* with the qualities he found so attractive in *her*, someone who also had the fortune and connexions he was expected to find in a bride.

What a useless endeavor this was! The *ton* was full of matchmaking mamas and social climbing ladies. The women of the *ton* were all variously annoying versions of Caroline Bingley, and he loathed their behaviour toward himself more than he had ever before. He felt as though he were a prime piece of horseflesh at market.

While his duties called Richard away at times, he attended a few of these same events and saw what Darcy was up to. He would hear his mother, Lady Matlock, speak to Darcy about the ladies he had spent time with that evening and would hear Darcy rattle off a list of attributes which they lacked. When he had heard a few of these conversations, he realized everything Darcy was naming was present in Elizabeth. Richard was not sure whether he should have a discussion with him about it or not. He decided to leave it alone for the time being in the hopes Darcy would move beyond this, but he was not confident that he would. Richard was going to have to leave London for a while, and so he put off the conversation till he returned, hoping time would affect Darcy in a positive way while he was gone from Town.

Darcy tried to keep himself busy during the day as well so he would not think of *her*… spending time at his club, fencing, boxing, and riding—to the point of exhaustion every day. Chess was attempted but abandoned since he found himself thinking all through the game of his never-played match with Elizabeth. He also found playing billiards was no longer enjoyable since he could think only of the fantasy of teaching her the game.

No matter where he went, she crept into his thoughts, and he found himself comparing all women to Elizabeth. All of his efforts had been futile. Instead of forgetting her, his attachment to Elizabeth grew stronger, and his misery was growing with each passing day.

The little reed, bending to the force of the wind, soon stood upright again when the storm had passed over.
--Aesop (Greek author, 620 BC – 560 BC)

Thursday, January 9, 1812 – The Collins' Wedding Day

~Longbourn Estate

Mr. Bennet had been sure that Charlotte's wedding would be just the thing to induce some sort of reaction from Elizabeth, but now he was more concerned than ever. He had watched his second eldest carefully at the ceremony and wedding breakfast. She had remained composed with a slight smile throughout, without one look of concern or disgust at what her good friend Charlotte Lucas was doing to her life by marrying Mr. Collins.

Mr. Bennet realized he had allowed this to go on too long. He was afraid if he did not do something soon, his Lizzy might never be herself again.

When the family returned from the wedding breakfast at Lucas Lodge and the ladies had changed into their everyday dresses, Mrs. Bennet decided that they should all go to her sister's house in Meryton to discuss the wedding. Mr. Bennet thought this the perfect time to speak to Elizabeth and asked if she would stay behind and join him in the study in a few minutes.

He was pacing the room when she entered. He sat in a chair in front of his desk and motioned to its match across from him. As she sat, he cleared his throat and began, "Lizzy, I must speak with you. I have left you to yourself during these six weeks, but I can do so no longer. The morning after Mr. Bingley's ball, you woke up a different person, my dear. You are slowly wasting away right before my eyes, and I cannot bear to see it."

"Papa, I know not of what you are speaking. I am as I always have been."

He sat up straighter, his voice booming, "Elizabeth Bennet! You are *not* as you always have been!"

Mr. Bennet began to panic when he saw that Elizabeth had not even flinched at his outburst. He leaned back into the chair once more, closed his eyes and took a few deep breaths to calm himself before continuing in a lower tone, "I apologize for raising my voice, Lizzy." He cleared his throat and began again, "I am not the only person who has noticed this, my dear. Your sister, Jane, is very worried about you as are your Aunt and Uncle Gardiner. Mrs. Hill has asked me several times if there was anything she or the other servants could do to help you. Both Jane and Mrs. Gardiner have spoken to you, and though they did not betray any confidences, they told me you did not wish to speak with them much, if at all, of your troubles. Now you will speak of it, whether you wish it or not. I will not allow this to continue any longer, Elizabeth!"

Elizabeth was looking at him with a blank expression.

Am I too late? thought Mr. Bennet. "Lizzy… if you will not tell me what happened, I will go to London and speak directly to Mr. Darcy himself."

At these words, the wall around her emotions crumbled. Elizabeth gasped and jumped up out of the chair. She blushed furiously and her eyes filled with tears. "NO! You must not, Papa!"

At that moment, the aching emptiness she had felt in the carriage after the Netherfield ball suddenly exploded within her, but to a much more intolerable degree. Somehow, she knew she was not dying, but in the midst of this pain, she wanted to. Elizabeth's breathing had increased at an alarming rate, and her heart was beating so forcefully that it felt as if it would explode. She suddenly turned cold—so very cold! She could not continue standing; as she folded in upon herself her father caught her in his arms and gently lowered them both onto a nearby sofa.

Mr. Bennet was terrified; he had never seen anything resembling this behaviour in Elizabeth and knew not what to do. He pulled his Lizzy onto his lap and rocked her for a very long time, while silent tears escaped his eyes.

Eventually, her sobs slowed to sniffles, and Mr. Bennet slowed his movements. He reached for his handkerchief and handed it to her without breaking his embrace.

Elizabeth said, "I am sorry for that, Papa. Thank you. I feel much better now, but I do think I have ruined your coat!" She laughed a little.

Mr. Bennet sighed shakily and thought, *My Lizzy has returned.* He had to clear his throat before saying aloud, “If it was necessary to reclaim you from the state you have been in for the past few weeks, I would be glad to have you ruin *all* my coats, my Lizzy!”

Elizabeth laid her head on her father’s shoulder as she said, “He… Mr. Darcy has left, Papa. He said he would not be coming back. I shall never see him again.”

They were both silent for a while until Elizabeth broke the silence. “In the carriage on the way home from the ball, I did not want to cry in front of everyone. Once I had gained control of my sorrow, I did not know how to let it loose again. I have felt nothing since then… until now. I must say that I do not know which I prefer, Papa.”

“It is best to feel, Lizzy. Grieve if you must, but please do not do that to us again. We thought we were losing you, my dear.”

“Papa, I do not want you to think badly of Mr. Darcy. It was not his fault that I could not stop myself from loving him. He did not mean for me to love him—I could see it in his eyes.”

Mr. Bennet sighed. He moved her off his lap, took her face in his hands and kissed her forehead. “Thank you for speaking to me, dearest Lizzy. I think you could probably do with a rest now. We will talk again soon. Shall I ask Mrs. Hill to send you a tray for dinner tonight?”

Elizabeth stood. “Yes, please, Papa. Say that I have a headache—it is not an untruth after all that crying. And I think that I need a full night’s sleep before hearing every detail of the wedding again from Mama.” She said this with a slightly teasing tone as she made her way toward the door, then stopped and turned toward him.

“Papa, Charlotte has asked me to visit her at Hunsford Cottage in March.”

Surprised, his eyebrows almost reached his hairline. “Are you actually considering it, Lizzy? I did not think you were at all comfortable with Mr. Collins under the same roof.”

“I am considering it, sir. I believe his behaviour will be less distasteful now that he is married.”

“I will say only that I will think upon it, my dear.”

When a man has lost all happiness, he's not alive. Call him a breathing corpse.
--Sophocles (Greek Dramatist 495 BC – 406 BC)

~Darcy House, London

Darcy had expected after his removal to London and the initial shock of her absence had passed, that Elizabeth's image would fade from his mind, and life would continue the way it was before he had met her. It was well into February before he gave up the lie he had told himself; he now knew that he could not forget her. She was embedded within his soul.

What a dark, dark time it was!

Darcy withdrew almost completely from society, locking himself in his study or his chambers, and surrendered to drink, his only source of "nourishment" being images of *her*. On the rare occasion when he was found in the hallways in between his two solitary retreats, Georgiana and Mrs. Martin, the housekeeper, would converge upon him, attempting to convince him to eat. He ate a little just to get them to leave him to himself, grumbling at them throughout. He went weeks without being home to callers, with little concern for personal hygiene, snapping at the servants, even becoming rude to his beloved sister.

He could not see how close he was coming to commitment to Bedlam! What great fun *that* would be for the London gossips.

The true measure of a man is how he treats someone who can do him absolutely no good.
--Samuel Johnson (English Author, 1709-1784)

~Longbourn Estate

The weather during this part of the winter usually meant there would be fewer walks for Elizabeth, but this winter there was also no Jane or Charlotte with whom to visit. She spent some time with her father playing chess and discussing whatever book she was reading at the time. She also employed her time writing to Jane, Charlotte, and Aunt Gardiner, though reading their letters was of more interest since there was a distinct lack of activity in Longbourn's neighbouring areas.

If one took Charlotte's letters at face value, she did *sound* very content in her new life, though there were hints here and there which gave Elizabeth the impression there was more to Charlotte's situation than what she admitted to with words. The general mood of the letters was not in her usual style, and her choice of words seemed very well thought out. Elizabeth wondered if her friend was attempting to hide her true feelings without telling a falsehood. She described the house and grounds with alacrity, and these passages were in her usual tone. It was clear Charlotte took her dual duties as mistress of her own home and wife of a parson very seriously. Lady Catherine was described as "a most attentive neighbour" and Charlotte wrote of the lady's "suggestions" to improve the house as well as Charlotte's style of housekeeping. Elizabeth inferred from these declarations that rather than advising, Lady Catherine was demanding and interfering. Most concerning to Elizabeth was that Charlotte wrote of her loneliness and repeatedly mentioned how much she missed all her friends from Hertfordshire. She knew that Charlotte would not mention these feelings unless they were becoming overwhelming. She decided that she would like to visit Charlotte after all.

From Jane's letters, Elizabeth surmised that Aunt and Uncle Gardiner were attempting to keep Jane occupied in order to raise her spirits, but Jane's melancholy tone changed little. Jane wrote part of a letter daily, entertaining Elizabeth with descriptions of the visits, teas, offerings, and assemblies that she attended as well as the antics of the Gardiner children, while avoiding Elizabeth's queries about how she herself was faring. It distressed Elizabeth that none of the outings served to improve Jane's spirits.

There was one letter that Elizabeth had postponed writing but thought about often, and that was to her chess partner. She had been delaying her reply for months. The lady in question knew Darcy and had been wishing for them to meet for years. When she had first met Darcy, Elizabeth was biding her time until she knew what sort of relationship would develop between them before informing her friend that she had made his acquaintance, but after the ball, Elizabeth simply did not know what to say to her. She did not know whether Darcy had mentioned her to the lady and dreaded having to answer any questions about what she thought of him, or worse—her feelings for him.

There were few parties or dinners at this time of year in Hertfordshire, and only occasional trips to Meryton for shopping due to the unpredictability of the weather. Since Jane was in London, Mary accompanied Elizabeth on her visits to the sick and poor of the area. Over time, Mary became quite animated and sociable during these visits. Elizabeth was happy to see that Mary had finally discovered something of interest outside the bindings of Fordyce's sermons.

Mr. Bennet continued to be unsure about Elizabeth's going to Hunsford Cottage to visit Charlotte Collins. Every time she received a letter from Charlotte, Elizabeth read it to him, and they discussed her increasing worries. Elizabeth made it abundantly clear to her father that she missed Charlotte as much as Charlotte missed her. After much consideration, Mr. Bennet reluctantly agreed to allow her to go, but only under one condition—that he send her with enough money to buy a ticket on the post. She could then leave at any time for her Aunt and Uncle Gardiner's house in London if she felt uncomfortable or unsafe. Elizabeth agreed to the condition without hesitation and with a brilliant smile. It would be nice to see Charlotte again!

Mr. Bennet was so relieved to see the appearance of the most genuine expression of cheer spread across her face that he felt his decision to allow Lizzy to go to her friend was the prudent thing to do for her sake as well as for that of Mrs. Collins. He thought that perhaps *this* was what Lizzy needed to begin to heal.

A few days later, Mr. Bennet called Elizabeth to his study once more. Though Elizabeth's behaviour had returned to some of her previous spirit, she continued to be noticeably depressed, and he thought it was time for some serious questions to be answered.

"This discussion is long overdue, my dear." He hesitated a moment. "I have noticed that you have never treated the shopkeepers, servants, tenants, and labourers as if they were low the way some others do. Why do you not, Lizzy?"

Surprised and more than a little confused about the subject of his choosing, Elizabeth thought for a few moments before beginning. "I believe that people are… people, Papa. They should not be judged by their station in life or how much money they have; they should be judged by their character. The fact that a person is a servant or labourer does not make him unworthy of notice or attention as long as he is good at heart. Being born among the gentry does not make a lady or gentleman a good person. How they *behave* towards others matters more than who they are, in my opinion, sir.

"To illustrate my meaning… you may remember hearing this story, Papa, but I do not think you know all the details associated with it. A few years ago while visiting in London, I was shopping with my Aunt Gardiner. We happened across a man who was dressed only in a shirt and breeches which were very dirty and torn, and he was begging for help. Quite a few ladies and gentlemen walked past him with their noses turned high in the air, pretending not to see him. A few people did stop to see if they could assist the man, as well as the proprietor of the shop that he was in front of. Aunt Gardiner and I approached and offered our assistance as well. The man insisted that someone take him home, and since we were the only two with access to a carriage, Mrs. Gardiner sent for it, and we accompanied him home. As we were waiting for the carriage, the man was quite upset and insistent on taking down all the names of the people who had stopped to help him. To soothe his agitated state, we did as he asked.

"When we arrived at his home, we found he was actually a duke who had been robbed and abused; his coat and shoes had been taken along with his other valuables. With most of his clothing gone and with what remained dirty and torn, there was no way of knowing his rank in society. He had mud smeared on his face and was not recognizable by anyone passing by who might have known him previously.

"The following day, we received a summons from His Grace, who was healing nicely. His mood was pensive, and he spoke of being discouraged with society. It concerned him that none of the *gentlemen* he had asked for help had stopped. After reflecting upon it all night, he told us that he had realized that if these same gentlemen had been able to see the fine quality of the cloth of his coat, they would have come to his aid immediately. It shamed His Grace to admit that one day earlier he might have acted in a similar manner.

Only those who were tradesmen, labourers and servants had paused, even risking their own livelihoods by returning to their duties later than required by their masters, in order to assist their fellow man—to do what was right without accounting for his station in life first. He was convinced that the gentry would have left him there to bleed to death! Though I do feel he exaggerated the situation a little," Elizabeth smiled and went on, "it certainly changed *his* view of people and society in general, Papa.

"Each of those who had helped His Grace received a monetary reward in thanks, as well as an offer of a well-paid position on his staff. The shopkeeper received His Grace's business from then on, and he was recommended to others among His Grace's acquaintance. His Grace attempted to reward Aunt Gardiner and myself as well, and after he would not be denied, we asked that he send ours to the orphanage that Aunt Gardiner visits and to which I accompany her whenever I am in Town. His Grace decided to take the donation to the orphanage himself as part of his new view on life." Elizabeth's smile appeared, wider than before, as she continued, "I understand he is now a frequent visitor and has a wonderful time with the children.

"His Grace has told me that his father was very strict when he was a child, and that when he walks through the door to the orphanage, it is as if he enters a childhood that he never had the pleasure of enjoying in his own younger years. While the children have always been well taken care of, they now have conveniences that they could not have dreamed of in the past. In return, the children make gifts of paintings, drawings, wooden figures, and embroidery for His Grace.

"They give to each other what they can, sir, but the most important of all is affection—and respect." Elizabeth's countenance turned serious. "This is also my view of how people should be treated, Papa. I refuse to look down on people who are 'below' me, as Miss Bingley, Mrs. Hurst, and many others of the *ton* do, and even at times the country gentry. I will not treat someone 'above' me with *more* respect only because of the family into which they were born, though I will follow the dictates of propriety when it comes to manner of address. *Every* person deserves respect, and they shall have mine unless I find their characters are lacking in some way, and that they should be treated otherwise, no matter what their station in life. However, it does not follow that they deserve my *trust*, a view which has recently been fortified. Whether they deserve my affection—that decision may take a while to puzzle out." She hesitated, and then asked, "Do you believe I am wrong, sir?"

"No, Lizzy, you misunderstand me. In my opinion you are quite correct, and it is admirable that you should see at such a young age what so many do not understand after living a lifetime. It took His Grace two and sixty years to come to the same conclusion."

"Then why do you question me about it, Papa?"

Mr. Bennet leaned forward in his chair and looked at her pointedly. "It has come to mind that you do not believe that *you* deserve the same respect that you give to others, my Lizzy. Why is that?"

Elizabeth's mouth dropped open, and she was speechless for a few moments. When she recovered, she answered, "Of what are you speaking, sir?"

"You believe Mr. Darcy cannot care for you because you are below his station, do you not?"

It took her longer to recover this time. "Sir, I do not believe I am inferior to those of the *ton*, if that is what you are asking me, or even that Mr. Darcy believes so. But I know that Mr. Darcy would not allow himself to *care* for me in that way, let alone offer for me, because of how the *ton* would react to it—if not for his own sake, then for the sake of his sister."

Mr. Bennet gave her a look of reproach and began to speak, but Elizabeth interrupted. "Papa, you know what happened with Mr. Hainsworth and how he was treated afterwards. I was much relieved when more interesting news came about just after our situation, or he surely would have been subjected to such ridicule for a much longer period of time. I am certain that Mr. Darcy knows that this sort of behaviour is exactly what would occur were he ever to offer for me."

Mr. Bennet replied, "I have watched Mr. Darcy very carefully, my dear, and you can rest assured that if *any* man has loved a woman, Mr. Darcy loves you. It is possible he will come to see the error of his ways—mayhap with the help of some of your friends in Town. Until then, I will enjoy your company here at Longbourn. That is, unless you are still determined to leave me to visit Mrs. Collins."

Elizabeth stood and walked around the desk to stand in front of her father, taking his hands in hers. "Papa… I will visit Mrs. Collins as promised and then return to Longbourn. I have spent many hours contemplating this lately, sir. Whether Mr. Darcy cares for me is irrelevant, as I am sure he would not have left Netherfield the way he did if he meant to make me an offer. Do not depend upon being rid of me any time soon."

"If this be the case, then he does not deserve you, my Lizzy." Mr. Bennet stood and kissed his daughter on the forehead.

Her smile faded as she sighed and left the room. Seeing this caused Mr. Bennet's heart to ache for his daughter's lingering despondency. It was obvious to him that whether Darcy deserved her or not, Lizzy still loved him.

~Gracechurch Street, London

March dawned, which meant that the time had come for Elizabeth to visit Charlotte in Kent. She planned to stop in London for two nights along the way. The welcome she received at Gracechurch Street was quite enthusiastic. Elizabeth and Jane were so happy to see each other that they held each other for a full minute before Elizabeth was surrounded by the Gardiner children demanding that it was only fair for Cousin Jane to share Cousin Lizzy's attention. Before her arrival, Jane had shared with her aunt that Mr. Bennet had written to her saying that Elizabeth was much more like herself again, and it was a relief to see it with their own eyes—though both ladies could see she was still not fully recovered.

Elizabeth and Jane spent much time together walking and talking over the next two days. Elizabeth could see that Jane was becoming more adept at hiding her sadness over the loss of Bingley, but it had endured… just as she still grieved Darcy.

The Gardiners offered to take the young ladies to the theatre the second evening Elizabeth was with them, but Elizabeth declined saying she would much rather spend her limited time in London with the family. It was only partly true, though neither of the young ladies would say it aloud, they both knew: Elizabeth did not wish to chance seeing Darcy while in Town.

~%~

Thursday, March 5, 1812

~Hunsford Cottage, near Rosings Park, Kent

As Elizabeth's carriage arrived at Hunsford Cottage, Charlotte rushed out to meet her and embraced her friend as if she had not seen her in three years rather than three months. Immediately, Elizabeth knew that she had done the right thing by coming. Mr. Collins came out to meet her as well, chattering about all the benefits of his home and the excellent condescension of Lady Catherine de Bourgh. He showed his guest every corner of the house, detailing every improvement that Lady Catherine had either made or recommended for him to make. The highlight of the tour, judging by the number of times it had been mentioned, would be the shelves in the closet of the room Elizabeth would be occupying. When they finally arrived at Elizabeth's bedchamber, the closet was opened and presented in such a way that Elizabeth felt obliged to make a comment about how pleasing was the arrangement of the shelves. A satisfied Mr. Collins finally left the ladies to themselves, much to *their* satisfaction.

After Elizabeth had rested a while, she joined Charlotte in her sitting room. They talked, and after a while, they were all caught up on what little news they had not shared by letter. Since Charlotte had some household matters to attend to, Elizabeth went to her chamber to unpack and plan how she would arrange her room to guarantee that there would be no unwanted visitors.

Over the next day or two, Elizabeth became acclimated to the routine of the household. It seemed Mr. and Mrs. Collins spent little time together during the day, which was a great relief to Elizabeth. When able, she worked with Charlotte mending, embroidering, or visiting parishioners, but there were quite a few daily tasks and errands which did not allow for Elizabeth's attendance, and she would be on her own for hours at a time. When Mr. Collins went out, she would stay home and write her letters. Though Mr. Collins had been on his best behaviour since her arrival, Elizabeth made every attempt to be out of the house as much as possible whenever Mr. Collins was within and Charlotte was busy, fearing to spend time alone with him after all that had happened at Longbourn and Meryton.

The one thing about Charlotte that was of most concern to Elizabeth was that occasionally Elizabeth would look up to find her with an almost frightened expression in her eyes before she realized that she had been caught out and schooled her features. On several occasions Elizabeth asked Charlotte if anything was bothering her, but her friend dismissed it and declared herself to be content with her new life.

Elizabeth found a bench in the shade of a grove of apple trees where she would go to read her letters or books. Though she tried to hide it, Elizabeth could tell Jane's spirits continued to be quite depressed at the loss of Bingley's attentions. She allowed a mirthless snicker to escape her lips while wondering if Jane was thinking the same about herself and Darcy. If so, Jane's thoughts would be accurate.

Foolishness is indeed the sister of wickedness.
--Sophocles (Greek dramatist, 495 BC – 406 BC)

~Rosings Park

"Our guest has arrived, Lady Catherine. You will meet her at church on Sunday."

"Mrs. Collins mentioned that one of her former neighbours from Hertfordshire would be visiting this month. I have told her it is good practice for her to be entertaining so soon after your marriage. I shall show my approval by inviting you all to tea tomorrow afternoon. And which of your future neighbours will I be meeting, Mr. Collins?"

"You are very gracious, Lady Catherine! It is my cousin, Miss Elizabeth Bennet."

"Elizabeth Bennet? Elizabeth Bennet!" She turned a very odd shade of purple. "Why would you allow that *harlot* to visit your wife, Mr. Collins? This is the minx who has used her arts and allurements in an attempt to cheat my daughter, Anne, of her rightful betrothal to my nephew! How could you *do* such a thing to me—me, for whom you say you would do anything, Mr. Collins? You shelter her under your roof, entertain her, and feed her? Did you expect me to invite *her* to my home? No! You will not disgrace Rosings by bringing that little wench to tea! You will turn her out of your house this instant! Do not give her money or lend her transportation. Put her out on the streets where she belongs!"

Mr. Collins bowed and apologized more than ever he had before. His cowering served to calm Lady Catherine at first, and then she ignored him while her eyes tightened to slits as she contemplated the opportunity the situation presented.

"Stop, Mr. Collins! That is quite enough. It has occurred to me that having the detestable Elizabeth Bennet close by where I can make sure she is not using her wiles to lure my nephew in would not be a bad thing after all. Keep her here at Hunsford. But I will not allow her to pass through the doors of Rosings, and this will mean your wife will lose the pleasure of my company and that of my daughter while that hoyden is staying under your roof—unless she comes without her!"

Chapter 32

One who knows how to show and to accept kindness will be a friend better than any possession.
--Sophocles (Greek dramatist, 495 BC – 406 BC)

~On the grounds of Rosings Park

Over the next fortnight, Elizabeth spent much time walking the beautiful grounds of Rosings, finding new paths to explore almost every day, and at times she went searching for a peaceful place to sit and read a book. She often came across the gardeners on the grounds and talked to them if they had the time. She also spent some time at the stables admiring a new litter of puppies the gardeners had told her about, and enjoyed watching a young horse being trained.

When near the stables she would often see a boy of about nine years of age with very straight, almost white hair and intelligent green eyes. He was always working diligently, cleaning out the stalls and other menial tasks. She attempted conversation with him a few times, but he would not answer her. She found out through the other stable hands that his name was Johnny and that he did not speak to anyone; some guessed that he *could not* speak.

Elizabeth at first suspected that if he did not speak then it was possible that he could not hear—she knew a boy who could not hear at the orphanage she visited with her Aunt Gardiner—but it was soon proved that was not the case since she saw him follow directions without any trouble even when he was not looking in the direction of the speaker. He also reacted to her approach by looking around to see who it was, even when she came up from behind him.

Johnny carried a toy ship with him whenever he was at leisure, and she always saw it nearby when he was working. Sometimes she would see him walking on the grounds, the toy ship in his hands, and she assumed he was going somewhere to play with it. It appeared that he had no playmates, and the ship seemed to be his only toy.

Johnny was followed around by a tall, burly boy with wavy black hair and dark eyes. The others told her this boy, whose name nobody knew, followed Johnny everywhere, and that there had been a man who had done the same before this boy replaced him. That man had spoken a little about what his job entailed when someone had asked him for assistance a few times; he was being paid to watch Johnny to the exclusion of all else, no matter how urgently he might be needed elsewhere.

Elizabeth guessed the older boy was about sixteen or seventeen years of age, though he was much more muscular than she had ever known a boy of that age to be. She had never witnessed the older boy speaking either. The two never approached each other—he just watched Johnny from afar at all times. Elizabeth thought everything about the two boys considerably strange, and she had become excessively curious about them both.

One day, Elizabeth was exploring the grounds and followed a stream to a beautiful pond. Though much larger, the meadow surrounding the pond was reminiscent of her special place near Longbourn and, in turn, it was comforting to her, so she found a place to sit and read. After reading her book for a while, a movement at the far side of the meadow caught her attention. Johnny moved through the bushes, followed by the older boy. Johnny sat by the pond and placed his ship in the water. The older boy sat on a fallen log and simply watched Johnny while he looked at the boat as it sailed across the pond.

Elizabeth observed the boys, and when nothing changed for a several minutes, she wandered to the opposite side of the pond where the boat had come ashore, paying attention to both boys' reactions. The older boy stiffened as she approached and then relaxed his stance when she turned the boat around and pushed it out into the pond toward Johnny. The two continued on this way for a few minutes before the older boy stood up and whistled, and then Johnny took the boat out of the water and waved to Elizabeth before disappearing into the woods with the older boy following him.

"How singular!" she thought.

Elizabeth decided to go back to the pond as often as possible when she went for a walk over the next few days. She explored the area surrounding the pond and made a plan for the next time that she would meet Johnny and the older boy. She went at different times of the day as her time with Charlotte would allow, but came upon the boys again only at the same time of day as she had met them before. This time when the boat crossed the pond to her side, Elizabeth removed it from the water and began to walk upstream, motioning for them to follow.

The threesome walked until Elizabeth found the place that she had been looking for. The stream feeding the pond entwined through the woods from this point, where a small waterfall traversed a rocky slope. She placed the boat in the water below the waterfall. Johnny's eyes lit up, and they all followed the ship as it travelled down the stream toward the pond. They repeated this one more time before the older boy whistled; Johnny waved and both boys disappeared into the woods.

Elizabeth tried to go to the pond whenever she could at the time she knew the boys would be there. After a few meetings, Johnny talked to her. He would not say much, but he did tell her that he had worked in the stables for the past two years, and that he was only allowed to play during a certain time of the day when his duties allowed. He also told her with a proud air that his great-grandpapa had made the toy ship for him. Elizabeth tried to talk to the older boy, but he did not answer her inquiries. She could not even find out his name. Were the boys simply shy or were they *afraid* to speak to her? Elizabeth could not decide.

Since Elizabeth was one to be active and Johnny seemed to have only one toy, she decided to make Johnny a kite. One day when she walked into the village with Charlotte, she used a portion of the money her father had given her to spend as she pleased to buy supplies she could not fashion herself, such as twine, cloth, a long length of ribbon, glue, and a knife to carve with. The next time she met the boys, she cut two thin branches as she made her way to the waterfall. When they reached the pond, Elizabeth sat on a boulder and began shaving the branches smooth with the knife. Neither of the boys asked what she was doing, but since she had removed the knife from her pocket, she noticed the older boy staying further away from her than usual and watching her more carefully. She did not enlighten them about what she was doing other than telling them it was called a kite—hoping one of them would ask for a further explanation, but neither did.

Every day that they met in the meadow, she worked on the kite a little bit more after the ship took a ride down the stream. The day came when the kite was finished, and it was the perfect weather for kite flying. Both boys seemed very excited when she declared the kite ready.

Johnny asked, "What's a kite for?" Elizabeth just smiled in reply. She hiked up her skirts and ran across the field. The kite took flight, and Elizabeth looked back to see the boys standing *next* to each other. Observing the boys wearing the first smiles she had ever seen upon either of their faces was more than enough payment for the time and effort Elizabeth had spent making the kite. The boys walked toward her.

"It's like a bird!" Johnny said in awe.

The older boy nodded and said, "Johnny, time to return to the stables."

Both Elizabeth and Johnny were stunned. Neither had ever heard the boy speak.

When Elizabeth had recovered, she said, "When next we meet, I will teach you both how to fly the kite. Goodbye, Johnny! Goodbye…" she raised her eyebrows in anticipation.

"My name is Abe, Miss Lizzy."

"Goodbye, Abe!" She flashed him a brilliant smile. The "queen of kites" had surpassed all of her expectations for the day.

Elizabeth continued to meet Johnny and Abe when she could and taught them some kite tricks that she had discovered through the years. Abe wanted to make a kite of his own, and Elizabeth helped him only by directing a few of his actions. Obviously Abe had paid very close attention when she had made Johnny's kite and was quite accomplished at crafting things. Elizabeth presented the first kite to Johnny as a gift.

Friday, March 20, 1812

~Darcy House, London

If not for Georgiana and Richard's actions, Darcy might have been trapped in his pitiful state, headed for Bedlam or worse. Georgiana could not get through to her brother, so she sent a letter requesting reinforcements—Richard.

On the night of Richard's unannounced late arrival, Darcy had forgotten to lock the door to his chambers when entering. Richard burst in upon him at a time when he was in an advanced state of inebriation, and

Richard insisted on Darcy's answering for this recent behaviour. After the argument between the two added to the exhaustion from his lack of sleep, Darcy had no trouble falling asleep for many hours. While he slept, Richard made Georgiana familiar with a portion of what he could understand of Darcy's ranting, and the two of them devised a plan to save his sanity.

~%~

Saturday, March 21, 1812

The next day, once Darcy had sobered, bathed, dressed in fresh clothing, and eaten the meal Georgiana and Richard had insisted upon, they moved to the library and the two worked on him.

Georgiana began shyly, "Brother, I know you still think of me as a child, but I am a young lady now. You have been so good to me and helped me through many difficult times. It is time that you allow me to do the same for you. Now that I am older and have experienced some difficulties myself," she continued as a blush made its way up her neck, "I hope you can trust me to be more understanding than I could have been in the past. Richard told me that your recent behaviour is related somehow to Miss Bennet, whom you wrote about in your letters. Will you please explain to us both what happened so that we may be of help to you?"

Several minutes passed in silence as Darcy paced between the fireplace and the window, feeling two pairs of eyes watching his every move. Though he loved and trusted his sister and cousin, Darcy was at odds with himself about whether to speak to them of his heartache. He had always been a private man, and laying out his heart for examination by others would make him feel even more vulnerable than he already did. But then, last night when he had made a slurred confession of sorts to Richard, it seemed to have helped lighten the weight just a little. And he had little experience with romantic love… maybe this was something he could not face alone.

While Georgiana and Richard remained quietly seated, Darcy continued pacing as he told them much of what had passed between Elizabeth and himself in Hertfordshire, and how he had decided not to propose, still *not* including the promise to his mother. He revealed to them that he did not know how to go on without her in his life.

Richard, quiet till now, decided it was time to speak. "I agree that Miss Bennet's character has been portrayed correctly by your brother,

Georgiana. Even though you might think he is besotted with her by praising her so highly—if anything he has not done her justice." Turning to Darcy, he asked, "So, what is next, Darce? What are your plans now that you know you cannot live without her?"

Darcy looked surprised. "Plans?"

At Richard's exasperated look, Darcy added after a few moments, "If you mean plans for myself… I have no plans other than my usual business affairs."

A look of anguish overtook Darcy's features as he tried to put his feelings into words. "I suppose it is my duty that I someday provide an heir to the estate… and I must resign myself to spend the rest of my life shackled to a vain and selfish creature of the *ton* who has good social standing, a healthy dowry, and not the brains to put two words of sense together… all the while knowing what I could have had if society had allowed it! Maybe that would be rightful punishment for my sins!"

Richard said, "You *will* stop this stupid talk of duty and honour, and you will end your misery and go court Miss Bennet with the intention of marrying her!"

"Richard, I knew even when I left Hertfordshire what I was losing… but I cannot marry her because of what is *expected* of me. I have a responsibility to Georgiana and my family. It would damage Georgiana's hopes of being accepted into society if I married someone of whom they did not approve, no matter how wonderful she may be! Scandal would not be welcomed by anyone in the family, and so she certainly would not be accepted there either. I cannot ask her to marry me just because I am selfish! I must think of others, and I must think of *her*! How could Elizabeth be happy if all of society and my family rejected her? She would grow to hate me… and I could not live with that."

"Brother, please! I want you to be happy! I care not about anyone who would snub me because you chose love. You *deserve* to be loved!" Georgiana said as tears filled her eyes.

"You might not care now, Georgiana, but you will when the families of the first circle give you the cut direct whenever you walk into a room!" Darcy boomed. His brow furrowed and utter misery enveloped his countenance as he moved to reach for the brandy decanter.

Richard stopped his hand. "Darcy, you will listen to me now. You will not go *there* again," he said as he pointed to the brandy, "Not if

Georgiana and I can help it. I will not allow you to go back to that hole from which I pulled you up last night! You have people depending on you, Darce, and depending upon your actions. What good can come from abandoning all matters of business? What do you think Miss Elizabeth would think of you then? Do you have any inkling what your behaviour is doing to Georgiana? Even your housekeeper has come to me since I arrived to voice her concern about you! The entire staff is worried. You are lucky that Mrs. Martin did not write to Mrs. Reynolds and have her come here to London! Or worse, yet, to my mother! No, Darce, you will not be drinking again anytime soon!"

Darcy was ashamed of himself when Richard spoke of Elizabeth, remembering all that she had said to him on Oakham Mount. If nothing else, he owed it to *her* to strive to be the man she thought he was, and keep to his responsibilities. He sighed deeply.

"Speaking of my mother, you both are invited to tea tomorrow afternoon, and then a family dinner if you would be so inclined to stay. You *must* come—it was more of an order than a request, Darce. I was told that if you do not come, she will come here and drag you across to Matlock House by your ear in front of all of London!" Richard laughed heartily. "By the bye, I do not believe she was joking.

"I also should remind you of something you seem to have forgotten. Since you have distanced yourself from the world lately, you may not be aware, but it is almost time for our annual visit to Rosings. We are leaving in two days' time, Darce."

Darcy was shocked. "We are not leaving for Rosings until the third and twentieth day of March!"

"Yes, that is in two days."

Darcy blinked a few times. "But… is it not February?" Darcy asked confusedly.

"No, William, it is not." Georgiana pointed to the brandy decanter. "*This* is what happened to part of February *and* most of March, Brother."

Darcy closed his eyes and rubbed his temples. "Georgie, I am so sorry. I am ashamed of myself." Then he turned to Richard, "Tell your mother we will be there for tea *and* family dinner, Richard."

Sunday, March 22, 1812

~ On the grounds of Rosings Park

It warmed Elizabeth's heart when she approached the meadow while Abe was flying the kite and Johnny was standing near him. She was too far away to hear, but she could see the two were conversing! The kite made a wrong turn, falling to the ground, and the boys began to laugh. Elizabeth's eyes filled with tears of joy. She watched the scene for several minutes unnoticed before returning to Hunsford Cottage to write a letter to Jane.

Sunday, March 22, 1812

~Matlock House, London

Lady Adelaide Fitzwilliam, Countess of Matlock, was in her sitting room reading through some old letters when the Darcys and her son Richard arrived for tea. As they followed the footman to the door, they could hear her laughter ringing down the hall. The footman announced the three, and they entered the room before she could calm herself long enough to acknowledge their arrival. Georgiana, Darcy, and Richard could not help but smile in response to her mirth.

"Hello, dears! I am so glad to see you—Georgiana… William," she kissed them both on the cheek as she said their names, "and Richard, as always." He received a kiss as well.

"Aunt Adelaide, it is a pleasure to see you," Darcy replied. Georgiana was nodding with a wide grin.

"Why were you laughing like that, mother? Is it a letter from your chess partner?"

"Yes, she always sends the most pleasant and entertaining letters along with her next move for the game we are playing. Receiving her letters is a poor consolation for not having her in London, though, as she is one of my favourite friends."

At this point, Lord Matlock entered the room. After everyone was greeted properly, he said to his wife, "Adelaide, I heard your laughter all the way down the hall in my study. You must have received a letter from Miss Elizabeth."

Darcy twitched at the name, but thought himself rather silly since it was not possible that it could be *his* Miss Elizabeth.

"Unfortunately not, my dear, I only have been reading over some of her old letters."

"It has been a while since she has written, and I know you have missed her terribly. I do hope nothing is wrong. I know you are exceedingly fond of her, as am I."

"I must say, I have been worried. Something particular must have happened to delay her from writing for such a long time. She is usually a much more faithful correspondent than she has been for the past few months," she stated thoughtfully, and then remembered who else was in the room. "But you do not want to hear about my chess partner, do you?" The maids entered with a grand tea service and assorted goodies. "Ah, here is tea. Let us talk of what my niece and nephew have been busy with lately. And you, Richard, are always running here and there in the service of the Prince Regent. I have not seen William since… well, for at least a month." She looked at Darcy a bit suspiciously as he had been turning down her invitations lately, and she was always told he was not at home when she called at Darcy House to visit with Georgiana.

The tea was served, and a few of the usual subjects were discussed, yet Lady Matlock's mind shifted back to the subject of her chess partner. During a lull in the conversation, a concerned expression passed over her face, and she walked to her writing desk to shuffle through a neatly tied bundle of letters to check the date on the last one.

She stood staring at the wall for a minute before Lord Matlock asked, "Adelaide, what is wrong?"

"Lizzy has not written since the tenth of October, Robert. I *am* worried now. Do you think Thomas would have written if something had happened to her? Or Madeline, she would have let me know, would she not?"

"My dear, you are quite the worrier. Of course Thomas, Madeline, or Edward would have told you. We saw Madeline, Edward, and Jane just this past month, and they said nothing at all about Lizzy to me."

"When I asked after Lizzy, both ladies were very evasive. Madeline said only that Lizzy seemed not herself when they saw each other at Christmas. And Jane did not seem well either; she barely spoke and was quite depressed in spirits."

Darcy began choking on his tea, *Lizzy and Jane… Madeline and Edward… Thomas …could it be?* Once he recovered from coughing, Darcy asked, "Is that Mr. and Mrs. Gardiner you speak of?"

"Yes, do you know them? Of course you do, he owns the bookshop you frequent, does he not? Lizzy, my chess partner, is his niece. Jane is Lizzy's sister. I have known them for years through Madeline Gardiner. I have often tried to have you two young men meet Lizzy and Jane, but you both slip out of any of my matchmaking schemes too easily. Lizzy would be perfect for *you*, William…"

It was Richard's turn to choke on his tea.

"Now, now, my dear, you promised not to try to play matchmaker again!" Lord Matlock chided.

"Oh, Robert, you and I have discussed many times how perfect Lizzy and William would be for each other. Do not try to lay the blame solely at my feet!"

The earl cleared his throat as he picked up a newspaper to thumb through.

My aunt and uncle would approve? Darcy's heart was beating so fast that he thought it would burst. Could they not hear it? He took a deep breath to try to calm himself.

Darcy appeared so flustered that Richard thought he should make an attempt to distract his parents' attention from his cousin by asking, "How did you first make Mrs. Gardiner's acquaintance, Mother?"

Lady Matlock smiled. "A few years ago, Edward Gardiner's book shop had been highly recommended to your father. After a few visits there, Robert and Edward became friends, and he invited Edward to be his guest at his club. One morning, Robert had been at the shop to ask Edward to search for a first edition of a particular book, and Madeline Gardiner was introduced when she came in to speak to her husband. As impressed with Madeline's manners and good breeding as he had been with Edward's, he thought I would enjoy Madeline's company and extended an invitation to dine at Matlock House. We have been good friends ever since."

Trying to look as disinterested as possible Darcy said, "You are correct, Aunt. I do know the Gardiners. I also met the Bennets at Netherfield Park, the estate my friend Charles Bingley is leasing in Hertfordshire."

Finally Georgiana caught on, and her eyes were opened wider than her aunt and uncle had ever before seen them. Lady Matlock looked around her at the odd reactions of all the young people. This certainly was becoming curious… unless… could it be?

Lady Matlock's smile brightened the room. "I did not know you had met Lizzy and her family, William! Why did you not tell me?"

Richard was the only one at that moment with a mind able to respond. "Neither Miss Bennet nor Miss Elizabeth made any mention of knowing you, Mama. They are not the type of ladies who advertise their connexions to gain favor—that much is obvious!"

Darcy was struck with a remembrance from Oakham Mount… he could hear Elizabeth saying, "Sir, by *all* accounts I have heard, and I do not mean Miss Bingley... for you do not know of some of my more excellent sources."

She was talking of Aunt Adelaide and Uncle Robert!

"That is correct; neither Jane nor Elizabeth would use their connexion with us for their own gain as so many other ladies would not hesitate to do. They would not dream of using others in such a way," said Lady Adelaide. "But Richard! You met them as well? When was this?"

"I was at Netherfield in the middle of November and remained until we returned to London—about a fortnight, I believe. Darcy arrived in Hertfordshire much earlier than I… Michaelmas, was it not, Darce?"

"Yes… yes," was all Darcy could manage to say, while wondering, *Why is this information bothering me so? Why am I not happy at this news?*

"Oh… Michaelmas was just before Lizzy's letters stopped."

Darcy visibly started at this realization.

"What did you boys think of Miss Bennet and Miss Elizabeth?" Lord Matlock asked to break the silence.

"Miss Bennet is a very good sort of girl—kind and gentle. But Miss Elizabeth… she is absolutely charming," Richard replied glancing at Darcy, who had turned about as red as was possible, short of a high fever. "So… you were trying to match Darce and Miss Elizabeth, eh, Mama? You would not characterize her as a *mercenary* lady then?"

Darcy gave Richard a sharp look.

Both Lord and Lady Matlock began to laugh at Richard's question. Lord Matlock recovered first. "Elizabeth Bennet, mercenary? Then you have not heard about Mr. Hainsworth and his pursuit of her two seasons ago…

or was it three?" He waited till all three young people shook their heads in the negative, their faces showing their extreme interest. "Hainsworth is the grandson of a duke and has more wealth than Darcy and I put together! Or he will, once he inherits from his father, but he is no pauper now with what he has already inherited. He saw her twice after he accompanied his mother here for a dinner party that Miss Elizabeth attended with her aunt and uncle, was completely agog, and made an offer. The poor man would not take 'no' for an answer! Miss Elizabeth had to leave her aunt and uncle's home in London to escape his attentions. She said she felt it unfair to her uncle to ask him to be constantly turning away such a highly placed gentleman from his door." He guffawed. "It was a good thing he could not remember the name of the estate she lives on, eh, Adelaide? I do think the man would have set up camp on Longbourn's drive if he had!" Lord Matlock laughed again.

Lady Matlock spoke up, "Yes, and he made it quite difficult for us when we would not tell him where she lives! Really, you children do not listen much to gossip, do you? The *ton* was all abuzz about it for a few days. Though, it is possible you did hear of it and did not know it was Lizzy since the talk did not include her name. They were referring to her as 'a country nobody,' which is quite unfair based upon her success among my acquaintance. Those of us who did know it was Lizzy felt it was a blessing that her name was not included in the gossip. It was just short of a miracle that the whole of the talk was of short duration, since a few days later a married woman ran off with a single gentleman, which was immediately followed by a divorce announcement from the husband. Since these events were far more entertaining to the *ton* than a refused proposal, Lizzy's story was quite forgotten about."

Richard was quite amused. "So, are you saying Miss Elizabeth is accepted by the first circles, Mama?"

"She has been accepted by some of the highest placed ladies in society for years when she has visited me for a morning call, tea, or dinner, and I myself have taken her along to call on some ladies. She does not often come to Town, and so she has not as wide a range of acquaintances as she could have. I am aware that upon meeting her, members of the *ton* are usually initially prejudiced towards her due to her station, but those who have actually spent time with Lizzy approve of her greatly. The only people who did not find her acceptable were those who had their eye on Mr. Hainsworth for their own daughters, but only *after* he had not been discreet about telling others of his preference for her while in company.

It seems the news of his proposal being refused began to spread after he indulged too liberally in spirits at his club one night.

"But you have met Lizzy, Richard! What do *you* think?"

"I believe she would be a smashing success in the first circles, Mama." He smiled at Darcy.

"I am afraid the gossip did affect poor Lizzy in a way. She began to see herself as a 'country nobody,' at least in respect to marriage, and refused to allow me to introduce her to any gentlemen in the *ton* after that—though I must admit I did try to sneak a few gentlemen through, including the both of you. I doubt that she would ever be rejected by the *ton* as she is our particular friend, as well as that of the Duke of Beaufort. The Duke and I have attempted to set her to rights about it, but it does not seem to help. She only seems to remember what was said of Mr. Hainsworth when he offered for her and… oh, how did she put it, Robert?" Lady Matlock inquired.

Lord Matlock replied, "Miss Elizabeth announced she would refuse to leg-shackle any man to a 'country nobody.' It is nonsense."

"Ah! Miss Elizabeth is a friend of the Duke? How did *that* come about?" Richard was enjoying himself greatly.

Lady Matlock laughed. "If you hear the Duke tell it, Lizzy and Madeline Gardiner saved his life. However, Lizzy and Madeline are not quite as prone to exaggeration as the Duke is. Several years ago, he was injured while being robbed, and the ladies happened upon him in a state of great anxiety. The ladies helped care for him and took him home in the Gardiners' carriage. The Duke has formed a special bond with Lizzy. She is almost like a daughter to him."

Lady Matlock was thoughtful for a moment, and then a smile spread across her face. "Georgiana, you have met Lizzy and Jane as well! Do you not remember?" When Georgiana shook her head, Lady Matlock continued, "It will be four years ago this summer that you and Lizzy were here for tea at the same time, though you were so young I do not believe the two of you spoke on that occasion. But you did meet again about two years ago." She turned to Lord Matlock. "Robert, it was two years ago that Mr. Hainsworth offered for Lizzy, not three, as it was the same time that Lizzy and Jane were in London and became reacquainted with Georgiana." Turning back to Georgiana. "When I came to sit with you, Lizzy was telling you a story about how she learned to ride a horse… oh, I do not remember exactly, but she made you feel much more comfortable whilst among all the ladies at the tea. The Bennet sisters entertained you all afternoon and…"

Georgiana was so excited that she interrupted her aunt—something she normally would not do. "Oh! Yes!" she clapped her hands and giggled, and then her words came tumbling out so quickly it was difficult to understand how this could be the same shy girl they all knew. "I felt comfortable enough with them to speak a little and had asked them if they liked to ride! Miss Elizabeth told me that when she was a young girl, her friend and she learned to ride in secret because they wanted to compete with the boys in a race that they were having in a nearby village. They would sneak away one of their father's horses from the stables, and since they could not saddle a horse, they taught themselves to ride bareback! And she won, too, but after all that, she was not recognized as the winner of the race because she was a girl. She told me that she never did learn to ride sidesaddle.

"Oh, yes, Aunt! I do remember them now. Miss Bennet and Miss Elizabeth were so kind to me, and when I told them I had no sisters, they both entertained me with amusing stories of what it is like growing up in a house full of girls. But I must admit I enjoyed hearing stories of Miss Elizabeth as a young girl most of all!" Georgiana beamed.

"No one would guess by her manners in the drawing room or ballroom now, that she was a hoyden as a child," Richard added to help complete the picture of Elizabeth for Georgiana.

Georgiana had been watching her brother through the corner of her eye during the entire conversation about Elizabeth. He was sitting completely still as if in shock, though it was obvious to her that he was absorbing every word quite attentively. She had to look directly at him for a few moments to see whether he was breathing at all, but found his breath was quite shallow and too rapid. His colour kept changing from pallor to a deep blush, then back again.

Richard, trying hard to keep the mirth from his voice, spoke next. "Darce, will you tell my mother and father what *you* think of Miss Elizabeth?"

Darcy jumped up out of his seat and walked quickly over to the window, but remained silent.

Georgiana could not hold in her excitement any longer and spoke up,

"He is in love with Miss Elizabeth but was too afraid that she would not be considered a proper marriage partner for a man of his station!"

Darcy did not even turn around to see anyone's reaction… he simply walked to the door and left the house.

~%~

Lady Matlock's elated heart fell at Georgiana's words as she watched her nephew walk out the door, and plummeted further still when she looked to her niece and saw her expression of dejection.

Georgiana buried her face in her hands and began to cry. "I did not mean to betray his trust so! I was so happy about what you said, Aunt, and I thought he would be as well. Everything you said about Miss Elizabeth negated everything he told us was keeping him from offering for her!"

Richard was sitting next to Georgiana and put his arm around her, handing her his handkerchief. "I thought the same, Georgie. He had practically drunk himself to death over her these past few weeks! One would think he would be ecstatic with today's news! I cannot account for this reaction at all."

Lady Matlock allowed a slight gasp to escape her lips and looked to her husband, who was reeling in shock from all that had been revealed in the past minute or so.

Richard got up from his chair, obviously about to follow his cousin, but Lady Matlock moved quickly and stopped him with a hand on his arm. "Richard… let me go after him. There is something I must do… I – Anne was so insistent on the timing of it… but I now see that I should have done this a long time ago."

"Anne? My mother?" Georgiana asked.

"Yes, my dear. I am glad you spoke when you did, dear Georgiana, for if you had not, William would have been in pain for a long time… possibly for the rest of his life.

"Georgiana and Richard, please keep Lord Matlock company for dinner… I will return when I am finished, but I know not when that will be. I would like you both to stay here until I return, even if it takes all night."

Everyone watched in confusion as she crossed the room to her writing desk and unlocked the bottom drawer. After removing a thick envelope, she left the room.

“Father, do you know…”

“No, Richard, I do not know of what your mother was speaking or what was in the envelope. Whatever it is, I do hope it helps William… and Miss Elizabeth.”

Darcy walked out of the house, completely numb inside. He had shut down all his emotions when Georgiana spoke. He knew she was only trying to help… knew that the reason she said it was to make the point that Uncle Robert and Aunt Adelaide had taken away every reason he had *stated* for not proposing to Elizabeth. But none of them knew the true reason he could not do it, and he had no intention of telling them. He was too ashamed of the promises he had already failed to keep. He *must* honour his word to his mother! He could not betray her trust in him completely.

The thought that it most certainly was *not* his mother’s fault that he was so miserable kept recurring to him as he walked on and on.

He knew not how long he had been walking, but the next time he was able to think clearly, he found himself staring into the front display window of Mr. Gardiner’s bookshop. Startled to find himself there, he quickly walked away and got into the first hackney cab he could find, giving directions for Darcy House.

Once inside the cab, he reached into his pocket and took out the treasure he carried with him every day… Elizabeth’s bookmark. It was his only physical link to *her*. She had chosen the ribbon for herself; she had held it in her hands with her delicate fingers; she had worked on the stitching, and she had done most of the work *for him*!

At Netherfield, he had planned to use the plain white ribbon with her initials in the corner as a keepsake of her, beginning the instant he realized that she had placed it there two years prior and had become desperate to take it out before she borrowed the book. He could not do it without anyone’s seeing him, so he reluctantly allowed her to leave Netherfield with the bookmark still within the book.

The night she had returned the book and he was just out of sight of Longbourn, he stopped his horse. He could not wait for another moment to pass before retrieving it. When he gently pulled her bookmark from the book, he gasped when he saw what she had done to it.

As they had spoken during their shared breakfast in her little clearing, Elizabeth described its appearance in the spring, the time of year she loved it best. She shared how she had planted her favourite spring flowers there in the little grassy area across from the boulder where they had sat.

Even in the low light of the moon, he had recognized that she had embroidered all of her favourite flowers on the bookmark. His heart had swelled with joy… Elizabeth had embroidered it *for him*! She gave of herself, expecting nothing in return.

He had never received such a heartwarming gift!

Darcy also knew that he never would receive anything that meant more to him. In a future devoid of Elizabeth, there was no chance of that happening.

The only time he had seen her after that was at the ball. With his high emotions that evening, he had forgotten all about thanking her for it. She would never know how special it was to him.

Darcy lightly brushed his fingertips over the bookmark once more before returning it to the pocket over his heart.

~Hunsford Cottage

After seeing the boys conversing so nicely, Elizabeth was anxious to write to Jane to make her aware of the boys' most recent progress. She arrived at the parsonage and was headed for her room to write her letter when a strange scraping noise coming from Charlotte's sitting room caught her attention. Concerned that her friend might be in trouble, she went to investigate. When she grasped the door handle, she noticed that it was locked and was about to move away, but the latch was not engaged properly and her touch pushed the door open part way. Peeking through the opening while reaching to close the door, she met with a strange sight and froze in place.

Mr. Collins had moved a heavy chair and had rolled the rug off to the side of the room. Part of the floor was pulled up as if it was a hatch door and it was leaning on the chair which had been moved. A large metal box was open on the table beside the chair. Mr. Collins was facing away from the door, thankfully, and was mumbling to himself. Several papers and a ledger book lay on the table before him.

Afraid Mr. Collins might detect her presence, Elizabeth backed out of the room, being careful to close the door quietly behind her. She took up her things and rushed out of the house as quickly as she could, deciding that her original choice of staying outdoors when Mr. Collins was home alone must have been a correct assessment. She would wait until she was certain that Charlotte had returned home before going back to Hunsford Cottage.

Elizabeth took a long walk trying to sort out what Mr. Collins had been about, but could only determine one thing. Whatever it was, he meant for it to be kept a secret, and now that she knew about its existence, Elizabeth wondered if she was in any danger… and if Charlotte was in danger as well.

~Darcy House

As Darcy walked into his house, the footman attempted to speak to him, but Darcy waved him off and headed straight for his study. When he opened the door, he had a feeling he knew what the footman had been trying to convey. His Aunt Adelaide was waiting for him within, curled up in his most comfortable chair by the fire with a book laid across her lap—sleeping. He wondered how long she had been there.

He walked across the room to where the brandy was usually kept, but he found the decanter empty and slammed his fist on the table. *Richard!* he thought, *Have I been so bad that Richard does not trust me to drink in moderation, even after I promised?*

Darcy heard his aunt stir and sighed. "I am sorry, Aunt Adelaide; I did not mean to wake you."

She stretched a bit, and then stood. "I am glad you did, William. I need to speak with you… or rather I have to tell you something and give you a letter. I will wait in another room for you to read it in case you have any questions. You should not have to wait any longer for answers, my dear."

Darcy was curious. This was not what he had expected her to say when he saw her waiting for him. He motioned for her to sit, and then sat in the chair across from hers and waited.

"As you know, after giving birth to Georgiana, your mother was seriously ill. She knew she would leave us soon. Anne and I were closer than sisters. I was there attending the birth and stayed at Pemberley for a few days, but I had to leave because Richard had fallen quite ill while at school. I must say leaving her just then was one of the most difficult things I have ever done, but she understood that my son needed me. Before I left, she dictated two letters to me since she was too weak to write them herself. One is for you, and one is for Georgiana."

Lady Matlock let what she had said hang in the air between them for a minute, and then continued, "Your mother gave me specific directions about when to give the letters to the two of you. It was to be only when you were seriously thinking about getting married. I have respected her wishes, though—knowing what it says—now I think I should *not* have waited. I should have given it to you sooner, William, and I apologize. I do believe that I will give Georgiana her letter just before her coming out."

She handed him the letter. "Remember, it may be my handwriting, but these are your mother's words, not mine." She hesitated again. "I will be in the drawing room. Please come to me when you are ready. You may ask me any question at all. I do understand the way she thought, William; we had spent many hours discussing what we wanted for our children. I will *not* leave until I hear from you, even if it takes all night." She rose, kissed him on the forehead and left him alone.

Darcy sat staring at the letter for some minutes before he found the courage to open it.

My dearest William,

I am having your Aunt Adelaide write this letter for me as I know my time on this earth is limited. There is much I wanted to be able to teach you, to tell you, my son, but I will not be here to say these things to you.

I should wish to know with what difficulties you will meet so that I know what advice to share with you here. Alas, what will happen in your life I know not; I can only imagine, just as I have spent countless hours since you have been born imagining what your life would be like. I tend to imagine only good things for your future, William, but I do know there will be unpleasant happenings in your life as well. I prefer not to think forward to the unpleasant, just as I prefer to look upon the past only as it gives me pleasure.

You are a shy boy, and I wonder if you will remain shy as you become a man. I regret not being able to know the adult you will be.

I know you will be handsome and strong, honourable and kind, intelligent and loving. You will be an excellent master of Pemberley when the time comes, a good brother, a good husband, and a good father. Of that I have no doubt. Have confidence in yourself, as do I, that you will do your best in all things.

I see in you a person who has difficulty tolerating his inability to do everything perfectly. Please forgive yourself for any mistakes you may make, dear. Be assured I was far from perfect! Your father is not perfect, though he might be less inclined than I to admit it. We are all imperfect creatures; it is how God intended us. It is expected of us to make mistakes, William; please understand that.

I worry about what your father will do after I am no longer in this world. He loves me so deeply and completely—as I love him. I worry that he will never be the same once I am gone, and I hope this does not harm you or your sister. Please know that he loves both of you deeply as well, my dear, and that his love will never change. It is not in his nature to display it the way I would. Will you be more like your father or me in this way, I wonder?

I know how difficult the **ton** *is, dearest. Do not let them frighten you into doing anything that you do not know in your heart to be the correct thing for you. Yes, there are things we all must do that make us uncomfortable, but if you know it to be wrong, then it is wrong, son. Trust your judgment.*

The most important people in your life will be those who love you for who you are inside—the man who is Fitzwilliam Darcy—not your name, social standing or wealth. You may have many acquaintances in your lifetime, but choose your friends well. Choose those who would care for you, no matter what.

I think the most important lesson I have learned is to love. Choose your wife well, William. Do not let anyone talk you into marrying only to increase the wealth or rank of the family. I warn you, your Aunt Catherine can be a strong-willed woman, but do not allow my sister to tell you that you must choose her daughter for anyone's sake but your own, and then only if you love her, son. I know you could never choose someone who would disrespect our family or harm your sister. Do not allow Catherine to convince you to think otherwise!

Your father and I were happy every minute we were together, even when we disagreed. We respect each other and have many of the same interests, but most of all we love each other deeply. There is nothing that could come close to a life filled with love, I promise you. If you cannot remember us together, look to your Aunt Adelaide and Uncle Robert as an example of great love.

When you have thought any situation through and are still undecided, choose your heart over duty. That is the only way you will be happy. Love can help you answer most questions, even those you think have nothing to do with it. Love can do great things – I do believe the only reason my heart continues to beat at this moment is in anticipation of seeing the three of you just once more before I go.

My love for you, Georgiana, and your father will never end, dearest William. Please know that I will be with you always.

Mother

~Hunsford Cottage

Upon returning from her second walk of the day, Elizabeth checked with the maid to see if Mrs. Collins was within before removing her pelisse and bonnet. Once assured that the mistress was home, she braced herself for any possible reaction to her discovery.

The evening progressed as it normally did, though Elizabeth retired earlier than usual; placing her trunk against the door after locking it, as usual… and spending the next hours in thought since sleep would not come.

Observe your enemies, for they first find out your faults.
--Antisthenes (Greek Philosopher 444BC – 371BC)

~Darcy House

Lady Matlock waited in the drawing room for what seemed to be a long time. She did not quite remember every word of the letters she had written for her sister-in-law sixteen years ago, but she remembered the general ideas. She did remember many of her conversations with Anne, their hopes and dreams for their children's futures. How different things had turned out for their children from what they had expected, but still… they were all good to the core. She spent this time reviewing many of the happy moments she had shared with William's mother, many of which had recounted for her children over the years which had elapsed since her passing.

It took Darcy quite some time to read the letter in its entirety, for often his tears would not allow him to see the words clearly. By the time he had reached the end, he felt as if a great weight had been lifted from him.

Once he recovered, he went searching for his aunt. She stood when she saw him enter the room and held out her arms to him.

Darcy crossed the room quickly and embraced her. "Thank you; it is exactly what I needed. I feel like I can breathe again, Aunt. I have not felt this way since… since before mother became ill, to own the truth." He took a deep breath to prove it. "I will be leaving for Longbourn at first light tomorrow!"

"I am glad to hear it, dear; I am sorry I had not given it to you sooner. But William… while I agree with your reasoning to do this as soon as possible, I do think that you are going to have to wait a bit longer. You are forgetting that you are to be leaving for Kent tomorrow with Richard, are you not?"

Darcy closed his eyes and sighed. "Yes, of course. Aunt Catherine! I had trusted her, you know. Mother called me to her rooms shortly before she died, and she was so weak… she had me make promises to her. One of them was to 'marry well.' I fault you not, my dearest aunt, for you had good reasons, but you were not there to help in deciphering what my mother had told me. Aunt Catherine *was* there, and I made the mistake of asking her what my mother could have meant. She gave me *her version* of what my mother proposed by those words, and she has trounced me with it often over the years. Until reading my mother's letter just now, I believed what she told me!

"I thought that by marrying Elizabeth, I would be going against the promise that I had made to my mother—which is the true reason I left Hertfordshire, Aunt. It is also the reason I left your house today. If nothing else, I had convinced myself that if Elizabeth married me, the *ton* would make her miserable with their judgments of her, and that their rejection of Elizabeth would cause Georgiana to be rejected as well.

"Under no circumstances did I ever want to blame my mother for making me feel so wretched, but the conversation today at your home took away all the reasons I had used to convince myself that I could not marry Elizabeth. All that remained was my mother's wishes. Part of me began to blame Mother for how I felt, and I now know that I was trying to run away from that part of myself this afternoon.

"The irony of the situation is that as I read her letter just now, I realized that if I *did not* offer for Elizabeth, only then would I be failing to act according to my mother's true wishes!" Darcy looked away from her. "It shames me that I did not see that she would want only my happiness."

Lady Matlock touched his cheek, causing him to meet her eyes once again. "She also said to forgive yourself your mistakes, William. I remember that clearly. I think you have already endured more heartache over this than you deserve, and you should heed your mother's advice."

Darcy swallowed hard and took a deep breath before continuing. "To think that Aunt Catherine has lied to me for sixteen years! Mother said things in her letter that were the exact opposite of what Aunt Catherine told me her sister wanted! Why would she do such a thing? Did she believe it? I cannot even begin to comprehend why she would choose to exploit my mother's death. I do not understand her at all. And you say that I must go visit *her* instead of rushing to Elizabeth's side to begin courting her properly, as I so desperately wish to do? Why do you say this, Aunt Adelaide?"

"Dearest William, I think you know my opinion of Catherine has never been favorable. Something inside me is telling me that you *must* go to Rosings. I do not understand it, but I feel it intensely. If nothing else, go for long walks and think of precisely how you will ask my good friend Lizzy to marry you."

William nodded. Most of those in her family had learned through experience never to act against one of Lady Matlock's *intense feelings*. "You believe I should offer marriage instead of courtship then?"

"Absolutely!" Lady Matlock smiled brilliantly.

He answered her smile with one of his own, with a display of dimples that his aunt hoped would no longer be a rare occurrence. "I have waited this long, I believe I can wait a few more days, Aunt… but no longer!"

The clock on the mantel chimed, and Lady Matlock said, "I do believe I am hungry, William. Shall we return to my house for dinner?"

"I did not realize it was so late, Aunt, I am sorry. I will freshen up and meet you in a few minutes. Is that acceptable?" he asked.

"Yes, my dear," she answered with a great sense of relief and a kiss to his cheek.

~Matlock House

When Lady Matlock and Darcy arrived at Matlock House, they were met with a room full of worried faces. Darcy walked directly to his sister, picked her up and twirled her around as he had used to do when she was a young girl. She giggled and looked up at her brother in time to see a grin she had not seen since before the death of their father. "I am glad to see your mood much improved, Brother!"

"Yes, and I have *you* to thank for it, Georgiana. It would not be so if not for your disclosure earlier today, my dear." He twirled her one more time, and her giggles filled the room.

Richard and Lord and Lady Matlock were enjoying the display, though their hunger overruled its continuation, and all moved to the dining room. The remainder of the evening was passed in an agreeable way, with much laughter filtering into the halls of Matlock House.

The only low point in the conversation came when Georgiana mentioned that she had received a letter from Aunt Catherine the day before. She thought it a most normal thing to speak of since her brother and cousin were going to visit her the next morning, but it seemed to dampen the high spirits of her brother and aunt.

After watching the young people's coach depart, Lord Matlock asked his wife, "What on earth did you do to William, my dear? I have never seen him in such good spirits!"

"It was not I, Robert, it was your sister Anne who had the words of wisdom; I was only the messenger."

"Are you speaking in riddles, Adelaide?"

"No, my dear, Anne left a letter in my care to be given to William when he was seriously considering marriage. I have one for Georgiana as well, but after this experience I do think giving it to her just before her coming out would be more appropriate."

"You know the contents of the letter?"

"Yes, Anne was too weak to write, so she dictated the letters to me. They are similar, though Georgiana's had a bit more, oh dear, how shall I say it... ladies' talk."

"Ah, well!" Lord Matlock shifted in his chair, feeling very uncomfortable at the mere mention of *ladies' talk*. "I trust your judgment, Adelaide. If you think it should be given to her before her coming out, then I do not doubt that it should."

It is impossible to love and to be wise.
--Francis Bacon (English Philosopher 1561 – 1626)

Monday, March 23, 1812

~Rosings Park

Every year Darcy looked toward his obligatory visit to his aunt with apprehension and displeasure, but this visit he was absolutely dreading. Though he knew Aunt Catherine was selfish, he had never thought that she would take advantage of his sorrow at the loss of his mother. To find that she had been lying to him every time he was in her presence for the past sixteen years was astounding! How could he ever look upon her again without contempt? He had already informed Richard that he would only be staying three days—long enough to see that their cousin Anne was well and to see that Rosings' ledgers were in order, as he had promised to do for *Anne's* sake. Darcy also decided that he would take this opportunity to confront Aunt Catherine with his newly found awareness and put an end to this gnawing feeling of having been betrayed.

In four days' time he would be on his way to Elizabeth! His thoughts wandered to seeing her again—her loveliness, the words he would say to her, the way that entering her presence always felt as if he were coming home.

His mind was pleasantly engaged in this manner as the coach entered the parklands surrounding Rosings. When Darcy first caught a glimpse of a lady walking in a glade near the road, as usual his mind compared her to Elizabeth. The lady usually would come up lacking… but when *this* lady looked toward the noise of the passing coach, Darcy found he could not breathe. It *was* Elizabeth!

Darcy was about to signal the driver to stop the coach, but he hesitated. He had to think.

Suddenly remembering that disgusting cousin of hers, he panicked. Last night when Georgiana mentioned Aunt Catherine's letter, she said that Mr. Collins had taken a wife!

NO! It could not be possible that Elizabeth has married her revolting cousin! Mr. Bennet would not have forced her to marry him after our talk, would he? Why did I ever leave Hertfordshire?

Darcy could not stop images of Elizabeth with that vile man from appearing in his mind, making him feel ill.

~%~

Richard saw a lady who looked very much like Miss Elizabeth as they passed. He turned to ask his cousin if he had seen her, when he heard Darcy repeating, "NO!" in a panicked tone of voice. Darcy began breathing so rapidly that Richard became concerned. He had seen similar reactions to stress on the battlefield, but what was going on now? He grabbed hold of Darcy's shoulders and shook him vigorously. Trying to ascertain whether or not to slap him, Richard watched Darcy's breathing. As his breath began to slow, Richard sat back and watched. By the time they had arrived at Rosings, Darcy had summoned *The Mask.*

Well, that answers that question—it must have been Miss Elizabeth! But what on earth is causing this reaction to seeing her? Her cousin is Aunt Catherine's parson and Georgiana said Collins got married recently, but I know Charlotte was engaged to him when we left Netherfield. If anyone, I should be the one reacting to having to see Charlotte with that odious man! But if Darce did not know about Charlotte's plans, he might assume Miss Elizabeth was the new bride. Perhaps I should enlighten him? But... I had better confirm just who the new Mrs. Collins is before I mention it. If I am wrong and Miss Elizabeth is now Mrs. Collins after I told him it was not so... it might have even worse effects than I am seeing now. I had better prepare for anything to happen today!

~%~

As far as Darcy could recall, he had not said anything about seeing Elizabeth, and Richard had not asked him what was wrong. He thought this was odd, especially when, after Richard had motioned to the footman to leave the carriage door open, Aunt Catherine and Cousin Anne came outdoors to meet the carriage and, after the usual civilities, Richard immediately inquired about Mr. Collins's wife. Richard kept his hand on Darcy's shoulder and seemed to be prepared to push him into the coach and head back to London if the answer was not to his liking. Darcy knew his relief did not escape Richard's close scrutiny when he heard that Mrs. Collins was the former Miss Lucas… but Darcy did also catch the look of disappointment and disgust that passed over Richard's face and wondered at the reason for it—and at the violence of the shudder that followed it. However, the thought of *any* lady having to suffer being the wife of that man was disgusting, after all.

~%~

After somehow enduring through an agonizingly long time cleaning off the dust from the road, Darcy went for a walk. *Elizabeth is here!* He was ecstatic, but he also did not want her exposed to his aunt's probable reaction to his behaviour toward her. He had to think of what to do and say before he saw Elizabeth again, since he knew that the minute he did see her, all hopes of rational thinking would be lost!

Elizabeth had been walking most of the day, exploring an area of Rosings she had not seen before. She made her way around some bushes and stopped at seeing some movement in the distance across a clearing. A group of men were in front of a small cabin. They were close enough for her to see what they were doing and catch a few words of what they were saying. Though there was something about the scene that made her feel uneasy, she felt fairly safe from being noticed as her presence was mostly hidden by a large bush.

There were six men in all: five were unloading two wagons filled with crates and barrels. She could not imagine how it all could fit into such a small cabin—unless there was an immense cellar. All of them were large men, and all were carrying guns! One of the men was standing with a rifle, acting as a guard, and he looked familiar somehow. The whole of the scene was suspicious. She wondered if anyone at Rosings knew that this cabin was here.

When the laughter of one of the men caught her attention as being familiar, she looked more closely. It was Wickham! *This* must be how

Mr. Collins and Wickham knew each other. That they were hiding their knowledge of each other while in Hertfordshire made this situation all the more dangerous. Now, more than a little frightened, Elizabeth rethought the situation and decided that she should remain hidden until the men were all inside the cabin, afraid that if she stirred, they might notice her.

After a few minutes, three of the men began to move in her direction, Wickham among them. Wickham called to the men who were still unloading the last of the crates, saying that they were going to see Collins at Hunsford. Elizabeth knew Mr. Collins was not home today, but obviously Wickham did not.

Elizabeth needed to make a decision quickly, before the men came too close. They were walking at a leisurely pace but the risk that they would see her was high if she stayed where she was, especially with her light coloured dress. The men might have longer legs and could walk faster than she, but she could stay ahead of them if she ran. She certainly did not want to be found alone in the woods by a group of men carrying guns, especially when one of them was Wickham! She backed away from the bush slowly and then once she was sure that she was out of sight, Elizabeth hiked up her skirts and began to run at full speed in the direction of Rosings. She thought she would make an excuse to stay in the stables for a while, hoping that by the time she returned to Hunsford, Wickham would have found Mr. Collins gone, and they would have returned to the cabin.

After running a while, a need to catch her breath overcame her, and she pushed through some bushes to hide in the midst of them. Her face and arms were scratched, and her dress had been torn, but she cared not as long as the men did not find her. She only paused long enough for her breathing to slow a little before beginning to run again. Elizabeth tripped and fell twice, adding to the dirt and scratches, but she barely noticed.

Seeing a group of large trees and judging it a good place to hide again to catch her breath, she headed in that direction. As she rounded an enormous tree trunk, she ran directly into Darcy! Instinctively, his arms caught her, but the force of such an unexpected impact knocked him off balance, and they both fell to the ground.

Darcy was startled, but calmed knowing that Elizabeth was in his arms. Elizabeth, in too much of a panic to realize who held her, struggled to free herself. He pulled her closer in a gentle but unyielding embrace and whispered, "Elizabeth!"

She stopped struggling and looked up at him.

He had seen her frightened before—in Meryton with Collins and Wickham, and in the woods as they had heard the plan to poison her father—but those times were nothing compared to the look of complete terror in her eyes right now. Recognition dawned in her eyes, and she froze.

What is he doing here? she thought, but cared not. He was here and in her heart, she knew that meant everything was going to be all right. She had to make him aware of what was going on, but the first priority was to hide the both of them; she could not allow the men to find them, for she knew what would happen. He would try to protect her and end up being injured… or worse! She had recognized the look in Wickham's eyes in Meryton, and she did not want him anywhere near Darcy while he was carrying a gun!

Darcy looked more closely at her and was horrified by what he saw. She had scratches all over her skin, her arm and face were bleeding, and she had dirt everywhere. Her hair had mostly escaped from its pins and was in disarray, her dress was torn in several places, and she could barely breathe from running. *What has happened to my Elizabeth?*

Elizabeth saw Darcy's eyes travel over her person. She could not imagine what she looked like, but she knew it could not be good based upon the expression of alarm that overtook his features. When he opened his mouth, she was afraid he would exclaim loudly due to seeing her condition and give their location away. She put her hand over his mouth and shushed him. She then pushed herself away from him and got up off the ground; moving her hand in a gesture for him to get up. Darcy righted himself while Elizabeth looked around wildly at the landscape, trying to find a place to hide.

She knew she was ahead of Wickham and the other men, but she could not discern how far! For now, it was *her* job to get them to safety since he had absolutely no idea what was happening. She saw a thick clump of large bushes a little way down the path, grabbed Darcy's hand and began to pull him along. He was not following fast enough for her liking, so she moved behind and pushed him into the bushes, and then followed closely behind him. Finally catching her breath enough to speak, she managed to say in a soft voice, "We must hide!"

She stopped when she felt they were securely hidden. Darcy was becoming more and more concerned and was about to ask her to explain what was going on when she covered his mouth again. Elizabeth stood up on her toes and whispered close to his ear, "I will explain, but please, for now, just hold me and be quiet."

She shocked even herself with her forwardness, but she decided that she did not care about propriety at the moment; she needed to feel the safe warmth of his embrace. Elizabeth wrapped her arms around him and buried her face in his chest. His arms came up around her, holding her gently, and he began to run his hand along her back as his other hand caressed her hair.

Darcy's thoughts were careening wildly, envisioning how Elizabeth had come to be in this state and just what she needed to hide from. Judging by her appearance, he could not help but assume the worst. Why had he not stopped the coach and rushed to her side when he had perceived her earlier in the meadow? Elizabeth would be safe right now had he followed his heart when he had first seen her!

He had to force himself to think of other things. Elizabeth needed him now, and he could not fail her again. Darcy concentrated on the feel of her in his arms, the way her arms were wrapped around him, listening to the rhythm of her breaths becoming slow and steady. He remembered how she had *asked* to be held by him. Her trembling was subsiding, and she was beginning to relax, letting her body fall into him.

His hand touched her face, and he moved away a bit to look into her eyes. Darcy's fingers caressed her cheek and turned her face up to his. His eyes took her in; even now she was the most beautiful thing he had ever seen! His eyes rested on her lips.

Elizabeth looked up into his eyes and what she saw made her breath catch. *He loves me!* She was beginning to smile, but then suddenly she stiffened, and her eyes were filled with fear again. Elizabeth's heightened state of anxiety for such a prolonged period of time allowed her to hear their voices before he did, and she pulled herself closer to Darcy.

At first, he was confused and worried that he had frightened her… but then Darcy heard them. His muscles coiled instinctively, readying for a fight. His mind raced, and all his senses were clear. He planned to put his body between her and these men if they found their hiding place, but he did not want to move and call attention to them. Nobody would hurt her again unless they killed him first.

Darcy's blood turned to ice in his veins, and his arms tightened around Elizabeth as he recognized one of the voices. *Wickham! What is he doing here? What has he done to my Elizabeth? I will kill him if he has hurt her, I swear!* Elizabeth clung tighter to him in turn.

The men passed by without noticing them, and Elizabeth and Darcy both let go of the breaths they had been holding as the men passed closest to them. They waited in silence until they were sure the men were out of hearing range, and Darcy resumed his caresses.

Once the danger had passed, Elizabeth relaxed into Darcy's arms and began to pay more attention to *him*. She had wrapped her arms around him within his frock coat, and she could feel his muscles move through his waistcoat—and realized this was quite a pleasant position to be in. She had not realized he had wrapped her within his greatcoat, in all probability to help hide her light brown dress from standing out within the dark bushes. It was as if they were wrapped in a world of their own. Her ear was pressed to his heart, and she could hear its rhythm slowing from one of a frantic pace. She filled her lungs with his scent of musk and cloves. Though she could have remained this way all day, she realized there were some things which must be said. What must he be thinking of her?

Though not willing to give up his embrace completely, Elizabeth leaned away from Darcy a bit and looked into his eyes as she said softly, "I know not why you are here, but I must say that I am thankful that you are! One would think by now that I would be more accustomed to stumbling across Wickham involved in suspicious activities in the woods!" she laughed a little without mirth. "Though it might have been the other five men and all the guns which unnerved me today."

Darcy's eyes widened at her statement, and he wanted to hear more about this, but he needed to know something else first. "Then, he… they did not hurt you?"

Elizabeth knew exactly what he meant and gave him a little reassuring smile. "No, I was running blindly for a while—not paying much attention to what was in front of me except to be conscious of running in the direction of Rosings, but mostly my attention was on who was *behind* me. I was caught by some thorn bushes when I hid to catch my breath and tripped over a few roots along the way. I cannot imagine what I must look like!" Her hand went up automatically to smooth her hair, but when she realized it would do no good, she laughed a bit and returned it to its former position around his waist. Afraid she might never have this chance again, she fully intended to take advantage of the position in which she found herself.

He said, "Elizabeth, even in this state, you are the most beautiful woman I have ever seen!" Darcy coloured.

Elizabeth coloured as well, but flashed him a dazzling smile. "I thank you, Sir Knight! You have saved me yet again." She cocked her head to one side. "One day you shall have to explain to me just *how* you know about that." Darcy's colour deepened, and Elizabeth continued, "But I think the more pressing matter is what has happened in these woods today, and some other strange goings on I have witnessed since I have come to Kent."

Darcy smiled as he realized that Elizabeth had leaves, twigs, and grass stuck in her hair as well as several pins which were no longer doing their duty. "Tell me your tale while I make an effort to rid your hair of the elements of nature," he said while picking out a twig with a leaf still attached and showing it to her.

She stifled a giggle, and then said quietly, "I must look the part of the Dryad for certain!" Then her countenance turned serious. "I do think we first should remove ourselves from Wickham's path between Hunsford and the cabin. I heard them say they were going to speak to Mr. Collins, and I know Mr. Collins is not at home today. Come, let us go to a place which, according to my sources, not many others seem to know of. It is well out of the way of their return. I think I could use a face washing as well!"

Darcy peered out from the bushes to make sure they were alone, and then helped Elizabeth out into the path, holding back some branches as best he could. "If that is the case, then let us begin walking, and you can tell me about the cabin and the men with guns." Then he gave her a scolding look. "But first, I would like to know why you are here staying with Mr. Collins, of all people!"

Elizabeth explained that after much consideration, her father and she did not feel that Mr. Collins knew about the poisoning. "And we both felt that now Mr. Collins is married, he would not be as… forward in his attentions toward me as he had been in the past." Elizabeth coloured as she admitted, "I have taken the precaution of locking my bedchamber door, sir, and devising a way of telling whether someone has been in my room or disturbed my personal items." With that confession, her colour deepened as she continued, "But it has not appeared to have been necessary.

"I dare say if I was not so concerned about Charlotte, I would not have come. Her letters showed that she was lonely and unhappy, though she attempted to hide it. I did not wish to deny her the visit of a friend in a new place. But once I arrived… Mr. Darcy, there is more to Charlotte's state than loneliness and being discontent with her situation. There are brief moments where I catch a look that leads me to believe that Charlotte is *afraid*! I could not make sense of it at all, but now that I see Wickham and the other men here, it does make me think that it has something to do with them and whatever it is that Mr. Collins and Wickham are involved in."

Elizabeth then told him all that she had seen and heard at the cabin, and she shared the details of Mr. Collins's odd behaviour at Hunsford the afternoon before, and that she now thought that the two were connected.

When she finished imparting her information, they walked in silence for a little while, and then Elizabeth stopped and turned to face him. "Mr. Darcy, I must ask you… do you know why Mr. Bingley has left Netherfield?"

Darcy's surprise was obvious. "I had no idea that Bingley had left Hertfordshire. Other than that he had planned on going to Scarborough during the Christmas holiday to visit his relatives, his plans were to be staying at Netherfield." Suddenly embarrassed, thinking of the reasons *why* he had no idea of Bingley's current location, he continued, "I had received a letter from Bingley, but I have been…" he blushed deeply and cleared his throat, "*indisposed* for quite a while. I have only just… regained some part of my former… *constitution* before leaving London." Darcy faltered awkwardly. "I came to Rosings with Colonel Fitzwilliam for our annual visit to our aunt. I never did read Bingley's letter, though I had assumed it was an announcement... May I be so bold as to ask—did your sister not receive an offer from Bingley before he left?"

Concerned and confused, Elizabeth answered, "I am sorry to hear you were not well, sir, and glad to know you are much improved. To answer your question, my sister is not engaged. Mr. Bingley left three days after the ball. I will be honest, Mr. Darcy… Miss Bingley wrote to Jane that

Mr. Bingley was attached to your sister, implying they would soon marry, and the Bingleys would not be returning to Netherfield."

"My *sister*? Miss Bingley wrote that Charles Bingley and *my* sister… Georgiana?" When Elizabeth nodded, he said, "There has never been, nor will there ever be, an attachment between them. While they do care for each other, their feelings are almost as brother and sister. I do not understand where Miss Bingley would get such an idea. Though it may be one of Miss Bingley's *wishes*, that does not make it true. It is disturbing to me that she should pass along such false information to you and your sister, and involving *my* sister in her deception! I cannot begin to imagine what she must have told Bingley to get him to leave. I will do my best to look into the entire matter when I return to London."

"Thank you, Mr. Darcy," she said with a dazzling smile. "You may be assured of our discretion, sir. Neither of us would ever repeat what Miss Bingley has asserted."

His eyes softened. "I already knew that you could be trusted, Miss Elizabeth."

Darcy followed Elizabeth as she turned off the path they had been following and moved through some bushes into the meadow where she usually met Johnny and Abe.

He looked around at the beautiful meadow filled with spring crocuses, blue bells, snow drops, and other early spring flowers and smiled. "How do you find these places?"

"Ah, we Dryads know all the beautiful sights to see in the woods! But this place is not mine alone. I share it with good friends."

She approached the pond, sat on the shore, and began to wash the mud off her arms. "I do not believe sitting in the dirt will make my dress much worse." Elizabeth smiled. Darcy was not able to tear his eyes away and was amazed at how such a simple sight could stir him so.

When she was finished, he offered her his handkerchief to dry her arms, and then took it back. "I will need this to cleanse the scratches on your face. But first, I think we should remove the leaves and twigs from your hair and pin it back so that I may clean the dirt away more easily."

Elizabeth blushed and put her hands on her cheeks. "Oh! I had forgotten! But I have no mirror, sir; you will have rid my hair of nature for me." She searched her hair for any remaining pins and plucked out anything else she could find while walking to a nearby rock to sit upon it.

Darcy stood behind her—running his hands through her hair was something he had been dreaming about since the moment he saw her, her hair down, in the hallway at Netherfield. As she removed the pins, her chestnut brown curls tumbled down her back and its highlights glistened in the sun. He tried his best to concentrate on the leaves and twigs and not on Elizabeth or her hair, attempting to identify the plant each came from—but it was impossible to achieve. When he was finished intently removing the leaves, he ran his fingers through her locks with the excuse of needing to work out any knots that might have remained before she pinned it up again. It was like no other sensation… it was liquid silk flowing through his fingers. Mesmerized, he proceeded carefully, precisely, and thoroughly, and all the while his ardor rose to a level higher than he had ever previously had to suffer. When he could no longer endure this pleasant but torturous employment, he thought, *How am I to face her just now?*

Elizabeth's voice was husky when she asked, "Thank you, Mr. Darcy. May I pin it up now?"

He had been trying not to look at her before, but now his eyes moved down her figure and he noticed her breath had quickened considerably, and her skin was flushed. Darcy closed his eyes at the question of whether his almost selfish ministrations could have affected her as it had him. It was absolutely impossible for him to look in her eyes just then. If the look there was anything like it had been in the hall after the ball at Netherfield just before they said goodbye… the memory of the passion in her eyes had tortured him almost constantly since November, and he did not know what he would do if he saw *that look* just now!

He cleared his throat. "Yes," he croaked, and he walked away to pace in the meadow behind her while she arranged her hair as best she could without a mirror. He did not return until he was certain he could behave properly.

When he came back to the rock, *The Mask* was in place. Upon seeing his expression, Elizabeth's speculation on what caused the change in his countenance was quite close to the truth, and she was delighted.

"What?" he asked a bit gruffly.

"Oh, nothing!" Elizabeth giggled a little before stifling it. It was a glorious feeling to realize he was as attracted to her as she was to him.

Darcy took off his greatcoat and handed it to her, saying in a commanding voice, "You will need this to protect your dress from getting wet while I wash the dirt from the scratches." He walked to the pond to wet his handkerchief as Elizabeth donned his greatcoat, still suppressing a smile.

The last thing I need right now is Elizabeth in a wet dress! He groaned inwardly when the thought conjured up an image that almost sent Darcy off to pace again. He splashed his face with water a few times before dampening the handkerchief and returning to Elizabeth.

The Mask remained upon his face as he gently washed her face, refusing to look into her eyes. He ground his teeth as he forced himself to concentrate on washing the mud from the scrapes, so he did not notice her increased colour or rate of breath. But when her hand touched his, he met her eyes and his breath caught. The chance of maintaining his control was beyond hopeless when he saw *that look* in her eyes. *The Mask* fell away, and Darcy began to lean toward her—but just before his lips met hers, Elizabeth seemed to pull away from him. In the next instant, someone else was pushing between them.

Johnny began slamming his fists into Darcy's chest, forcing a confused Darcy to back away from Elizabeth. Abe caught up a moment later and pushed the entangled pair into the pond. When his head emerged from the water, Abe yelled, "Run, Miss Lizzy, run!"

After an instant of shock, Elizabeth recovered and cried, "Johnny! Abe! This is *my good friend*, Mr. Darcy."

Darcy stood up, his lower half still submerged in the pond. *What excellent timing! I deserved a dip in the pond for what I was thinking just then!* Whether he was angrier at himself for losing control or at the boys for interrupting what was about to happen, he would never know.

Elizabeth bit her lip to stifle a laugh at the sight of Mr. Darcy, soaking wet, wearing a cross expression upon his face. Her efforts were almost completely nullified when he repeatedly slipped and fell while labouring to exit the pond. "The bottom is slippery!" an abashed Darcy explained.

Elizabeth had to bite down harder upon her lip to keep from laughing aloud as she nodded and walked toward the shore, holding out her hand. "Would you like some help?"

Considering the difference in their weight, the likelihood of his pulling her into the pond with him was greater than that of her pulling him out of the water. Though for the slightest instant he was tempted, the gentleman in him knew if that happened, he certainly would be completely undone—and so he waved her off.

Both boys were already standing on the shore, bracing themselves for the worst of consequences.

Once Darcy was standing on dry land, he removed his coat saying, "Excuse me, Miss Elizabeth, but this coat is now too heavy with water to wear any longer" and began wringing it out. Assuming Mr. Darcy was distracted by the task, Elizabeth's gaze briefly shifted down the length of his body as she appraised the way his wet clothing clung. At Darcy's gasp, their eyes locked; her approving thoughts were apparent for a fleeting moment before she regained control over her features. If one had made the attempt, it would have been difficult to determine whose resulting blush was a deeper crimson.

Removing his greatcoat, Elizabeth said, "Mr. Darcy, I do believe that you have more of a need of your greatcoat than I." As he took the coat, he saw that Elizabeth's eyes were full of amusement. Darcy turned away from the group to don the greatcoat.

Surprising even Elizabeth, as Darcy turned back to the group, his dimples were showing, and his laughter began to resonate throughout the meadow. It was infectious—the boys began to laugh in relief, and Elizabeth was delighted that she no longer had to stifle her natural tendency toward enduring difficult situations by finding some measure of amusement in them.

After the laughter settled down, a blushing Abe spoke up, "I'm sorry, Mr. Darcy! We met some men in the woods and thought you were one of *them* bothering Miss Lizzy."

"If that is the case, there is no need for apologies! It is admirable that you are such brave boys who would fight for Miss Elizabeth's honour. I cannot express how grateful I am to know that you would do so," Darcy said with a bow to the boys, and then smiled at Elizabeth. "I assume these are the good friends with whom you share this beautiful meadow?"

Elizabeth made proper introductions, or as proper as could be done when one is introducing three dripping wet young men, two of whom she did not even know by surname. It was then that she noticed a mark on Johnny's cheek. "Johnny, have you been injured during your adventure in the pond?"

Johnny eyes moved to the ground, turmoil passing over his features. He remained quiet for several moments, and then answered with more emotion than she had ever heard from him, "No, 'twas the Wickedman who did it!"

"The Wickedman?" A flash of understanding made Elizabeth gasp. "Wickham? Did Mr. Wickham do this to you, Johnny?"

Johnny nodded the affirmative.

"Why would Wickham hit you?" Darcy's colour was rising, in outrage this time.

"No reason… he always does, anytime he comes across me," Johnny replied angrily. Abe nodded and rubbed his own chin.

"He is here often then?" Darcy asked.

Johnny looked to Abe as if to ask permission to speak on the subject. "Abe, I trust Miss Lizzy, and she trusts Mr. Darcy."

Abe looked to Elizabeth. "Isn't he staying with Lady de Bourgh? Yet you *trust* him?"

Elizabeth was about to answer, but Johnny had already begun, "I didn't recognize him when we got to the meadow, but I've been here two years and seen Mr. Darcy twice before. He's not the same as *her*."

Abe was thoughtful for a minute or two. It was obvious by the change in his countenance that he had decided to trust Elizabeth and Darcy. Abe said to Johnny, "Then maybe he can help. This has gone too far!" Turning to Darcy, he continued, "Wickham is here every few weeks. Whenever a ship comes in, they come. They made my father work for them, too."

"Ship? Do you mean the crates and barrels the men were unloading into the cabin in the woods today came off a ship?" Elizabeth asked.

"Yes. I worked with them before the man who watched Johnny was needed somewheres else. The things they sell in England come here first, but some of it stays on board to go to America. Then they bring more from America here. Some goes to France."

Darcy rubbed his chin, deep in thought. "Where do the shipments come from originally?"

"India," Johnny replied.

Both Elizabeth and Darcy understood the meaning of this at the same time.

“India!” Elizabeth repeated.

Darcy’s blood turned to ice. “They take some of it to France and America? Is that the merchandise stored under the floors of the ship?” Abe nodded.

Darcy looked to Elizabeth, whose eyes were wide. “The saltpetre! Is not saltpetre used to make gunpowder?”

Not surprised that she would have knowledge of that, Darcy nodded.

Abe said, “Yes, my father says they are stockpiling it in America.”

Elizabeth continued, “That is treason! They will use it to kill British troops!”

“Supplying the Americans is not treason—yet. We are not at war, though it looks as if we will be soon. But you are correct; supplying it to the French *is* treason!” Darcy’s expression turned bleak. “I must tell Richard, his father, and Lady Catherine. We must put a stop to what is happening on our lands.”

“You mean Lady Catherine de Bourgh, sir?” Abe asked. Darcy nodded.

“Lady de Bourgh knows, Mr. Darcy. She bosses most of us. Wickham, Collins and some of the others work with her.”

Darcy’s eyes widened as he raked his hand through his hair and began to pace.

“How are you under her control, Abe?” Elizabeth inquired.

A small, mirthless laugh escaped Abe’s lips. “She knows something about us or is holding someone we care about—sometimes both. Johnny is here to force his great-grandfather to do what she wanted after he refused. I don’t know what she wants him to do. With my father and me it was my sister… what Wickham done to her!” Darcy’s pacing stopped abruptly, and Abe realized what he just said and blushed. “Excuse me, Miss Lizzy; I shouldn’t have said that in front of a lady!”

After Elizabeth murmured her understanding, Abe continued, “Lady de Bourgh found out and took my sister somewheres and said she was ‘safe’; I don’t know where. At first we were thinking she was kind, but now if we don’t do what she says… well, I don’t know what will happen.

My father don't wanna tell me." Abe's air turned worried. "I hope my father and sister will forgive me for what I've said today, but I can't allow her to keep on doing this to people. It's not right!"

They spoke for a little while longer before Elizabeth urged, "It is getting late. I should like to get to Hunsford to change my dress before Mr. and Mrs. Collins return, to avoid questions about the condition of my attire, and you all should depart as well. If we are not careful, we will all be missed."

"Wickham should be on his way back to the cabin if Collins isn't there, but we know a way to the parsonage and Rosings where we won't see Wickham again," said Johnny.

"Good. Let us be off." Darcy said. As they followed the boys, Darcy was lost in silent contemplation. Finally he said, "I do not like to think of your staying at Hunsford any longer, or even in this area. I shall take you away from here tonight!"

"I have been quite safe at Hunsford for almost three weeks, sir. I cannot think of an excuse to leave so abruptly tonight without raising suspicion. My departure will have to wait until the morning at the very earliest, Mr. Darcy. I will stay in the house, with my door locked if necessary!" Elizabeth took his offered arm. "Abe mentioned that the men stay at the cabin for a night or two after making a delivery; there is no need to worry that Wickham will be at Hunsford." Elizabeth turned thoughtful for a few moments before saying, "I do not like to think of leaving Charlotte here when I go, Mr. Darcy."

"No, I supposed you would not. I have been making plans, Miss Elizabeth. If Mrs. Collins is willing, we can take her with us when we leave. This business must come to an end very soon. Colonel Fitzwilliam and I will take Mrs. Collins and you to the Gardiners' tomorrow and speak to the earl and also to Fitzwilliam's commanding officer to see what we can do. Johnny and Abe can stay at Darcy House with me. I am thankful that my sister removed to Pemberley when I departed London this morning. She need not be involved with any of this."

"I think I should look under the flooring in the sitting room before we leave, Mr. Darcy. Mr. Collins was sorting through papers when I saw him." She arched an eyebrow. "A brief act of espionage may provide the evidence you shall need to convince the authorities. Tonight Mr. and Mrs. Collins are scheduled to attend dinner at Rosings, though I am *not* invited. The only servant on duty is the cook, and I intend on having a severe headache and retiring early, giving her permission to have the evening off."

"You do have a sly mind, Miss Elizabeth! I do believe that I, too, must miss dinner this evening for I have some urgent business to attend to which cannot be delayed, not even for an hour." Darcy returned her brilliant smile. *How I love you, Elizabeth!*

Chapter 36

~Rosings Park

After seeing Elizabeth safely to Hunsford and observing the prearranged signal from the window informing him that Wickham was not inside, Darcy returned to his rooms at Rosings through the servants' corridors so that his aunt and cousins would not see the condition of his clothing. Upon arriving at his chamber, he found a note from Richard. While Darcy was out, Richard had received an express from his regiment requesting his immediate return to London. He had borrowed a horse from Lady Catherine and departed post-haste.

Darcy was disappointed to have missed Richard, but since he would be leaving the next day with Elizabeth and Mrs. Collins, he would be able to speak to him upon their return to London.

After a bath, Darcy joined Lady Catherine and his cousin for tea. He would no longer call her his "aunt" out of the revulsion that he felt for her dishonest schemes. "Lady Catherine, I must inform you that I will not be staying at Rosings as long as I had thought. I have much business in Town to attend to and must return on the morrow. I have an appointment with your steward after tea today and will then need to attend to some business which cannot be delayed; therefore, I will not be at dinner this evening. Tomorrow I will finish my business with your steward and quit Rosings immediately following our meeting."

Lady Catherine was enraged. "First you tell me that you must greatly reduce your visit to three nights, now you tell me that you will stay but one? I demand to know the details of your business so that *I* may decide whether it is important enough for you to abandon your duty to your family."

Darcy's eyes tightened to slits. "I have stated that I will do *as I have promised* and meet with the steward to review the accounts. This is *all* I owe to my cousin Anne, Lady Catherine. You have no need to know the details of my business nor will I divulge that information."

"I am almost the nearest relation you have in the world and am entitled to know all your dearest concerns, Nephew. After all I have done for you these many years, you maintain that you owe me nothing more than reviewing the accounts? You refuse to spend time with your aunt and cousin? Is nothing due to me on that score? Do you forget all that you owe to Anne? It is unfair to ignore her as you plan to do. I insist that you will attend dinner tonight at the very least."

Fully aware that she only intended to manipulate him into spending more time in Anne's company, Darcy answered, "Lady Catherine, I am unable to attend dinner. I am devoting time to you and my cousin at present."

"It is my wish that you become reacquainted with my parson and his wife, Mr. and Mrs. Collins, and so I have invited them to dinner as well."

Darcy tried to remain detached, but his temper was rising. "I understood that Mr. Collins has a guest staying at Hunsford. May I ask why a gentleman's daughter was so obviously slighted by you and excluded from the invitation?"

Lady Catherine smirked. "She is a young woman of inferior birth, of no importance in the world! True, she is a gentleman's daughter. But who is her mother? Who are her uncles and aunts? Do not imagine me ignorant of their condition—they are tradesmen, all! And I have heard stories of her, Nephew. She is a hoyden and a Jezebel! Her presence in this house would pollute the shades of Rosings!"

Becoming enraged, Darcy stood and boomed, "Enough, *Madam*! I have been acquainted with Miss Elizabeth Bennet for many months now, and I can assure you that you are completely in error in your opinion of her. Since I know it will do no good to discuss the matter, I refuse to expend my energy upon it, but I will not allow you to insult her in any manner!"

Darcy had never raised his voice to her before! Beginning to panic at his obvious regard for Elizabeth Bennet, Lady Catherine raised her voice further. "Nephew, you have been intended for Anne since she was in her cradle—it was the favourite wish of your mother! You have not asked her to marry you as of yet, but you *will* before you quit Rosings on this visit!" Lady Catherine's crimson flush of anger continued to deepen throughout her speech. "You are formed for each other… descended, on the maternal side, from the same noble line, and, on the father's, from respectable, honourable, and ancient—though untitled—families. Your fortune on both sides is splendid. You are destined for each other by the voice of every member of your respective houses, and nothing is to divide you!"

Throughout her speech, her words replayed in Darcy's memory…but he could not place it. By now he was incensed. "Anne and I have discussed the subject of marriage on several occasions throughout the years, and I will have you know that neither Anne nor I have any wish to marry—at least not each other. In marrying Anne, I would make us both *unhappy*, and neither of us wishes to spend our lives in such a manner."

Lady Catherine tried to interrupt, but Darcy would not allow it. "Lady Catherine! After all these years, I now have it in my mother's own words that she wished me to marry for love, not for status or wealth. She bade me to be happily married, and she also wrote that my father's wishes concurred with her own. My mother actually stated that she had no wish for Anne and me to marry unless we were in love with each other!" Darcy's voice boomed, "I will have you know I am now aware of the *lies* you have told me for the past sixteen years, madam! Whether you insist upon demanding that we marry is your choice, but I will not remain in your presence if you do continue this charade!"

Lady Catherine's anger was evident as she screeched, "You *will* marry Anne and unite these two great estates! I have not been in the habit of brooking disappointment! You will do as I say because honour, decorum, prudence, and interest demand it. If you willfully act against my inclinations, you and your sister will be censured, slighted, and despised by everyone connected with you. You both will be a disgrace; your name will never even be mentioned by any of us."

Darcy countered, "Madam, I am a child no longer; be convinced I answer to no one—including you. I am my own man. You have attempted to force your will upon me, but the completion of your plans depends on me, and I will not be influenced by *you* ever again, Lady Catherine! You may depend upon it!"

"You refuse, then, to oblige me. You refuse to obey the claims of duty, honour, and gratitude. You are determined to ruin yourself and your sister in the opinion of all your friends, and make both of you the contempt of the world!"

Darcy gasped quietly when suddenly his mind turned to the dream he had of his mother while at Netherfield. He now realized why he was so confused in the dream… it was *not* his mother's voice at all, it had been Lady Catherine's voice in the dream saying many of the same words that she was saying now—those words that she had spoken throughout the years signifying why he should marry his cousin Anne and not someone else!

Using his "Master of Pemberley" voice, Darcy announced, "I will summarize what I have declared over the past few minutes and then will no longer discuss any of this, Madam. I will *not* give you the details of my business. I will *not* be attending dinner this evening. I *will* be leaving in the morning after I have completed reviewing the ledgers with your steward as I have promised to do for my *cousin's* sake.

"You should not expect anything further from me than what I have stated here today, *Lady* Catherine. Ever! I must warn you that you have interfered in my life for far too long. I now know of it, and I will not allow it to continue! When I leave Rosings tomorrow, it will be the last time you will lay eyes upon me, and you will *not* be permitted into the presence of my sister again, nor will you be allowed to correspond with her."

Darcy took a deep breath attempting to cool his ire. Turning to Anne, he bowed and said, "I do hope that I have not upset you, Cousin Anne. Know that I wish you health and happiness. *You* are welcome at Darcy House or Pemberley at any time to visit… *alone*."

Anne nodded. Darcy turned and walked toward the door.

Lady Catherine rose and followed him. "You pay no regard to the wishes of all your friends. You are lost to every feeling of propriety and delicacy. I am shocked and astonished! Is this to be endured? It must not, shall not be!"

Turning back to Lady Catherine, Darcy concluded, "If any of what I have said displeases you, so be it, *Madam*. My conviction will never recede. Excuse me; I have an appointment to begin reviewing the ledgers." Darcy left the room, ignoring his aunt's continued ranting.

~*~*~*~*~*~*~*~*~*~*~*~*

~Hunsford Cottage

Darcy made good time in reviewing most of Rosings' books, and then informed the steward that he had business to attend to and would meet him at an early hour in the morning. He surreptitiously left Rosings using the servants' entrance and walked through the woods to Hunsford Cottage along the path that Johnny and Abe had shown him the previous day. Darcy watched Mr. and Mrs. Collins leave the building and walk towards Rosings, and then saw the cook leave as well before approaching the house. As they had arranged earlier, Elizabeth opened the door to the kitchen, and he slipped inside.

Darcy was standing in the kitchen looking at Elizabeth, the room barely lit by a dying fire. *In the dimmed light she is even more beautiful...*

After having experienced the torture of being separated from her for four months, he never wished to leave her side again. This was the woman who drove him to distraction... who could drive all reason from his mind with one look from those bewitching eyes or a trace of her scent as she passed him... whose touch reached his soul... who he had held in his arms today. She was so close and looking at him in such a way that made his heart race and his breath quicken. As his ardor was rising, he suddenly recollected that he was *completely alone* in the house with this beautiful, soft, enchanting creature that had become the primary reason for his existence.

As he was about to take a step toward her, Darcy's protective nature tugged at his conscience. *This is the worst breach of propriety I have ever made, and if found out, I could be responsible for damaging Elizabeth's reputation. I have vowed to protect her, not ruin her! Perhaps I should leave? No, she is determined to find something to show the General, and I will not allow her to do it alone. We must do this together and had best finish it quickly before we are discovered.*

Elizabeth smiled with a familiar glint in her eyes that could lead to his undoing in any state of mind, let alone the one he was experiencing just now. "Good evening, Mr. Darcy."

Darcy blinked a few times before he was able to think. Needing a distraction, he said, "I did not speak to Richard as of yet; it must wait until tomorrow. Before I returned to the house, he had departed due to a summons from his regiment."

"Let us get to work so that we have information for his commanding officer, shall we?" Elizabeth said as she turned to leave the room.

Yes, ***work****! That is why I am here. I must leave as soon as possible! I can watch the house from outside until Mr. and Mrs. Collins return,* he reminded himself as he followed her from the room.

Once in the sitting room, she showed him which chair he should move. As he did so, she rolled up the carpet, which revealed the hatch door. Underneath was a storage area containing a few barrels and crates along with two metal boxes like the one Elizabeth had observed Mr. Collins rummaging through the previous day. Uncertain as to how much time it would take, Darcy lifted out both boxes, and they each began to search through one, informing each other as to what they found as they went along.

One box was filled with ledgers and ships' manifests for the Bradstowe Company indicating goods brought from India to England. There was a ledger for silk, cotton, and indigo dye from India, and a separate ledger for the saltpetre from "Bradstowe Mine."

The other box held the same accounting for ships sailing from England to America. While on British shores, some of the saltpetre did indeed remain on the ships as its destination was America, the rest was unloaded in England. They would load the ships with British goods to trade at the Isles of Scilly off the coast of Cornwall and then sail across the Atlantic to America with the remainder, returning to England with tobacco and spirits. On the return trip, they stopped again at the Isles of Scilly before unloading the remainder of their cargo in England.

It seemed they had several ships making these voyages in a staggered fashion so that there was a new shipment arriving in England every three months.

Guinea boats at home were running goods nearly weekly to and from France; when they had saltpetre, they would deliver that to France. It seemed that when they did not have saltpetre shipments to disperse, they would pay in gold for brandy, wine, and lace.

Elizabeth glanced at the clock. "Mr. Darcy! Look at the time! It is late—we must hurry!"

"I will take a few of the ships manifests to show to the General when we reach London… some older ones so that the loss is less likely to be detected. That should be enough to begin an investigation. Knowing where the records are hidden, they can easily find the rest, as long as nobody suspects we have found them." Darcy folded a few pages from each box and placed them in a pocket inside his coat.

The fire was dying as they returned the boxes into the compartment and the room to its prior condition.

Darcy suddenly became overwhelmed with all they had found out. He shuddered and closed his eyes. An expression of pain consumed his countenance.

Elizabeth could not stop herself from gently taking his face between her hands. His eyes opened, and she whispered, "Please stop… others are culpable, not you. You had no reason to suspect that she would be involved in such matters."

Darcy sighed as the warmth of her touch, and the love in her eyes flowed like water through his body and soul. He bent down, placing his forehead to hers and his hands upon her shoulders. As he closed his eyes again he whispered, "Elizabeth," in a way that made her heart sing.

They drew comfort from the intimacy of the moment as all the tension from the past day drained away. Opening his eyes, he saw that hers remained closed. She was such an incredible woman; she knew just what he needed to hear without his ever having to ask a question. She was truly half of his "self." Elizabeth was everything!

He ached to gaze into her eyes to see if he could read her thoughts there. As Darcy pulled his head back slightly, she opened them. His gaze drifted across her features and rested on her lips. His eyes darted to hers seeking permission, and his breath caught at the passion he found there.

Darcy's hands slowly moved from her shoulders to her cheeks, his fingers caressing her skin as they passed. Elizabeth's hands drifted to his chest. Moving ever so slowly, he leaned closer to kiss her.

"COUSIN ELIZABETH!" Mr. Collins shrieked.

Elizabeth and Darcy jumped away from each other and turned toward the door to see Mr. and Mrs. Collins standing in the open doorway. Mr. Collins rushed across the room and took Elizabeth by the arm, pulling her away from Darcy so roughly that Elizabeth cried out.

Darcy, incensed at his presumptuous behaviour, immediately stepped between Mr. Collins and Elizabeth, grabbing hold of Mr. Collins's arm. Darcy towered over Mr. Collins and roared, "Remove your hand! You do *not* wish for me to remove it for you!"

Mr. Collins released her and jumped back a step. "Cousin Elizabeth!" Mr. Collins cried as he peered around Darcy's form, "Lady Catherine warned me about your being a harlot! Alone in a house with a man—with Lady Catherine's nephew! You have lured him in!" Mr. Collins gasped and his eyes widened. "You are his mistress!"

Darcy heard Elizabeth gasp behind him. His thoughts moved quickly—the only way he could salvage her reputation… a private audience with Elizabeth would be acceptable only if he was making an offer of marriage. Had they had only a few more uninterrupted minutes, he *would* have asked her! Would she have accepted? Brushing his doubts aside, Darcy knew he had to save her.

"Mr. Collins! You will apologize for injuring *and* insulting my fiancée immediately!" Darcy boomed in his "Master of Pemberley" voice. "I came here this evening to propose marriage to Miss Elizabeth, and she had accepted me only a moment before you entered."

Darcy felt Elizabeth place her hand on his arm, wondering what she meant by it.

This was not what she deserved! Oh, how he wished he could turn around and see the look in Elizabeth's eyes at this moment, but he had to keep his attention on Mr. Collins! Would she be angry at him, despise him, for saying what he did?

Mr. Collins gasped loudly and stood completely stunned for several moments. "That is impossible! You cannot be betrothed to Cousin Elizabeth; you are already betrothed to Miss Anne de Bourgh!"

Darcy scowled. "Mr. Collins, no matter what Lady Catherine has led anyone to believe—including herself—I *am* not, I never *have* been, and I never *shall* be betrothed to my cousin."

Lady Catherine will blame me! I was supposed to watch Cousin Elizabeth, not allow her to trap him under my own roof! Mr. Collins was becoming more upset by the moment. "Lady Catherine will be most seriously displeased with this turn of events, sir!"

"Then she need not attend our wedding." Taking a step closer to the dumbfounded parson, Darcy almost growled, "I have yet to hear your apology, Mr. Collins!"

Mr. Collins moved away and began pacing. He repeatedly wiped the sweat from his brow with his handkerchief, and tried to show some courage that might be reported back to Lady Catherine. His words were bold, but his voice was trembling. "That is correct, and you will not, Mr. Darcy. She has trapped you into this betrothal when you are promised to someone else! You must return to Rosings and never again step foot in

Hunsford while my cousin remains here. I will not allow clandestine meetings to take place under the parsonage roof! You will tell Lady Catherine about this when you return to Rosings!"

"I will not be announcing the engagement to anyone until I have gained consent from Mr. Bennet." Darcy moved towards Mr. Collins again. "You *will* apologize to Miss Elizabeth! NOW, Mr. Collins!"

"I will do so unwillingly!" Mr. Collins cowered and said, "I apologize, Cousin Elizabeth." Then he scurried to the front door and held it open for Darcy, visibly trembling. "This is my house, and you must leave at once, Mr. Darcy."

Darcy turned around to face Elizabeth, blocking her from Mr. Collins's view. He could not decipher the look in her eyes at all, and it made his stomach lurch. He needed more time with her just now and could not have it! Taking her hands in his, he whispered, "I apologize for this. Meet me at dawn outside the parsonage to make plans to leave here." Elizabeth squeezed his hands in agreement.

As Darcy made his way toward the front door, he schooled his expression into such a menacing look, it made Mr. Collins shrink a step or two away. Darcy stopped and straightened to his full height. "You, sir, *will* treat my fiancée with respect and dignity. If I hear you have done otherwise, you *will* answer to me!" Darcy left the house.

Once Darcy had passed through the entranceway, Mr. Collins slammed the door behind him, walked straight over to Elizabeth, and began a lecture on the immorality of the situation. Elizabeth thought, *Such a hypocrite! Trying to put on a good show of being a parson! "Preachers say, 'Do as I say, not as I do.'" Indeed!*

After several minutes had passed, Mr. Collins suddenly stopped speaking to her, turned to Charlotte, then exclaimed, "I must go to Lady Catherine immediately!" and he scrambled to the door mumbling to himself all the way.

As Mr. Collins left the house, Charlotte rushed to the window to watch him stalk away. When she was sure he was heading for Rosings, she crossed the room and took Elizabeth's hands in hers.

"Oh, Lizzy, I am so happy for you! What wonderful news! I had always told you he loves you, did I not?"

Elizabeth's heart was aching. How she wished that she really was engaged to Darcy. This was too much! "I am sorry, Charlotte, but all is not what it seems to be. We are not engaged. Mr. Darcy used it as an excuse for his being found here by Mr. Collins. We need to speak quickly before Mr. Collins returns. Charlotte, there is foul business afoot at Rosings, and Mr. Collins is involved. I am afraid for you, my friend! You have been putting on a good face to convince me that you are content here, but I have seen your looks of fear when you think no one is watching." Elizabeth waited for Charlotte's reaction.

Charlotte walked to the window, obviously lost in deep thought. Several minutes passed before she sighed and met Elizabeth's eyes once again. "Yes, you are right, Lizzy. I cannot define it, but there is something not right here. I have had reason to be afraid at times. I almost wrote to tell you not to visit, but I knew that if I did that, you would have been determined to come."

Elizabeth laughed mirthlessly. "I would have at that, Charlotte. In fact, it might have forced me to come sooner, and I am glad that I did not, for we would not have had help! Dear friend, Mr. Darcy and I are leaving tomorrow, and I must insist that you come with us. Say what you like to your husband or say nothing at all, it matters not to me, but you must not reveal to him the true reason we are departing. We were here this evening searching for evidence for an investigation that is about to begin. Under the very chair behind you there is a compartment in the floor hiding documents. We will tell you more about it on our way to London tomorrow. I will meet Mr. Darcy at dawn to arrange the details and return to the house before Mr. Collins is awake. Johnny and Abe will come with us as well; they are being kept here under duress. You will come with us, will you not?"

Charlotte furrowed her brow. "I will. I cannot remain here any longer, no matter what vows I may be breaking by taking my leave. I believed myself to be marrying a respectable gentleman, but he is not." She paused. "Lizzy… I must apologize for not allowing you to speak about Mr. Collins at the ball. I did the same to Colonel Fitzwilliam. If I had listened to either of you…"

Elizabeth crossed the room and embraced her. "Hindsight is always clearer than foresight. I blame myself for not talking with you sooner, Charlotte. If Mr. Collins travelled to Lucas Lodge in the rain, then I could have as well. But we cannot change the past, and I hope that you can forgive me for not being more effective in my attempt to speak to you.

"Besides, if you had not married Mr. Collins, we would not have found out what is happening at Rosings and abroad. It may never have been found out! Many people are being harmed by this, Charlotte—some have died, and more will die if this is not stopped. Your presence here has put into motion that which will bring about the end to the suffering of many innocent people." Elizabeth took Charlotte's hands in hers and squeezed them.

Charlotte's eyes opened wide. "Well! I will patiently await your explanation, Lizzy. Meanwhile, we had better retire to bed before Mr. Collins returns from seeing Lady Catherine. Lizzy… I do fear her reaction to your supposed 'engagement.' Not a day has passed that she has not mentioned her plans for Miss Anne to marry Mr. Darcy."

"Do not fear, Charlotte. We will be away to London before many hours."

The two friends ascended the stairs and bid each other goodnight. As Elizabeth entered her bedchamber, Charlotte called out, "Lizzy?" As she turned, Charlotte continued, "I am sorry that you are not engaged. I still do believe Mr. Darcy is in love with you, dear."

Elizabeth's attempt at a smile failed miserably. "Good night, Charlotte."

~*~*~*~*~*~*~*~*~*~*~*~*

Elizabeth's mind was full, and she could not fall asleep. She tensed when she heard Mr. Collins upon his return from Rosings, but relaxed a bit as she heard his heavy footsteps pacing the floors downstairs. He paced for an hour before a knock on the front door made her jerk to a sitting position in bed. The sound of someone's opening the front door was heard, followed by a pair of footsteps leading away from the house.

Elizabeth moved to the window. From her position hidden behind the drapes, she could see Mr. Collins and Mr. Wickham standing in a way that reminded her of their confrontation at Meryton. Their voices were raised, and she could hear a little of what they were saying.

Wickham was angry. "Collins, why were you not at Hunsford this afternoon as we had arranged? I walked the distance from the cabin to meet you."

"I left a letter in the usual place explaining that Mr. Darcy and Colonel Fitzwilliam had arrived. You know that when they are here, Lady Catherine does not allow you near Rosings. You should not have come to Hunsford during the day."

"I would love to come across William or Richard at Rosings. It would be great fun to clash with one of them!"

"Lady Catherine wishes to see you..." Mr. Collins said before the two began to move further away from the house and out of her hearing.

Self-conceit may lead to self destruction.
--Aesop (Greek Author, 620BC – 560 BC)

~Rosings Park

It was well after midnight and Lady Catherine was on a rampage of unequaled proportions. Tonight's upset surpassed that of a fortnight ago when Mr. Collins had told the mistress that Miss Elizabeth Bennet was visiting at Hunsford, and was worse than that of yesterday afternoon when Mr. Darcy informed the mistress that he would not be marrying Miss Anne. Neither of these events provoked a rage that could compare to this evening after Mr. Collins had come to Rosings to impart some new information to the mistress.

The staff had suffered her wrath for years, but none had ever seen her like this, and none of them knew what to do to pacify her. She had been screaming for hours without end, pacing the entire first and second floors. Only bits of what she uttered could be made out, the rest was incomprehensible. The only information any of them could piece together was that Mr. Darcy was engaged to that nice Miss Bennet. Some of the staff were happy for the newly engaged couple; others knew their mistress had been speaking of Miss Anne's marrying Mr. Darcy for years, and this would mean that their own lives would be much more difficult from this day forward.

The housekeeper knew that there was only one person who could soothe her mistress when she was on a rampage of this proportion. Though she had heard through the usual sources of gossip that *he* was on the grounds, she hesitated to contact the rake. The last time he had stayed at Rosings, she had lost two of her female staff a few months later when their "conditions" had become visible, and the mistress had dismissed them summarily. She went to see Miss Anne to ask if there was anything she could suggest they do to calm her mother.

Anne had been able to hear her mother from two floors up since she began her vociferous rant and had begun hiding in her bedchamber. She shook her head and said, "You know as well as I that there is nothing that will pacify her. It must run its course. I do not believe that I have heard her quite this angry in all of my life!" Anne turned and retreated into her room.

Lady Catherine saw the housekeeper descending the stairs and screamed, "You! Bring me the cook! I want to see him, now! Is he trying to make me ill with this horrible food? This indigestion is not to be borne!" She placed her hand on her chest. "Get him, now… NO! Tell him to leave Rosings immediately; he is discharged. Hire another cook!" Having made that pronouncement, she rushed down the hall into the sitting room, mumbling to herself.

As the housekeeper headed for the kitchen, she thought that perhaps it was not the cook's food causing this "indigestion," but rather Lady de Bourgh's unparalleled state of agitation. She would have difficulties reassuring the cook who she was sure had heard the exchange since the mistress's voice could be heard all over Rosings tonight. She was certain Lady Catherine would reconsider when her emotions had settled, as she usually did.

~%~

Wickham entered the house through a servant's entrance and artfully made his way to the sitting room undetected. Lady Catherine noticed him enter. She shook her cane at him. "How could he do this to me? To *me*! After all I have done for him! Engaged! He has ruined all my plans! That harlot must be stopped, do you hear me?"

Wickham laughed, "Yes, my lady, I could hear you from *outside* the building, and I am sure everyone indoors can hear you as well! I do believe you will need to lower your voice if you wish for me to assist you." He flashed a wicked smirk.

Lady Catherine's nostrils flared, her eyes narrowed, and her face turned purple, but part of her mind was reviewing what he had said, and she could see the value of it. There would be some danger if the staff knew what she was about to plot with Wickham. The pain in her chest worsened. She took several deep breaths, rubbed her chest and spoke at a lower volume, "The cook is trying to poison me with rotting food!"

"He served you rotting food because he is engaged to a harlot?" Wickham asked, confused.

"No, no, you rag-mannered coxcomb! My nephew, Darcy, has got himself *engaged* to that tart Elizabeth Bennet!"

Wickham's eyebrows almost reached the ceiling. "Ah! Has he now? How interesting!"

"Interesting? Interesting! It is not interesting! I told you to ruin her, and you did nothing! This is *your* fault!"

"Now, now, Madam, you are mistaken. I would have been eager and willing to carry out that order, but you told me to wait for your permission before ruining her, and so I have. Do I have your permission now?"

"You will do more than ruin her, Wickham. You will take her away from Rosings and away from Darcy, forever! He is just the bleeding-heart who would marry her after she is ruined because he felt responsible for it—because it was *your* doing! I will not have her using her arts and allurements on him any longer."

Wickham's eyes were full of amusement. "Lady Catherine, I cannot leave this moment. I have the…" he cleared his throat, "*business meeting* locally in the morning and must be there personally to make certain that *you* are not cheated. I am due to meet with Captain Sharp in two days, and so I begin my journey to Broadstairs tomorrow after the meeting nearby—at which time I could take Elizabeth Bennet with me if you so desire."

"Yes, I desire it; of what do you think we have been speaking? Take her away from here… and ruin her in every way possible, Wickham! How dare she try to destroy all that I have worked for? You shall disgrace her family as well! This is all her father's fault! If he had given permission for her to marry Collins, none of this would have happened. No one will marry any of her sisters if her ruin is made public, and you will make certain it is made public! I will make it absolutely clear to Collins that he will throw them from Longbourn the moment her father is dead. They will all be turned out onto the streets." Her eyes glistened with revenge, her hand pressing against her chest once more.

"Ah, your plans are always so amusing, my lady! It shall be my pleasure," he said as he bowed to kiss her hand.

Chapter 38

Thursday, March 24, 1812

~Rosings Park

5:30 A.M.

The next morning, not able to sleep whilst knowing Wickham to be nearby, Elizabeth had risen and dressed early and had set out before the sun had made its appearance in the eastern sky. She had heard Collins return and enter his bedchamber a few hours earlier, so she knew that neither he nor Wickham was about. She was surprised when she saw Darcy already at their meeting place. His pacing stopped upon noticing her approach, and relief was evident across his features. They began to walk away from the house as soon as she joined him.

"Good morning, Miss Elizabeth. You are early."

"Good morning, Mr. Darcy. Yes, I could not sleep. Wickham was here last night arguing with Mr. Collins outside my window before they went elsewhere."

Darcy was visibly upset by this news. "We should have left last night! It was too dangerous to leave you here unprotected. What if he…"

Elizabeth raised her hand to stop his speech. "He did not come into the house. I was perfectly safe; there is no need for chastising yourself, sir. Mr. Collins left the parsonage shortly after you did last evening to speak with Lady Catherine—is that why you do not look as if you slept last night?"

Not willing to admit he had been awake all night worrying about her staying the night at the parsonage and thinking about all that had happened the previous day, Darcy grimaced before saying, "Lady Catherine was ranting all night. While I was able to avoid being in her direct line of fire, she made herself heard throughout Rosings."

Surprised, Elizabeth said, “Rosings is such a vast building, how is that possible?”

Darcy smiled. “You have never met Lady Catherine, have you?” Elizabeth noticed he was no longer calling her “aunt.”

“I have been introduced to her only at church, but otherwise we have not conversed.”

They walked for a while, and then Darcy broke the silence. “I do not feel I owe any allegiance to Lady Catherine, but I do feel a responsibility to my cousin Anne. Every year I come to Rosings to review the ledgers and make certain her future is secure; it is a standing promise. My uncle comes once a year to do the same. I have almost completed my review, but it will take me a little longer with the steward before I will be finished and able to leave for London. I should be ready by ten o’clock. Do you know where the triple copper beech trees are by the bend in the road leading into the village?”

“Yes, I do.”

“Will you and Mrs. Collins be able to meet my coach there at half past ten? If so, I will go directly to the stables after leaving you and inform Johnny and Abe of our plans.”

“We can. I spoke to Charlotte last night after Mr. Collins left to speak to Lady Catherine. She is frightened and has been for a long time, but she had not wanted to tell me for fear of my reaction. She is more than willing to leave. Mr. Collins should be out of the house well before that time. If we are late, it will be because he has been delayed in leaving.”

They walked a little while in silence, Darcy deep in thought.

“Do you think Miss de Bourgh is involved with all this?”

Darcy smiled a little. “I was just pondering that very question as you came upon me. I honestly do not know if Anne is aware of any of this, and I was trying to decide whether I should take her with us. From what Johnny and Abe have told us, what we saw yesterday has been normal at Rosings for a long time… but as far as I can tell—I am not sure what to believe anymore when it comes to Rosings—Anne lives a sheltered life and may not have been exposed to the criminal activity occurring there. I believe she is safe here since she has been safe all this time—and I cannot imagine a way of asking her if she knows about it, either. I also do not wish to alert Lady Catherine to our discoveries. There is too much evidence that she and her men could dispose of before Richard's commanding officer sends his men to investigate! If I take Anne with us, or even if I leave before completing my purpose here, she might become suspicious that I have unveiled her scheme."

Elizabeth made her way through the bushes into the meadow she shared with Johnny and Abe. She wanted to see it one last time before she left Rosings, so she had led the way there without Darcy's realizing their destination.

The sun was rising as they entered the meadow, and they stood watching it for a few minutes. "Beautiful!"

Darcy answered, "Yes… I agree. Beautiful!" Giving himself a few moments to enjoy Elizabeth's blush when she realized he was looking at her as he said that, he continued, "I apologize about last evening. When the Collinses walked in—I did not know what to say. I did not want him to think… for him to spread rumours…"

She could not look at him lest her eyes betray her disappointment. "Yes, I do understand, Mr. Darcy. There is no reason to worry about duty, sir; Charlotte knows we are not engaged, and she understood the need for saying that we were last night."

Taking her hand, Darcy whispered, "Elizabeth, this is not progressing the way I had planned."

Confused, Elizabeth looked into his eyes for clarification, but found none. "Events rarely unfold exactly as one has planned."

She began to move away, but Darcy clasped her hand tighter and brought it to his lips. He stepped closer to her and placed her hand on his chest over his heart. "Elizabeth, please do not walk away. I must speak to you even though I know this is not the best time or best place to do so. I know not when I will have another opportunity to be alone with you."

Elizabeth closed her eyes. *"He will say goodbye again."* She did not believe she could survive another goodbye—she almost lost herself after the ball, what would happen this time? Her eyes filled with tears. "I do not wish to say goodbye again, Mr. Darcy. Let us allow our goodbyes at Netherfield to last our lifetime. When we return to London and our time is done, you will leave with no goodbyes."

Darcy's expression was one of confusion at first, but then turned to one of panic. Elizabeth wanted to say goodbye and never see him again? His breath became ragged as it had when he had seen her from the coach upon his arrival at Rosings. Fearing the overwhelming anxiety that threatened to return and not wishing for Elizabeth to see him in that state—he looked deeply into her eyes, full knowing that he would lose himself there.

"Elizabeth, please? I would do anything never to hear you say goodbye to me again."

Elizabeth's brow creased in confusion.

He took her other hand and held it with the first over his heart. "Do you not know how ardently I admire and love you?" Elizabeth gasped as he continued, "Please, I ask you… no I *beg* you to end my suffering and make me the happiest man who has ever lived. You are already the best friend I have ever had… please say that you will become my partner, my companion, and my wife. Elizabeth, I live for you alone. There is no one else with whom I would wish to share my life, or whose opinion I value more. I am acutely aware that I do not deserve you, but I promise to do everything in my power to work toward becoming worthy of you. I love you with every fibre of my being, body and soul. I beseech you, Elizabeth, please marry me?"

Elizabeth could not believe she was actually hearing any of this, and she stood watching him closely.

Darcy began to panic again when she did not answer him, and his hands pressed hers flat against his chest. She could feel his heart racing faster and faster, his chest rising and falling more quickly with every moment that passed.

"Is this real?" Elizabeth asked.

Darcy's breathing stopped, and he blinked a few times before he said, "Real?"

"Yes, real. This is not a dream? I was expecting you to disappear as you would in a dream… or that I would awaken."

Darcy had no idea how to interpret this… was this a good sign or a bad one? "This is not a dream, no."

"Then you did ask me to marry you just now?"

"Yes—though *beg* would be the more appropriate term."

Elizabeth smiled brightly. Darcy's soul filled with hope.

But then his hope faded and was replaced with foreboding when her smile slowly dimmed and changed to an expression of utter despair, then to steely indifference as her body stiffened. Her words came astonishingly fast and in a toneless voice, “Mr. Darcy… I must say that I do return your affections and admiration at every level, and so I must refuse your offer.”

His throat had tightened with suppressed emotion, but he managed to choke out, “You love me… and yet will not marry me? May I enquire… please, will you explain further?”

Elizabeth refused to meet his eyes, looking at their hands pressing against his chest instead. “I care too much for you to expose you to the censure and caprice of the *ton*. Mr. Darcy, you know as well as I do that the reactions of Mr. Collins and Lady Catherine are only the beginning of the scandal you would suffer at an engagement between us. I have seen firsthand how the *ton* reacts when they only *suspect* a ‘country nobody’ will encroach upon the upper circle. If I accomplished this feat, they would surely be much more cruel, not only to you but to your sister. I cannot be that selfish, sir. You would grow to resent me for it, and I could not cope with that once it happened.” Her eyes finally met his, and her voice was filled with the love she had been trying to suppress. “You deserve happiness, not a life full of despair.” Elizabeth could not endure seeing the pain in his eyes, and she returned her gaze to their hands.

Darcy saw the irony of her arguments being almost identical to the ones he had used to convince himself to leave her. “Elizabeth.” Afraid she would run off, he refused to let go of her hands and waited until she looked at him. “There could be nothing—absolutely nothing—worse than the despair I have experienced these past months since I left Netherfield. I told you I was indisposed, but that was a colossal understatement of the truth… I was too ashamed to tell you what had actually happened. I will say it has been proven, without question, that I cannot live without you, Elizabeth… there would be nothing *but* despair in my future without you as my wife. I know beyond any doubt that achieving happiness without you is absolutely impossible.”

“But your sister…”

“My sister has lived through these last months in agony as well. She has heard of you from Richard, remembers you from your past meetings and more recently has heard of you from my aunt and uncle. My sister approves my choice wholeheartedly, as do my aunt, uncle, and cousin.”

Desperate to convince her to marry him, he decided to lay everything before her. "Surprisingly, I left Netherfield for many of the same reasons you have just stated. I did not wish for you to despise me for exposing you to the censure of the *ton*. But something has been pointed out to me, and after much reflection, I know it to be *truth*. You may not understand the power Lord and Lady Matlock have within the *ton*, Elizabeth, as well as our mutual friend the Duke. I do not believe either of us, or Georgiana, will experience derision with these advocates. Lady Matlock asserts that you are already accepted by many in her acquaintance in the first circle.

"That is not to say that we will not meet with difficulties, but to be perfectly candid these would happen with anyone I married. Pemberley, and the purse that goes with it, have been vigorously sought after since even before I had come of age. I am afraid there may be a few matrons and young ladies within the *ton* who will strive to make our experience in society unpleasant when we are first married.

"Elizabeth, please understand—I have *never* been comfortable in society; my experience would be absolutely intolerable without you by my side in the future. The only people who matter to me are those who would wish us the joy of a life filled with love. Georgiana feels the same way.

"There is one more reason why I left Hertfordshire, but I have come to find it was a combination of misunderstanding and the cruel betrayal of the trust of a child. I innocently turned to Lady Catherine to explain something my mother said in her final moments. I was deliberately lied to. I had no reason to doubt what she said… until my Aunt Adelaide gave me this—only just this week." He reluctantly released her hands, and then gave Elizabeth his mother's letter and gestured for her to read it. As she did, Elizabeth was visibly moved by it.

When she did not speak for a few minutes, he took one of her hands and laid it upon his chest once more. He then continued, "I left Hertfordshire thinking I could never have you… and I did not think it possible to survive witnessing your falling in love and marrying another. But after experiencing life without you in it—Elizabeth, the only reason I was able to emerge from the pit I fell into was Richard's asking what *you* would think of me if you found out how I was behaving!

"After receiving my mother's letter, I had planned to ride directly to Longbourn to beg you to marry me. My Aunt Adelaide told me she felt I *must* come here, though she did not know why… but finding you here causes me to believe it was providence.

"Elizabeth, I am bound to you, married or not. If you insist on refusing me, I do not believe I could survive without at least having you in my life as a friend.

"If you love me as you say you do, please, I beg of you once again—marry me, Elizabeth. It already is my life's ambition for you to be happy… please allow me to make the attempt at accomplishing this in person."

Elizabeth closed her eyes and was silent for several minutes.

"Will it help if I throw myself at your feet and grovel? I am quite prepared to do so!"

Elizabeth opened her eyes and smiled the most dazzling, brilliant, heart-stopping smile he had ever seen grace her ethereal face.

"Elizabeth?"

"Yes!"

His dimples made the grandest appearance ever. "Say it, please—I am afraid I will not believe it unless I hear you say the words."

The fire in Elizabeth's eyes ignited something deep within him as she said, "William, I love you with all my heart and wish to become your wife."

His grin widened and hers matched it. "If you were correct in thinking this is a dream, I do not wish to awaken."

Elizabeth stretched up on her toes and kissed him gently on the cheek. "Does that feel like a dream?"

Darcy whispered, "My dreams, although wonderful, have never come close to the real you, my dearest, loveliest Elizabeth."

His hands moved to her face, caressing her smooth skin. Darcy leaned in and kissed her gently… lingering again and again. She pressed herself against him; her fingers wrapped themselves in his hair, pulling him closer to her. He responded to her passion by deepening the kiss gradually. Her response at first was surprise—but she learned quickly as she suddenly became much more passionate, almost crushing herself against him. In an attempt to restrain himself, he broke the kiss and instead continued with a series of tender kisses drifting across her jaw line and neck to her shoulder. Her lavender scent driving him wild, he retraced the path to just under her ear and tasted the sweetness of her skin. He whispered her name into her ear and felt her begin to tremble in his arms. At her quiet moan, he was almost overcome with desire and pulled away quickly to regain control.

"Did I do something wrong, William?"

Darcy answered breathlessly, "No, my Elizabeth, it is that you do everything *too* well!"

Thrilled at her ability to evoke such feelings in him, she replied simply with a certain combination of a saucy grin and arched brow which had almost driven him to kiss her several times in the past. Now that he could—he did.

With every intention of continuing, Darcy pulled away slightly to draw breath, but when he saw her eyes filled with a passion he had not even dreamed possible, his instincts nearly overtook him. Fortunately, a brief moment of rational thought emerged, and it forcefully occurred to him that Elizabeth had no idea how quickly he could lose his self-control just now. Reluctantly, Darcy knew it would be up to him to put a stop to this before it went too far. He held her shoulders and gently pushed her away from him.

"Elizabeth, I do think we ought to start walking back, my love, or I will do something I will regret. You know not what you do to me."

"No more kisses?" she pouted.

The pout almost did him in completely, and he closed his eyes and took a deep, trembling breath. "Not at present. Elizabeth, I do not think I can withstand even one more of your kisses at this moment. Perhaps we can stop on the way back to the house as a reward for your compliance," he teased. *We had better have the first banns read next Sunday and get married as soon as possible!*

~Hunsford Cottage

8:00 A.M.

When Elizabeth returned to the house, Mr. Collins was still abed and Charlotte was in her sitting room, seated in the chair that rested on the hidden compartment. She had a very thoughtful look upon her face when Elizabeth entered the room, which changed when she saw her friend's countenance.

"Lizzy, what is it?"

"Charlotte! You were right! Mr. Darcy *does* love me, and we now are really engaged!"

Charlotte rushed across the room and embraced Elizabeth. "Oh, Lizzy! I am so happy for you! I knew it would be so!"

"Thank you, Charlotte. I am very happy!" She took Charlotte's shoulders and held her at arm's length. "I must speak with you before Mr. Collins awakens. We will meet Mr. Darcy at the triple copper beech trees on the road leading into the village at half past ten. We should both pack a small bag to bring along. Perhaps we should hide them somewhere outside the house?"

While they were both in their rooms to pack, Mr. Collins awoke; he met them in the breakfast room when they came down. All through breakfast, he continued to chastise Elizabeth for her meeting with Darcy and their engagement, telling the ladies how displeased Lady Catherine was upon hearing his account last evening.

Elizabeth was too happy to allow Mr. Collins's chattering to bother her in the least. Mr. Collins informed the ladies that he would visit Lady Catherine to ascertain if her health had improved since last night, for she had been plagued with terrible indigestion when he had visited to deliver the news of the engagement.

After they were sure Mr. Collins had gone, both Elizabeth and Charlotte retrieved their bags and left the house when they were sure no servants would see them. They took a short walk to hide their bags in some bushes near the road to London. Darcy was not due for another hour.

On the return to Hunsford to make some final preparations before their journey, they came across Johnny and Abe. The ladies showed them where to hide their sacks. Johnny apologized for not being able to take the kites with them and Elizabeth promised to make another for Johnny and provide Abe with the means to make his own.

As the boys began to return to the stables to prepare Darcy's horses for the trip, they heard a lady scream, and turned back to investigate.

9:30 A.M.

George Wickham licked his lips and smiled devilishly as he stood just inside the tree line near Hunsford Cottage. His eyes followed the sway of the young maid's hips as she walked off toward the village with the housekeeper.

"When we next return to Rosings, I must make certain to help myself to a taste of that sweet thing!" Wickham said to the burly man who was standing nearby. He chuckled when a glance at the brute revealed that he was glaring at him with disapproval. "Do you not like women?"

The large man obviously did not feel the question worth answering. He turned away from Wickham and walked a few yards further into the woods.

Wickham laughed a little louder and said, "Most likely they went to the market which means they will be gone quite a while. That leaves the two ladies and Collins at home, and I happen to know that he has an appointment with her ladyship soon."

As the two servants walked round a bend in the lane and out of sight, Wickham's attention returned to observing the cottage. Several minutes later, Mr. Collins scurried out the door and headed toward Rosings manor house, mopping his forehead with a handkerchief as he hurried along. After seeing the state that Lady Catherine had been in last night, Wickham could understand why the parson would be nervous!

"The ladies are alone. Follow me; we will go in through the kitchen. Stay out of sight until I give you the sign, and then you will use the same strategy with Mrs. Collins as you did with the men at our meeting this morning. The woman with the dark hair is *mine*."

The brawny man followed at a distance as Wickham searched the house. He watched the smaller man's features darken further with anger as he found each chamber empty. The two men slipped out of the house unseen and circled the area around the cottage.

~%~

Wickham thoroughly enjoyed the expression of fear that briefly crossed Elizabeth's countenance the moment she saw him and his man step out from the bushes into the ladies' path. Wickham stayed where he was, but the burly man moved next to Charlotte, though they remained within Elizabeth's view.

Charlotte's pallor betrayed that she might faint.

Wickham bowed to the ladies. "Good morning, Mrs. Collins. It is a pleasure to see you again," he said in a most polite tone, but his leer at Elizabeth's form was anything but gentleman-like.

"Mr. Wickham." Elizabeth threaded her arm through Charlotte's and attempted to direct her around the men. Wickham side-stepped, blocking their path.

Elizabeth took a deep breath to bolster her courage. "You *will* let us pass."

Wickham laughed loudly. "And just why should I do that, my dear Lizzy?"

Elizabeth's eyes flashed at the familiar use of her name. "I am sorry, Mr. Wickham, but we cannot stay to talk. We are in a hurry to return to the parsonage. Good day, sir." She pulled Charlotte around to the other side of Wickham, but again he stepped in their way.

"Mrs. Collins may soon go, but if you do not cooperate, my friend will not like it." The large man crossed his arms over his chest. "You do not wish to see him when he is angry." He gestured for them to continue down the path toward the parsonage and stepped out of their way.

Elizabeth tugged on Charlotte's arm and they began to walk quickly ahead of the men.

"Do not get any ideas of an escape; I fear that neither of you could outrun us."

They rounded a turn and stopped short. There in the road that intersected the path was a carriage. A glimmer of hope passed through Elizabeth's mind until she realized that the man in the driver's seat was one of the men that she had seen in the woods at Wickham's cabin.

"I have a long carriage ride ahead of me and am looking forward to your company for the journey, Lizzy."

"I certainly will not come with you!" she stated firmly.

"I was afraid of this," he said to the large man as he shook his head. "I can see my man here is becoming impatient to leave. Do not force him to demonstrate his temper; poor Mrs. Collins may be injured."

Elizabeth eyed the huge man. She had no way of knowing whether he would make good on the threat. "You will allow Mrs. Collins so go free, unharmed?"

Wickham laughed, took hold of Elizabeth's arm and roughly guided her to the carriage. "Why, of course!" He opened the carriage door, and they stood staring at each other with matching glares.

"Take me instead!" Charlotte called out.

"Ah, poor lady! Had enough of your husband already? I apologize, but I must take Lizzy on this trip. Perhaps when I return to the area, we will meet again?" Wickham grinned.

"Goodbye, Charlotte." Elizabeth said and then quickly stepped into the carriage. Wickham and the large man followed close behind her. Charlotte watched the carriage pull away.

"Lizzy!" she gasped.

Once they were out of sight, Charlotte ran in the direction that Johnny and Abe had gone.

~Rosings Park

Johnny was the one chosen to sneak into Rosings to tell Darcy. After living there for two years, he knew of several entrances into the manor and also knew his way around the house a little since Lady Catherine had summoned him a few times. Charlotte had told him that Darcy was in a meeting with the steward, and Johnny knew they would most likely be found in the room where Lady Catherine had met with him. Johnny slipped through the door soundlessly. He stood where Darcy could see him but the steward could not and waved his hands to attract Darcy's attention. After he was sure that Darcy had seen him, he hid behind a sofa.

~%~

Movement caught Darcy's eye. When he saw Johnny, he knew something was wrong. Panic gripped him when he saw the fear in Johnny's countenance. Thankfully, he had just completed his work with the steward, so he said his goodbyes quickly, and the steward left the room.

The moment the door closed, Johnny came out of his hiding place and whispered, "Mr. Darcy! Wickedman and Jeremiah took Miss Lizzy!"

"What? Took her, what do you mean? Took her where? To the cabin in the woods?"

"They took her away in a carriage! Mrs. Collins came running after us and said Wickedman and a big man, who sounds like Abe's cousin Jeremiah, put her into a carriage and drove away—probably going to Broadstairs."

"Broadstairs... near Ramsgate? Why would he take her there?"

"After a delivery, Wickedman goes back to see my great-grandfather."

Ramsgate! Wickham is often near Ramsgate? So it was probably a coincidence and not by design that he came across Georgiana there last summer, Darcy thought to himself as he began walking toward the door to the hall. "Hurry, I must saddle a horse and go after them!"

Johnny took hold of Darcy's arm to stop him. "Mr. Darcy—I don't know what Jeremiah's orders are, sir, but he won't let any harm come to Miss Lizzy from Wickedman. I'm not sure what he'd do if you go after them. He's nasty when threatened. Jeremiah is… big, sir. I've never seen any man so big, not even you, sir. Miss Lizzy might get hurt."

Darcy closed his eyes and took a deep breath. "Then what do you suggest I do? Sit here and do nothing?"

"Go to Broadstairs and talk to my great-grandfather."

"You will come along, Abe as well. I promised Miss Elizabeth I would not leave Mrs. Collins here. We need to move more quickly than a coach will allow, can you and Abe ride a horse?"

"Yes we both can, but I don't know 'bout Mrs. Collins."

"Let us find out." Darcy made his plan as he followed Johnny through the servant's corridors to the stables where Charlotte and Abe were waiting. On the way out he saw Hughes, his valet, and had him follow them.

Darcy took Hughes aside. "Hughes, this must be kept absolutely confidential. Miss Bennet has been kidnapped. Time is of the essence! Mrs. Collins, the boys, and I are riding into London on horseback, taking our horses. I need you to hire horses from the village and take the coach into London with all haste. I will meet you at Darcy House. As soon as preparations are made with Colonel Fitzwilliam, I will be going after Miss Bennet. You will follow us with the coach to Broadstairs as soon as is possible. I do not know what to expect once I get there, Hughes." He gave the valet a pointed look as he said the last. With no doubt that his directions would be followed, Darcy did not wait for an answer.

He quickly crossed the distance to Charlotte. "Mrs. Collins, Johnny has told me what has happened. We are going to London to seek the help of my cousin Colonel Fitzwilliam, and then on to Broadstairs. We will escort you as far as London where you can stay with Mr. and Mrs. Gardiner. My carriage horses are trained for riding in case of emergencies. Can you ride? We need to proceed to London post-haste, and I cannot leave you here with Mr. Collins."

"Mr. Darcy, I grew up with Lizzy! Of course I can ride! Our bags are in the bushes by the road where we were supposed to meet, and I am willing and prepared to leave this very moment."

The boys had already begun to saddle the horses, and Darcy started saddling one as well. "Oh yes, of course. Georgiana told me a story… let me guess, you were the one training with Elizabeth for the race and cannot ride sidesaddle?"

"That is partially correct, sir. Lizzy never did learn to ride the proper way, but I did." Charlotte said with a little smile, which quickly faded.

Darcy realized that since they met again in Kent, he had not the time to speak to Elizabeth about so many things—about her knowing his aunt and uncle and Georgiana, and the amusing stories they all had shared about her. He wanted to be having this conversation about riding with *Elizabeth*, not her childhood friend. Meanwhile, *his* childhood friend had kidnapped his Elizabeth!

Suddenly overwhelmed with worry for Elizabeth, he leaned heavily on the horse and closed his eyes. The horse whinnied, reminding him of the urgency of the situation, and his attention returned to the saddle. There would be much time to think on their ride to London… and then on to Broadstairs.

10:00 A.M.

The group stopped at the bushes where they had left their bags. Darcy took Elizabeth's bag and attached it gently to his saddle, as if it were a fragile object. The group then rode on to London as fast as was possible. Darcy put the time to good use making plans, and as they neared Town, he updated the others as to what course of action he had decided to pursue next. They would all go see Colonel Fitzwilliam first, since they would pass near his General's office on the way into London.

He had come to the conclusion that he could not ride into a smugglers' lair without the aid of his cousin if he wished to be of any assistance to Elizabeth. He would be of no use to her if he were dead.

~%~

~London

12:30 P.M.

Colonel Fitzwilliam happened to be leaving the building with General Curtis as the group approached. He saw them nearing, and after one glace at Darcy's face, he asked General Curtis to wait to hear what his cousin had to say.

After Darcy greeted both soldiers, his words quickly spilt forth, "Fitzwilliam, I need your help! Lady Catherine is involved in the India problem, and it is much worse than we thought. Richard, it is treasonous! My fiancée, Miss Elizabeth, and I were bringing proof, which I have with me now, to show to you, General Curtis... but then Wickham kidnapped her earlier this morning. We believe he has taken her to Broadstairs in Kent, near Ramsgate."

General Curtis and Colonel Fitzwilliam stood wide-eyed in shock during Darcy's speech, and when he had finished, the general suggested that they go to his office to discuss the matter further. The group then proceeded indoors; the boys sat in the hall while Mrs. Collins and the gentlemen entered the general's office. They quickly came to the conclusion that Mrs. Collins should *not* be taken to the Gardiners' house since Mr. Collins could potentially find their address. Instead, she would be taken to the house of Captain Walsh, a trusted friend of Richard, to stay with his wife. Mrs. Collins agreed to the scheme as long as Darcy would include a note to her father when he sent his express to Mr. Bennet informing Sir William that she was under the Army's protection.

General Curtis said they could have four men go along with them to recover Elizabeth in order to take into custody the deserter Wickham and find out more about the saltpetre smuggling. The general did note that he knew Captain Sharp, the leader of the smugglers in that area, and doubted very much that he was involved in anything treasonous.

"You *know* a smuggler, General? Why is he able to continue doing business?" Darcy asked, dumbfounded.

General Curtis replied, "The authorities know of these smugglers and their usual activities. It is the nobility and highly placed gentry, even the judges themselves, who are ultimately buying most of the contraband items, and some even have monetary interest in the endeavors. As a result, the military ignores them *unless* an innocent becomes involved or there is a threat to the Mother country from something they are smuggling. If this be the case, a conflict will result, but the authorities usually punish only the underlings to the full extent of the law, which could be death. Those in charge of the smugglers, if caught, must pay a fine, and are freed with the understanding that there will be no more of the specific activity they had been engaged in which resulted in such an action."

Though Darcy was thankful for the general's assistance, he was also disgusted by this information. "Sir, you are aware of the ledgers I found detailing the saltpetre being supplied to the French? That *is* treason, sir! Are you saying Captain Sharp will go free?"

Colonel Fitzwilliam sighed. "Probably, Darce. Sharp is one of the main providers to the upper classes of spirits and tobacco from America. He will most likely be warned not to engage in supplying the French with any further saltpetre and be allowed to continue on as he has been for years. You said yourself that Sharp was being coerced by Aunt Catherine. You have to understand, Sharp is only transporting from one port to another whatever goods with which he is supplied, Darce; it is truly Aunt Catherine who is committing treason. I personally believe that they are both guilty of treason, but I believe that this is how the authorities will look upon this situation. Because Aunt Catherine is so highly placed in society, she will most likely get a warning and not be prosecuted."

"When will we be leaving for Broadstairs? I must speak to Mr. Gardiner and the earl about this matter."

"My men should be about ready to go in a couple of hours—but *you* are not going, Darce."

In his "Master of Pemberley" tone, Darcy answered, "Of course I am going! Elizabeth is to be my wife! I *am* going, Richard!"

Richard put his hand on Darcy's shoulder. "I had at least to make the attempt to keep you out of harm's way, Cousin. We will meet you at Darcy House when we are ready to leave London."

~Matlock House

2:00 P.M.

While Richard escorted Mrs. Collins to her temporary home, Darcy brought Johnny and Abe with him to Darcy House. He arranged with Mrs. Martin, the housekeeper, to feed the boys and pack three saddlebags, and to have three horses ready to leave at a moment's notice. He changed quickly and headed off to see his uncle at Matlock House.

"Stand ready," told the coachman as he walked toward the door of his uncle's house. Once announced, Lord Matlock took in his nephew's agitated appearance as Darcy began to speak. “Uncle Robert, I must speak with you, but time is of the essence. Will you accompany me to Mr. Gardiners’ residence, and I will tell you the details in the carriage? Elizabeth has been kidnapped.”

“Lizzy, kidnapped?” Lady Matlock’s startled voice came from behind Darcy.

“Oh—Aunt Adelaide, I did not see you there, I apologize.” Darcy raked his hand through his hair and blurted out, “Yes, Elizabeth has been kidnapped. Richard and I will be off as soon as his men are ready. I am to go to the Gardiners’ to notify them and have them send an express to Mr. Bennet. I must return to Darcy House as soon as possible. There is much to tell; will you both come with me?”

Lord Matlock crossed to his nephew and said, “William, why do you not tell us now, and we shall go to the Gardiners’ and send the express to Mr. Bennet?”

“That would save a little time, thank you. A message must be sent to Sir William Lucas by express as well. Lady Catherine’s parson, Mr. Collins, is under investigation. Mrs. Collins is Sir William’s daughter. I am to notify Sir William that Mrs. Collins is safe and under Army protection until further notice.” Darcy’s hand was visibly trembling as he raked it through his hair once again and looked directly into his aunt’s frightened eyes. “Richard and I will do everything within our power to bring Elizabeth home safely, Aunt Adelaide.”

Darcy began pacing in front of them. “Aunt, your intuition was correct. I did need to go to Kent. Elizabeth was at Rosings visiting her friend Mrs. Collins! It’s too much to explain now, but you must know that Lady Catherine has been employing George Wickham; as soon as I knew he was in the area, I knew that Elizabeth was at risk. You know as well as I do that Wickham has not an honourable bone in his body.

“India is Lady Catherine’s doing as well, Uncle! I am sorry, but I will no longer refer to your sister as my aunt. She is a traitor to the crown, shipping the saltpetre to France to make gunpowder to kill British troops, as well as to America, a country we might be at war with any day now. Elizabeth and I had several ‘adventures’ in Kent over the past day during which we found evidence of Lady Catherine’s misdoings. We were to bring the evidence to London today, but Lady Catherine discovered that I am engaged to Elizabeth and had George Wickham kidnap her. She was gone before I could stop it." He shuddered.

"William, you are speaking so quickly that it is difficult to understand you. Did you say you are betrothed to Lizzy?" Lady Matlock asked.

Darcy closed his eyes, his voice full of many emotions all at once. "I begged her to marry me but two hours before she was kidnapped. She accepted." Neither Lord nor Lady Matlock could think of anything to say in response, for congratulations hardly seemed appropriate at this juncture.

Darcy's eyes snapped open. "I have no doubt that Lady Catherine had Elizabeth kidnapped because she wants me to marry Anne. I should not have left her side once I realized that Lady Catherine knew… I should have brought her to London immediately… I know not what Wickham will do to her… I just… I just did not think Lady Catherine capable of something like *this*! I should have realized…" his trembling voice trailed off as Lady Matlock took his hand in hers and squeezed it in an attempt to comfort him. After a few moments, he cleared his throat and said, "I must go. Thank you for informing Elizabeth's family in my stead." Darcy bowed to his aunt and uncle and left the room.

Lord Matlock followed him into the hallway. "William, just a moment… I want you to be aware that when Mr. Bennet arrives, I will be accompanying him to Broadstairs. I must do what I can to help to clean up the mayhem my sister Catherine has created."

Darcy nodded, quickly exited the building and entered his waiting carriage.

~Gracechurch Street, London

2:30 P.M.

When they arrived at the home of their good friends the Gardiners, Lord and Lady Matlock exchanged looks, bracing themselves before climbing the stairs to knock on the door.

The servant showed them into the entryway. Hearing voices in the hallway, Mr. Gardiner came out to meet them. "Good afternoon, Adelaide… Robert! It is such a pleasure to see you both. Will you join the family for tea?"

Lord Matlock shook his hand. "Edward, I thank you, no. We are here on an urgent matter of business regarding Miss Elizabeth."

"Lizzy?" Mr. Gardiner looked at their grave expressions and prepared himself for the worst.

Mrs. Gardiner and Jane heard the exchange through the open door and rushed out into the hall.

"Lord Matlock, is something the matter with Lizzy?" Jane asked.

Mr. Gardiner saw his friend tense his jaw and decided the hall was not the place for this discussion. "Shall we move into the sitting room?"

Lady Matlock took Mrs. Gardiner's and Jane's arms and led them into the room as the gentlemen followed. The children said their greetings and were ushered upstairs by Mrs. Gardiner.

When everyone was seated, Lord Matlock decided on an abbreviated version of what he knew of the situation in Kent. There would be time to sort out what Miss Elizabeth wanted her family to know later, after she had been retrieved.

"My nephew Fitzwilliam Darcy happened to be at Rosings visiting my sister, Lady Catherine de Bourgh, at the same time Miss Elizabeth was visiting her friend Mrs. Collins. This morning, Miss Elizabeth was kidnapped by George Wickham. I understood you to have met him in Hertfordshire, Miss Bennet. We have reason to believe she has been taken to a village near Ramsgate. Darcy has enlisted my son Richard to help find her. General Curtis has been so kind as to provide men to assist in the search. As they are to be leaving London shortly, Darcy asked me to come in his stead while they prepared provisions for the trip."

"My sister's parson is under investigation in a related matter. We must also notify Sir William Lucas that Mrs. Collins is safe and under Army protection until further notice."

Mr. Gardiner began to cross the room to the writing table. "Robert, would you like to write the express to Thomas, or shall I?"

Lord Matlock answered, "I think it would be better from me, Edward. I will ask Thomas to meet me at Matlock House, for I have every intention of going with him to Broadstairs. I will send a note to Sir William Lucas as well. I do believe I have met him at St. James once or twice; a rather jolly fellow, is he not?"

"Yes, that he is. Thank you, Robert."

"I should like to wait and speak with Madeline when she is finished with the children, if you do not mind," Lady Matlock said to her husband.

~%~

~Darcy House, London

2:30 P.M.

Arriving at his own home, Darcy verified that Johnny and Abe were ready to leave the moment that Richard and his men appeared. He then retreated to his study to write a note begging Bingley's assistance. Darcy briefly explained that Elizabeth and he were engaged, she had been kidnapped, and that Miss Jane Bennet was staying at her relatives' house in London, noting the address.

You could be of service to the family. I do not know what the situation will be when I find her, Bingley. Elizabeth may need her sister. Please, be ready to bring Miss Bennet to Broadstairs if necessary.

Shuddering at these thoughts, he requested his butler to have the note delivered to Bingley immediately.

Just as he finished speaking with his the butler, the door opened and Richard's voice boomed, "Time to go, Darce! I hope you and the boys are prepared to ride hard. Thankfully, it is almost a full moon and we will be able to ride all night. If all goes well, we should be at Broadstairs at about sunrise."

There is no witness so terrible and no accuser so powerful as conscience which dwells within us.
--Sophocles (Greek Dramatist 495BC - 406BC)

~Rosings Park

After looking in the mirror and noticing the bluish colouring of her skin, Lady Catherine was beginning to think her discomfort was not indigestion after all. The apothecary had told her years ago that there was something amiss with her heart. He had given her powders to help and cautioned her to avoid becoming overly excited. With all that had been happening in the past few days, she only realized just now that she had forgotten to take the powders… and she had certainly been highly excited. In hindsight, she also could see that the pains had worsened the more upset she had been, and a few times they had become quite severe.

She knew she had to face the truth… she was going to die, and soon. Surprisingly, this did not come as a shock, but more of a relief. Lady Catherine looked from the mirror to the portrait over the mantle. It was painted upon her coming out at age seventeen. What had happened to that young girl with all the hopes and dreams for the future? What had changed her so drastically that she had become the bitter woman she was now?

She knew exactly what had gone wrong. Those hopes and dreams had been disappointed in a single moment—the first time *he* had looked at her sister. She could never release the hatred she felt for George and Anne Darcy, who had only followed their own hearts and made a love match. Their son, whose very existence pained her to the core as he was living proof of their love for each other, had come to her for comfort when his mother died, giving her an opportunity to take her revenge upon them both through him!

But now she could see that by refusing to forgive them, she had not experienced one moment of happiness in her lifetime since that portrait had been painted.

Suddenly, her life was so clear to her. Would anyone mourn her death? She could not think of anyone who would—not even her own daughter! She dictated to her daughter, Anne, but had never taken the time to come to *know* her. She did not know any of Anne's true likes or dislikes, or what her hope and dreams were. Had she ever wished to marry her cousin? Would she be disappointed about his engagement? Or was it as young Darcy had said—that she, too, did not want a marriage of convenience? Did her daughter care for her?

Perhaps Collins would mourn her death, or had he merely acted his part to avoid her scorn? It mattered little for he was a man she could not respect in the least.

Of one thing she was certain... her death would be celebrated by people all over England who would rejoice in the release from bondage that her passing would grant them.

Lady Catherine felt something she had not felt since she was that girl of seventeen in the portrait. She was ashamed of herself, of how she had striven to revenge her bitterness upon the world, of how she used people to try to achieve a sense of relief which never came, of how she mistreated her own daughter, and of how she had consistently lied to young Darcy.

Deciding that she would not allow her daughter to suffer after her death as she had done during her lifetime, she knew she would need to prepare her estate for her death… not the estate that everybody was aware of, but the one very few knew existed.

She would write a letter to her brother Robert, the Earl of Matlock, and ask him to take care of things for Anne… a confession so he could clean up the chaos that she had created with her greed. He would do it, though not for *her*—for Anne… and to save the family name from disgrace. He was a much better person than she had ever been—he would do it for the good of all of those she had injured in her lifetime.

Laughing mirthlessly, she remembered the many lectures she had given Darcy about not doing anything to disgrace the family name. Yet, it would *not* be he who threatened to destroy it—she herself would be responsible for disgracing them all if word of what she had done was ever made public!

When she finished her letter to her brother, Lady Catherine wrote a letter of apology to her daughter, Anne.

Several hours later, Lady Catherine's maid entered her chamber to check upon her since she had not rung for assistance in changing for dinner. She found that her mistress was laid out upon the bed with her hands folded perfectly—almost lifeless.

~In a carriage on the road headed away from Rosings Park

10:00 P.M.

Elizabeth awoke with a start to darkness. Though disoriented, by the movement she could tell that she was in a coach, but other than that, she could remember nothing. As her eyes adjusted to the lack of light, she saw Wickham and Jeremiah—the big, burly man from Rosings—and her memories of the past few hours came flooding back upon her.

Afraid he might take her gold watch if he saw it, she waited until Wickham closed his eyes to sleep before she glanced at the time. They had been traveling a little more than twelve hours. They had not stopped in all that time but to change horses. Wickham had gone into inns and taverns every time the horses were changed, reeking of alcohol when he returned. A couple of times he brought them a basket of food and drink, while he brought only a bottle for himself.

When Wickham would leave to imbibe, Jeremiah would allow Elizabeth to walk around a little each time after she promised she would not run away. She doubted she wanted to face *this* man's ire if he caught her! He was particularly tall and muscular—probably the largest man she had ever seen. He had weather-beaten skin, and his curls were bright orange. The coach ride must have been very uncomfortable for him with his having such long legs, and he was so tall he had to slump to have his head merely graze the ceiling of the coach.

There were other reasons she did not wish to escape; she had no idea where she was and had no money. The only thing she had to sell was her pocket watch, and since it had belonged to her grandmother Bennet, she did not want to sell it unless it was absolutely necessary.

Elizabeth was forced to sit across from Wickham to give Jeremiah room for his legs, and that was not an experience she wished to repeat in her lifetime. Wickham's comments and leers made her uncomfortable enough, but he also kept rubbing his legs against hers and a few times tried to do more.

So far, Jeremiah had kept her safe from Wickham, and she trusted him… limitedly. The last time Wickham had attempted to make advances, Jeremiah threatened to harm him if he tried it again. She might be in a worse situation if she left Jeremiah's protection. She shuddered to think that if she attempted to escape and failed, Jeremiah might grant Wickham a free hand with her.

Elizabeth had engaged in some conversation with Jeremiah during the times that Wickham was indoors. She had begun by calling him Mr. Jeremiah, and he had laughed and told her it was his first name. She had thanked him for helping her. He had answered only that he worked for a man named Captain Sharp, and Captain Sharp did not approve of such goings on with ladies. She had attempted to gain more information about Captain Sharp and where it was that they were travelling to, but Jeremiah had seemed unsure of what he should reveal to her and had remained silent on these subjects other than telling her that they would continue to ride at night. He had seemed to enjoy speaking to her about other subjects, especially the sea, and so she had continued to talk and listen to him—but whenever Wickham returned, neither of them had spoken at all.

She felt lucky it was almost a full moon, for she did not want to consider what would have happened had it been too dark to drive on and had they been forced to stay overnight at an inn. Not knowing what to expect when they finally arrived at their destination, Elizabeth had been trying to sleep as much as possible, which was not much under the circumstances, and had hidden some bread and biscuits in the pockets of her dress and pelisse. She was sure Wickham had been too drunk to notice, but she thought she had seen Jeremiah hide a grin once while she had transferred a biscuit to her pocket.

Some four hours later, the coach passed through a village about the size of Meryton. She had been able to smell the sea air for hours and had heard the waves breaking at times, but had not been able to espy anything of the sea itself. After they passed through the village, Elizabeth looked out her window and could see the moon reflected upon the water, but something was wrong with the scene. The water seemed to be much lower than the road they were traveling on. She moved a bit closer to the window to take a better look and became frightened, pulling away from the window when she realized that they must be riding alongside a sheer cliff. She looked at Jeremiah, who was stifling a grin. Elizabeth smiled a little when she realized how silly the move had been. If the coach veered off the cliff, being further away from the window would not signify in the least!

Wednesday, March 25, 1812

~Broadstairs, Kent

2:00 A.M.

The coach slowed near a large building that was teeming with life, surprising Elizabeth, for when she had peeked at her watch last she had seen it was just after two o'clock in the morning. A sign on the front of the building read "Digby Ale House." The coach stopped behind the building, and Jeremiah handed out Elizabeth.

Wickham moved toward a door and whistled three high-pitched shrieks. Elizabeth assumed they were a signal that he had arrived. A barmaid came rushing out to talk and flirt with Wickham for a few minutes.

"Jeremiah, are we waiting for something to happen here, or are we stopping here to change horses again?" Elizabeth asked.

Jeremiah jutted his chin out toward the building to bring her attention to an older man who had just appeared in the doorway and was now approaching them. He was a tall man, with skin darkened and weathered from the sun and sea, bald on top with grey hair in a half halo around his head. His eyes were clear, bright green, and intelligent. There was a sense of kindness and humour about him which comforted Elizabeth, but she reminded herself to be on her guard.

"Jeremiah? Why are ye here wit' Wickham? And who be this lass?"

Elizabeth watched both men closely.

"She's a *lady*, Mr. Mott. Wickham knows more, but I'll say she has been kept safe from the likes of him, sir. All he told me was Lady Catherine wanted her away from Rosings and ordered him to take her. I made sure we rode all night, sir, and *he* was never alone with her," pointing his thumb at Wickham.

"Good thinkin', Jeremiah." As Mr. Mott took in Elizabeth's form, she straightened her back and raised her chin in a determined manner as her eyes took on a steely quality. Mr. Mott smiled. "A real spitfire this one is! Don't ye worry, missy, nobody will hurt ye here." He raised his voice, "Ye hear that, Wickham? *Nobody!*"

Wickham took a moment to break away from his hold on the barmaid before joining them. "That is not what Lady de Bourgh ordered! She *gave* her to me!" he said throwing a rakish glare Elizabeth's way. Elizabeth's eyes widened.

Jeremiah moved closer to Elizabeth as Mr. Mott moved toward Wickham. "Ye listen to Cap'n Sharp when in Broadstairs, Wickham. I don't care what the duchess wants or don't want." Turning to Elizabeth he asked, "What's yer name, missy?"

"Elizabeth Bennet."

"Well there, Miss Bennet. We'll be takin' ye to see Cap'n Sharp. Come on now."

Mr. Mott led the group through the Ale House kitchen and along the outskirts of a large room full of men drinking, gambling, and flirting with barmaids and other… women. Elizabeth saw some behaviour that shocked her and heard some language she had never known existed—and she did not think she wished to know what it meant.

The group stopped in front of a door which Mr. Mott opened. He motioned for her to enter. "Ye wait here, Miss Bennet. We're goin' to talk to Cap'n Sharp to find out what to do with ye. Jeremiah, ye hold the key since the missy here trusts ye. It might take a little while, missy. Cap'n be sleepin' up the road a ways."

Elizabeth entered the room and looked about. It was a small room with a crude wooden table and four uncomfortable-looking chairs. There were two windows on the far side of the room, looking out over the sea. Elizabeth turned back toward the door and asked, "Jeremiah, may I have something to drink, please? Some water, perhaps?"

"I'm guessin' you don't need anything to eat, Miss Bennet… but I'll see what I can do." Jeremiah flashed a smile at her before closing the door. She could hear the lock slip into place.

The room seemed very quiet compared to the noise of the Ale House. She paced the space, and then went to the windows to look out. From there she could see the cliff extended as far as she was able to ascertain down the shore. It was pure white in the moonlight, and jutted out toward the water with what looked like an arch toward the sea end of it. She opened the window a little so she could hear the ocean and let the sound of the waves calm her, as the sound of water usually did.

It is beautiful! Based on the length of time it took us to arrive, Broadstairs must be near Ramsgate, but I do not know which way that would be from here. So far, Jeremiah and Mr. Mott have treated me well. After seeing what is happening in the tavern room, I am probably better off staying with them! I wonder if Johnny's great-grandfather is here, or Abe's father. Perhaps one of them can help me get word of where I am to William or my family.

After a few more minutes, Jeremiah returned with some tea, a glass of water, bread and cheese. "I thought you might want to hold on to your stockpile, ma'am, so I brought you some food as well." He flashed another smile. "It took them a while to find a decent tea cup, or I'd have been here sooner."

"I thank you, Jeremiah, you have been a great help. I cannot tell you how much I appreciate all you have done for me, sir."

Jeremiah seemed surprised and touched by her words. Had he never heard sincere appreciation from a lady?

"You're welcome, Miss Bennet. I hope the tea isn't too bad; they don't make that here much," he said as he left the room.

Elizabeth finished her meal before the men returned, Wickham not among them. She was standing by the open window when they did. A man she had not seen before, whom she assumed was Captain Sharp, entered first. He crossed the room and stood before her, sizing her up as she did the same.

He was older than Mr. Mott, though he had a full head of strikingly white hair. His green eyes were wise, and he had many laugh lines surrounding them. He reminded her of Johnny. His skin was even more weather-beaten than that of any of the other men she had met so far. His stance was that of a younger man; in fact, she was having a difficult time making out his age due to his good health.

They stood in silence for quite a while. Since Captain Sharp was not inclined to speak, Elizabeth asked, "Good… morning, Captain Sharp. May I ask if you are Johnny's great-grandfather? He looks so much like you."

Captain Sharp had been waiting to see what she would say first. He was surprised that she would begin with this subject, expecting demands for her comfort or to be released. "Aye, Miss Bennet, that I am."

"He speaks of you quite often, sir. I am guessing you are the one who made the ship for him. It is wonderfully crafted. We sailed it down the stream and across the pond and had much fun with it. Johnny taught me how to make the sails furl and unfurl; when they were torn, I repaired them. He is a wonderful boy, sir; you should be proud. I also met a boy named Abe who says his father works for you. He has been taking good care of Johnny."

Captain Sharp's eyes narrowed. "Miss Bennet, why are you tellin' me all this?"

Elizabeth's eyebrow arched and her eyes narrowed a bit in challenge. "Sir, perhaps I was wrong to assume that you cared about Johnny since Lady Catherine has been using him to force you to do her bidding. As you have not seen him in two years, I thought you would want to have news of him. But I do not believe I was wrong, sir. That boy cares for you a great deal, and he would not carry his ship with him everywhere he goes if you did not care for him as well."

"Aye, that I do. But you couldn't be tryin' to get on my good side, eh?" Sharp countered.

"Honestly, sir, not when I first began speaking—but I must admit as I continued, it did cross my mind that my friendship with Johnny would not *harm* my interests either."

Sharp laughed loudly. "I do 'preciate honesty, Miss Bennet, that I do. I think I'm startin' to like you." He sat down in one of the chairs, and it creaked loudly. "But now I have to figure out just what to do with you, ma'am. You see, we're not allowed to take on innocents in this business. The law looks the other way for a lot a things on account of they buy our cargo, but they're not goin' to look elsewhere from this one. The duchess and Wickham got us in a heap o' trouble here. Though I'm glad he brought you here, ma'am, instead o' somewhere else. Anywhere else *you'd* be the one in trouble."

"I assume when you and Mr. Mott speak of 'the duchess' you are speaking of Lady Catherine de Bourgh?" At his nod, she continued, "Well then, does the law look the other way when it comes to treason as well, Captain Sharp? You do know that supplying saltpetre to the French *is* treason, sir? I understand she is holding your grandson, and that is why you are doing it, but getting away without the authorities finding you out is another matter completely."

Sharp slapped his knee and laughed loudly. "Ooooh, missy! You sure have the nerve! Don't she, Mott? Here I am holdin' all the cards, and she's accusin' me of treason! Well there, Miss Bennet, since I'm likin' you more and more every minute, and I can tell she ain't no friend o' yours or you wouldn't be here, I'll tell you a secret. The duchess thinks we are, but we are *not* sendin' saltpetre to the Frenchies. It all goes to America. Maybe we be smugglers, ma'am, but we also be loyal Englishmen. It ain't treason to bring it to America, not yet anyways, and once the war starts, we won't be doin' it anymore, that's for sure. We'll sell the stuff somewheres else if we has to, but we wouldn't be doin' anything with India if it weren't for Johnny. We pay gold and tobacco for the high class lace, wine, and brandy we get from the Frenchies."

Elizabeth smiled brightly. "Well, sir, I am glad to hear it. I must say it was difficult forcing myself to think badly about Johnny's kin, especially since I have met you this morning—I do believe I like you as well!" They all laughed, and then Elizabeth said, "There is something else I do not understand, Captain Sharp. If you knew where he was, why have you never taken Johnny from Lady Catherine?"

"How do you know so much, missy? The duchess has a spy amongst us, she does, other than Wickham. Can't figure out who it is, but she knows things she shouldn't. I've been afraid she'd hurt Johnny if we planned anything. Up till Abe went to Rosings, she had another man there to watch him, and he was one o' hers, too. Just been waitin' for the right time is all, ma'am. Maybe now's the time, eh Mott?"

"Sir, if all has gone as we planned before I was kidnapped, Johnny and Abe are already safe with my fiancé in London. The mine in India is actually on his land, and he found out about it only recently. He is outraged at the treatment of the workers there. While at Rosings, we found the ledgers for the smuggling business, and Johnny and Abe helped us put it all together. She *will* be stopped, sir. She will be blackmailing people no longer."

"Ledgers, books! She's got to have all those papers all the time. That duchess'll send us all to the gallows with her books! And just why are you here, Miss Bennet? Why did the duchess want Wickham to ruin you?"

Elizabeth's eyes widened. "She told him to ruin me?" It took a minute for her to recover enough to speak again. "Well, it does make sense, Captain Sharp, for I have committed the unpardonable sin of becoming engaged to Lady Catherine's nephew." Sharp and Mott looked at each other, confused. "The nephew she had planned on marrying to her daughter."

He slapped his knee. "Aye, that'll do it! This doesn't happen to be the one that owns Pemberley, does it?"

"I believe he does, sir."

Sharp and Mott both laughed heartily. When Sharp recovered he explained, "Miss Bennet, the duchess has had her eye on Pemberley for years. It's all part of her plan to move the stuff up north, or so she says, but I'm thinkin' it's more than just that. When her man comes with messages, we give him a bit o' drink, and then he sure can talk! One story goes that she had her cap set for Pemberley's owner, but he went and married her sister instead, and she's been the meanest hag you ever met since."

Elizabeth's mouth opened in a silent "O," and Sharp continued, "Well, there now, missy, here we are gossipin' like a bunch o' old ladies! Truth is, I've got to decide what to do with you. I don't want to just send you out on post all the way to Town. You think your man is goin' to come lookin' for you?"

Elizabeth was thoughtful for a few minutes. "I do think he would if he knew where to look! Would Johnny or Abe know where Wickham has brought me… and would they tell Mr. Darcy? I think those are questions that need to be considered."

"You want to send him a message sayin' where you are? You tell him you be safe here so he don't come in with guns drawn. I'd put you up with my family, but then Wickham can get to you there cause I have no guard for you tonight. You be better stayin' with us. Mott here and Jeremiah, I trust them and so should you." Turning to Mr. Mott, he continued, "Mott, you take the watch at the lookout cave, and bring Miss Bennet with you. That'll keep her hidden for a while."

Sharp opened the door and let Jeremiah in. "Jeremiah's got some things to do, but when he's done, he'll take you to my granddaughter's house to get some sleep and uhhh… whatever you need, missy. Jeremiah can handle Wickham if he comes after you, eh, Jeremiah? I sent a man with Wickham to the Seven Maidens, but I ain't takin' any chances that he's there for sure."

Elizabeth's eyes opened wide. "The Seven Maidens?"

"The Seven Maidens be the caves we store our cargo at, missy. Wickham was sent to unload a batch from the Frenchies. That's where most o' my men are tonight."

"Captain Sharp, not that I mind, but I was wondering why you are telling me so much about your smuggling business so openly. I thought this would all be secret."

"Miss Bennet, we ain't no secret. Everybody around here knows all about us. Like I said, the law looks the other way for us because o' all the high class customers who want our cargo. It's only when an innocent gets mixed up in the business, or something like what you said about treason, where they'd be comin' after us. That's why I want you to send that there letter to your man to come get you, so they know we ain't keepin' you here against your will. We'll tell him about the saltpetre when he gets here. The duchess makes enough trouble for us—I don't need no extra."

They brought her some writing material, and she wrote to Darcy explaining where she was, that Captain Sharp was keeping her safe, and that she needed someone to come get her as soon as possible. Sharp sent the message with one of his men who he was sure he could trust.

4:00 A.M.

Mott led Elizabeth out of the Digby Ale House and down a path. As she was walking, she reflected on how she had never heard such a mixture of accents in someone's speaking voice before as she had since she met these smugglers. She wondered if it was a result of their being onboard ships for long periods of time with sailors from other parts of the world, mixing together different accents and ways of speaking.

After walking for a while, Mott moved behind some rows of bushes which overlapped. Well hidden behind the bushes, there was a fissure in the rocks, leading downwards. Mott directed her to a tunnel which branched off in two directions, and he took Elizabeth to the right. The tunnel ended abruptly with a turn into a cave which had an opening that bore a short ledge.

At the side of the opening, there was a man sitting on a stool with his back to them, and there was a lantern on a small stool near the cave's opening. Elizabeth thought the lantern was placed in a strange way, and other than providing light for the man, it might be a signal to the ship they were expecting. Mott put his hand on the man's shoulder and motioned for him to leave. "Walker's deaf as a door from bein' too close t' the cannon!" Mott said. "Ye don't need ye ears to be on lookout duty, so he does that now. He misses sailin' though."

As she inched closer to the hole, Elizabeth peeked out and saw evidence that she was above the arch in the chalk cliff that she had seen from the window of the Ale House. Looking around the inside of the cave, she could see there were several stools, a blanket, burnt-out candles, and old cigar ends littering the floor. Bottles of wine and more potent spirits, some empty and some half full, were scattered about—all evidence that this cave was well used by the smugglers.

Elizabeth asked Mott whether he still sailed, but he said he was too old for that now, and then went on to tell her quite a few stories about his adventures on the high seas, much to Elizabeth's amusement.

5:48 A.M. – Sunrise

Their attention was drawn by dawn breaking over the water. It was breathtaking to watch, and Elizabeth thought back to the last sunrise she had seen with William, just before he proposed. So much had happened since then—it was difficult to believe it was only one day ago. She worried about how he had reacted to the news of her kidnapping and wondered what he was doing now. How long would it be before he could get to her?

Just as she was thinking this, she heard a crash come from behind her and turned quickly. Mr. Mott lay on the ground bleeding from his head, and Wickham was standing over him with a broken bottle in his hand. As Elizabeth tried to run for the tunnel, Wickham quickly caught hold of her. She struggled but it was of no use, he pulled out a knife from his boot and held it up so she could get a good view of it.

"Good morning, Lizzy!" he said, his face close to hers, his breath reeking of alcohol. He pulled her closer to him and forced a kiss upon her. She successfully pulled away before he said, "Worry not just yet, little Lizzy, there will be plenty of time for enjoyment later. But for now, I will make certain you do not decide to leave me."

Wickham put the knife away and pulled some rope from his pocket using it to tie her hands together, and then pushed her down on the floor near Mott, ordering her to stay there. Taking one of the half-full bottles off the floor, Wickham began guzzling from it.

Elizabeth was relieved to see that Mott was breathing, though he was unconscious. The bleeding from his head wound had slowed considerably since he had been hit. She hoped that he would be well once he woke up… but she knew she could not expect any help from him in the meantime.

~Broadstairs

6:00 A.M.

The sun had just broken the horizon as the party from London arrived at Broadstairs. They had ridden hard all night, stopping only to change horses, and were exhausted, but when Abe told them that they were very close, the group felt a burst of renewed energy.

Johnny had insisted on coming with them, convincing Darcy and Colonel Fitzwilliam that since his great-grandfather was the leader of the smugglers, he would not be harmed and could convince them to let Miss Lizzy go if they were not inclined to do so already. A few hours earlier, Johnny had been falling asleep in his saddle so Darcy had taken him onto his horse and held him upright while he slept. As they approached Broadstairs, Darcy woke Johnny gently.

Johnny guided them to his grandfather's house, but nobody answered the door. Abe suggested trying Digby's Ale House next since that was a meeting place for the smugglers, and they set off down the road.

Meanwhile, Captain Sharp had heard of some soldiers in the village, and he had brought Jeremiah to the street to meet them.

"Grandpapa!" Johnny jumped down from his horse at the sight of Captain Sharp and ran toward him. The two embraced and Captain Sharp wiped his eyes as the other men dismounted and approached. Darcy got there first.

"Where is Miss Bennet?" Darcy demanded.

"Ah, and you must be Darcy! No need for those pistols or swords, neither, mister; the little miss is just fine. A spitfire that one is!" he laughed. "She's over on lookout duty with Mott for now to keep her out of Wickham's way. Jeremiah was just about to bring her over to my granddaughter's house. We weren't expectin' you for a while yet. How'd you get her letter so fast? Did you meet my man, Jackson, on the road?"

Darcy, Richard and his men were confused.

"No, grandpapa, we didn't see Jackson. Me and Abe brought them here, sir. Miss Lizzy and Mr. Darcy are my friends. Miss Lizzy is the queen of kites! She made a kite for me and showed Abe how to make one, too. We came to get her before Wickedman hurt her."

"Good thinkin' lad, though she's been just fine! Jeremiah took good care of her on the trip here, and Wickham didn't lay a hand on her." He mussed his grandson's hair. "Johnny, 'tis good to see you! Miss Bennet said I'd be proud of you, and so I am. She's a friend of yours, eh? I'm likin' her, too. I hear she fixed the toy ship's sails to unfurl, did she?"

Johnny nodded.

Richard chuckled and said to Darcy, "It *would* be just like Miss Elizabeth to make friends with smugglers!"

Turning to Colonel Fitzwilliam, Sharp said, "If you didn't get her letter, then you don't know—we ain't been doin' no treason no matter what the duchess thinks. Those papers were just to fool the duchess so she wouldn't hurt Johnny here. We be in business to make money, but we be Englishmen, Colonel—we don't supply nothin' more than tobacco to those Frenchies, and for a grand price! The saltpetre all goes to America for now."

His patience growing thin, Darcy took a step closer to Sharp. "I demand to see Miss Bennet immediately."

"And so you will, Darcy. I don't blame you one bit; fine lady, that she is." Turning to Johnny, Sharp said, "Johnny, take Mr. Darcy to the lookout. She's there with Mott. You remember the way?"

"Yes sir!" Johnny straightened his posture, taking his responsibility seriously.

~%~

For never, never, wicked man was wise.
--Homer (Greek poet, dates of life unknown BC)

~Lookout Cave, Broadstairs

Not knowing how Mr. Mott would react if a stranger walked through the cave entrance, Darcy gestured for Johnny to lead the way. The boy started inside, only to stop dead so abruptly that Darcy collided with him. Peering through the opening, he met Elizabeth's terrified gaze. His heart constricted as if gripped in an icy fist.

Mott lay unconscious on the floor, a deep cut on his head spilling a pool of blood onto the dirt beneath him. Elizabeth sat on the floor at his side. Dried blood smeared her bruised face, and someone had stuffed a filthy rag into her mouth as a gag. Her dress was torn, revealing flashes of pale silken flesh. His childhood friend towered over her, swigging from a liquor bottle held in a blood-stained hand. His free hand gripped her bound wrists.

Darcy pushed Johnny gently aside and strode toward his betrothed.

Pivoting, Wickham dropped the bottle as he pulled Elizabeth up in front of him. Smoothly slipping a knife from his boot, he held the blade against the delicate flesh of Elizabeth's neck.

Darcy froze in horror.

"Oh, this is perfect! How good of you to come, Darcy! Did you wish to join in the entertainments that Lizzy has provided me?" Wickham smiled widely.

"Wickham! This is between us, is it not? Let her go; come for me!"

"But your fiancée is too tempting to resist; I will not be robbed of my amusement. I have yet to break her spirit." Not taking his eyes from his adversary, Wickham pressed his cheek against Elizabeth's. "Tell me, Darcy, does she respond as passionately to you as she does to me?" He snickered as his hand wandered licentiously over Elizabeth's figure.

Elizabeth squirmed, her protest muffled by the gag. With a warning snarl, Wickham pressed the knife closer, and she arched her back, straining to pull her neck away from the blade.

On the verge of bursting with rage, Darcy reminded himself, *Elizabeth needs me—there is no telling what Wickham will do if I do not keep my temper under regulation!*

The fiend turned his head to speak into Elizabeth's ear. "No, I forget to whom I am speaking. I am certain that *he* has not sampled your favors... 'Pious Darcy' has always been too proper to allow himself such pleasures! Perhaps he would like to watch!" Head snapping up to meet Darcy's glare, Wickham growled, "Which grieves you more, old friend? To know that I had her first, or that your own aunt *paid* me to ruin her?" Wickham chuckled as Darcy's face coloured further with anger. "Marry your sickly cousin as your family wishes, Darcy. If you still want this spoiled wench, keep her on the side."

One thought echoed through Darcy's mind: *I **will** kill him this time!*

~%~

Darcy's eyes betrayed his thoughts, and Elizabeth knew he could not endure this situation much longer.

Neither man had noticed Johnny inching along the cave wall. The boy had sent her a pointed look before he disappeared from view. She wished she knew for certain what Johnny would do so she could be better prepared to act! Several possibilities moved quickly through her thoughts, and she planned how she might react if Johnny was successful.

She knew the amount of liquor that Wickham had consumed could only assist her efforts.

Elizabeth coiled her muscles as she slowly raised her bound hands to her chest, extending the fingers of one hand and making a fist with the other in anticipation. She attempted to catch Darcy's eyes to alert him, but he would not release Wickham from his incensed glare.

The sound of a bottle shattering rang out, and Wickham's stance changed in the same moment.

She moved quickly, using her hand like a hook, catching hold of his knife hand and pushing outward. Twisting out of Wickham's hold, she threw herself onto the ground, in the direction opposite the opening that would send her plunging down the cliff wall.

Darcy sprang forward, seizing Wickham as Elizabeth rolled away. Taking hold of the knife arm with his left, he pushed Wickham up against the wall and pummeled his face with his right.

Wickham brought his fist up into Darcy's stomach, the blow perfectly aimed to knock the wind from his lungs.

Darcy stepped back out of his adversary's reach to regain his breath. Wickham recovered first and lunged at Darcy with the knife.

Darcy grabbed the knife arm once again, and struck it against the cave wall, causing Wickham to release the blade. As it fell, both men scrambled to retrieve it. In their struggle, the dagger was kicked out the cave opening, sending it bouncing down the cliff wall.

Wickham twisted, striking Darcy in the jaw. Darcy's hand wrapped around his adversary's collar, and he lifted Wickham by the neck, choking the rascal.

"You have gone too far this time!"

Elizabeth feared the emotion she saw in her fiancé's eyes. *Between what Wickham did to his sister and what he has now done to me, he will seek revenge. I must prevent him from becoming a killer!*

Elizabeth's struggles to remove the tight gag gained Johnny's attention and, with his help, her mouth was freed. As Johnny worked on the knots binding her hands, Elizabeth begged, "Stop, William, please! He lied! He put his hands upon me and tried to kiss me, but that is all."

Darcy's expression changed. Abruptly, he dropped his opponent and stepped back, trying to regain his breath once again. Wickham fell to the floor, coughing and gasping for air.

"NO!" Wickham sputtered out phrases between hacking coughs, "No! Hurt you... the worst way. Took her from you."

Elizabeth stated in a steady voice, "You lie."

Faster than anyone could have predicted someone in his condition could move, with a guttural howl, Wickham dashed towards Elizabeth in a frenzy. Darcy moved to stop him.

Surprising everyone, a stool collided with the side of Wickham's head. Losing consciousness, Wickham stumbled into Darcy, who pushed him away roughly. Wickham fell like a sack of grain near the cave opening to the cliff.

"Serves ye right, Wickham!" Mr. Mott spit out as he dropped the stool.

He was unsteady on his feet, and Johnny rushed over to support him. In all the ado, the previously unconscious Mr. Mott had been forgotten.

Elizabeth quickly got to her feet, and Darcy pulled her into his arms. His rage began to cool with *her* safely in his embrace. After a few moments, he took her face in his hands. "My Elizabeth, are you well? Where have you been injured?"

"I will have some bruises, but I am well. Wickham did not do all that he implied."

"There is blood on your face."

Elizabeth blushed. "Oh! I… I was forced to use several… *extreme* tactics my father taught to all his daughters so we could protect ourselves from unwanted advances. The blood is Wickham's, not mine. At one point I found it necessary to bite him—with considerable force. There was one thing that I found quite surprising, though; one would think that he would be warned after the first, but I was able to use a certain manoeuvre involving my knee twice. He began drinking more heavily after the second time."

Darcy and Elizabeth turned toward the tunnel entrance upon hearing a noise to find Colonel Fitzwilliam and Captain Sharp standing there. When Darcy and Johnny had not returned with Elizabeth, Colonel Fitzwilliam had become concerned, and Captain Sharp had led the way to the lookout cave. They had just entered the cave as Mr. Mott struck

Wickham with the stool and had stood quietly watching.

Colonel Fitzwilliam crossed the cave as he dampened a cloth with water from his flask and moved toward Elizabeth. "I must say you did an excellent job defending yourself, Miss Elizabeth!" As he handed her the cloth to wipe her face, he continued, "Though I do not think *that* is Wickham's blood." He said pointing at her hand.

"Oh! How did that happen?" Elizabeth said, moving a little away from Darcy, though Darcy protectively held onto her waist. "I did not feel it before." She winced at the burning ache in her hand.

Darcy removed his cravat and gently wrapped it around her hand. "Most likely when you were twisting your way out of Wickham's hold after Johnny hit him with the bottle. You grasped his hand which was holding the knife, and it must have cut you."

"All the excitement must have masked the pain. It happens often on the battlefield," Colonel Fitzwilliam replied, directing the next to Darcy. "Darce, we need to get her to a doctor as soon as possible."

Trying to distract her from the pain as he wrapped the wound, Darcy asked, "Elizabeth, I must ask how you knew to make that movement to release Wickham's hold on you?"

Elizabeth raised her brows. "Ah… the hoyden I truly am has finally exposed herself to you fully, sir. When I was a young girl, I used to wrestle with the Lucas boys. Because I was so small, I was always the best of the group at escaping from holds. What prevented me from acting sooner was the knife. All I needed was a distraction, which my young friend kindly provided." She nodded her thanks at Johnny. Johnny beamed with pride.

They turned toward the tunnel door at Captain Sharp clearing his throat. "I've noticed bein' hoydenish as a lass can come in handy at times."

"It did today, that is certain. You are a brave lady, Miss Elizabeth!" Colonel Fitzwilliam said with a small smile.

Darcy took the damp handkerchief and carefully wiped the dried blood off Elizabeth's face as she stared into his eyes. Elizabeth was moved by his tenderness and surprised that he should still seem to care for her after what had happened. In that instant, a movement off to the side caught her attention, and she cried out as Wickham rose from the ground.

Terrified, his eyes darted around taking in the scene. The colonel began to move toward him, and Darcy moved to place himself more fully between Elizabeth and Wickham.

Panicked at being surrounded, and disoriented by the blow to the head in combination with his intoxicated state, Wickham glanced behind him at the cave opening and smiled as he leaned toward it. His gaze moved between the colonel and Darcy as he backed away from them.

Realizing Wickham was too confused to be aware of where he was, the colonel grabbed Wickham's arm to stop him. Wickham reacted by hitting the colonel's arm in such a way that it forced him to released his hold.

Darcy yelled, "Don't…!" but at the same moment Wickham broke free and dove through the cave opening.

Wickham's scream echoed through the cave, ending abruptly.

The group stood blinking at the cave opening for a few instants in shock before the colonel took another few steps forward. Holding onto the cave wall, he carefully leaned out and looked down the cliff face. His sickened expression told everything he could not put into words.

The silence was broken when Elizabeth cleared her throat and said something similar to what they were all thinking, "I am certain as the only lady present, and in accordance with what I imagine propriety would demand, at this juncture I *should* say 'Poor Mr. Wickham.' But I must confess, gentlemen, based on my experience with the man—my opinion of this most recent event is profoundly… undecided."

~Fig Tree Inn, Broadstairs

Elizabeth was taken to the Fig Tree Inn, and the local doctor was called for. Captain Sharp sent for his granddaughter, Cassie, to attend the examination. The doctor waited for Cassie to arrive before commencing.

During Doctor Brown's examination of Elizabeth, Darcy was afraid he would run mad if he did not attempt to distract himself from his thoughts. He made certain that his horses were being cared for adequately, inquired after his coach, which had not yet arrived, arranged for a place for his servants to stay when it did, and took rooms for all those in his party, including Mr. Bennet and his uncle who were expected before the end of the day.

None of this was enough to divert his mind from the worry he had for Elizabeth's health—nor did it keep at bay the haunting memory of the mixture of fear and disgust he had seen in Elizabeth's eyes while Wickham held a knife to her throat… and the way he handled her. He could not repress the violent shudder that ran through his body every time this thought forced itself upon him, nor the bitter taste of bile that rose in his throat at the recollection of his own feeling of helplessness as he watched the scene unfold before him.

Completing his own duties well before the doctor had completed his examination, Darcy joined Richard in the private sitting room that he had rented for the duration of their stay in Broadstairs and continued to brood as he paced. Richard, seeming to understand his cousin's aversion to conversation at present, returned his attention to his newspaper after a short greeting.

The rage Darcy felt toward Wickham and Lady Catherine was extreme, knowing fully that the *only* instances that he had *ever* witnessed Elizabeth as fearful or helpless were as a direct result of their actions, and yet his own behaviour could not escape the harshest self-censure. He felt that Lady Catherine would not have blamed Elizabeth for his choice of marriage partners if, through the years, he had been more forceful in his attempts to convince her that he would not marry his cousin under any circumstances. And why, after all they had learned about Lady Catherine in the past few days and all that he knew of Wickham for *years*, had he not anticipated a plan such as this from the pair?

He prayed that Elizabeth would forgive him for he knew not what he would do if she would not or could not.

Darcy hoped the doctor would be finished with his incessant examination shortly as he was unsure how much longer he could fight the intense urge to burst into Elizabeth's chambers and demand to see her.

Finally, Doctor Brown entered the sitting room. "Miss Bennet has given me permission to advise you of her condition, sirs. Her ribs are not broken but are badly bruised. There will not be permanent damage to her hand as long as she follows my instructions. It is imperative that Miss Bennet *not* use her hand at all. I suggest you arrange for a lady's maid for her, sir, for she will surely require the use of her hand if she does not have a great deal of help. Since Cassie has experience as a lady's maid, I hope it is agreeable to you that she has agreed to stay the night.

"If the salve I provided is used every time the wound is cleaned, and it is cleaned and redressed frequently, it should lessen the chance of infection. If a fever develops, I have left some powders for her to take, but I should be called immediately. Though Miss Bennet refuses to take any now, I have left instructions with Cassie to give her laudanum if the pain becomes unbearable."

He hesitated and looked quite uncomfortable before saying, "What worries me most at present is how *favorably* Miss Bennet is enduring her ordeal. Most ladies would not be carrying on this well. I have left extra laudanum with Cassie if Miss Bennet needs it to calm her. I have also left a draught for her to take if she has trouble sleeping."

Darcy said, "Doctor, Miss Bennet is an exceptionally brave lady. In the past, I have seen her face some situations with equanimity in which other ladies would have been incapacitated, but those were not as… personal as this was. However, I expect that she would react in a calmer manner than most ladies would to any situation."

Doctor Brown took a deep breath, struggling to decide how much he should reveal, then replied, "Mr. Darcy, with all due respect, sir, I must speak plainly. You have not seen the extent of the injuries to her ribs and the other bruises her body bears. The man who did this had experience in causing a great deal of pain without lasting damage. I must insist on warning you that a more severe reaction than Miss Bennet is currently displaying is more than likely to appear in a delayed fashion."

Darcy nodded thoughtfully. His glance toward his cousin was hint enough to Richard to hide himself behind his newspaper once again. Darcy spoke in a low voice, "Doctor… I am engaged to marry Miss Bennet… I must ask, sir…" he could not finish. He had thought on this during his ride to Broadstairs and had decided that if it had been so, if she had been defiled, it would not be of consequence to him as long as Elizabeth was safe—he loved her too much to live without her. He did feel it a vital fact to *know*, though, for Elizabeth's sake. She had said Wickham did not… but she must have recognized him to have been in a complete rage at the time. Had she said it only to stop him from committing murder?

"She was not violated, Mr. Darcy."

A sense of relief washed over him. "Thank you, Doctor." The gentlemen shook hands as Darcy continued, "Before you leave, will you please tell Cassie that I would like to speak to her?"

"Certainly, Mr. Darcy. I will return in the morning unless I am sent for sooner." Doctor Brown took his leave of the gentlemen.

Not wishing for Captain Sharp's granddaughter, Cassie, to leave her charge for long, Darcy met her in the hallway outside Elizabeth's chambers. She was hired by Darcy to assist Elizabeth for the remainder of their stay in Broadstairs. Darcy asked her to notify him if Elizabeth needed him for any reason, and if she required anything at all to make her more comfortable, she was to get it without delay, regardless of cost. As Cassie departed through the door to Elizabeth's chambers, he peeked through the doorway in an attempt to catch a glimpse of his beloved. A brief hint of a smile passed over Cassie's features before she could check herself, revealing to him that he had been caught in the attempt.

With a slight blush, and hoping he spoke loudly enough for Elizabeth to hear, Darcy said, "Please relay to Miss Bennet my best wishes for a good night and a speedy recovery."

Elizabeth did hear her betrothed's message and smiled. As she readied for bed, she was quite put out at having to depend so completely on anyone, but was grateful for Cassie's assistance just the same. After a much needed hot bath, and a meal in her room, Elizabeth gladly followed the doctor's orders to sleep.

~%~

After having a meal tray sent up to Richard's room and leaving the door slightly ajar so they could hear if Cassie summoned them, Darcy and Richard were discussing how to go about informing Mr. Bennet of the day's events upon his arrival at Broadstairs when they heard a scream come from across the hall. Not about to risk her life for the sake of propriety, a panicked Darcy burst into Elizabeth's room with Richard close on his heels.

Elizabeth was sitting up straight in bed, her arms flailing about as if she were hitting someone, and she was still screaming. After quickly looking about the room and seeing no one else there, Darcy rushed to Elizabeth while Richard searched the room more thoroughly. Meanwhile, Cassie had heard the screams from the servant's corridor as she returned with a pitcher of water and some fresh linen. She rushed in, taking in the scene before her.

Darcy kept repeating Elizabeth's name, but she was not responding. He sat on the edge of the bed and, gently restraining her flailing hands, said in a voice full of concern, "Elizabeth! Please tell me, what is the matter?"

She stopped screaming and thrashing at his touch and looked at him; her trembling was visible to all. Darcy recognized the same terrified look in her eyes as from the woods at Rosings. He glanced at Richard with a questioning look. Richard, who had just completed his search of the room, shook his head and shrugged his shoulders. Darcy turned back to Elizabeth. "I promise that you are safe, Elizabeth."

Elizabeth looked around the room frantically and then back to Darcy. "William?"

Her confusion now was frightening him even more than the screaming and thrashing had. "Yes, Cassie, Richard, and I came into your room when we heard your scream. I think you were dreaming, Elizabeth. There is no one else here."

"But Wickham was here!"

Darcy was unsure of how to respond without upsetting her further, but felt the brutal truth was best. "Wickham is dead; he can no longer hurt you."

Her countenance slowly changed from terrified and confused to one of understanding. "Yes, a dream… not real… just a dream," she said more to herself than to anybody else. Elizabeth broke down into sobs. "Oh! I am sorry, William… I am so weak!"

Since propriety had been already completely abandoned the moment he stepped through her bedchamber door, nothing was going to keep him from taking her in his arms now when she needed him. Hesitating for a moment, thinking it was possible that contact with his person might frighten her, he recalled that in the cave when he had taken her into his embrace it had served to soothe her a great deal. He gathered her close, and she clung to him tightly. Taking a shaky breath, he said, "You are the most valiant lady I have ever met, Elizabeth! It is only natural to have nightmares after such an experience." Darcy closed his eyes. Emotions tightened his throat, but he was able to whisper sweet nothings past it, and he rubbed her back gently to help settle her, remembering that this tender motion had proved helpful with Georgiana on a few occasions after *her* problems with Wickham.

Elizabeth slowly quieted. Darcy wished to kiss her tears away but could not do so in the present company. Instead, he retrieved his handkerchief from his pocket and gently blotted the tears from her cheeks, handing it to her when he was done.

Darcy said in a tone of gentleness and commiseration, "Is there nothing you could take, to give you relief? A glass of wine; shall I get you one?"

"No, I thank you," she replied, endeavoring to recover herself, wiping her eyes with his handkerchief. "I shall be well. I was only distressed by that dreadful dream."

Richard cleared his throat to remind Darcy that he and Cassie were still in the room.

He loathed having to release her—there was nothing he wanted more at that moment than to hold her all night so he could make certain she felt safe—but once Elizabeth had steadied her emotions, he had no acceptable excuse to hold her any longer. He rose and stepped away from the bed.

Cassie spoke up, "I will stay with you the rest of the night, Miss Lizzy. I am sorry I stepped out to get some fresh water. I will not leave you again."

"There is nothing to apologize for, Cassie," Elizabeth answered.

He knew he could linger no longer, and though Cassie promised to remain with her, it was difficult for Darcy to tear himself from Elizabeth's side. The gentlemen bid Elizabeth and Cassie a good night and *pleasant* dreams as they left the room.

For the next couple of hours, Darcy paced and startled at every noise. After several instances of Darcy's going so far as having knocked on her door to inquire as to Elizabeth's state of well-being, Richard assigned one of his men to sit outside her door, with the promise that Darcy would be awakened if anything out of the ordinary occurred, so that his cousin could get some rest.

Darcy had been attempting to remain awake long enough to greet Lord Matlock and Mr. Bennet when they arrived, but he fell asleep at almost the same moment as he sat down in a chair by the fire in Richard's room. Richard roused him enough to move him to the bed and left him there to sleep, leaving the door open a few inches so his man could awaken Darcy without delay if there was a need.

Being used to the irregular hours of army life, Richard bided his time until the arrival of his father and Mr. Bennet in the dining room, and enjoyed a good meal and a few pints with two of his men, Captain Sharp, Mr. Mott, and Jeremiah—all at Darcy's expense of course.

Lord Matlock and Mr. Bennet arrived by horseback a while later, guided to the correct place by the man Richard left waiting for them on the road leading into Broadstairs. Lord Matlock informed Richard that when Elizabeth's letter had reached Darcy House, Mrs. Martin had forwarded it to Matlock House. Richard told both the gentlemen of the happenings in Broadstairs and Elizabeth's condition. After dispatching an express to Matlock House, the Gardiners, and Longbourn relating the news of Elizabeth's relative well-being, all of the gentlemen then retired for the night since Elizabeth and Darcy were not expected to wake until morning.

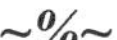

Thursday, March 26, 1812

Elizabeth heard the sound of sea gulls and filled her lungs with salty air before she opened her eyes the next morning. When she sat up, she was reminded of Wickham's rough treatment of her, but she knew the bruises would soon heal. Though the doctor had said she would regain full use of her hand if she rested it, she knew that having her activities curtailed was going to be frustrating for her. She hoped Cassie had a patient temperament, for that was what she would need to put up with an independent lady such as herself in such a state as this.

The reminder of Wickham caused her mood to turn pensive. She had passed a restless night filled with dreams echoing all that had happened the previous two days. After her screams had alerted William of her nightmares, at Elizabeth's request, Cassie moved from sleeping on the couch in her room to sharing the bed with her so that she could wake Elizabeth every time she began to thrash around—*before* the dream became too deeply involved and her cries became loud enough to disturb others. Elizabeth prayed these dreams would not continue.

Remembering how William had been with her after she had the first of many dreams a few hours ago, she could not help but think of how wonderfully safe it felt to have him hold her just then. Every time she had awakened during the night, she had wished he had been there to make her feel that way again.

Some of her nightmares were not of what had happened to her… not directly anyway. The worst of them were of what might happen as a *result* of the past days.

Yesterday, William had acted very protective toward her and his feelings seemed to have been unchanged, but she wondered whether his intentions toward her would alter after he had time to reflect upon what had happened to her. Wickham had put his hands upon her in a way she had never experienced before, and most of it was done directly before William's own eyes! She doubted any man could look past how she had been sullied, and she could not blame William in the slightest if he held it against her.

She wondered when he would ask to end their engagement. Perhaps she should do it—to make it easier for him? Or should she take advantage of every minute they spent together before he said the words? Once those words were uttered, she doubted she would ever see him again.

Cassie helped her dress into a gown borrowed from the Innkeeper's wife while Elizabeth's was being mended and laundered. William had brought her bag, but the bag had been too small to fit in a gown—she had thought she would wear one of her aunt's gowns when she reached London. While she dressed, Cassie told her that Lord Matlock and Mr. Bennet had arrived while she was sleeping, and that Darcy had sent his valet to the kitchen to wait for Cassie so he could inquire about how Elizabeth fared this morning. Elizabeth's mood lifted slightly at the last piece of information; at least he still cared for her a little.

Leaving her room to find her way to breakfast, she found Mr. Bennet sitting in a chair in the hall waiting for her. He rushed forward and embraced her, his eyes glistening with unshed tears, too moved for words.

"I am well, Papa," she whispered.

"I am glad to have had the foresight to meet you upstairs. I cannot express how concerned for you I have been, my dear," Mr. Bennet croaked out as he wiped at his eyes, then looked more closely at his daughter. "You look tired, my Lizzy… excessively tired. Are you certain you have rested enough?"

"Yes, Papa, I have rested as well as I am able to just now. I have no wish to return to bed. I must admit that I hope to have fewer dreams this night. I am hungry, and that must be a good sign!" She smiled at her father as best she could, trusting that it would help to belay his fears for her.

Mr. Bennet nodded and then escorted Elizabeth to the dining room. All of the gentlemen stood and exchanged greetings with the newcomers. Darcy left the table to fill a plate of food for Elizabeth from the sideboard and returned just as Mr. Mott approached them.

"Good mornin', Miss Bennet! It's good to see ye up and about. Good mornin' gentlemen! I been sent to check on ye by the Cap'n. They better be treatin' ye good here at the Fig. If they don't, ye let us know." Turning to Elizabeth, Mr. Mott continued, "How is Cass workin' out for ye?"

"Good morning, Mr. Mott. I am happy to see you have recovered so well! Cassie is a great help, sir, and I think highly of her. I have not had time to do much more than sleep since my arrival at the Fig Tree Inn, but I am just now discovering the food is delicious. Would you like to join us for breakfast?"

"Thank ye, missy. I'd join ye, but I've broke my fast already and I have work this mornin'. The Cap'n wants to know if ye, Miss Bennet, and all ye gentlemen would want t' join the rest o' us for a picnic on the morrow at the beach since the weather is so fine. It's a party for Johnny's homecomin', and ye all had much t' do with that. Miss Bennet, Cap'n wants t' take ye t' Seven Maidens if ye game, and Cass can help ye t' pick out some lace for ye dress." Mott glanced at Darcy, and then back to Elizabeth, displaying an almost toothless grin.

Elizabeth looked at her father whose eyebrows were high on his forehead, and then to Darcy's shocked expression. She blushed and said, "Since the doctor has forbidden me from removing from Broadstairs at present, and we have no plans, I am certain we shall attend the party, Mr. Mott. I would like to see everyone again before I return home."

Richard had spoken to Mr. Bennet earlier about a certain subject, and received permission to discuss the subject in Elizabeth's presence. Richard said, "Mr. Mott, before you leave us… I thought I should inform everyone at once… Wickham will be buried this morning at eleven o'clock. The parson will say a few words at the graveside."

"Well now. I fer one won't be goin', but I'll pass the word on, Colonel. Don't ye go waitin' on any of us, though; there ain't no friends of Wickham 'round here." Turning and bowing to Elizabeth, Mott said, "Have a good day, Miss Bennet. Hope yer feelin' better. Good day, gentlemen." Mott bowed to the gentlemen and left the group.

Elizabeth was concerned about William's reaction to Wickham's burial. "Will you be attending the burial, Mr. Darcy?"

A dark look briefly passed over Darcy's face. "I have no wish to attend. The boy I grew up with was not the same man who died yesterday. I have already grieved his loss many times over the years… too many times." Elizabeth nodded and Darcy asked, "I know it is not customary for a lady to do so, but do you think it would be helpful for you to attend, Miss Elizabeth?" He intended on accompanying her if she felt it necessary to go. Darcy noticed they had Mr. Bennet's full attention.

Elizabeth looked down at her plate and simply stated, "I would prefer not to."

Judging the subject to be at an end, Darcy asked permission from Mr. Bennet to escort Elizabeth for a walk along the beach after breakfast. After receiving a silent nod of approval from Elizabeth, Mr. Bennet agreed. When Elizabeth had finished eating, Darcy rose to hold Elizabeth's chair, and then she returned to her room briefly to retrieve a borrowed pelisse and bonnet and ask Cassie to accompany them.

~%~

Elizabeth and Darcy walked out in silence for a few minutes. Cassie stayed a few steps behind them to allow for private conversation, doing her best to appear interested in her shoes, her gloves, the village, or the waves rolling onto the shore—anything *except* Elizabeth and Darcy, though that is where her attention was truly focused. She watched her temporary mistress for any signs of excessive distress.

Though she had only known her for a few hours, Cassie had already grown quite fond of Miss Bennet. Cassie had spent years in service as a personal maid to Lady Howell in London, and had been spoiled by having such an excellent mistress. When Lady Howell died, she had left Cassie a little money—enough to live on for a while. At the time, Cassie had thought she would never find another lady as fine as her former mistress, so she had left London to go home and see if she could find work near there. She had only agreed to help Miss Bennet as a favor to her grandfather, her cousin Johnny, and Doctor Brown. Now she thought it possible that Elizabeth was just as fine a lady as her former mistress.

During her time with Lady Howell, she had learned a few things about the gentry that would apply to this circumstance. She knew that if Elizabeth's experiences yesterday were to become public, she would be considered "ruined" by the *ton*, that gentlemen do not usually marry ruined ladies unless they were the one to ruin her and were forced to do so, and that most times those of the highest circles of society were shallow enough that the wishes of their hearts would never win out over the unwritten rules of society.

Elizabeth had spoken often in her sleep last night, and so Cassie had a good idea as to what this conversation was going to be about… or at least what Elizabeth *feared* it would be about.

Seeing the look of concern when Darcy spoke to her after meeting with the doctor, the look of love and torment in Darcy's eyes last night after Elizabeth's first nightmare, and the interaction between the two that followed, Cassie was praying that his heart would rule and all would turn out well with this couple who were so obviously deeply in love.

The next few minutes would prove what kind of man Darcy really was.

~%~

Darcy attempted to speak several times before he could force himself to say the words, "Miss Elizabeth… I would certainly understand if you would wish to…" his voice cracked, "end our engagement after all that has happened…" he ceased speaking when she stopped walking.

Elizabeth's heart was breaking—it was as she feared, he wished to end their engagement. She took a deep breath, hoping it would help her to hold back her tears and could not meet his eyes as she said in a steady voice devoid of all emotion, "Mr. Darcy, you need not say another word. I know very well that I have been compromised by the events of late, and I understand your wish to end our engagement. I release you without any need for further discourse on the subject."

Darcy's eyes widened. "NO! No, *I* do not wish it… that is to say, I am to blame for this entire ordeal, and I would understand if *you* would wish to end our engagement. Thankfully, Wickham did not do all that he implied, but even if he had, I would have honoured our engagement!"

"I would not wish you to *honour* an engagement out of duty or obligation. I do not wish you to marry me out of guilt or pity, sir."

"Elizabeth, I wish to marry you out of pure *selfishness*, not obligation, guilt, or pity. Without the need to think about it, I realized on the ride from London that it did not matter… whatever Wickham had done, it would not have been your choice..." His voice again broke with emotion, and he paused a moment to collect himself before saying, "My affections and wishes are unchanged, but one word from you will silence me on this subject forever." He swallowed hard.

Elizabeth closed her eyes and sighed as a wave of relief passed through her soul. It took several heartbeats to recover enough to speak. "William, please explain to me how you think it was your fault that Lady Catherine ordered Wickham to kidnap and… to kidnap me."

Darcy answered very quickly, as if the words would burn his tongue, "Lady Catherine had you kidnapped because she wanted me to marry her daughter, not you."

"And you are to blame because…?"

"I should have made it clearer that I would not marry her daughter. I should have…"

Elizabeth interrupted, "Mr. Darcy, had you not expressed the fact that you had no interest in matrimony with your cousin?"

"Yes, I had, but…"

"Was it ever within your power to control Lady Catherine's thoughts, wishes, or actions?"

"No, she has never been swayed by the opinions or arguments of anyone or anything but her own wishes."

"Then you are to blame because…?"

Darcy blinked a few times before admitting, "I am not to blame."

"But you think I am such an irrational creature that *I* would blame you for what Lady Catherine and Wickham did?"

After a few moments of careful consideration he replied, "No, I do not."

"Good. Then we have nothing left to discuss on that matter, have we?" Elizabeth said, but her countenance darkened. "You do know this will cause even more gossip, William? I will be considered damaged… ruined. Are you absolutely sure you are not just honouring our engagement because of a sense of duty? Are you certain you wish to subject your sister and family to my dis honour?"

"Elizabeth, please rest assured that that will not happen. Our friends here in Broadstairs have already agreed not to mention this incident to anyone who does not already know about it. It was Lady Catherine who put these events into motion. *My* uncle, *her* brother, the husband of your *particular* friend, a man who cares for you almost as a daughter—the Earl of Matlock—is determined that all involved in this incident remain silent on the matter. There will be no gossip; it will not be talked of. He does this to protect not only your reputation, but the family names of Fitzwilliam and de Bourgh, which Lady Catherine has dis honoured. *You* have dis honoured no one, Elizabeth!"

Darcy hesitated for a moment, looking deeply into her eyes and then almost whispered, "I beg of you, do not ask me to disappear from your life—you are more necessary to me than the air I breathe." Then he smiled a little, repeating what he had said during his proposal at Rosings, "Will it help if I throw myself at your feet and grovel? I am quite prepared to do so and have been for some time now."

She stood looking into his eyes for a minute or two before saying, "I am a selfish creature, William, and for the sake of giving relief to my own feelings, at this moment I care not how much I may be wounding your reputation if this should ever be found out."

Darcy's eyes shone with hope. "Then you *will* marry me, Elizabeth?"

She smiled brilliantly, sending his heart racing. "I would be a fool not to marry the man I love more than life itself, would I not?" Then she added with a hint of teasing in her manner, "Besides, who else would make certain you understand you that you take too much upon yourself?"

His arms ached to hold her. "I will speak to your father!" His smile widened. "Immediately—before you change your mind!"

"I will not change my mind about marrying you, my William!" she said with so much affection in her voice that he felt it to his very core, and his throat tightened again with a much different emotion.

They walked for several minutes before he could speak again. "Do you think your father expects my petition after Mr. Mott spoke of lace for your wedding gown earlier?" His dimples made a glorious appearance, and Elizabeth's heart skipped a beat.

"I do not think my father realized Mr. Mott was referring to my *wedding* gown. And living in a house with so many women, he does tend to ignore any talk of lace." Elizabeth's eyes twinkled with amusement. "Oh! Speaking of Mr. Mott calls another subject to mind. I will need your assistance in an undertaking which must be completed before we leave Broadstairs. I promised to make Johnny another kite, and since we will be leaving soon, I should like to do it today, but I can scarcely do it with my hand injured so."

"I am embarrassed to admit that I know not how to make one. A member of my father's staff would make them for me, though I do know how to fly one. Under your wise instruction, your loyal knight will do thy bidding, my queen of kites," Darcy bowed and pressed his lips gently to her uninjured hand.

Elizabeth laughed. "You *will* tell me how you know about that someday, sir, but for now, I am satisfied. I have devised a plan! We are in need of supplies and will be able to acquire them on our return to the Inn. Once there, I suggest you speak to my father, and then we shall spend the remainder of the day together assembling the kite. Does my plan meet with your approval, William?"

"Have I told you what it does to me when you use my Christian name?" His eyes were so alive with passion that it stirred powerful feelings within her. She blushed and broke the gaze swiftly, afraid of what *she* might do if she became lost in his eyes at this time.

His voice brought her back from her reverie. "Any plan that includes spending the day with you meets with my approval." His countenance turned worried as he asked, "Do you believe your father will consent?"

"I believe he will, but you must remember that he and I are very close, William. He might be a bit… difficult."

Darcy winced. *Will everything involved in my relationship with Elizabeth be difficult?* His eyes were caught by hers anew, and he sighed, losing himself to her once more. *To have only the privilege of gazing into these eyes for the remainder of my days would certainly be worth any difficulties life will put in my way!*

During their exchange, Cassie let out a sigh of relief, comforted by Elizabeth's smiles proving that Darcy would not abandon her to abide by the expectations of the *ton* after all.

The course of true love never did run smooth
--William Shakespeare (English Playwright/Poet 1564-1616)

~Fig Tree Inn

Darcy returned to his chamber at the Inn to refresh himself before seeking an audience with Mr. Bennet. Having taken care of his appearance, he began to pace the room as he saw the necessity of using the next few minutes to perfect what he should say to Elizabeth's father when requesting her hand.

Once his appeal was settled upon, Darcy thought himself quite prepared for this interview. As he left his room, he told himself that he was not *very* apprehensive. Nor was he *very* nervous when he descended the steps. Nor was he *very* agitated when he entered the sitting room where he found Mr. Bennet, the room's only occupant, reading.

But then, quite unexpectedly, as he entered the gentleman's presence and sat across from the father of his future happiness, the rational portion of his mind gave way and all was in an uproar. Darcy's preparation was for nothing; it was as if his planned words were written on a slate that had been wiped entirely clean. All that remained within him at the moment was his love for Elizabeth and a sudden and extreme apprehension about the outcome of this interview.

Indeed, had it been any other man that he was to petition, Darcy would have been confident of immediate approval. But this was Elizabeth's father! From what Elizabeth had told him, she had spent quite a lot of time with him while growing up. Having met her mother, he knew it must have been through her father's ideals that Elizabeth learned to value a man for more than his material worth or the social gain one might expect when connected to him. This man was not going to be impressed by his wealth or social standing any more than was Elizabeth.

Darcy wondered if Mr. Bennet was expecting his petition for her hand.

"Mr. Bennet… Sir, I am here today to request… it would be a great honour, sir, to… I respectfully beseech your consent to a marriage between your daughter, Miss Elizabeth, and myself…sir." Darcy fumbled out and breathed a sigh of relief.

~%~

A mirthless snort slipped from Mr. Bennet's throat, and he watched Darcy's eyes widen.

I am not prepared for this. I have not yet decided if he is worthy of my Lizzy!

Mr. Bennet's eyes tightened as he examined more closely the man sitting across from him. Darcy, though impeccably dressed as usual, had something about his countenance today that was very different from anything he had observed in their earlier encounters. The impression the young man projected today was more akin to a frightened deer than the commanding presence of the master of one of the largest estates in all of England. It was most astonishing.

The older man frowned deeply as he recognized that he still harboured resentment toward his daughter's petitioner. He *knew* that some of his feelings were unreasonable. After all, the man had just saved Lizzy's life! But still… his saving her life did not imply that she owed him the remainder of her years in return.

When he had left Lizzy in November—plunging her into that resultant dark state of mind and the melancholy that followed his departure—after witnessing ***that****, how can I now believe that he respects her as he should… that he recognizes Lizzy's worth?*

He knew that Darcy had been in love with Lizzy—that much had been obvious during their time together in Hertfordshire… but then he had left her behind. Had Darcy come to terms with the concerns that had persuaded him to reject her and leave months ago?

Was Darcy's offer today an extension of his protective nature brought about by the ordeal they had just endured together? Once the reality of the situation set in, would he abandon her again, just as he had last November, this time leaving her in disgrace after a broken engagement as well?

Did he now offer her marriage out of some misguided sense of duty? Was he assuming responsibility for all that had recently happened to her since his own aunt and childhood friend were responsible for her trauma?

Mr. Bennet could *not* allow Lizzy to marry a man who could not fully respect her for the wonderful person she was. He had daily proof of the consequences of not being able to respect a marriage partner, and he would not wish his own fate upon any of his daughters, especially not Lizzy. Although Mrs. Bennet showed no indication of noticing his own lack of respect for her, he knew that his Lizzy would be miserable if Darcy withdrew his affections from her after they were married. If this petition was being made out of a sense of obligation for the past few days' experiences, it was quite likely that, in time, Darcy's regard would turn into indifference—or worse, resentment—and their marriage would become unbearable for them both.

Would Lizzy be good for him? Yes, without question! She drew him out of his reticence and helped him to reveal the amiable man within.

Now was the time that he was required to give an answer to the question that had plagued him for a long time —would Darcy be good for Lizzy?

~%~

Mr. Bennet's silent stare was causing Darcy's anxiety to rise precipitously. A number of emotions had passed across Mr. Bennet's face during this extended silence and none of them were positive! He had to say something, if only to remind Mr. Bennet that he was waiting for an answer.

"Mr. Bennet?"

Several minutes passed before Darcy could wait no longer. "Mr. Bennet, sir?"

Mr. Bennet blinked a few times, bringing himself back to the present and sighed quite audibly. "Mr. Darcy, you know not what you ask of me!" A few moments later he shook his head and added, "I am very concerned that this is a hasty reaction to the experiences that you both have undergone the past few days."

Darcy looked at Mr. Bennet carefully to see if he could detect any of Elizabeth's teasing in his eyes, but he could not. This was serious. Icy fingers of fear wrapped around his heart. Darcy rose quickly from his chair and walked to stand by the window. Closing his eyes, he took several deep breaths in an attempt to control his emotions.

Mr. Bennet's voice betrayed the anger toward Darcy which had finally been unleashed. "You left her months ago without a word in all that time. Do you know what she went through after you left? Our Lizzy disappeared, and she became a shell of her former self. She was almost lost to us, Mr. Darcy! *You* were not there to see what had to occur to bring her back. It was almost the most terrifying experience of my life, second only to that of her being kidnapped! For the past several minutes I have been thinking on the matter and, to be honest, I cannot help but be of the opinion that you, sir, do not deserve her."

The anxiety that had been building within Darcy had suddenly been transformed into anger—at *himself.* He knew that to reply now would give the impression that he was angry with Mr. Bennet, which was the last thing he wished for. Well... close to the last thing he wished to happen. Mr. Bennet held his future in his hands.

Being of a private nature and not knowing the gentleman well, he was more than hesitant to expose the depth of his feelings for Elizabeth, even to her father. Words were insufficient to communicate what he so deeply felt, but he knew that he had to try to find a way to help Mr. Bennet understand before he could gain this man's approval.

More important than his fear of exposing his feelings was the certainty that he knew that the man he had become since he had met Elizabeth could not survive without her. With Elizabeth as his wife, he would live; without her, he would simply *exist*, emotionally dead as he had been during the months following his removal from Hertfordshire.

Focusing on what Mr. Bennet had said, Darcy realized that Elizabeth had experienced a similar reaction to their separation. A violent shudder ripped through him at the thought. No! He could not allow her to live that way and neither could he do so, especially not now—not with the absolute knowledge that Elizabeth returned his love in full measure. To face life separately, that was unthinkable to him. From Mr. Bennet's speech, it had been so for Elizabeth as well.

Elizabeth trusted her father, and he decided he would have to trust him as well. He would need to pour out his heart and soul to Mr. Bennet if there ever was to be happiness in their future.

The final wall of reserve tumbled down, and he turned to Mr. Bennet and began, "I would like to be completely open with you, sir, if you will give me leave to do so?"

Mr. Bennet's eyebrows rose almost to his hairline. This statement piqued his curiosity to no end. "Yes, yes, of course, I value honesty very highly. Go on."

Darcy took a deep breath and continued, "From the first moment I saw your daughter last autumn, I felt a connexion to her unequaled to anything I had ever experienced. At the very beginning, her lack of fortune and connexions kept me from courting her. Though I care little for the opinions of society in general, in the past, I had witnessed a few matches that were unequal in these respects, and they caused a great deal of censure from the *ton*. In some cases, the circumstances led to regret, bitterness and resentment between the couple, and I felt this would best be avoided. I thought I was denying only myself, sacrificing my own happiness for Miss Elizabeth's sake, and that of my sister.

"So, I tried my best to stay away from Miss Elizabeth and foolishly thought that distance would be enough to lessen my attachment to her—though I struggled, I could barely keep my eyes from turning toward her. I discovered this plan of action worked in reverse, sir, because what I found when I watched her only served to strengthen my regard. This, of course, intensified my already favorable opinion of her goodness, her intelligence… her unequaled wit, beauty, elegance, and grace… her liveliness, her love of nature… her mastery of conversing with anyone in subjects ranging from ribbons and lace to philosophy… her brilliant impertinence, her glorious independent spirit, the quickness of her mind… her impeccable manners in the face of even the most adverse of situations, and so much more. Even her imperfections are perfection itself, sir. She is strikingly so… full of life!

"As each meeting would progress, I would find myself unwittingly drawn to her as a moth to a flame, until she would open a conversation with me, and I could not stop myself from responding. I had selfishly convinced myself that the attachment was mine alone and that my friendship with her would not raise her expectations. It proved that I had little control over my actions, *within* the bounds of propriety, of course, and every time I was with her, I could not resist having one more 'last chance' of experiencing the joy which accompanied spending time in her presence, nor could I restrain myself when she would honour me with being the person with whom she was willing to share her thoughts and opinions.

"After leaving her presence, I would examine my behaviour and reproach myself, resolving never to repeat the experience—only to begin the entire process again every time we met. I thought it best for her sake to withdraw from the vicinity before I risked engaging her heart in more than a friendship, though my own had long since been irrevocably and completely lost to her.

"The most difficult thing I have ever done in my life was to leave Hertfordshire, Mr. Bennet. It would be impossible for me to explain the torture I experienced in being away from her, thinking I could not ever have what my heart most desired—Elizabeth by my side for the remainder of my life. Let me only say my misery was complete, indeed.

"You may not know much of my personal history, sir. Would you please allow me to enlighten you further?"

Mr. Bennet only nodded, for he knew more than Darcy could probably guess but did not want to break the young man's concentration.

Darcy averted his eyes from Mr. Bennet and began to pace slowly in front of the fire. "My mother died when I was but a lad, shortly after my sister, Georgiana, was born. As she was dying, she asked me to make several promises to her. When she died, the warmth that was once a part of everyday life died as well. Pemberley became a very cold place—a house, no longer a home. My father became withdrawn, and I felt I had failed in one of my promises to my mother. I did not understand the one last thing my mother asked of me, and so I went to my only adult relative at Pemberley at the time, other than my father—my mother's sister, Lady Catherine de Bourgh.

"Based on Lady Catherine's explanation of this promise, I could *not* have married Miss Elizabeth and fulfill the promise I made to my mother on her deathbed. Only now do I realize that Lady Catherine was manipulating me with her version of what my mother had meant, only said to further her own selfish goals." Darcy closed his eyes and ground his teeth for several moments before recollecting where he was. His eyes snapped open and he glanced at Mr. Bennet.

"Excuse me, sir. I need a moment before continuing." It took several moments to master his anger before Darcy could speak again.

"My father died several years ago, leaving the care of the estate to me. The guardianship of my sister, more than ten years my junior, was left to my cousin Colonel Fitzwilliam and myself. Since my cousin is in the army and had spent some considerable time on the continent, most of the responsibility of her upbringing was left to me. An event occurred last summer concerning Georgiana, and I felt I had failed to uphold my second promise to my mother.

"As for myself, I existed only to perform my inherited duty in a way that I thought would honour my parents and fulfill my obligations to my family.

"But when I met Miss Elizabeth, I realized that I was not really 'living,' sir. Being in her presence brought an awareness of *life* within me… warmth I had never known, not even when my mother was alive.

"After battling within myself, I decided that I was *willing* to fail in carrying out what I believed to be the final promise to my mother, sir, until my attention was quite forcefully turned once again to consider that if I did marry Miss Elizabeth, she would grow to regret our marriage if the *ton* rejected her. I knew that *she*, at least, deserved every happiness; I, in my selfishness, could not be the cause of plunging her into a life of misery and suffering. I had no reason to believe the *ton* would not reject her, and so I deemed it necessary to leave Netherfield.

"To be honest, leaving Miss Elizabeth behind almost destroyed me. I was in such a state that I might have ended up in Bedlam had my cousin Richard not reached me when he did. It was only the thought of disappointing Elizabeth that saved me. I hope that I have come through that dark time a better man.

"Providentially, my Aunt Adelaide came to me with a letter which had been dictated to her by my mother when she had the strength to explain her wishes… stronger than she had been when she had spoken to me. She was instructed not to give it to me until a certain time in my life, though I wish that I might have had the opportunity to understand her wishes much sooner, since much of the heartache of the past months would have been avoided."

Darcy stopped pacing and a short mirthless laugh escaped his lips. "It seems her wish for me to 'marry well' did not mean what Lady Catherine told me it did, after all. In her letter, my mother explained that she and my father wished me to be *happy*… to love and respect my marriage partner, and not to give in to the expectations of the *ton*. It does me little credit to admit that, for sixteen years, I had listened to Lady Catherine's interpretation of those words. Instead, I *should* have had more faith that a woman who loved her husband so deeply would want the same for her children."

Darcy stared out the window for a few long moments before turning back to Mr. Bennet. "There is only one woman whom I could ever love, respect and be truly happy with—and that is Miss Elizabeth Bennet."

He began to pace once again. "As to my former concerns that Miss Elizabeth would be miserable if she was not accepted within my family and social circle, I now realize these concerns were ridiculous. I have always known that she is far superior in character to many in the first circle. I have enough wealth for the both of us; I am not in need of acquiring more through marriage. Miss Elizabeth brings a sense of joy and life to all she meets, and those who cannot recognize this are fools and will *not* be tolerated by me nor will they be permitted in Miss Elizabeth's presence. I will do my utmost to protect her, sir."

Darcy stopped pacing and took a determined step toward Mr. Bennet. "I can promise you, Mr. Bennet, that if you consent to our marriage, I am quite able to provide for her material comforts. While I know we are both of very stubborn constitutions and will not always agree, I can guarantee that Miss Elizabeth's opinions will always be *respected* by me. I have, in fact, taken quite a bit of pleasure in our past debates, and I look forward to many more in our future together. She has such an admirable mind; it is a delight to hear her express herself, even when the opinions she expresses are not her own!

"You were perfectly in the right to say that I do not deserve her, sir; I am painfully aware that I do not. But please know that I will spend every day of my life striving to make her happy and to continue to better myself under her gentle tutelage. I know that I am not worthy of her love and acceptance of my offer, but by some miracle I *have* gained it, and I give you my word that I will not disappoint her!"

Mr. Bennet's expression changed and was unreadable after this statement.

Darcy panicked and, with even more passion than before, he concluded, "I beg of you, Mr. Bennet, will you please allow me to be the man to share her thoughts, dreams, hopes, and vivacity for all the days of her future life?"

Emotionally exhausted after this speech, he sat down to await the verdict, briefly closing his eyes and saying a silent prayer.

Mr. Bennet was quite moved by Darcy's words. Though he was surprised at the young man's honesty, all that he had suspected months ago of

Darcy's feelings for Elizabeth was confirmed, and all his hopes for his favourite daughter were met by what he had revealed today. "Mr. Darcy? I have one further question."

"Yes, sir?"

"*When* did my Lizzy consent to be your wife?"

"Miss Elizabeth had accepted my offer the morning before… while at Rosings, sir. I have confirmed her wishes only just now before coming to you," Darcy almost whispered.

Mr. Bennet's eyebrows rose. "*Before* she was kidnapped?"

"Yes, sir."

Mr. Bennet sighed and shook his head slightly. "It might have been wise to have made me aware at the beginning of this interview not only that Elizabeth had accepted you—twice—but just *when* she had accepted you. Though that was a very moving speech, it might have saved us both a great deal of unease had I been informed of this sooner."

"I did not?"

"No! You did not."

"Ahhhh." Darcy shifted uncomfortably in his chair.

After a few moments, Darcy leaned forward in his chair and rested his face in his hands, with his elbows on his knees. As Darcy's shoulders started to shake, Mr. Bennet became concerned and knew not what to do. *Well, well! The tension must have been too much for the man! But I daresay if he has broken down to the point of weeping by* ***this*** *interview, he certainly will not be able to handle a lifetime of sparring with Lizzy!*

"Mr. Darcy?" Mr. Bennet said tentatively.

When no answer came he said more forcefully, "Mr. Darcy!"

Darcy removed his hands from his face and Mr. Bennet was shocked to find he was laughing! It turned out to be infectious and, before long, Mr. Bennet was laughing as well.

Once he had recovered enough to speak, Darcy said, "Sir, after all Miss Elizabeth and I have been through to get to this point, I cannot believe I was nervous enough not to have been more clear about when Miss Elizabeth and I came to an understanding."

"I can, Mr. Darcy. I believe we could both use a glass of port at the moment, do you not agree?"

At Darcy's nod, Mr. Bennet crossed the room and poured them each a glass.

~%~

Outside in the hall, Elizabeth had been pacing, wringing her hands with worry. Though she could not hear what they said, she could hear the deep voices of the two most important men in her life. She paced for a long time… and then a strange sound began emanating from the room. Was that laughter? Very confused, Elizabeth knocked when she heard the men quiet a bit.

As he was handing Darcy his glass of port, Mr. Bennet said, "I am guessing my poor Lizzy is wondering what tortures I have put you through to keep you in here this long…" Mr. Bennet raised his voice and called out toward the door, "Enter!"

The door opened slowly, and when Elizabeth's head peeked around it with a concerned expression and wide eyes, the men broke out again in what sounded almost like… giggles?

Elizabeth stepped into the room with a mischievous twinkle in her eye. "If I did not know better, I would suspect you gentlemen have overindulged in drink."

Both gentlemen stood as she entered the room. As she approached, Elizabeth's eyes were full of questions. Darcy put her at ease with a smile.

Elizabeth took the seat next to Darcy as Mr. Bennet said, "No, no, my dear Lizzy, we have not yet partaken. We simply had a bit of a misunderstanding!" Both men burst out laughing once more.

Elizabeth was bewildered, but could not help but laugh with them.

Once the group's nervous laughter had been spent, Mr. Bennet turned to Elizabeth and asked seriously, "Lizzy, do you wish to marry this man?"

Elizabeth looked upon Darcy, and her eyes reflected every bit of love and respect for him that Darcy had expressed for her earlier. At that moment, Mr. Bennet was absolutely certain this was the match he had hoped for his favourite daughter after all.

"Yes, I do, Papa, very much!" Elizabeth said wholeheartedly.

With a touch of sadness, Mr. Bennet said, "Off with the both of you then." He closed his eyes for a moment and sighing, thought, *I have lost my Lizzy!*

"Mr. Bennet… do I have your consent to marry Miss Elizabeth?"

Mr. Bennet looked to Elizabeth's hopeful face and back to Darcy. "Yes, son… yes, you certainly do." Moving toward Elizabeth he added, "I do believe you have found the one man who can appreciate you the way you deserve. I could not have parted with you, my Lizzy, to any one less worthy." He leaned down and kissed her forehead.

Darcy put down his glass, stood, and extended his hand to Mr. Bennet. "Thank you, sir! Thank you very much!"

Weeks later, Mr. Bennet would look back on this moment and think that the brilliant smiles which spread across the couple's faces as he shook Darcy's hand were rivaled only by the ones they both displayed on their wedding day.

Elizabeth, her father, and William, sought out Lord Matlock and Colonel Fitzwilliam to share the happy news. Congratulations abounded and letters were written to London, Longbourn, and Pemberley. Elizabeth and Mr. Bennet both reflected on their relief that they would not be at Longbourn when Mrs. Bennet received hers.

Colonel Fitzwilliam, having no official reason to stay any longer and no desire to attend the burial, had already made arrangements to return to London with his men, so they said their goodbyes and were on their way. He promised Elizabeth that his first order of business after delivering their letters to his parents would be to call on Mrs. Collins and see how she fared. Elizabeth had suspicions about his planned visit, as she had noticed the wistful expression in the colonel's eyes whenever Charlotte's name was mentioned.

Lord Matlock and Mr. Bennet enjoyed reminiscing and sharing those memories with the newly betrothed couple as they gathered on some pleasantly situated benches near the beach, while Elizabeth spent more than a little time instructing Darcy in proper kite construction. Before afternoon tea, Darcy had finished the kite and the foursome planned to walk to Johnny's house to present it to him after enjoying their refreshments at the Inn.

During tea, Lord Matlock received an express forwarded from London from Anne de Bourgh. She wrote that her mother was very ill indeed, and was only partially conscious, at times barely holding onto life. The doctor had shared with Anne that her mother's heart had been deteriorating for years, and he felt that it finally was giving out. They had been able to spoon a bit of broth and water into Lady Catherine, but the doctor felt it was only a matter of time before her heart would give way, and she would pass on.

In Lady Catherine's chamber, two letters had been discovered upon her writing desk; both appeared to have been written just before her episode.

One was addressed to Anne, the other to Lord Matlock. Anne had enclosed the letter from his sister within the express, and he excused himself and retreated to his room to read it.

Lord Matlock was surprised to discover that the letter from his sister was a confession of sorts. He would leave for Rosings to help his niece as soon his valet could pack, but first, he wished to share the contents of the letter with Mr. Bennet, Darcy, and Elizabeth—he felt they were owed that much after all that had happened—so he made his way to the sitting room once again.

Lord Matlock read a portion of the letter aloud:

"I have been aware that I have acted abominably for most of my adult life, and until today, it has not mattered to me in the least. I am ashamed to admit that if I were not dying, I would have continued on in this manner indefinitely without the smallest measure of guilt.

"Earlier today, knowing that I was teetering on the threshold of death's door, for the first time in years, I reached into a bedside drawer to retrieve the Book of Common Prayer. Feeling it was providential that it happened to fall open to the Commandments, I read, 'Hear the commandments which God has given to his people, and examine your hearts,' and so I did. In doing so, I can clearly perceive that I have not upheld God's Commandments. With my greed, I have worshipped money—the only idol of my existence! I have done no better with any other direction written within His book.

"Upon this realization, I have concluded I am undoubtedly bound for the infernal regions when my time comes. I can only hope that my eternal fate will be a little less unpleasant if I make an attempt at redemption by telling you all, and charging you, my good brother, with making reparation in my stead. Please do what you can to compensate those I have injured, used, and abused, Robert, and do what you can to set things as right as possible.

"I shall begin with telling you that my husband tried his hand at mining saltpetre in India. He had requested of you and our brother Darcy to buy adjoining land there, planning to buy the land from you both when he had more available monies, since his cash had been used to begin the mining company. Because the conflicts with France had begun, Sir Lewis had already been financing a smuggler, John Sharp, who was bringing wine, lace, and other goods from across the

Channel. Sharp was willing to help him smuggle silk, cotton, and indigo dye from India if Sir Lewis provided the ships. Since the East India Company held a monopoly on trade with India, the only way for others to do so was by smuggling; the saltpetre mining would legitimize the endeavor. When Sir Lewis found that the men he had sent to run the mine were mistreating the workers, he put an end to the mining operation, but kept up the rest, though it was more risky.

"I had learned about all this while Sir Lewis was alive, and after he passed on, I continued the business with Sharp, expanding the smuggling to the Americas. No matter how much money I had acquired through this or any other means, it was not enough! I recommenced the mining operations when I learned that the British had halted all saltpetre deliveries to the French. I expanded the operation by having some of my men convince the Americans to stockpile saltpetre before another war began with the British, furthering my endeavor.

"When Sharp refused to supply saltpetre to France, I am ashamed to say that I had his great-grandson taken from him and kept the boy at Rosings under guard for more than two years. Most of the other workers were similarly threatened or blackmailed into doing my bidding.

"There were few who worked for me willingly, Robert, but George Wickham and William Collins were my main accomplices. There are several others who were less intimately involved, and I have a list of their names stored with the ledgers in a box under the flooring in the parsonage sitting room.

"Collins is not fit to be a minister, though I had financed his schooling to become a cleric so that he could replace my former parson, who had grown a conscience.

"Wickham has ties to all sorts of evil people and could get things done easily—I had cared not who was hurt in the process as long as my desired ends were met. I am certain you will find enough evidence in my papers to have Wickham convicted of any number of crimes.

"Please see to it that a proper minister is placed at Hunsford for Anne's sake, Robert, and do not allow either of these men to take his revenge upon me by harming my daughter."

Lord Matlock took a drink of water and sighed before continuing, "My sister here reveals where the proceeds from the smuggling are hidden and asks for it to be distributed to the families that she has mistreated over the years. She asks to have the people she had removed from their families to be restored to them. As for the materials she used for blackmail, she suggests that they be burnt or returned to their rightful owners. Captain Sharp should be gifted the ships he has been using for the operation, which is what Sir Lewis had requested to be done upon his own death.

"The letter continues…

"I ask you, Robert, to extend my apologies to my nephew Darcy for my lies and manipulations over the past sixteen years, although I know I do not deserve his forgiveness. I confess I had allowed jealousy and bitterness to transform into hatred and a personal vendetta against my sister's family. I hope my nephew is able to find his fiancée, Miss Elizabeth Bennet, before Wickham harms her.

"And then she gives directions on where Miss Elizabeth could most likely be found.

"I also wish to apologize to Miss Bennet's family, not only for the kidnapping of Miss Elizabeth, but for the attempt at poisoning Mr. Bennet in an effort for Mr. Collins to gain control over Longbourn. I had planned to use it, along with Pemberley, to facilitate the distribution of the smuggled goods to a greater number of people.

"Finally, I ask you, brother, to look after Rosings for Anne's sake, and help her to live a happier life than the one I—her mother—have previously offered her. Anne is completely ignorant and innocent of all; she knew nothing of this enterprise."

An uncomfortable silence settled over the room for several minutes as all those present considered Lady Catherine's admissions.

Elizabeth shot her father a look of warning when he seemed ready to say something. She did not feel it their place to comment upon Lady Catherine's letter before the woman's own family, and she was afraid her father might make an offhand remark, as was his way. She took William's hand in hers and gave it a gentle squeeze, hoping it would help to soothe the conflicted emotions she could see in his eyes.

Darcy cleared his throat, and shaking his head, said, "Lady Catherine is selfish to the last."

Lord Matlock was shocked. "Pardon me? Does not this letter prove that, in the last hours of her conscious life, my sister had become ashamed of her actions and wished to make amends? She wished to protect her daughter and to protect the family names! How is this selfish?"

With a mirthless laugh, Darcy replied bitterly, "Did you not hear the same letter as I? Yes, she recognized her errors and sins! But, while having you follow her orders *will* be helpful to others and they should be carried out as she said, Lady Catherine has not suddenly become altruistic, uncle. I can only see that she thinks of what she can do to make her own eternal life easier! She thought only of herself, sir."

Lord Matlock reviewed the letter again before nodding. With a deep sigh, he said, "Yes… yes I do see it now. And yet I *will* do as she wished… for the sake of all those whom she has injured if not for my sister's." He hesitated a few moments before continuing, "I must bid you all goodbye for now. I must depart for Rosings."

Mr. Bennet responded, "Robert, you must be as exhausted as I from our frenzied journey to Broadstairs. Perhaps you should rest tonight and depart in the morning?"

"I promise I will stop at an inn tonight, but I would feel more comfortable in beginning the journey as soon as possible."

~%~

Elizabeth passed the remainder of the day with her father and betrothed. Although William was clearly thinking through all that had been learned from his cousin's express, he was adamant that they continue on with their plans to deliver the new kite to Johnny.

Cassie had accompanied them to visit with her family as the kite was delivered to a very appreciative Johnny, and all were invited to stay for the evening meal. They were introduced to more of the family, and had an enjoyable time; the invitation to the picnic was renewed and plans were discussed.

Elizabeth could detect that William was, at first, quite uncomfortable with Elizabeth's suggestion that Cassie accompany them. She could imagine that spending time with a servant and a family that was now his employee's family was not among the usual ways he expected to spend his afternoons, and that he agreed only to please her. As the visit progressed, the Sharp family was so welcoming and friendly that even William could not help but respond with good humour. During their return walk to the Inn, he admitted that it had been an enjoyable evening, and he asked her opinion on planning a trip with Georgiana to visit Broadstairs after they were married.

Elizabeth could not help but smile widely at this admission, and at his having sought her opinion on making plans for *their* future. Only just engaged and already he wished to consult her before making any decisions! Elizabeth had every confidence that they would have the marriage that she had always dreamed of.

Friday, March 27, 1812

The following morning, Elizabeth again woke to the sound of seagulls and the smell of salt in the air. She was feeling much more rested than the previous morning. Though she had still had nightmares, they were much less numerous and less severe than the night before. She had made it through most of the night without Cassie's having to wake her.

When Elizabeth stretched, she noticed she was doing so with less discomfort. Perhaps the doctor would give her leave to ride in the coach sooner than expected. Cassie had opened the windows and the sheer white curtains were floating through the air on the sea breeze as if they were clouds. Through the curtains she could see something outside the window and moved closer to investigate. There, flying high in the sky, was Johnny's new kite.

Elizabeth smiled—Johnny and Abe were home. Darcy was nearby, and they were officially engaged to be married. All was right in the world!

As she bathed and dressed, Elizabeth's thoughts turned toward the immediate future; she was looking forward to seeing the caves where the smugglers stored their goods, as well as Kemp's stairs, which climbed the cliff face to the top where they loaded their goods into wagons to be delivered. Elizabeth greatly anticipated giving Captain Sharp a letter that Lord Matlock had written before he had departed for Rosings, informing the Captain of the long overdue fulfillment of Sir Lewis's dying request. Sharp *should* have been gifted all the ships and boats he had been using in his service years ago.

After Cassie had finished arranging her hair, Elizabeth smiled at her maid. "Oh, Cassie, I am sorry I was not attending. I have been lost in thought all morning. So much has happened the past few days, it is difficult at times to believe it occurred at all." As she stood from her seat before the mirror, her expression changed at a stabbing pain in her ribs. Holding up her injured hand she said, "Well… at least until I try to do something for myself or move the wrong way! I feel like a small child again since I am not able to cut my own food with a knife!"

Cassie only nodded and then moved on to her duties.

As Elizabeth left her room to go down to breakfast, she was surprised to find Darcy asleep in a chair just outside her door. Elizabeth stood gazing upon his peaceful countenance for several minutes, examining every feature of his face and every curl of his hair. He looked so much younger when asleep, as if he had not a worry in the world.

Her mind wandered to think of what it would be like to wake up and see this face every day for the rest of her life, and she felt a stirring within her that made her reach out to touch his cheek. When she did, he turned his face toward her hand, and she gasped as he kissed her palm.

His eyes opened and he smiled. "What a nice way to awaken," he murmured, his voice low and raspy with sleep.

Darcy's breath caught at the passion in her eyes. His thoughts returned to how it had felt the other night… sitting on her bed holding her in his arms… she had been wearing only a thin cotton gown… *We are too near her bedchamber for her safety!*

He stood and offered his arm to lead her away from her door and toward the dining room.

"Were you waiting long for me?" Elizabeth asked.

"I have been waiting for you all of my life," Darcy replied, his eyes filled with longing.

Elizabeth's smile twinkled in her eyes. "I meant this morning in the hall chair, my love."

"Ah, that." He teased, "Say it again, please?"

She beamed brightly, "My love!"

The warmth of Darcy's smile filled Elizabeth's soul. "I could not sleep the first night until Richard posted a guard at your door who would notify me if you became upset again. Since the soldiers were gone to London, last night the only way I could be certain of your wellbeing was to take up the position at your door myself." He examined her, noticing that she looked less tired than the day before. "I am glad that you slept better last night."

Elizabeth's expression turned to one of concern, "You spent the entire night in the chair?"

He stopped walking, took her hand from his arm and tenderly kissed it. "I am not ashamed to say that you are more important to me than anything else, Elizabeth, more than life itself. I will have you in danger no more."

A door opened further down the hallway, admitting a family on their way to breakfast, and startling the couple back into the world. Darcy replaced Elizabeth's hand on his arm and continued on their way to meet Mr. Bennet for breakfast.

One does not love a place the less for having suffered in it, unless it has been all suffering, nothing but suffering.
--Jane Austen (English author, 1775-1817), Persuasion

As the arranged time for the picnic drew near, Elizabeth, Darcy and Mr. Bennet walked out. Since it was low tide, Elizabeth expressed an interest in passing through the Kingsgate Bay arch under the lookout cave. The gentlemen agreed, neither willing to deny her anything within their power to give her pleasure.

While passing through the fissure, Elizabeth stopped at the tunnel entrance that led to the lookout cave and said, "Papa, would you like to see the view from the lookout cave? I received permission from Captain Sharp to take you to see it today."

Both the gentlemen wore surprised expressions.

"I suppose so. But Lizzy, do you truly wish to revisit the cave after all that came to pass within?" Mr. Bennet's concern was heard plainly in his voice.

"Yes, I would like it very much, Papa. Not all of my memories associated with Broadstairs are bad ones, including this cave. I prefer to think of the past only as its remembrance gives me pleasure."

Darcy remembered similar words from his mother's letter, and a sense of tranquility washed over him as he thought, *Mother would have loved Elizabeth.*

"I fully intend to forbid the unpleasant memories from intruding again by facing at least the *place* where those events occurred," Elizabeth continued as she moved to enter the tunnel.

Darcy reached out his hand holding her elbow firmly to delay her. "*I* will go first, Elizabeth! I want no surprises this time." Elizabeth nodded, allowing Darcy to enter ahead of her, and then she and her father followed.

Darcy called out before reaching the end of the tunnel, just in case someone was on lookout duty. Peering around the corner, he ensured the cave was empty before stepping aside and allowing Elizabeth to enter.

Both gentlemen's eyes were fixed on her face as Elizabeth looked around the place.

When her gaze settled on a broken bottle on the floor and the cave opening, a look of fear briefly swept over her face, and passed just as quickly. She walked closer to the cave opening and looked out over the ocean while saying, "Mr. Mott and I had a nice conversation here for an hour or two before…" She hesitated quite a few moments. Both gentlemen held themselves back from their natural desire to go to her and comfort her—knowing it was important for her to work through this in her own way.

Elizabeth continued as if no time had passed since her last utterance, "…before we were interrupted." She then smiled a little before saying, "He told me stories of his sailing days—some were rather exciting! We watched the dawn break over the ocean. It was beautiful, but at the time my thoughts were upon the previous sunrise." She looked at Darcy, who was in awe of how she was concentrating on the good which had happened here rather than the unpleasant. She was such an amazing woman! That she had been thinking of his proposal was not lost on him, and he was deeply touched.

Not breaking her gaze with Darcy, Elizabeth almost whispered, "William saved my life here." Darcy's heart swelled at the love within her eyes.

Mr. Bennet's eyebrows rose as he cleared his throat to remind the couple that he was still present before their shared look turned into something more. After having to clear his throat a second time, he chuckled and said loudly with a teasing tone, "And for that, I shall be eternally grateful, though I do think allowing him to take my favourite daughter away from me, halfway across England, is an overly generous reward for it." When they still did not break their gaze, Mr. Bennet began to move toward the tunnel. "I think I have seen all that there is to see here, my dear."

Elizabeth released Darcy's eyes and looked at her father. "Perhaps today I can persuade Captain Sharp and Mr. Mott to tell us more of their adventures."

With a parting glance around the cave, Elizabeth moved toward the exit, and the gentlemen followed. They continued downward along the path to the beach and through the arch to Botany Bay using Johnny's kite as the marker for their destination.

As the trio approached, Johnny and a group of children were flying his kite at a little distance from Cassie, Captain Sharp, Mr. Mott, Jeremiah, Abe, and their families. Abe was just completing the construction of his new kite but was having trouble with one piece and asked Elizabeth for advice.

Johnny recognized Elizabeth's laughter in response to something Abe had said, and a smile spread across his face. He handed off the kite string to another child and then ran to embrace her, almost knocking her down in his enthusiasm. "Thank you for the kite, Miss Lizzy!" Bowing to Darcy, Johnny said, "Thank you for being Miss Lizzy's hands, Mr. Darcy!" Johnny said and then ran away again to play with the other children.

Johnny's father, Jim Sharp, was standing nearby. "We have you both to thank for Johnny's return to us."

"It was all Miss Bennet's doing, Mr. Sharp."

Elizabeth's eyebrow arched. "*You* brought Johnny home, Mr. Darcy!"

Darcy smiled, "Ah, but it had been my third visit to Rosings since Johnny had been there, and though I had seen him, I had never thought anything amiss. I only assisted once I knew something was awry. If it were not for you, Miss Bennet, Johnny might still be at Rosings."

"Perhaps, but it all would have been for naught if you had not come to Rosings and brought him home yourself, sir. I hardly could have uprooted him from Rosings and taken him to Broadstairs myself. Johnny would have remained there when I departed."

Darcy's eyes twinkled in challenge. "I do not agree. Will it not be advisable, Miss Bennet, before we proceed on this subject to arrange with rather more precision the circumstances surrounding your presence and my absence at Rosings?"

Elizabeth's eyes sparkled in reply, remembering his use of similar words in a previous conversation at Netherfield. "By all means, let us hear all the particulars."

Captain Sharp and Mr. Mott came up beside Mr. Bennet as Elizabeth and Darcy set the framework for their discussion. "What are they two arguin' about?" asked Captain Sharp.

"Debating, Captain Sharp! They both love a good debate," Mr. Bennet laughed. "And I think it is safe to say they are both so stubborn they might never come to a solid conclusion on any subject. It is a good thing they will have a lifetime to work it out, eh?"

Elizabeth overheard the gentlemen and thought it best to end this discussion… for now, anyway. The look in her eyes changed to amusement as she recalled more of Mr. Bingley's words from Netherfield when Jane was ill. She cocked her head to the side a bit before saying to the group, "We must not forget the comparative height and size of those debating, gentlemen, for that will have more weight in the argument than you may be aware. I assure you that if Mr. Darcy were not such a great tall fellow in comparison with myself, I should not pay him half so much deference."

The corners of Darcy's mouth turned up a bit. "Yes, and I remember once hearing that there is no more awful object than myself on particular occasions, and in particular places—at my own house especially, when I have nothing to do."

Elizabeth began to laugh, "Principally on Sunday evenings, from what I was led to believe."

"Most decidedly on Sunday evenings, Miss Bennet." Darcy bowed to Elizabeth, his dimples gracing the company with an appearance, and then held out his arm to escort her to a blanket to sit with the others.

Low enough only for Darcy to hear, Elizabeth added, "Well, then, Mr. Darcy, we must find something to keep you occupied at all times after we are wed!"

The look of passion in Darcy's eyes let Elizabeth know he understood her thoughts and agreed.

Confused, Mr. Mott said, "Strange way t' be courtin' a lady."

"Aye, but it all depends on the lady!" Captain Sharp observed. "Ain't it true Mr. Bennet?"

"That it does, gentlemen—that it does," Mr. Bennet said, laughing heartily.

They proceeded to join the rest of the group, where Elizabeth presented Captain Sharp with the letter from Lord Matlock. In accordance to Sir

Lewis's original intentions upon his death, all six ships owned by the de Bourgh family, in addition to all the Guinea boats they used for their runs to France, were now Sharp's to do with as he willed, but Lord Matlock specified it should be nothing that could be considered treasonous. The goods aboard the four ships which were already enroute to or from India and had not yet arrived in England would all be his to profit from. There was also one ship due in from America.

Captain Sharp said that he would make an anonymous gift to the British military of the four saltpetre shipments that were already enroute to England. Darcy offered to arrange the deliveries with General Curtis.

Sharp asked about the mine, and Darcy spoke of soon closing it. With the time it took for his letters to reach India, he did not know how long it would be before the authorities in India could accomplish that purpose. His expression darkened as he thought of all the workers who were suffering, perhaps dying, during the time it would take for his letter to be conveyed to the British Army post there.

Elizabeth noticed the change in his mood and slipped her arm through his, the warm tingle of her touch spreading through him, bringing him back to the present. The love shining from her eyes warmed his soul, and he felt as if a weight were being lifted from his shoulders once again. Without breaking their gaze, he placed his hand over hers and squeezed it gently, bringing it to his lips for a kiss which lingered a bit longer than it should have. *Elizabeth is here with me, safe. She loves me and will soon be my wife. With this dream come to fulfillment, I must have faith that all else will be well.*

All in attendance had an enjoyable afternoon; the Bennets and Darcy heard tales about the smugglers' adventures, and when the meal was done, they were taken to see the Seven Maidens caves, where they heard the story of a battle on Botany Bay beach with another smuggling gang taking place thirty years earlier. Cassie helped Elizabeth choose from the finest French lace for her wedding dress, and the gentlemen were each treated to a bottle of superb brandy.

Earlier in the day, Cassie had agreed to travel with them to London, and Elizabeth had asked Cassie if she would consider becoming her maid permanently when she married Darcy. While exiting the caves, Cassie informed Elizabeth that she had discussed the position as lady's maid with her family during the day and had decided to accept.

Since the doctor had given Elizabeth permission to return to London the next morning as long as they proceeded slowly and she rested often, they said their goodbyes upon rejoining the others. There were some tearful goodbyes between Cassie and her family, and Elizabeth promised that they would visit Broadstairs after she and Darcy were married.

Before darkness set in, they were shown up Kemp's stairs. Darcy and Mr. Bennet were nervous for Elizabeth's sake, for they did not want her to re-injure herself, but Elizabeth thought the climb exciting, though she had to take it more slowly than she would normally have done. At the top of the cliffs, carriages and carts awaited, one of which would return them to the Fig Tree Inn.

~On the road between Broadstairs and London

When traveling at a normal speed, the journey between Broadstairs and London could be completed in two days including an overnight stay. However, to ensure Elizabeth's comfort, Darcy insisted on dividing the miles over a period of three days. Cassie rode inside the coach sitting next to Elizabeth, and Darcy's valet rode atop with the driver. Cassie and Mr. Bennet were soon lulled to sleep by the rocking of the coach.

Darcy's coach was well supplied with books as always, but instead of reading as he usually did on long trips, when he was not engaged in quiet conversation with Elizabeth, he spent the time rejoicing in the opportunity to sit across from her and take pleasure in just looking at her. The first time he was "caught" by Elizabeth, he worried that after her recent experience, she would feel uncomfortable, and he feared he had gone too far. He was relieved to find that the sparkle in her eyes was one of approval and amusement—and it pleased him to no end when he caught her closely inspecting his form several times as well.

Elizabeth slept through parts of the trip and had awakened on several occasions with a start, wild-eyed and confused. Not wishing to awaken the other passengers and unable to take her into his arms, Darcy leaned forward to take her uninjured hand in his with a look filled with concern, which she answered only by squeezing his hand. He would sit, caressing her hand until someone would stir, and Elizabeth would pull away with a blush.

Upon setting out, Elizabeth voiced her objections to their planned three stages of the trip, feeling it was too cautious… until her ribs began to ache severely after about fifteen miles upon the road. Elizabeth tried to hide the pain by pretending to fall asleep, but Darcy knew her every movement too well. At seeing her distress, he had the coach stop at the next village with an inn.

The pain in her eyes the first afternoon spurred Darcy to suggest that they stay another night at the inn before continuing two days hence, but Elizabeth insisted she would be feeling much better with rest, and that they should continue as planned. In the morning, after a careful examination of her countenance assured him that she was not in extreme pain, he agreed to continue the journey, but he reduced the number of miles they would travel, extending the trip by one more day.

Mr. Bennet was amused at Darcy's coddling of his daughter and quite impressed with the way he handled her stubbornness with firm but gentle ease and respect. His observations over the four-day journey relieved him of any lingering doubts; Darcy *would* be good for his Lizzy.

~%~

Tuesday, March 31, 1812

~The Gardiners' house

Upon their return to London, Darcy's carriage took them directly to Gracechurch Street where, as soon as the bustle of their arrival was heard indoors, Mr. and Mrs. Gardiner, Jane, and Bingley came to greet them.

Mr. Gardiner greeted Elizabeth with a kiss to her cheek and a gentle hug. "It is good to have you safe, Lizzy," he said, his voice thick with emotion.

After thanking him, Elizabeth stepped directly into her sister Jane's tearful embrace. "Oh, Lizzy! Lizzy!" Struggling to regain control over her emotions, Jane could say no more.

"Jane! I am well; truly, I am!" whispered Elizabeth.

A teary-eyed Mrs. Gardiner stood behind Jane, and Elizabeth extended her arm out to include her in the embrace with Jane.

Bingley and Mr. Gardiner had moved close to Darcy and Mr. Bennet where the gentlemen exchanged greetings. Darcy kept a watchful eye on the ladies, worried that their enthusiastic greeting might hurt Elizabeth, and in a concerned tone of voice, he stated a little too loudly, "Please be careful! Mind Miss Elizabeth's injuries!"

Mrs. Gardiner and Jane both released their hold on Elizabeth immediately, but shared a knowing look and a smile with her about Darcy's disregard for niceties in order to ensure everyone was aware of Elizabeth's needs.

Elizabeth smiled. "I never saw a more promising inclination. Could there be finer symptoms? Is not general incivility the very essence of love?"

Darcy smiled and his colour deepened as he moved closer and bowed to the ladies. "Excuse me, Mrs. Gardiner, Miss Bennet. I am happy to see you again. I hope you will forgive my lack of manners."

Mrs. Gardiner said to him, "You are very welcome, Mr. Darcy. It is quite understandable under the circumstances. Mr. Darcy, Elizabeth—may I congratulate you on your engagement?"

After congratulations were said all around, the travelers were all offered the opportunity to freshen up before Mrs. Gardiner called for tea and more substantive refreshments.

Bingley was so eager to ask for consent to marry Jane that he requested a private interview with Mr. Bennet as he descended the stairs.

Mr. Bennet laughed openly as he noted Bingley's agitated state, saying, "Hello to you as well, Mr. Bingley! May we at least go into a private room before you petition for Jane's hand, or shall we discuss it here in the hall?"

Just then, Darcy came down the stairs. Bingley stuttered out something nonsensical, and then Mr. Bennet answered, "Very well then! You have my consent to marry my Jane. *Now* may I go have my tea?"

Bingley's face turned quite red before displaying a wide smile. He shook Mr. Bennet's hand and thanked his future father-in-law thoroughly.

Mr. Bennet turned and saw Darcy's jaw drop open at the ease of Bingley's consent "interview," which must not have taken half a minute in total. The older gentleman chuckled and said, "Mr. Darcy, observing your countenance can be exceedingly diverting!"

Darcy's colour rose. Mr. Bennet was amused at his "skill" of having been able to turn the faces of both his soon-to-be sons-in-law bright crimson within a few moments' time.

As Mr. Bennet passed through the door to the sitting room where the others had already gathered, he heard Darcy mutter a little too loudly, "I should have gone to him while he was still astride his horse arriving at Broadstairs!" He could not help but laugh again so vigorously that he needed a handkerchief to wipe his eyes.

Tea was served promptly along with some bread, cold meats, and cheeses, for Mrs. Gardiner was an excellent hostess and knew that the travelers would be in need of a meal upon arrival. Shortly after the tea things had been cleared away, Darcy recognized from the grimace upon her face that Elizabeth was again in pain. He dreaded leaving Elizabeth's side after having been in her company almost constantly for days, but he knew that she needed to rest as soon as possible.

Mr. Bennet had learned to trust Darcy's judgment about Elizabeth's state of health, and after seeing his concerned expression directed at Elizabeth, decided a quick announcement of Jane's betrothal was in order, followed by an insistence that Elizabeth go directly to bed.

More congratulations were heard for Jane and Bingley. Mrs. Gardiner suggested a double wedding, the idea of which was quickly accepted by all concerned.

Darcy and Bingley were walked out to the hall by Elizabeth and Jane, where the two newly engaged couples separated as much as possible in the foyer.

Darcy took Elizabeth's uninjured hand and pressed it between both of his. "I have been used to being near you for the past several days, and I do not want to leave you. Promise me you will take care of yourself, Elizabeth? Please do not stay up all night conversing with your sister as you told me you tend to do."

"I will try to go to bed after a short conversation with Jane as she helps me change into my bedclothes, though I cannot guarantee that once we start I will not let my mouth run over. If I do stay up late tonight, I will sleep later in the morning. Is that acceptable, sir?" She smiled teasingly, but her expression fleetingly turned into one of discomfort before she was able to repress it.

Darcy nodded, knowing that he did not have much control over the situation. "May I return in the morning to see how you are feeling?"

"My aunt did invite you for breakfast, William. Did you not hear her?"

His eyes brightened knowing that he was welcome so early. "No, I was… distracted. I will see you in the morning then. Please rest well, my love." Darcy kissed her hand as he bowed over it, lingering a little while longer—but not long enough for either of their preferences.

~%~

~Darcy House

Darcy and Bingley left together in Darcy's coach. Bingley had moved out of the Hursts' house after discovering Caroline's deception and had been staying at his club ever since. Now that he was engaged, he thought to look for a house of his own in London instead of relying upon the Hursts or Darcy when he wished to come to Town. Darcy offered accommodations at Darcy House for the time being, and his offer was heartily accepted.

Upon arriving home, Darcy went to his study to write a few letters: the first to his doctor asking him to visit Elizabeth the following day, the next to Richard asking after Mrs. Collins and her plans, and finally one to Matlock House notifying his aunt of all that had occurred since his last communication and asking for an update from Rosings as a postscript.

He then went to his study to unlock the iron chest that held most of his mother's jewels. He took out the blue diamond ring that his father had given to his mother upon their engagement and sat looking at it. Darcy imagined it on Elizabeth's hand and hoped that she would like it.

~*~*~*~*~*~*~*~*~*~*~*~*

~The Gardiners' house

Once Jane and Elizabeth were in their room, Jane asked gently, "Lizzy, will you tell me what happened?"

They sat on the bed with Jane holding her sister's hand gently in hers.

"Oh, Jane! But I am afraid to tell you… It troubles me to think that my story will taint your view of the world."

"I do admit that before the unsettling experiences with Mr. Collins and Mr. Wickham at Meryton, I had thought very differently about the world, but since then I have had to concede that not *all* people have good intentions. When we heard that Mr. Wickham had kidnapped you… I was forced to realize how evil people could be. But to know that evil *does* exist does not necessarily force me to believe that all people are evil, Lizzy—and it has made it easier for me to identify deceit in others that I would not have believed possible a few months ago. Perhaps, for me, now being able to accept the truth in certain persons' actions is a *positive* outcome of all that has happened."

Jane was resolved to listen to anything her beloved sister wished to tell her, and she inwardly braced herself for the worst and tried to school her features.

"In that case, I will tell you. I suppose it was not as bad as it could have been. On the trip to Broadstairs, I had so much time to think… I confess I had been imagining the worst! I could not think of any way to escape that would not put me in greater danger than I already was, and I had no money to make my way home if I did get away. If it were not for the goodness of a gang of smugglers who, only a few days ago, I would *never* have believed able to be honourable in the least, I do not believe William would have ever found me. If not for them, most likely would not have seen you again, Jane."

The two ladies embraced again before Elizabeth continued, "Jeremiah protected me from Wickham's advances during the journey to Broadstairs, and then Captain Sharp and Mr. Mott were kind and gentleman-like and tried to keep me safe until William could come retrieve me. Wickham had to hit Mr. Mott on the head with a bottle to be able to get near me! Wickham had been drinking during the entire trip to Broadstairs and then he must have had more once he got there—and he certainly was drinking in the cave. His impaired state made it easier for me to defend myself, I think, so I cannot complain… but not allowing his advances angered him." Tears began to fall as she continued, "He hurt me, but I was able to prevent him from doing more. What Father taught us to protect ourselves worked, Jane! Though I was running out of things to try… If William had not arrived when he did, I do not know what would have happened!"

Elizabeth closed her eyes and when she opened them, Jane could see the pain her sister was feeling was magnified tenfold. "Oh, Jane! What William witnessed! I do not know how he could still wish to marry me! Wickham taunted William… he touched me, but he was holding a knife and neither William nor I could stop him… and Wickham then told William that he had… that he had…" Elizabeth could not finish the thought and she shook her head. "And from the look in William's eyes, I thought he would kill Wickham. For such a good man to be forced to that level—and it was my fault!"

Elizabeth began to sob at this point, hiding her face with her hand. Jane comforted her until she was confident Elizabeth had checked her emotions well enough to understand what Jane wished to say.

"None of it was your doing. William loves you; of course he would still wish to marry you. Do not take any of the blame upon yourself, dearest Lizzy!" Jane stroked Elizabeth's hair for a few moments before going on to say, "You do not know what a state William was in when he asked his aunt and uncle to tell us of your kidnapping. Lady Matlock told us he looked as if he could barely contain himself from searching for you before the soldiers were ready to leave."

Elizabeth raised her head to look at Jane, and said, "Afterward… the following day, he told me that he would understand if I wished to end our engagement. He blamed himself and assumed I would also blame him. Jane, I thought he did not wish to marry me because I had been compromised by what had happened, and I agreed to end it. He explained that he did not wish it… and it was settled after talking for a while.

"But, Jane, I still cannot fully reconcile myself to it. When I am with him and I see the way he looks at me, I do not doubt his love, but once he is no longer with me, I cannot help but fear that he will change his mind once he has had time to think it through more thoroughly. Every time I have a nightmare, I wake up fearing he will no longer love me." Her tears began to fall once again. "And I would not blame him for it at all! Sometimes I think it would be better for him if *I* ended our engagement so that I would not have to see him become disgusted with me when he stops loving me. Jane, I never felt truly worthy of his love, but now… now this feeling… I feel much less worthy and question everything I do."

"He loves you, Lizzy, with all his heart. It is quite obvious that to William, you are his life!"

Elizabeth wept for a little while longer and knew more discussion on this subject would be futile, so when her emotions settled down once again she said, "I suppose all will be revealed with time, Jane." She sighed. "But tell me about what happened here. How have you all faired through this?" Elizabeth smiled slightly. "And what of you and Mr. Bingley? Please tell me all!"

"It has been difficult for us, Lizzy. At first we were all in a state of shock, and we felt so useless here in London—there was nothing we could do but worry! Charles came to see us a few hours after your Mr. Darcy wrote to him of what had happened, and he was so kind and compassionate. He spent the entire day and evening with us, supporting us in any way he could, and the following days as well. I was torn about what to do… whether to go home to Longbourn to comfort Mama or stay here and await your return. Charles helped me decide to stay—he told me that Mr. Darcy asked him to be ready to bring me to Broadstairs if you needed me.

"While we were waiting for news, Charles and I took the children for several walks, and he explained to me what had happened to keep him away from Netherfield. He revealed to me that Mr. Darcy told him where to find me. Charles was here when we received the express letter notifying us that you were safe. Oh, Lizzy, you know not how relieved we all were!

"And then, the next day, Charles asked Uncle Gardiner if he could speak to me privately. He confessed that he loved me and had always loved me, and he asked me to be his wife! I did not know how I should bear so much happiness—and I so wished you here with me to share my joy!" Jane's smile was wider than Elizabeth had ever seen it before.

"I am so happy for you, Jane!" Elizabeth embraced her sister once more.

When they parted, Jane said, "You must get some sleep now, Lizzy. You are here now, and we can talk more on the morrow."

Jane helped Elizabeth get undressed and into her night clothes. As Jane brushed Elizabeth's hair, Elizabeth said, "Jane, I must warn you… I have been having nightmares since…" She took a deep breath and continued, "They seem to be getting better, but I must ask you… if you find me thrashing about, please wake me. Cassie has been kind enough to do so since it all happened, and we have found that it has been better to wake me rather than to allow the dream to continue." Elizabeth blushed.

"Oh, Lizzy! I am sorry you have been having nightmares! I promise I will wake you, dearest. Now please, get some sleep. I assured Mr. Darcy that I would not keep you awake too long talking, and I have already done so! I would not wish that your betrothed should be disappointed in me." She tucked Elizabeth in and kissed her on the cheek. Elizabeth fell asleep before Jane joined her in bed.

Wednesday, April 1, 1812

~The Gardiners' House

Albert Somerset smiled when he received the note from Darcy. He was only too glad to assess the future Mrs. Darcy's state of health and visited the Gardiners' house during the course of the morning.

Darcy and Bingley were eager to see their betrotheds and so arrived at Gracechurch Street early for breakfast. They joined Mr. Bennet and Mr. Gardiner in the sitting room and awaited the doctor's report on Elizabeth's progress.

The gentlemen stood as the doctor entered. Darcy turned to make introductions, but Mr. Bennet was greeting the gentleman before Darcy could begin.

"Albert! This is a surprise; I did not know you were Darcy's physician. I hope all your family is well."

"Good morning, Mr. Bennet, it is good to see you again, though I would rather it be under more pleasant circumstances. Mr. Gardiner, Mr. Bingley—good morning. The family is well, sir, I thank you. May we speak privately about Lizzy's condition, please?"

A bit rankled at his friend's referring to his Elizabeth in such a familiar way, Darcy checked his reaction, thinking, *Of course they know each other! Elizabeth is friends with The Duke of Beaufort and Albert is his seventh son. Although I did not realize they were friendly enough that she would know all the family.*

Surprising Darcy, Mr. Bennet asked him to join them in Mr. Gardiner's study to hear the news concerning Elizabeth's state of health.

Once the door was closed, Albert reported, "Lizzy's hand is healing nicely, and the treatment should continue the same as it has been.

Though no real harm has been done by the carriage ride from Broadstairs, it has, at the very least, delayed healing, and I am advising against any lengthy travel until her bruises are completely healed. I must admit to being surprised that with the extent of her injuries, the doctor in Broadstairs had allowed her such a long carriage ride so soon after they had been inflicted. All was explained, however, when Lizzy confessed that she may have exaggerated 'just a little' about how well she felt since she was looking forward to going home… and I know how stubborn she is once her mind is made up! Unfortunately, the doctor at Broadstairs could not know she was being less than candid with him.

"Mr. Bennet? I usually do not inquire, but in this case I feel I must. May I ask what happened to the man who inflicted these injuries? May I be of assistance in testifying to a judge as to the extent of Lizzy's trauma?" Both men could see that Albert was angry.

Darcy was surprised at the personal nature of his questions, but he had gone through Eton and Cambridge with Albert. He had become a friend over the years and attended to the medical needs of Darcy and his sister when they were in London ever since he had begun his practice—and he knew that Albert would adhere to the necessity of holding the matter in the strictest confidence. Albert had attended Cambridge with Wickham and had known, and disapproved, of Wickham's depravity almost as much as Darcy had. He also knew all the particulars of what occurred in Ramsgate due to Darcy's requiring his advice about Georgiana's behaviour afterward.

Darcy answered, "It was Wickham."

Albert started and paled.

"There is no need for your testimony, Albert. He will no longer be of concern to anyone. He was so drunk this time that when he saw Richard and me, he ran straight off a cliff."

Albert shook his head. "Well, if it had to happen to any human being, I could not have made a better choice as to whom. What a waste his life was!" Albert was thoughtful for a minute or two and then smiled. "I also could not have made a better choice of a wife for you, William. I have known Lizzy for years, and I cannot be happier that she will be the next Mrs. Darcy. Congratulations!"

After shaking hands with Darcy, Albert turned to Mr. Bennet and said, "And congratulations to you, Mr. Bennet! Darcy and I have known each other a long time, as we were in the same year at school, and I can attest that you will be gaining a truly good man as your son-in-law."

Mr. Bennet teased, "I would not have given my consent if I had thought otherwise! You seem to know Mr. Bingley as well, Albert? He will be taking Jane off my hands soon."

"Bingley was a few years behind us, but we met at Cambridge and have met on several occasions through the years through our mutual friendship with Darcy. Congratulations again, Mr. Bennet; Bingley is a good man as well and does seem a perfect match for Jane." Albert's expression became serious again before clearing his throat and changing subjects. "Gentlemen, it seems Lizzy is quite proficient at concealing her pain, but do not let her behaviour fool you. Her injuries are very painful ones. She does not need to be confined to her room or the house, but she does need her rest when she tires."

"Thank you, Albert," said Mr. Bennet. "I have noticed Darcy is acutely attuned to Lizzy's state of health and level of fatigue. I am certain Jane and Mrs. Gardiner are almost as perceptive as he is. Between the three of them, Lizzy will not have the opportunity to over-exert herself."

"Good! I should take my leave, now, as I have other patients to attend. I will return in two days to ascertain her progress. This afternoon, a messenger will deliver additional salve for her hand injury, and I have already given Lizzy's maid instructions. I do not anticipate there being any need, but if there are any changes for the worse, please do not hesitate to send for me at any time, Mr. Bennet. I assume the entirety of this situation is confidential?" Albert asked with a knowing look at both gentlemen.

"Absolutely, Albert, and my uncle will be using his influence to keep it that way," Darcy replied.

"Just as I thought, and I am glad to hear it. Have a good day, Mr. Bennet, Darcy." Albert shook hands with both gentlemen, and after making a stop in the drawing room to take leave of Mr. Gardiner and give his congratulations to Bingley, he was on his way.

"Mr. Bennet, before we return to the others, I have a request to make of you. May I have a few minutes alone with Elizabeth this morning? I have a gift for her in honour of our engagement."

"On one condition, Darcy… you must call me Thomas or Bennet from now on." Mr. Bennet raised his eyebrows. "And you may have only *ten* minutes alone with Lizzy."

Neither Elizabeth nor Darcy had realized that when they thought Mr. Bennet was sleeping during their carriage ride to London, several instances had occurred during which Mr. Bennet was actually observing their behaviour from under hooded lids—and he had witnessed some rather ardent looks being exchanged between the couple. He did not wish to leave them alone for too long! He also was of the opinion that this wedding should take place as soon as possible.

Darcy was thoughtful for a moment trying to decide which to call him, then answered, "Thank you, Bennet."

~%~

Soul meets soul on lovers' lips
--Percy Bysshe Shelley (English Poet 1792-1822)

As the two gentlemen left the study, they encountered Elizabeth descending the staircase; her countenance brightened by a smile the moment she espied Darcy. "Good morning! I hope you both rested well. Did you see Albert before he left?"

Mr. Bennet approached her and gave her a kiss on the forehead. "Good morning, Lizzy! Yes, he just gave us his report. I will allow Darcy to inform you of his opinion—why do you not use the study? I expect to see you in the dining room for breakfast in *ten minutes*." Mr. Bennet threw Darcy a pointed look and then left the couple alone.

"Good morning, Elizabeth. How are you? I hope you slept peacefully last night." Darcy said as he took her hand and then kissed it reverently.

Elizabeth moved toward the study. "I am much improved this morning, thank you. I am confident the dreams will soon be at an end. Jane had to wake me only twice. What did Albert say?"

Darcy opened the door to the study and stepped aside to allow her to enter before him, closing the door behind him. Moving closer to her, he took her hands in his, and answered, "He said you probably should not have travelled so soon, and he will not allow you to travel to Longbourn until your ribs are healed. Your hand is healing nicely and will continue doing so if you persist in the current treatment. There are no other restrictions, but you *must* rest when you are tired, Elizabeth. It is important."

"Well, that will not be too difficult to endure. It is much better than bed rest! It was good to see Albert again; spending time with him is always what I would imagine having an older brother would be like. He told me you and he went through school together."

"Yes, that is true… but I would like to speak to you of something else while we are alone, Elizabeth." Darcy's serious look frightened her, and the icy fears of her nightmares gripped her heart once again.

She realized her emotions must have shown upon her face when Darcy said, "Elizabeth? What is it? Have I said something to upset you?"

Elizabeth swallowed hard and said, "No… no. Please tell me what you must."

Darcy's features displayed his concern as he sat down beside her. "Elizabeth, please tell me what has you suddenly so disconcerted?"

Elizabeth blinked back unshed tears, and, as her vision cleared, the warmth of love in his gaze spread through her, melting away all her doubts. Sighing, she shook her head. "It is silly, really… what you said was reminiscent of my dreams of late." She moved into Darcy's willing embrace.

Resting his cheek against her soft, fragrant curls, he stroked her back for several minutes. His heart swelled with love for her beyond what he had hitherto believed possible at knowing that she wished to seek comfort in his arms.

After he felt her relax against him, he whispered, "I do not know what you were afraid I would say, my love, but I only wanted to give you something…" He reached into his coat pocket, took out the box that held his mother's ring, and shifted a bit so that he could see her reaction as she opened it.

Elizabeth opened the box to reveal a ring featuring an exquisite blue diamond. She gasped. "Oh, William! It is the most beautiful ring I have ever seen. This is for me?"

Darcy smiled. "Of course it is for you, Elizabeth. It was the ring my father gave to my mother upon their engagement. I had always hoped to give it to a woman whom I loved as much as he did my mother. That is you, my dearest, loveliest Elizabeth." He removed the ring from the box and took her hand. "May I?"

Elizabeth nodded, and he slipped the ring on her finger. It fit perfectly.

"Elizabeth, I cannot count how many times I have imagined this ring on your finger. I have not the words to express how happy you have made me by accepting me!"

His fingertips drifted lightly over the silk of her cheeks, and his thumb caressed her lips. When he saw her lips part slightly, he leaned in to kiss her. As their passion overtook the moment, and their kisses deepened, their arms wound around each other. Afraid he might hurt her, he kept himself from holding her as tightly as he wished to, but she was lost to him and pressed herself completely against him. The sensation of having his Elizabeth so close was causing him to lose focus of the warning Mr. Bennet had given them to limit their time alone.

That she would soon be his wife was the only thought that gave him the strength to pull away from her, but the images *that* thought conjured up in his mind did nothing to help his physical state.

Breaking the kiss, he leaned his forehead against hers while they both took several moments to catch their breath. His body was aching to do much more than kiss her, and he knew if he remained this close to his beautiful, warm, soft, *responsive* Elizabeth—who at this moment was stroking his back and looking up at him with a most arousing fire in her eyes—his self-control would not hold much longer.

Heaven help him, he needed to put some distance between them immediately, albeit reluctantly, and he needed some time to regain his composure before being seen in public again. Mr. Bennet had given them ten minutes, and he was certain they had been alone well beyond that time.

"Elizabeth, your father will be coming to look for us if we remain here. Will you go ahead to breakfast? I will join you shortly."

Elizabeth smiled saucily before nodding and moving toward a mirror near the doorway to fix a few curls which had come loose from their pins. As she did so, Darcy looked about the room for something to distract him and pulled from a shelf the book *Disquisitiones Arithmeticae* by Carl Friedrich Gauss. *Perfect!*

Darcy sensed she was closer than before and looked up to find Elizabeth peeking at the title of the book in his hands. Her eyes were smiling as she teased, "Higher Arithmetic in Latin before breakfast?" She rose up on her toes and brushed his lips gently with hers, whispering, "Thank you for the beautiful ring, William," before leaving the room.

~%~

Friday, April 3, 1812

~Matlock House

The Darcys, Gardiners, and Bennets had received an invitation for tea with Lady Matlock. Upon their arrival, Richard greeted them in the drawing room.

"Miss Elizabeth, my mother has left instructions for you to meet her in her sitting room for a private conversation—immediately," Richard stated.

Elizabeth nodded, and then asked, "And how does Lady Catherine?"

"As far as I know, there is no change in her condition."

"I shall join her directly, Colonel Fitzwilliam." Elizabeth curtsied and left the room with the footman.

Elizabeth was shown to Lady Matlock's sitting room and found it empty. After waiting a few minutes alone, Lady Matlock entered and crossed the room quickly, taking Elizabeth into her arms. After a few tears were shed, Lady Matlock sat down, regaining control over her emotions.

Since propriety dictated that the lady of higher rank speak first, Elizabeth sat and remained silent, waiting for Lady Matlock to begin scolding her for not writing, but she did not. Instead, Lady Matlock sat, eyebrows raised high, looking at Elizabeth expectantly. Thinking of the length of time two extremely stubborn ladies such as they might possibly sit across from each other waiting for the other to begin the conversation, Elizabeth repressed a smile.

Knowing she owed her friend an explanation, she decided to throw propriety to the wind and began, "Lady Adelaide, I must apologize for abruptly ceasing my correspondence with you last October. In hindsight, I can see that I should have written, but I did not know then all that I do now.

"I honestly did not know what to say to you. I felt it would be deceitful of me *not* to mention my meeting William, but I certainly could not tell you of meeting him without revealing my opinion of him. Writing of my opinion of him… it would have meant facing the feelings I was busy denying to myself, to Jane, and to my friend Charlotte. After some time, I could no longer deny that I loved him, but I had convinced myself that he thought of me only as a friend. I had observed some looks that told me otherwise, but I felt that I was seeing what I so desperately *wanted* to see, and not what truly existed.

"After William left Hertfordshire… I… I was not myself. If I had written then, knowing me as well as you do, you would have known that I was heartbroken, and I did not wish to concern you. That brings us to date—other than being kidnapped, and I certainly could not write during that time!" Elizabeth laughed nervously.

"And why did you think that William could not love you, Lizzy?"

"Lady Adelaide, I know that you have already made the correct assumptions, because we have discussed the reasons in detail several times over the past two years, but I will confirm them for you. I thought that he would recognize that he and his sister would be censured by the *ton* for marrying a 'country nobody.' In our previous conversations you may have told me that my connexions with you and the Duke, and my acquaintance with some of your friends, would make a marriage with any gentleman easier, but I could not believe it until I heard William speak the words. *His* opinion was more important… could *he* cope with the *ton's* disapproval? Until he told me that it mattered not—it did matter!"

"I must say that I was worried about you, Lizzy. All those months without hearing from you! First, you must promise never to stop writing to me again. Second, you must agree to address me as 'Aunt Adelaide' from this moment on!"

Elizabeth smiled brightly. "I am happy to agree to both conditions, Aunt Adelaide."

"Lizzy? If you ever wish to speak to someone about your recent experiences, please do not hesitate to seek me out. I will always be willing to listen, my dear—without judgment. I wish to make certain that you know that I do not hold you in any way responsible for what happened. You are very special to me, and you always will be!"

Elizabeth's eyes were brimming with tears. "I may accept your offer sometime soon, Aunt Adelaide, but not today. I thank you."

"Then I suggest that we join the others for tea, after which we will finish our chess game. It is long overdue!" As both ladies stood, Lady Matlock walked to Elizabeth and hugged her. "I am so happy for both you and William, Lizzy!"

Darcy and Richard were relieved to see Lady Matlock and Elizabeth walk into the drawing room arm-in-arm. After the usual greetings, Lady Matlock held her hand out toward Darcy, and as he moved closer and took it, she said, "If you had not been afraid of my matchmaking schemes, you would have met Lizzy years ago and saved much time, William!"

Displaying his dimples, Darcy answered, "I must agree, Aunt Adelaide, I should have accepted your invitations. If I had only known *your* matchmaking skills were so finely tuned, unlike most others I have been exposed to, I would have found perfection much sooner!"

Blushing, Elizabeth cried, "William! Even *you* have admitted that there are none without fault!"

"Ah! As I told your father a few days ago, Elizabeth, even your imperfections are perfection itself." Darcy's eyes were twinkling with amusement.

"Lizzy, I see you need no advice from us married ladies. You have him well trained already!" Mrs. Gardiner said as she approached the group.

Lady Matlock observed Elizabeth and Darcy throughout tea and was quite pleased to see the way each looked at the other and how happy they both were. She was impressed with the changes she saw in Darcy as well. He smiled much more often, and not only at Elizabeth. He carried on more conversations during tea than she had ever known him to do at social engagements, even when among family. They truly were in love, and they were good for each other. She looked at Mr. Bennet and realized he was watching her observe Elizabeth and Darcy. He approached her and said, "I must admit you were correct, Adelaide. I am impressed with your nephew, and he does seem perfect for my Lizzy."

"Of course I was correct, Thomas," Lady Matlock quipped, "and you owe me a shilling!"

Mr. Bennet chuckled as he handed her a coin. "Ah! So you do remember our bet, then? I wondered if you would. Though I am glad that Darcy resisted your matchmaking, or I would have lost my Lizzy much sooner. I will find it difficult being at Longbourn without her, I am afraid. Once she and Jane are gone, I will never hear two words of sense spoken together!"

Just then a message from Lord Matlock arrived; Lady Matlock read the missive immediately. A number of emotions were expressed upon her countenance, and at one point a gasp escaped her lips as she read.

"What is the news from my uncle?" Darcy asked, expecting to hear that Lady Catherine had died.

Lady Matlock knew she needed to share the contents of the letter with those present, but after their recent difficulties, she was unsure of whether or not to proceed. Her eyes moved to Elizabeth, and at Elizabeth's nod, Lady Matlock looked down at the letter while summarizing it for the group, "Lord Matlock is well, and Anne sends her congratulations and wishes for a happy life to William and Elizabeth.

"It seems that Mr. Collins had been quite upset at Lady Catherine's illness. Shortly after Lord Matlock's arrival, Mr. Collins declared to all present his longstanding love for Lady Catherine, and he refused to leave her side. He neither ate nor slept for days. Mr. Collins worked himself into a frenzy over her illness, had an apoplexy, and died! The doctor had attempted to give Mr. Collins something to calm him, but he was not able to do anything to save the man.

"Lord Matlock asks us to contact Mrs. Collins immediately. It seems Anne has offered for Mr. Collins to be buried there since he was so attached to Rosings and her mother, and Lord Matlock has already begun to make arrangements for a funeral there at Rosings but would like to know if that is what Mrs. Collins wishes. While Mrs. Collins is welcome to stay at Hunsford until a new minister is found, Anne offers the services of some of Rosings's servants to help Mrs. Collins pack her belongings when the time comes. Anne also asks for her affection for Mrs. Collins to be relayed and says she will be sad to see her go. Lord Matlock will be assisting Anne in filling the living.

"It seems that Catherine wrote Anne a letter of apology before falling ill which has left Anne quite confused about her mother. My niece has been sitting by her mother's bedside, speaking to her and reading from Anne's favourite books. Anne has also been sharing her thoughts and feelings about many other issues. Anne has explained to her uncle that after reading her mother's letter telling Anne of her regrets, she was giving her mother the opportunity to become acquainted with her daughter before she died—something she had never taken the trouble to do during Anne's lifetime.

"My husband says that they are unsure whether his sister understands what is being said, but Catherine has shed tears at times, so there is a chance she does. The doctor feels Catherine might continue in this state for several weeks before another attack, but he is sure one will come eventually."

After all that had happened with Mr. Collins, Mr. Bennet made it clear that he had no desire to attend his cousin's funeral unless Mrs. Collins was in need of his services, though he was certain that she would be escorted by her father to see to her belongings.

Richard left to see Mrs. Collins immediately. Elizabeth had offered to go along, but Richard declined the offer, saying that he would inform her at once if Mrs. Collins was in need of her presence. Seeing the pleading look in Richard's eyes, Elizabeth agreed. Perhaps it would be better for both her friends if Richard was the person that Charlotte turned to for comfort just now… mayhap leading to a more intimate acquaintance with time.

After the tea things were cleared, Lady Matlock and Elizabeth moved to the chess board to complete their game; it was a pleasure to play opposite each other, compared to the beginning of the game which had taken place through correspondence. Lady Matlock won, but she had to admit that Elizabeth seemed a bit distracted by the presence of her betrothed, and so a game *without* the presence of the gentlemen was planned between them while Elizabeth was still in London.

Over the next few days, Bingley and Darcy spent most of their spare time with their fiancées. Darcy was unable to spend as much time with Elizabeth as either of them would have liked; he had neglected his responsibilities far too long since his return from Netherfield.

Bingley had found several houses in London which he wished for Jane to see, and whenever Darcy was unavailable, Jane, Elizabeth, and Mrs. Gardiner often accompanied him to view them so that Jane could participate in the decision about their future home.

Elizabeth asked Lady Matlock and Mrs. Gardiner to accompany her on a visit to the Duke of Beaufort. The Duke was happy to see Elizabeth and overjoyed at the news of her engagement to Darcy. Unknown to Elizabeth, the Duke and Lady Matlock also conferred privately about making certain it was widely known they both thought very highly of Elizabeth in order to ease her acceptance by the *ton*.

The Duke held a large dinner party in honour of both couples. Invitations were sent only to the best company which meant that those in attendance consisted of clever, well-informed people who had a great deal of conversation—an event at which even Mr. Bennet was witnessed enjoying himself. The Duke told the story of how Elizabeth "saved his life" several times to anyone who would listen.

Another day, the Duke and Elizabeth took Darcy on a visit to the orphanage where they gave the children a special dinner and toys in honour of the couple's engagement—which gave Darcy an idea for a surprise for Elizabeth.

Mr. and Mrs. Hurst held a celebratory dinner to honour the engagements. The guest list included her siblings, the Bennets, and Darcy, as well as several other friends. Louisa Hurst was genuinely pleased at her brother's happiness. She welcomed Jane into her home with open arms and with the utmost respect, and treated Jane and Elizabeth the way that she always should have, regretting how she had allowed Caroline to influence her in the past. Louisa had done much to remove herself and her opinions from being under Caroline's influence, resulting in several outbursts from Caroline, but on the night of the party, Caroline behaved herself as well as she could.

Caroline Bingley was extremely vexed over her brother's engagement, and even more so about Darcy's. After seeing other people's reactions to Darcy and *Eliza* at the Hursts' dinner, she decided to feign acceptance. Her behaviour towards Elizabeth was so sweet that it was sickening, and it fooled no one, but she behaved well enough to gain invitations to all the festivities leading up to the wedding, knowing how her connexion to the Darcys would gain her invitations to other events as well.

She had been beaten in two battles, but the war was not yet lost—she needed to keep in mind her current goal was to find herself a new target on the matrimonial battlefield. At one of these parties she met Mr. Hainsworth, who had been refused by Elizabeth years earlier and had never come to terms with her refusal. When it was announced that Elizabeth would become Mrs. Darcy, Mr. Hainsworth became quite dissatisfied with his life and was an easy target for the *only* lady of the *ton* that he could find who disliked Elizabeth Bennet as much as he thought he did: Caroline Bingley.

The day following the Hursts' party, Darcy invited the Bennets, the Gardiners, and Bingley for dinner in two days' time; he planned to include an "inspection tour" of Darcy House for his future bride. Since

Doctor Somerset advised Elizabeth not to travel again for another fortnight, Mrs. Bennet, Mary, Kitty, and Lydia were due to come to Town to shop for Jane and Elizabeth's trousseaux in a few days' time. While Darcy planned to host all of the Bennets for dinner after they arrived, he knew that Elizabeth would enjoy seeing Darcy House *without* the energetic responses to every piece of furniture, rug, wall covering, and drapery that he expected would be heard once Mrs. Bennet and her youngest daughters were in London.

He trusted Elizabeth to redecorate Darcy House as she saw fit, and he wanted her to take pleasure in doing so. Mrs. Gardiner's and Jane's tastes were similar to Elizabeth's own taste, more than was Mrs. Bennet's, and Darcy knew that they would support Elizabeth's choices about decorating Darcy House more than Mrs. Bennet would. If the decisions were already made before Mrs. Bennet arrived, she could not attempt to coerce Elizabeth to decorate in her taste instead of Elizabeth's. He knew Elizabeth would stand firm, but neither did he wish her to find the need to cross swords with her mother. Again Mr. Bennet was impressed with Darcy's determination to do what was best for Elizabeth and his discretion in carrying it out.

~Darcy House

Mrs. Martin, the housekeeper at Darcy House, was at first amused at her master's nervous behaviour when he announced that he was bringing his future bride for dinner and a tour of the house. But his demands over the past two days had become an ever increasing anxiety to make certain that everything was absolutely perfect for this evening, and Mrs. Martin had begun to fear that the future Mrs. Darcy must have a very challenging and critical nature.

Having been with the family since before the previous master had married, she was extremely loyal to Fitzwilliam and Georgiana Darcy and felt quite protective of them. She did not know exactly what had happened to put the master in the state he was in these past few months, but she *did* know it had something to do with Miss Elizabeth Bennet.

Needless to say, Mrs. Martin was not predisposed to like her future mistress, though it was not her place to express this opinion. In fact, she was rather dreading to meet the lady whom she expected to be an even worse match than she had feared Miss Bingley would have been!

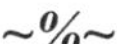

Friday, April 10, 1812

Darcy's personal preparations being completed much too early for his own good, he had spent the past hour alternating between badgering his staff repeatedly over the smallest details for the day's gathering, pacing the drawing room floor, smoothing wrinkles out of his clothing, removing invisible lint off his coat and standing by the window in nervous anticipation of his guests' arrival. As the reader may suspect, these extraordinary behaviours were largely the result of his anticipation of one guest in particular. Bingley had made a few jesting comments in an attempt to distract his friend, but Darcy's mood was beyond even what Bingley's good-natured humour could help.

Not only had he not seen Elizabeth for almost two full days, the longest separation since they had been reunited two and a half weeks ago, but this was the first time she would see Darcy House. And in only a few minutes, she would grace the halls of his home… or rather, *their* home. Darcy smiled at the thought.

He had imagined her at the London house and at Pemberley so many times that it was difficult to recall that she had never actually *been* there. What if she did not approve? What if she were expecting something larger or grander? He hoped she would not be disappointed.

The Gardiners' carriage approached the house, and Darcy was off toward the door, with Bingley not far behind. Rushing outdoors, Darcy's hand itched to open the door to the carriage himself but he restrained his eagerness enough to wait, rather impatiently, for the footman to perform the task.

The footman opened the carriage door, started, closed it very quickly and stepped away from the curb as the shade was drawn within the carriage. Darcy stopped at the bottom of the steps and blinked a few times before quietly saying to the footman, "Is something the matter, John?"

"The lady said 'not yet,' sir."

~%~

Elizabeth had been to Matlock House many times, as well as to the home of the Duke of Beaufort and some of Lady Matlock's acquaintances. Unlike *some* ladies of the ton, she had spent her time at these homes concentrating on the people, not judging the quality of the furnishings and draperies. Though she and Jane had helped Aunt Madeline redecorate the Gardiner's home in London, the only other times she noticed how a room was decorated was when the décor was ostentatious or bordering on the ridiculous. Elizabeth felt strange, and more than a little nervous, going into someone else's home and doing it over in her own tastes, even if it was about to become her home as well. What if William and Georgiana's taste in furniture or wall coverings was quite different from her own? What if they were unhappy—or worse uncomfortable—with her choices?

Upon the arrival of the Gardiner's carriage at Darcy House, Elizabeth's eyes widened. She did not know what to expect, but she did *not* expect it to be this majestic! When the footman opened the door to the carriage, Elizabeth blurted out, "Not yet!" The footman quickly closed the door, and then Elizabeth immediately pulled the shade, slumping onto the back of the seat.

Everyone looked at Elizabeth in confusion, but Elizabeth was looking at Jane. "Oh Jane! It is so grand! What am I to do?" she whispered and grasped her sister's hand with her own trembling one.

Though everyone in the carriage had been able to hear her and could see the terrified look upon her face, Jane was the only one who quietly acknowledged Elizabeth had spoken. "Lizzy, you are every bit as dignified, worthy, and able as the mistress of this house should be, perhaps more so than others due to your modesty and goodness. Lady Matlock and William would not have every confidence in you if they did not believe that you would be able to manage this house with ease after a time of adjustment. Do not underestimate your abilities, dearest!"

"Perhaps they overestimate my abilities!"

"Lizzy! You will be fine, please believe me. Think not of the house, think of who is in it."

"Yes…" Elizabeth took a deep breath. "Yes, William is here." Straightening her back, she opened the shade and looked out expecting to see the footman but found an anxious-looking Darcy standing in his stead.

As their eyes met, both felt much more at ease, and smiles spread across both of their features. Darcy handed Elizabeth out of the carriage and kissed her hand without breaking their shared gaze.

Suddenly remembering he was the host of the party and should be paying better attention to all the guests, Darcy turned and saw the gentlemen had already taken care of the most urgent duty of handing out the other ladies. Placing Elizabeth's hand upon his arm—where it should be—he smiled brightly and happily uttered, "Good afternoon, ladies and gentlemen." His gaze shifted to Elizabeth. "Welcome to Darcy House!" He turned and led his guests into the house.

Upon admittance to the entrance hall, Elizabeth was struck with the elegance displayed here and became overwhelmed once more, thinking of what the remainder of the house must be like. After the party had divested themselves of their cloaks and hats, Darcy introduced them all to Mrs. Martin, who would be accompanying them on the tour to hear any plans for the redecorating. Mrs. Martin kept a discrete but watchful eye upon Miss Elizabeth Bennet in an attempt to make her out.

The remainder of the group was busy admiring a painting on the far wall, leaving Darcy and Elizabeth with Mrs. Martin. He asked Elizabeth, "Would you like to begin the tour directly or shall I order tea before we begin?"

Elizabeth thought for a moment. She wished to put off looking about the house but did not think that she could eat or drink anything just now. It was better to get this done and then perhaps she could enjoy William's company. "I think we should begin the tour, William."

He took her hand to kiss it and noticed she was trembling. "Elizabeth? Is something wrong?"

Elizabeth's eyes filled with tears. "I… I am afraid I will disappoint you, William."

Darcy wanted to take her off alone somewhere and wrap her in his embrace to soothe her. Though the murmur of the voices at the other end of the hall did remind him that there were others present, so completely was he consumed by his concern for her that he forgot Mrs. Martin was close by. "My love, there is absolutely nothing you can do that could disappoint me. Every new thing I learn about you might surprise me or impress me, and some even leave me in awe of you—but you never disappoint me."

He was completely bewildered when his words stirred another flood of tears. Darcy swallowed with difficulty past the lump in his throat before being able to say, "Elizabeth? Please explain why my words have upset you so."

"William, do you not think it is possible you have overestimated my abilities to be a proper mistress of your homes? I have never expected to live in such a grand house. I have learned how to manage a small estate such as Longbourn and have helped my Aunt Madeline with her house in London… but neither is anything like *this*!" Her eyes widened. "Or Pemberley! Oh, William, today you wish for me to make plans to decorate your home, but I would not even know from which shops or warehouses to buy such elegant furnishings or wall coverings or rugs or draperies or…" Her emotions tightened her throat too much to speak any longer, and she struggled to maintain her countenance.

Darcy wanted to kiss all her fears away, but with the nearness of her family, words would have to do. "Elizabeth! I only wish for you to be comfortable in your new home, but you do not have to change anything if you do not wish it! I do not expect you to redecorate the entire house in one day.

"As to being mistress of *our* homes, there is no one I would trust more on this subject. You are more intelligent, well educated, and accomplished than most of the people that I have ever known, lady or gentleman! Aunt Adelaide and Uncle Robert feel the same way, and they are not among those who compliment others without good reason. No one will expect you to simply *know* everything about managing a house this size or an estate such as Pemberley the moment you become my wife, I promise you that. Mrs. Martin, Mrs. Reynolds, and I will be there to help you. Please believe me, my love."

Elizabeth nodded and forced a smile.

He took a deep, trembling breath and continued, "Let us take a tour of the house… I have often dreamed of sharing it with you. If you find anything you would like to change, tell me and, truthfully, I would greatly enjoy choosing something to replace it *together*."

Darcy swallowed loudly. "I would like you to pay special attention to your rooms, for they have not been updated in many years… though it is not proper for me to accompany you into your rooms *yet*." His breath caught at her expression, and it took a moment to recover enough to go on, "I am certain that Mrs. Gardiner, Jane, and Mrs. Martin can help you choose what you would like to replace or have redone, and I would be more than happy to help with the shopping." His eyes took on a far-away look for a moment when his thoughts filled with some of his imaginings of what would happen in her rooms in the future. Recalling where he was, he blushed and looked to Elizabeth only to find her gazing at him with *that look*—which could cause him to act quite rashly if he were not careful.

Mrs. Martin, who had moved away a little to fuss with a wall hanging so she could feign ignorance of what was being said—but who had heard every word—was greatly relieved by the conversation. Her future mistress seemed not at all as she had feared and very much in love with Darcy, as he was with her. She also was aware of the fact that the look the couple was sharing at the moment was not quite appropriate for the company they had obviously forgotten was in the same chamber with them. She cleared her throat rather loudly to help them become more conscious of the rest of the world around them. Little did she know that this was only the first of innumerable times she would be performing this duty for their benefit during the remainder of her years in service!

~%~

Elizabeth had relaxed quite a bit after their discussion and was able to take pleasure in the tour of the house more than she could have ever anticipated. Darcy and Mrs. Martin told family stories which had played out in the rooms. Elizabeth found those of young Master William most enjoyable.

Every room was more beautiful than the next, and Elizabeth found almost nothing she would change. Darcy had more suggestions to redecorate than Elizabeth did. Pieces he wished to discard that could not be recovered or renewed would be replaced; Darcy had made an appointment for the following day with a furniture maker. Their tastes were very similar, and there were few disagreements; she made plans to keep a few pieces that he wished to discard.

Mrs. Martin had fabric swatches and a book of sample wall coverings to go through, and the couple chose two or three for each item and then asked the opinions of Mrs. Gardiner and Jane before making the final choices.

~%~

Mrs. Martin had given the staff permission to "gossip" only on this one subject and only on this one occasion as long as none of what was said left the house. Naturally, the entire staff was curious about the future mistress and Mrs. Martin knew it would have been impossible to stop the talk even if she wished to do so. Threatening the loss of their positions, as she normally would have done for gossiping, would have resulted in her being the *only* remaining staff member at the end of the evening!

The servants gathered in the kitchen whenever their duties allowed. There was much interest in whether it was a love-match or a marriage of convenience. They were all fond of the master and wished him to be happy. While most were hoping for a love-match, many of them did not think it would be likely.

All wagers had to be placed before Mrs. Martin returned from the tour. The final determination would not be made until Mr. Darcy retired for the night for it was heartily agreed that more information might be obtained as the evening wore on.

It is a truth universally acknowledged among servants that the footmen stationed in the dining room would be the best source of information, and the second best reports were to be from the footmen who were present at their parting when the carriage came for the future mistress.

As the master and his guests moved to the dining room, Mrs. Martin's bright smile upon entering the servant's wing spoke volumes to the rest of the staff—showing that her opinion of her future mistress was very high indeed, verifying the opinions of staff who had already been in contact with Miss Elizabeth and shared their thoughts.

Mrs. Martin was relieved to find Miss Elizabeth personable with all the servants she came into contact with. She had watched Miss Elizabeth and Mr. Darcy's interactions closely and was more than impressed by her personality.

Each time a member of the staff returned to the kitchen, all attention was centered on any bit of news to be shared. Mr. and Mrs. Gardiner had been known to them all once before as a pleasant couple. Mr. Bennet was declared to be a highly amusing gentleman.

Miss Bennet, betrothed to the all-around well-liked Mr. Bingley, was a beautiful, serene, and admirable young lady. This was of great interest to some of the staff since their relatives were candidates to work for Mr. Bingley once he would purchase his house in London.

Most importantly, they learned that Miss Elizabeth was beautiful, intelligent, witty—an excellent young lady. She did not treat the staff members as so many ladies from the *ton* did—as if they did not exist or were lower than animals. She had a brilliant smile that could light up any room along with impeccable manners. They found that she was able to get the master to laugh openly, even at himself, and the cold exterior he usually wore while in company seemed to melt away when Miss Elizabeth was near. They had never seen Mr. Darcy smile so widely, nor so often, not even when he was conversing with Miss Darcy, playing games with Mr. Bingley, or jesting with Colonel Fitzwilliam.

By the end of the second course, it was decided that it was a love-match on Mr. Darcy's side, which was confirmed when he shockingly made absolutely no effort to hide his feelings as she played and sang in the music room after dinner—but one question remained. Was it a love-match on her side as well?

It was then acknowledged that the footmen stationed at the door would be a great source of information. They were instructed by all to pay close attention to every move and every look made by Miss Elizabeth Bennet, and the entire staff waited impatiently for them to return.

At the end of the evening, the footmen reported that Miss Elizabeth's eyes told all as she spent a few moments "alone" in the hallway with Mr. Darcy and outside before the master handed her into the carriage. It was announced that there had never been a woman more in love than Miss Elizabeth Bennet was with Mr. Darcy!

It was a love-match on *both* sides! All were pleased with the news—though perhaps those who lost their wagers were not quite as happy as those who had won.

Hughes, Mr. Darcy's valet, smiled. He and Cooper, Mr. Bingley's valet, had been disqualified from the wagering. Both were practiced in being excessively discrete and neither would give out any of the information they had gathered while at Netherfield… mostly because they did not want to spoil the others' enjoyment of the evening. But now, Hughes and Cooper told the staff the tales of Miss Bennet and Miss Elizabeth they had heard from the Netherfield staff to enhance the favorable opinions of the two ladies.

Mrs. Martin was glad she had delayed writing to Mrs. Reynolds of her opinion until after hearing from Hughes and Cooper, for she now had much more to report and set her mind at ease as well.

In honour of his engagement, Mr. Darcy had ordered wine for all the staff after their duties were completed this night, and so they drank, ate, and celebrated the good fortune of all soon to be associated with such truly fine ladies… which ended with one toast to their future happiness and another to commemorate the one evening when the staff at Darcy House had been permitted to gossip.

Wednesday, April 15, 1812

~The Gardiners' house

Mrs. Bennet, along with her three youngest daughters, travelled to join the rest of the family in London. Elizabeth was happy that Darcy's usual morning visit had been curtailed by his sister's impending arrival in London since her mother's effusions at seeing Elizabeth and Jane were extreme.

~%~

~Darcy House

Upon Georgiana Darcy's return to London later the same day, Georgiana was so excited that she opened the coach door herself and had rushed halfway up the steps in front of Darcy House before her brother was outdoors to greet Georgiana and Mrs. Annesley's coach. She threw herself into his arms and embraced him with such heartfelt emotion that she nearly knocked the breath from him.

Darcy separated himself from his sister and grinned widely. "I hope you do not mind that I sent for you so soon after you returned to Pemberley, Georgiana. To make such a journey twice in less than a month was difficult, I am sure."

"William! I am so happy at your news; you could not have kept me away. I would have come whether you sent for me or not!

Darcy walked toward the coach and handed down Georgiana's companion. "I hope you had a good trip, Mrs. Annesley."

"Yes, we did, thank you Mr. Darcy."

"When do we go to see Miss Elizabeth?" Georgiana said the moment her brother turned back to her to offer his arm.

"I thought tomorrow morning, after you have rested," he answered as he escorted his sister inside the house.

Georgiana's expression turned to one of disappointment as she gasped. "Tomorrow?"

"Georgie, you have spent much time traveling the past three days. You must be exhausted."

"Oh please, Brother? Please let us go today? I feel wonderfully refreshed already just from seeing you. Becoming reacquainted with Miss Elizabeth will be rejuvenating! I will just take a few minutes to change out of my traveling clothes and then we *must* go. Please, William?"

Darcy laughed. "If you are certain you are feeling well enough, then we may go. But we will only stay for a little while, and then you must come home to rest. Agreed?"

Georgiana clapped her hands and kissed her brother on the cheek. "Oh, thank you, William! You know not how I have been longing to meet Miss Elizabeth again! And Miss Bennet, too!" and with that she almost ran up the stairs to the family wing.

Darcy turned to a smiling, but weary-looking Mrs. Annesley and said, "I suppose you would rather rest, Mrs. Annesley, than accompany us to the Gardiners'?"

"Yes, I would appreciate that kindness, Mr. Darcy. I am not as young as Miss Darcy and do not take to traveling as well as she does. May I congratulate you, sir, on your betrothal? I am looking forward to meeting Miss Elizabeth soon."

"Thank you, Mrs. Annesley. I do think I am the happiest of men! Rest well, and we will see you on the morrow."

"Thank you, sir. Have a good evening." She curtseyed and was soon on her way to her room.

~%~

~The Gardiners' house

Bingley gladly accepted Darcy's offer to accompany his friends to Gracechurch Street. Georgiana had not realized that all of Miss Elizabeth's family would be there and was suddenly shy as she saw there were so many people she did not know. Elizabeth realized that she was overwhelmed, and so after Mr. Gardiner made the introductions and

Georgiana made her congratulations to Elizabeth and Jane, Elizabeth led Georgiana to a small sofa on the opposite side of the room from where her mother and sisters were sitting. Elizabeth smiled in reply to Darcy's grateful look directed at her, and she sensed his gaze on them often throughout the next few minutes.

Darcy had written to Georgiana a little of what had happened to Elizabeth, without giving too much detail. Though Georgiana wished to give Elizabeth a good impression of herself, she was unsure of what subjects might upset her future sister. This, in addition to her natural shyness, meant that Georgiana allowed Elizabeth to direct their discourse. They began safely by discussing the weather, Georgiana's journey, Pemberley, and then moved on to the wedding. By this time, Georgiana was feeling quite comfortable with Elizabeth. Elizabeth told Georgiana about Captain Sharp's giving her lace for her wedding dress, and when Georgiana expressed a desire to see it, she offered to bring it down from her room.

Georgiana forgot her bashfulness and exclaimed, "Oh! You must not bring it downstairs, Miss Elizabeth! I think it would be bad luck for my brother to see it!"

Elizabeth smiled and said, "Well, then—I am certain Mrs. Gardiner would not mind my taking you up to my room to see it, Miss Darcy."

Mrs. Bennet's attention was drawn by Georgiana's exclamation. "Are you speaking of the lace for your wedding dress, Lizzy? I will come upstairs with you, as will Kitty and Lydia since we all have been hoping to see it soon as well. Mary would have no interest in such things."

Elizabeth noticed Mary's blush. "Mary, you are welcome to come with us if you would like."

Mary would not be interested in lace that her mother or younger sisters had chosen because she found their taste to be too ostentatious for her liking, but in her opinion, Jane and Elizabeth had such good taste in clothing that she was always interested in seeing anything they had chosen. With a glance at her mother, Mary answered, "Yes, I would like to see it, Lizzy, thank you."

The six ladies removed above stairs to the room Elizabeth was sharing with Jane.

Georgiana had never seen such fine lace with such a delicate pattern. "It is beautiful, Miss Elizabeth!"

Upon seeing the lace, Mrs. Bennet exclaimed, "Well! I am impressed with the quality, Lizzy, but not surprised that you had such poor taste in choosing the design. By now you should know to get a more intricate design… and I do not understand why you had not asked for more for your sisters? Oh—and some for Miss Darcy, too, of course. You should have chosen some for each of them."

Georgiana seemed considerably uncomfortable.

"Mama! Do you not see it would have been rude to ask for more?"

"Rude? After all he put you through? Forcing you to stay in caves and having you exposed to a man such as Wickham! Captain Sharp owed you much more than a few yards of lace!"

Elizabeth saw Georgiana stiffen at the mention of Wickham and discretely took her hand in hers and pressed it gently. Georgiana was a bit shocked when she realized Elizabeth's action meant she knew of her past with Wickham, and looked at Elizabeth expecting to see a look of reproach in her eyes. When she found kindness there, she knew her future sister did not condemn her for what had happened the previous summer. Georgiana took a few deep breaths to calm herself.

Elizabeth answered her mother's charges, "Mama! Captain Sharp showed me nothing but kindness. He had nothing to do with anything unpleasant and was not responsible for my being injured. He owed me nothing and yet he fed me, sent a man all the way to London with an express telling Mr. Darcy where I was, and tried to keep me as comfortable as possible under the circumstances. He gave me the lace out of generosity as a *wedding gift*. Would you have me ask for more from *everyone* who gives me a wedding gift?"

"Do not be ridiculous, Lizzy! Of course not!"

Elizabeth looked at Georgiana and gave her a little smile in an attempt to communicate to her *not* to take her mother's reproaches to heart. "Perhaps it is time we rejoin the others?" Elizabeth suggested, and the ladies made their way downstairs once more.

When they returned to the drawing room, the subject of the wedding date was brought up by Mrs. Bennet. Eventually, it was agreed upon to have a double wedding in six week's time, on the twenty-ninth day of May.

Darcy was visibly disappointed at having to wait six weeks—after his conversation with Mr. Bennet, he thought it would be much sooner, and he exchanged a look with his future father-in-law. Mr. Bennet also felt that might be too long to wait after he had witnessed Darcy and Elizabeth's behaviour on their trip to London, but he knew he could not voice his reasoning without embarrassing his daughter. Mr. Bennet sent a look of warning to Darcy, which the younger man understood completely.

Mrs. Bennet would hear none of the arguments which *were* presented. "Six weeks will be short enough time to plan a wedding of this magnitude, and I will not settle for one day sooner!"

Darcy's countenance changed before saying, "Mrs. Bennet, I am sure you know Lady Catherine de Bourgh is very ill, and the doctor does not expect her to live much longer. She was my mother's sister and, when she dies, I will be required to go into deep mourning." To himself he thought, *to keep up appearances and protect Elizabeth's reputation,* and then he continued aloud, "It would be unheard of for me to be married during deep mourning, madam. I would rather marry sooner than later and forgo a more elaborate wedding. "

Mrs. Bennet did not wish to insult her prodigiously rich future son-in-law in any way. Confusion evident on her face, she was torn between his direct request to have the wedding sooner and having a less than perfect wedding ceremony and breakfast. After some minutes in silent calculation, Mrs. Bennet replied, "Three weeks… I can do it in three weeks, on the eighth of May. The banns will have been read three times by then as well. But we must begin shopping for the trousseaux tomorrow! I will not have much time to organize the wedding breakfast once we return to Longbourn!"

Mrs. Gardiner noted, "If anyone can do it, Fanny, I am confident that *you* can!"

~%~

~London

Georgiana and Elizabeth enjoyed exchanging visits, and Georgiana was included on all the Bennet ladies' shopping excursions; their rapport was splendid, and they were calling each other by their Christian names by the second visit. Elizabeth loved Georgiana's goodness and honesty. Georgiana loved Elizabeth's sense of humour and kindness—but her ability to make her brother happy was Elizabeth's best quality.

Georgiana was often surprised when she would find William smiling for no apparent reason or laughing out loud at something Elizabeth said or did. Even when she was not present, he spoke of her regularly with a smile reflected in his eyes. She had been a little shocked at the way the two "debated," but they both seemed to enjoy that time more than the silly, useless flirting she had seen other couples engage in. Georgiana was even getting used to laughing at her brother when Elizabeth teased him. All in all, she was growing to love Elizabeth as a sister—just as she had always hoped she would love the woman whom William would marry.

~%~

During one of Elizabeth's visits to Darcy House, Darcy was taking a short respite from his work, enjoying his time watching Georgiana and Elizabeth practicing a duet at the pianoforte. As Richard was taking his leave for the remainder of the day, a footman came in with a letter for Darcy. When Darcy saw who it was from, he wasted no time opening it. Darcy sat down heavily while reading, his face overcome by a pallor which caused all others in the room to become concerned.

Elizabeth crossed the room and sat beside him on the sofa, taking his hand in hers. "William, who is it from?"

"It is from Mr. Clark in India," Darcy paused and spoke directly to Elizabeth, "Diamonds! The saltpetre mining was hiding the fact that it is a diamond mine as well! It seems this is why they were not allowing anyone out of the mine… the men Lady Catherine hired to run the mine had kept their discovery of diamonds a secret from her, and they were keeping all the profits.

"One of Mr. Clark's men managed to escape from the mine, but he had been badly injured. He was able to make it away from the mine before he collapsed. Some men from the nearest village found him and took him home with them. They took care of him… weeks had passed before he was strong enough to send word to Mr. Clark of his whereabouts.

"Mr. Clark saw to it that the men running the mine have been taken into custody by the British Army for theft from British citizens. The local authorities are charging them with several murders, attempted murder, and kidnapping as well. He predicts that by the time I receive this letter, the trial should be concluded and the men brought to justice for their crimes."

Georgiana asked, “Theft?”

“Yes… the diamonds.” Looking back to the letter, Darcy continued, “The mine has been closed, and the people working there have been tended to. Mr. Clark asks what he should to do about the mine.”

Richard said, “Everything does make much more sense now.” All were quiet for a few minutes until Richard broke the silence, “So Darce—you own a diamond mine!”

Darcy blinked a few times before replying, “I suppose so. Along with your father, Richard… the adjoining land is in his name whether he bought it or not. I must speak to the earl about this as soon as possible.”

~%~

A frequent visitor at the Gardiners’ was Charlotte, who became closely acquainted with the Fitzwilliam family during this time. She was enjoying her time at Captain and Mrs. Walsh’s house and had agreed to stay to help with their children until Mrs. Walsh’s confinement was complete before returning to Lucas Lodge.

Her visits to Darcy House often coincided with the visits of Colonel Fitzwilliam. Richard was a frequent visitor to the Walsh residence whenever he could be spared from his duties as well.

Lady Matlock smiled whenever she saw Richard and Charlotte conversing together, for she could see clearly that Richard would have no need of her “finely tuned” matchmaking skills.

Mr. Bennet returned to Longbourn before the others to attend to business at home. It was settled that after the shopping for wedding clothes was complete, the Bennet ladies would return home in Darcy’s and Bingley’s coaches; the gentlemen would escort them, and arrangements were made for Netherfield to be opened for their return. Georgiana and Mrs. Annesley would accompany them to Hertfordshire to prepare for the wedding.

Over the next few days, much shopping was accomplished. Due to Elizabeth’s condition, each shopping session was shorter than most of the ladies would have preferred. With her family and Georgiana in Town, she had many willing assistants, but this also meant many opposing tastes. On different occasions, Lady Matlock, Mrs. Gardiner, Jane, and even Georgiana, helped to counter Mrs. Bennet and Elizabeth’s youngest sisters' insistence on “more lace” and “more elaborate designs” than Elizabeth would be comfortable with.

Monday, April 27, 1812

~Hertfordshire

By the time they were ready to depart from London, Elizabeth's ribs had healed completely and her hand was almost completely healed as well. Her nightmares had calmed considerably, and on some nights she did not have any at all. Once in a while memories of Wickham intruded upon her daytime thoughts, but it was becoming easier to quickly push them aside.

On the trip to Hertfordshire, Georgiana travelled together in Darcy's coach with the engaged couples, while the remainder of the Bennet ladies rode in Bingley's carriage. It was a most agreeable ride with the passengers passing the time playing word games and pleasantly conversing.

Having returned to Hertfordshire in the spring, Darcy was able to visit Elizabeth's special meadow at her favourite time of year. They made a day of it by planning a picnic for all their sisters and Bingley to share the place abloom in its entire springtime splendor.

Surprisingly, Mary especially loved the meadow, and Elizabeth and Darcy had no trouble finding a chaperone for walks there during the remaining days of their engagement… though Mary was *too* good a chaperone for their taste!

As a wedding present, Georgiana decided to paint a picture of the meadow that was so special to her brother and Elizabeth, and she enlisted Kitty to accompany her whenever she walked there. Watching Georgiana paint renewed Kitty's interest in art, which she had given up long ago due to Lydia's impatience with it. Georgiana shared her supplies with Kitty and gave her a few lessons. Kitty's natural talents had her catching on quickly, and in some ways she was even better than Georgiana, who had taken lessons from masters for years! Kitty created a sketch of Oakham Mount as her wedding present to them since Lizzy and Darcy seemed to enjoy walking there as well.

Georgiana, Elizabeth, and Darcy spent as much time together as the wedding planning would allow. For Darcy, the next best thing to having time alone with Elizabeth, which was extremely scarce, was sharing his time with her and his sister. There was no prouder man than he when walking out with the two ladies he loved best, one on each arm.

~%~

The minute I heard my first love story, I started looking for you, not knowing how blind that was. Lovers do not finally meet somewhere. They are in each other all along.
--Jlal Uddin Rumi (Turkish Sufi mystic poet 1207-1273)

Thursday, May 7, 1812

~Oakham Mount

The day before the wedding, Darcy woke up with an irresistible urge to ride to Oakham Mount. He set off after breakfast and as he approached the hill, he was treated to a sight that took his breath away… again.

There she was, *his Elizabeth*, standing atop the hill in the same position in which she had been the first time he saw her. Her eyes were closed and her face tilted upward, the breeze playing with some curls which had broken free from their pins. Her arms were extended a bit from her sides and slightly behind her. She was, as always, his angel.

The last time he had seen her like this, he had experienced difficulty in finding a way to ascend the hill, but now he knew the quickest route to the top, and he quietly made his way to her.

As he approached her from behind, Darcy whispered, "You were in that same pose when first I saw you. I could not help but fall in love with you instantly." He stepped closer and wrapped his arms around her waist. Eyes remaining closed; she leaned back into his embrace and covered his hands with hers. He bent down to speak into her ear. "I thought you an angel and expected you to sprout wings."

"I do not remember standing this way at the assembly," she whispered.

He smiled. "It was here, at Oakham Mount, a fortnight before the assembly. It was as if you were calling to me… I was drawn to you, as I was today—as I am every time I am near you. It was as if I was bewitched; I could not look away. I cannot explain the disappointment I felt that you were gone when I reached the top, though now I realize it was probably better that you were not here, for I might have taken you into my arms and frightened you off! You were, and always will be, the most beautiful sight I have ever seen.

"I thought you something my imagination had created since I did not believe a woman as lovely as you could truly exist—but part of me continued to hope you were real. I returned here every day to see if I could find you again, but you did not reappear. Your unnamed form haunted my thoughts and my dreams.

"When at the assembly you walked past me, and I realized I had insulted the only woman I could ever love, you cannot imagine how I felt!" He kissed her neck just under her ear and took a deep breath, filling himself with her scent.

Elizabeth smiled. "I remember that day! I was thinking of you, William… when I was standing here, all those months ago."

Darcy pressed his lips to her ear. "How so, my love?"

"I was wondering about the man I would love, imagining the man I would marry. You are more than I had ever hoped to find." Elizabeth turned in his arms to face him; the look in her eyes matched the love that was shining from his.

"Truly, Elizabeth?"

Her hands moved to his face, fingers smoothing the worried creases from his brow and tracing the lines of his face. "You are much more than I ever thought to expect, even in my imagination's conjuring of the ideal man, William."

An unknown feeling stirred deep within him. As her thumb traced his lips, he whispered, "I cannot understand what I have ever done to deserve your love, Elizabeth, and I do not have the words to express how thankful I am for it."

A teasing sparkle lit her eyes as she said, "Then *show* me!" She raised her lips to his, wrapping her fingers in his hair, pulling him closer… closer.

Their kisses slowly became more passionate than ever before. After several minutes passed in this manner, Darcy pulled away and gasped at the emotion in her eyes. He said breathlessly, "Elizabeth! I cannot tell you how I look forward to showing you *exactly* how thankful I am—tomorrow night, *after* we are married. But for now I need to walk you home… for if we continue in this manner, I do believe I will show you here and now!"

Elizabeth gasped. "Tomorrow!" She reached into his pocket and removed his watch. Her eyes filled with tears as she said, "I shall become your wife at this time tomorrow, William!"

He took her face between his hands, caressing her cheeks. "And I will be the most fortunate husband who has ever lived!"

They shared one tender, lingering kiss, before he took her hand and led her toward Longbourn.

Remember tonight, for it is the beginning of always
--Dante Alighieri (Italian Poet 1265-1321)

Friday, May 8, 1812

For months to come, Hertfordshire gossip would be full of praise for Mrs. Bennet on her arrangements for the double wedding of Miss Jane Bennet to Mr. Charles Bingley of Netherfield and Miss Elizabeth Bennet to Mr. Fitzwilliam Darcy of Pemberley—and all accomplished with only three weeks to plan!

The weeks leading up to the wedding saw the purses of the dressmakers and shopkeepers in Meryton and the surrounding villages become fat with the local gentry's attempt to impress the members of the peerage who were predicted to attend. The local butcher's tills were filled to overflowing with the purchases of sundry meats needed for the wedding breakfast and other entertaining which would surround the happy event.

The local matrons—including Mrs. Bennet—were cheerfully primping their single daughters in anticipation of all the single gentlemen friends and relatives of the grooms who were rumoured to attend, all said to possess large fortunes. Though not all were invited to the wedding breakfast itself, there was always the possibility of meeting with said gentlemen by chance in the village, and all of the families in the area with unmarried daughters had every intention of being present at the church ceremony.

Lady Matlock travelled to Netherfield a few days before the wedding. Since Lady Catherine's state of health had not changed for weeks, and the doctor had said that she could last for at least another week in this condition as she had been able to swallow some liquid nourishment, Lord

Matlock had convinced Anne de Bourgh to come with him to Netherfield for one night; they would leave for Rosings directly after the wedding breakfast. Georgiana would accompany Lady Matlock to London, where she would stay while the Darcys were away on a honeymoon tour.

The night before the wedding, Elizabeth and Jane stayed up late talking and enjoying their last time together as single sisters. They discussed many happy moments in their lives and some sad ones. They laughed as they shared their nervousness about beginning new lives and their happy expectations of marriage.

Lady Matlock and Mrs. Gardiner had invited the soon-to-be brides for a walk earlier in the day to give them "the talk" about what to expect on their wedding night, not trusting Mrs. Bennet to give them a reliable account. When Mrs. Bennet came into Jane and Elizabeth's room late that evening, what she shared was surprisingly similar to the information they had received earlier in the day— except that she was even *more* positive and more shockingly enthusiastic about what they should expect from their handsome, physically-fit husbands. The girls broke into a fit of giggles after Mrs. Bennet left the room, which lasted until they were too exhausted to stay awake any longer.

Lord Matlock took it upon himself to speak with Darcy and Bingley, since neither of them had a father living to perform that duty. Richard was in the room when Lord Matlock was about to begin, stating that since he would be standing up for both men he should not be required to leave. His father decided to proceed saying that he was saving himself from having to do this again some-day with Richard. There was more hemming and hawing heard than actual words, but the main ideas were eventually communicated... somewhat—with Richard's stifled chuckling in the background. The group then joined the other guests who had gathered at Netherfield to attend the wedding.

Contrary to what most of the gentlemen assumed, neither Darcy nor Bingley seemed nervous about getting married. It was the wedding itself that Darcy was worried about—standing up in front of all those people! The married gentlemen all assured him that the only time anyone would be looking at *him* was before the ladies entered the church. Instead of lessening his nervousness, this confirmed that he would be the centre of attention for part of the day, therefore putting his state of anxiety even higher than before, rivaling Mrs. Bennet's worst case of nerves.

The next morning, it took all of both Bingley's and Richard's attentions to keep Darcy from pacing or withdrawing to a window while they waited.

When the brides entered the church, there was no need for any further interference. Darcy had eyes only for Elizabeth, and she for him. They held each other's gaze through the entire service as long as the demands of the ritual allowed.

Months earlier, Darcy had worried about making his vows when he married. But on his wedding day, when he looked into his Elizabeth's eyes and vowed to love, comfort, honour, and keep her in sickness and in health; forsake all others, so long as he would live, he meant every word—wholly and completely—and there was not one person in attendance who would ever doubt it… not even Caroline Bingley. The same was true for Elizabeth's recital of her vows. Theirs was, without any doubt, a love-match.

As they left the church, Darcy told Elizabeth to look up, and the smile which no onlooker thought could become brighter, did. The sky was filled with colourful kites! At the look in her eyes, Darcy was tempted to skip the wedding breakfast and tell the driver to take them directly to Darcy House in London… but he knew his mother-in-law would never forgive him.

As a surprise for the "queen of kites," Darcy had hired some of the locals to make a kite for every child in the area as a gift, along with a shiny coin, from the couple on their wedding day. He had made certain that every one of them promised they would not tell Elizabeth about the surprise, and they had all kept their promise. There may have been evidence of some tangled lines and a kite or two stuck in a tree, but the children of Hertfordshire would have to make do without Elizabeth's assistance in that manner from that moment on.

The wedding breakfast was a complete success. There were many discussions on which lady was the more beautiful bride or which groom had been more handsome, but it was universally acknowledged that the ceremony was perfect in every way, as was the celebration afterward.

It was much talked of that Darcy and Elizabeth were inseparable throughout the event. In some way the two were always touching—they were holding hands, her arm was entwined with his, or his hand could be seen resting upon her waist.

As they left Netherfield, Elizabeth embraced her family and friends while bidding them goodbye, and though it was considered positively improper by *some* of the guests, she also embraced a few beloved members of the staff… but those people who were most important to Elizabeth and Darcy understood this behaviour completely.

Darcy sat opposite Elizabeth in the coach on the way to London, reveling in the fact that he now had the *right* to do more than just admire her from afar. This presented a challenge as she resumed her previous coach ride behaviour from the trip from Broadstairs to London and there was nothing to check his behaviour other than his desire to wait to arrive at their London home rather than embarrass them both by making her his wife there in the coach! Though from the look in her eyes he did not think she would mind very much, it was not the way he wished their wedding night to proceed.

He decided that, as a distraction for them, now was a good time to tell her about her father's veiled warnings in London, hinting at what he had witnessed pass between them in the coach on their previous trip. Revealing this information surprisingly only increased the look of ardor in her eyes and made it an increasingly laborious task to maintain his distance.

Remembering their conversation at the Lucas home months ago when she had requested to speak to him alone about their "friendship," Elizabeth said, "May I speak with you alone, Mr. Darcy?"

Confused, his eyebrow arched—of course she could speak to him alone, there was nobody else in the coach. That was his problem at the moment!

She continued with such a seductive look in her eye that he could barely breathe. "*This* time I *am* a 'dangerous' female about to compromise your honour! I wish to assure you that I *do* have the expectation of our acquaintance progressing well past friendship, sir. I would much rather not be the cause of any further suffering, and I will allow your future behaviour to guide my own… William." She extended her finger in a "come hither" motion—therein ending his endeavor to maintain his distance.

There is nothing nobler or more admirable than when two people who see eye to eye keep house as man and wife, confounding their enemies and delighting their friends.
--Homer (Ancient Greek Poet, dates lived unknown, BC)

Thursday, June 11, 1812

A strong sense of *déjà vu* came upon Darcy as he slowed his horse to a walk, his gaze swept across the landscape of the place he believed to afford the perfect prospect. The lake reflected a beautifully clear sky and a mirror image of Pemberley House. His eyes were drawn toward the vision of loveliness that strode in his direction. The sight of Elizabeth never failed to take his breath away; skin glowing with health that came from long walks in the sunshine, eyes sparkling with intelligence and wit. At the moment she noticed him nearing, a bewitching smile spread across her lips.

"Perfect!" he breathed.

He allowed the reins to fall to the ground as he dismounted and drank in her form, reveling in the grace of her movements as she approached him.

Elizabeth came to stand before him, their bodies almost touching, and her eyes captured his. His breath quickened; her scent nearly overwhelmed his senses.

She raised a hand to caress his cheek, and he bowed his head to meet her touch. Bestowing upon him the gentlest of kisses, she then pulled back to look in his eyes. His heart rejoiced to recognize his own feelings reflected within her soul.

Winding his arms around her waist, he delighted in the feel of every inch of her body pressed against his. Lips met again and again. As he savored the taste of her love for him, her delicate fingers laced through his hair. The kiss deepened.

Though he felt he should never need to breathe again as long as she was near, his lungs rebelled. They pulled apart after one last gentle kiss.

Elizabeth's saucy grin reached her eyes. "Have you had your fill of exercise for one morning, or would you rather join me?"

"A walk, perhaps, or would you like to receive the riding lessons I promised you?"

"I think not today, my love. My mind was turned more toward indoor activities. You are in desperate need of a bath, and I was looking forward to… assisting. I am certain the opportunity of other forms of exercise will soon present itself."

The expression in her eyes made him gasp softly. "I do believe that can be arranged," he responded, his voice husky, whilst bending closer for another kiss.

"Come." She turned toward the house, wrapping her arm about his waist. Elizabeth tugged him toward the house, and they began to walk.

"Do you think the staff is used to our scandalous behaviour by now, dearest?" Darcy's eyes were twinkling with a teasing light.

"If they are scandalized by our behaviour, it is for the best. I will not have anyone thinking that this is anything but a love-match!"

Happiness resides not in possessions, and not in gold, happiness dwells in the soul.

--Democritus (Greek Philosopher 460BC – 370BC)

Caroline Bingley did "catch" Mr. Hainsworth upon her return to London after her brother's and Darcy's weddings. Caroline Hainsworth, nee Bingley, received the wealth and beautiful estate she thought she wanted, and was able to write the names of the peerage on the finest paper for invitations and place cards, just as she had always dreamed of doing. Unfortunately, after the first two occasions for writing invitations, the thrill was gone.

The ladies of the first circle looked upon her as an interloper, the daughter of a *tradesman* who actually had the arrogance to criticize the taste and opinions of ladies *born* into the first circle. Whether they liked the ladies whom Caroline criticized did not matter, she did not have the right! They soon began to give her the cut direct—even physically turning their backs to her whenever the gentlemen were not present. Eventually, she was invited nowhere but to visit her own family, and none of the first circle would accept *her* invitations. What did it matter if she was able to wear the best gowns and decorate her house with the best materials available when she could not show them off to anybody of import?

Her husband was not at all supportive; he found he had unwisely rushed into making an error he would regret for the remainder of his life. Their dislike of Mr. and Mrs. Darcy was the *only* thing they had in common when they married, and that eventually changed on his part. In fact, he found that he and his wife could hardly be civil to each other, and he avoided her except when absolutely necessary. He did not worry about the servants gossiping for, judging by the way he saw her treat them, he felt they well understood his behaviour and wished only that they could do the same.

Whenever Caroline was in company with her siblings and their spouses, the Darcys, or any of the Bennets for that matter, she came to see the happiness and contentment which was missing from her own life… and became quite resentful towards them, blaming *them* for her dissatisfaction.

Her life was not at all what it was supposed to have been, and she was quite vexed! She should have *everything*! If events had followed her original plan, she would not be in this situation! Why had nobody listened to her?

The more discontented and irritable Caroline became, the less time Mr. Hainsworth spent with her—until Caroline found herself taking all her meals alone as well. The day dawned when she suddenly realized that in truth she had nothing compared to what any of her family or the former Bennet ladies had, but still she refused to give way to this thought and change her behaviour. Mrs. Caroline Hainsworth lived unhappily ever after.

Once Louisa Hurst had cast off her fear of her sister Caroline, she began to develop her own tastes and opinions on everything life had to offer. Alexander Hurst's attention was caught by the changes in his wife, which renewed his interest in life itself. He decided to court his wife for a second time… and the two slowly fell in love with each other. They became a happily married couple, bought an estate of their own, and had two sons.

Since Mr. Collins was deceased, the entail of Longbourn passed to a distant cousin who was the next in line, Archibald Baldwin, a rather sensible young man who had already come into a large inheritance and had no other family. It warmed Mr. Bennet's heart to know that such a worthy young man would take possession of Longbourn once he was gone. Having only a house in London, shortly after hearing of the entail, Mr. Baldwin came for an extended visit to learn estate management and soon became the son Mr. Bennet never had.

Lydia fell in love with Mr. Baldwin at first sight. To impress Mr. Baldwin, she joined Mary in taking over for Elizabeth and Jane in their heartfelt duties to the neighbourhood. Surprising everyone who had known her previously, Lydia found great pleasure in it and matured in the process. Over time, she became much more sedate but kept some of her liveliness in a perfect combination to attract the young gentleman. They married two years after Mr. Baldwin had first come to Longbourn.

Colonel Richard Fitzwilliam had placed Charlotte Collins with the Walsh family when she initially escaped from Hunsford. He had visited her there frequently and realized he truly was in love with her. Charlotte finally admitted to herself that she *was* a romantic after all. Following Mr. Collins's death, and an extended stay at the Walshes', Charlotte went home to Lucas Lodge. She spent much time visiting with Elizabeth and Darcy in London and at Pemberley over the next year. Richard visited his cousins as much as possible as well, and they often found themselves staying with the Darcys at the same time. He was also a habitual guest at Netherfield. When her mourning period was over, Charlotte was more than overjoyed to agree to marry the love of her life, Richard Fitzwilliam, and to live on a colonel's salary. A fortnight after their engagement, Richard received an express stating that a distant relative had died and, having no heirs, had left an estate to Richard, thrilling all who cared for them. Conveniently, the estate was little more than a two hour carriage ride from Pemberley. With the substantial increase in his income, Richard retired his commission immediately and married Charlotte as soon as was possible thereafter. Mr. and Mrs. Fitzwilliam lived a long and happy life together, making certain the Darcy children had many Fitzwilliam cousins.

Lady Catherine's heart gave out two weeks after Elizabeth Bennet wed Fitzwilliam Darcy. As Anne de Bourgh took possession of Rosings, though still weaker than most young ladies her age, her health and personality blossomed with the activity and responsibility of the inheritance. Anne had endured enough of someone else directing her life while her mother had lived and never wished to put herself in that position again. She would be the sole master of herself and of Rosings for the remainder of her years, and she named the second son of the Viscount Matlock as her heir.

Anne became fond of her new cousins through marriage, Elizabeth and Charlotte, and invited them to stay with her at Rosings often. Though Charlotte and Richard always declined the offer due to past associations with Hunsford, Anne was always welcomed to visit them—and she did so often.

Anne had met Elizabeth's sisters during her short visit to Netherfield for the Darcy's and Bingley's weddings when she became friendly with Mary. After correspondence was exchanged and their friendship had grown, Mary was invited to visit at Rosings—where she met the new, quite intelligent and respectable rector of Hunsford. Mary married the minister and became the perfect wife for a clergyman. They lived out their lives in quiet happiness.

Kitty and Georgiana continued their friendship begun during the time just before William and Elizabeth's wedding, and Kitty visited the Darcys often. While at Pemberley, Kitty met and fell in love with the clergyman of Kympton. They were married alongside Mary and her betrothed in Mrs. Bennet's second double wedding ceremony, which was almost—but not quite—as grand as the first.

Georgiana received her letter from her late mother before her "coming out." The influence of her mother's advice added to the example set by her family, especially William and Elizabeth, proved to Georgiana that it was indeed best to marry for love—though she did not do badly in matters of social status and wealth by falling in love with a wealthy baron.

Once Elizabeth and Jane were married, Mrs. Bennet settled down quite noticeably. Meeting Mr. Baldwin and believing his subsequent promise that she would never be "thrown out into the hedgerows" as long as she lived helped to calm her nerves as well. As Mary and Kitty's wedding drew near, Mrs. Bennet was almost unrecognizable by her two eldest daughters when they arrived for the visit. Without having to constantly worry about providing an heir, as she had for the first fifteen years of their marriage, or who would marry her daughters, as she had for the next eight years, she now had the time and the inclination to become involved in more intelligent pursuits, with her husband's guidance. Mr. Bennet began to see that the woman he had married years ago, though not of great intellect, was *not* just a pretty face. He fell in love with Fanny Bennet, and she with him. They lived the rest of their time together in blissful harmony.

Jane and Bingley did not live long at Netherfield. They purchased an estate not far from Pemberley and were able to visit the Darcys often with their own happy family, consisting of two sons and two daughters.

Elizabeth and Darcy lived a long and unquestionably happy life together. The heir to the Darcy legacy, Bennet Fitzwilliam Darcy, was born two years after their wedding, followed about every two years by another addition, in all four more children, two daughters and then two sons—Jane, Anne, Matthew and Richard.

The Darcys taught their offspring many things. Among them were the importance of duty and honour; the need to embrace their own happiness as opposed to allowing the expectations of other people to guide their lives, taking their happiness from them; the intelligence of judging the worth of others by their characters and not the standards of society; and the truth that trust is earned, not a thing to be given away casually.

All of the Darcy children followed the advice of their parents and lived to become truly generous and worthy individuals. They followed their parents' example by marrying partners with whom they shared mutual respect and the deepest love.

The story of Elizabeth and William Darcy's difficulties, adventures, and triumphant love influenced the lives of countless descendants. They lived on through stories passed from generation to generation for many years to come.

~Eight generations later…

Lizzy had followed in her father's footsteps in a choice of careers. Unlike some genealogists, they not only researched their clients' ancestral backgrounds using the internet and other modern methods, but also employed the old-fashioned, hands-on approach of tracing backgrounds through church records, graveyards, and family Bibles. Her particular success in the field came from going beyond merely handing over a family tree of ancestors to her clients as did many of her competitors. In order to relate a family's history as thoroughly as possible, she insisted on searching through the family's libraries and the dustiest corners of their attics for old letters, journals, and diaries which often revealed intimate information about their ancestors that gave her a sense of their personalities, all which would be included in the final report.

This time, though, her research was *personal.* Similar to the old adage that a plumber's pipes would always be leaking, her father had only sporadically researched their own family tree. Between assignments, Lizzy had continued this work with a vengeance. Most of her ancestors, dating back to the time of William the Conqueror, had been accounted for, but there was one family line which had a few branches missing. When she had traced the Bennet line to an estate called Longbourn, she had petitioned and was granted permission from the owner at that time for access to the library and attics. When she arrived, she fell in love with the place, and since it was for sale, she bought it. Her sister Jane moved in with her and did what she did best—restored the estate to its original condition.

In the attic, Lizzy found a chest full of letters that, to most people, would have been considered trash, but to Lizzy, they were a treasure. From them, she was able to trace several members of the Bennet family and fill in some of the branches of the tree. She also found a number of journals from a lady named Elizabeth Catherine Bennet, and Lizzy soon found herself becoming quite attached to Miss Bennet. They were kindred spirits, and Lizzy thought of Elizabeth almost as if she were an old friend. The journals ended abruptly after the year 1810. There were several rather general references to her in correspondence from later years found nearby, but she did not know exactly what Elizabeth's fate had been. She also could not find much information on Jane Mary Bennet, though there were several references to her living at Netherfield Park, a nearby estate. The church at Longbourn had suffered a fire in the year 1858, and most of the marriage and birth records before that time were lost. Several of the books were partially recovered, and on one page from 1812, Lizzy could make out that Jane and Elizabeth Bennet were married on the same day, but the part of the page that named the grooms had been destroyed.

Lizzy had petitioned the current owner of Netherfield Park, which had been closed for years, for access to the attics numerous times, but to no avail. Then gossip began to spread around the neighbourhood that Netherfield had been purchased by a wealthy man by the name of Charles Bingley. Quite the horseman, but not having a very good sense of direction, Mr. Bingley had become lost and upon seeing Longbourn, stopped for directions back to his new estate. Lizzy found Charlie very friendly, and Jane and Charlie soon became something more than friends. After being shown photos of what Longbourn's condition had been when Lizzy first purchased it and seeing the results of Jane's restoration firsthand, he asked Jane to restore Netherfield Park as well. While spending many months in each other's company during the restoration of Netherfield, Jane and Charlie fell deeply in love and were engaged to be married.

In the meantime, Charlie had given Lizzy access to the attics of Netherfield without a second thought. After much rummaging through the huge space, she was surprised to find some records indicating that a Charles James Bingley had leased Netherfield from 1811 to 1813. He left a simple note to the steward at the time with a forwarding address for any correspondence that might come after they had left, and for that of his wife—Jane Bingley nee Bennet! What a find *this* was!

The current owner of the estate in Derbyshire that the Bingley's had apparently purchased upon leaving Netherfield was happy to give permission to have her look through a box of old letters to Jane Bingley which they had found in with some family heirlooms. It seemed that Elizabeth Bennet, Lizzy's "old friend" from the journals at Longbourn, had married Fitzwilliam Darcy, of Pemberley, also in Derbyshire.

This information was bittersweet. She knew the current owner of Pemberley, as he was a good friend of Charlie's, and if it had been *anyone* else she would have been overjoyed… but *this* man was absolutely insufferable! Yes, he was probably the handsomest man she had ever seen, but he was such an arrogant snob! At their first meeting she had overheard an insulting remark he had made about her which she had never been able to forgive. Of course, the fact that he had never apologized for saying it played a large part in her resentment. Whenever they were thrown together, Lizzy and Will Darcy would either ignore each other or argue, and he was always glaring at her, probably trying to intimidate her, she had decided. Since he always seemed to be hanging around and coming back for more, she thought that either he was a glutton for punishment, or he was trying to make her feel so uncomfortable that she would be scared off. She would *not* give him the satisfaction of giving in to his bullying tactics, and therefore, any time she heard that Will was around, she would make sure to show up.

Months before, he had asked her out, and she literally laughed out loud thinking he was joking. From the way he reacted, she guessed he had *not* been joking. They had a terrible argument, and she told him exactly what she thought of him. Lizzy had not seen him since.

Charlie had insisted that Will had acted so rudely at first because he was very shy and very rich and always had women throwing themselves at him, which he absolutely hated, and he must have wrongly assumed that Lizzy would do the same. Jane had plenty of opportunities to get to know Will better while staying at Charlie's place in London and assured Lizzy that Will's personality was much different from what she had expected. Lizzy's opinion of him may have softened a little, but she had to see it to really believe it, and she knew that after the verbal thrashing she had given him, he would probably never want to be in the same room with her again, let alone get to know her better. Jane told her that she shouldn't be so sure about that, since the man was constantly asking about her, and she thought he was obviously head-over-heels in love with her. Lizzy just laughed in disbelief.

To avoid the awkward scenes that were inevitable when having to spend time with Will, she delayed her request to search Pemberley's attics, following the Bingley branch of the family instead through Charlie's relatives. She continued her explorations whenever there was a break in her work schedule –after all, paying clients still came first.

She would always remember the horrified look on Charlie's face when Lizzy informed him and Jane that they were all three descended from a union between Charles James Bingley and Jane Mary Bennet! Charlie immediately assumed that Jane and by being together all this time, they had committed a sin, had broken a law, and would be forbidden to marry since they were related, and he panicked. The expression of relief he exhibited when Lizzy informed him that it was not a problem since eight generations had passed was absolutely priceless.

Since her curiosity about her "old friend" Elizabeth continued to nag at her thoughts, and the blank space underneath Elizabeth Catherine Bennet Darcy's name began to drive her mad, when another lull in her work occurred, and only after all other leads had been exhausted, Lizzy finally relented and asked Charlie if he would talk to Will about allowing her to search the attics at Pemberley.

It was quite a shock to see Pemberley for the first time, and it helped her to understand his attitude a little better—seeing just *how* rich Will Darcy must be. The mansion seemed a castle straight out of a fairy tale and was perfect in every way possible!

When she arrived at Pemberley, Will surprised her by greeting her in person and would not hear of her staying at the Inn at Lambton, telling her that his staff had already prepared for her stay there for as long as she needed to complete her investigation.

He seemed a different person when she arrived, and at first, she was angry at him for not continuing with his spoiled-brat demeanor. She had become accustomed to despising the man, which went a long way in counteracting her physical attraction for him. This change in behaviour was playing havoc with her libido.

Will introduced her to the staff, and gave instructions for them to assist her in any way possible. He gave her a personal tour of the manor house explaining some of its history, and showed her parts of the grounds. Will even spent many hours with her helping her dig through the attics and dragging out several trunks that had been left untouched for generations, ruining his perfectly tailored clothing in the process. He treated her with the utmost respect the entire weekend and even stayed with her an extra day.

At one point Lizzy overheard the housekeeper, who seemed to treat him more like a son than an employer, saying how shocked she was that he had taken a day off from work when he hadn't for years. Will had replied in a defensive tone of voice saying that since he *owned* the company, he could take a day off if he wanted to. Mrs. Reynolds suddenly seemed to warm up to Lizzy after that, and she could not imagine why.

They spent the remainder of the weekend together, and after he left, she realized it had turned out to be very pleasant. By the time he departed for London early Tuesday morning, Lizzy had become very confused as to her feelings for Will Darcy.

Even the attics at Pemberley were beautiful. Since they had been servants' quarters generations ago, they were large and airy and had many windows—all of which, Mrs. Reynolds informed her, Will had opened the day before Lizzy arrived so that she would be more comfortable spending time up there.

The trunks that Will had recommended she investigate first were a goldmine! They contained Elizabeth Bennet Darcy's journals starting with 1811 and spanning the next few decades; though after the children came along, Elizabeth seemed to have much less time to write. Lizzy spent many hours sitting by an open window reading or skimming through her old friend's life story. Her relationship with her husband was wonderfully romantic and, though she hated to admit it, it seemed Will Darcy had a lot in common with Elizabeth's description of Fitzwilliam Darcy. Lizzy wondered if she would ever have a love like that.

When not researching, Lizzy kept finding herself in the portrait gallery with the excuse of needing to review all the people Will had "introduced" her to, but in reality she spent most of her time standing in front of Fitzwilliam Darcy's portrait. It was incredible how Will looked so much like his great-great-great-great-great-great-grandfather! It also seemed that there was a portrait missing from the wall and the pictures in that area had been rearranged recently. When asked, the housekeeper told her it was a picture of Fitzwilliam Darcy with his wife and children and was lately removed. Lizzy was very curious about why this had been done and became determined to ask Will about it when he returned at the end of the week.

She continued to search the attics for other information. Thursday around noon, as she was leaving the attic, she tripped over something and ended up on the floor covered with dust. Turning around, she noticed that her foot was caught in a large sheet… and her antics had pulled the sheet down off a portrait, exposing it.

Lizzy could not believe her eyes… it was almost as if she was looking into a mirror after dressing up for a masquerade party. The woman looked almost exactly like her! Was *this* the portrait that had been removed from the gallery? Could *this* be Elizabeth Bennet Darcy looking up at Fitzwilliam Darcy with such love in her eyes, surrounded by their children?

She startled and turned around quickly when she heard Will say, "The resemblance is uncanny, isn't it?" He had a pleading look in his eyes. "I had it hidden away before you arrived at Pemberley because… well, I didn't want you to get the wrong idea, Lizzy… that maybe you would think I'm a nut or something." Will closed his eyes and sighed. His voice was stronger when he continued, "It is a portrait of Fitzwilliam and Elizabeth Darcy, and their children, painted in 1825."

Lizzy could not find the strength to tear her eyes away from his. "I thought you were in London."

"I couldn't concentrate on work knowing you were here at Pemberley. No matter how hard I try, I can't seem to stay away from you, Lizzy." Hesitating for a few moments, but never breaking their shared gaze, he seemed to gather his resolve and continued, "I've never felt like this about anyone before, and it is a bit terrifying to know that you have so much power over me. I know I made a terrible first impression, but I would appreciate it if you would give me another chance."

Lizzy's thoughts returned to what she had been thinking while reading Elizabeth's journals. She had wished for a love like Elizabeth had had with Fitzwilliam. She had repeatedly thought that Elizabeth seemed so much like herself… and Elizabeth's descriptions of Fitzwilliam reminded her very much of Will.

Will seemed so *different* since she had met him again. Had he taken what she said to him months ago during their heated argument to heart? Could it actually work between them?

Realizing there was only one way to find out, Lizzy said, "If I remember correctly, I was not on my best behaviour, either. I think I would like a chance to get to know you better."

Will displayed the dazzling dimples that had set her heart racing when she had seen them for the first time the previous weekend. “Do you ride? It will be light for a while yet, and I’d like to show you more of the park...”

Lizzy smiled brilliantly, “Yes, I’d love that.”

They both looked at the portrait for a few moments before Will covered it with the sheet once again. “Someday you and I will have a similar portrait done, and we’ll hang it in the gallery across from this one.” His grin broadened at the sight of her wide eyes, and motioned toward the stairs. “Shall we?”

Lizzy nodded, and they continued on their way together… forever.

* The dream that inspired this story was of Elizabeth walking into Hunsford Cottage and finding Mr. Collins with the floor open. It still amazes me how *that* dream became *this story!*

* Dryads in Celtic and Greek mythology (and others) are beautiful woman tree nymphs whose joy is frolicking in nature. When a dryad does make contact with a human, you can't be sure whether they are there to help, play, or tease. They play wonderful music, as well as sing.

* The Isles of Scilly, off the shore of Cornwall, England, relied completely on smuggled goods at this time in history.

* *Preachers say, 'Do as I say, not as I do.* John Selden (1584-1654)

* Through my research I came across the history of Joss Snelling, a smuggler famous for being the head of the "Callis Court Gang", whom Captain John Sharp is based upon (Sharp was rumoured to be one of his aliases, actually). The settings in this book are based upon what can be pieced together about Snelling's operations. Snelling was fined £100 on several occasions, but was set free without any other punishments, while others from his "gang" were put to death. I highly doubt that Snelling ever smuggled anything that would be considered treasonous since my research showed that Princess Victoria (future Queen) at age 10, sought out "The Famous Broadstairs' Smuggler" to hear his stories while he was still in business. It is amazing for any era that Snelling retired from his business at age 89 and died at age 96. I guess the smuggling trade was good for one's health… as long as the death was due to natural causes! Jeff Mott is based on Joss Snelling's longtime associate Jeff Mutton.

* In the early 19th Century, safes were referred to as "iron chests."

"Capital!" exclaimed Mr. William Lucas, one fine spring day near the village of Meryton in Hertfordshire. Mr. Lucas was a jolly sort of man and a successful London tradesman who, several years earlier, had inherited an estate, and consequently, had promptly moved his family away from the foul city air.

His companion and neighbour, Mr. Thomas Bennet of Longbourn, chuckled. "What thought has caught your fancy just now, Lucas?"

Mr. Lucas stopped at a stream in the shade of a huge beech tree and allowed his horse to indulge in a drink. Mopping his forehead with a handkerchief, he answered, "A race is being held at the village of Bramfield in two months' time, Bennet! The local business owners in the village banded together and are putting up a prize purse of a guinea! All contestants must be under the age of fifteen years, which would make it more than likely that at least one adult family member would attend with them, spending their money at the local shops. It will provide some excellent sport for the locals to attend as well as a little competition for them, in addition to drawing in people from all over the area. I think it a splendid idea!"

"Ah, so they have revived the traditional race, have they? When I was a lad, I would enter the races at Bramfield. Perhaps we could attend the race and bring along your sons… and I do believe my Lizzy and your Charlotte might be interested as well," replied Mr. Bennet.

Little did the gentlemen realize that their daughters were at that very moment sitting on a high branch of the tree above their fathers' heads and having a difficult time stifling their giggles. Both girls had been admonished by their mothers all too many times for climbing trees and ruining dresses to risk being caught again.

"Capital idea, Bennet! Now we should move on, or we will be late for our meeting." Both gentlemen were soon on their way.

When their fathers were out of hearing range, a mischievous glint sparkled in Lizzy's eyes. "Oh, Charlotte! We must enter the race!"

Wide-eyed, Charlotte replied, "Lizzy! How could we possibly do so? Neither of us knows how to ride. Besides, I am already fifteen years old and would not be able to enter the race."

"Well, then… since I am eleven, I shall enter the race alone. I have watched my father ride for many years now, and it does not look difficult at all. I am certain I can teach myself within the two months before the race. Would you not like to learn to ride, Charlotte?"

"I would, Lizzy. My brother continues to say he will teach me, but he is always too busy between managing Lucas Lodge and my father's business in London."

"Then we shall learn without any help from anybody! I shall enter the race, and when I win, we will split the prize money."

"But Lizzy, do you not think the race will be only for boys? They will likely not allow you to enter."

Lizzy's eyes tightened. "You know very well that I can do anything a boy can do, Charlotte, and in more instances than not, I do better than most boys we know!"

"You cannot best my brothers at wrestling, Lizzy."

Lizzy's chin rose up defensively. "I *am* the best at breaking their holds! If I were only bigger, I would best them at the rest as well!" Lizzy's brow furrowed, and she was deep in thought for several minutes before a satisfied grin appeared on her lips. "Do you think you could borrow your brother John's trousers and shirt for a day or two without their being missed? If I wore a hat and John's clothing, nobody would notice that I am a girl!" She said the last while looking down at her own flat chest.

Charlotte nodded.

Lizzy began to climb down from the tree and jumped from a lower branch to the ground, tearing her skirt in the process. "Oh, bother! Now Mama shall be in a dither when I get home."

As she climbed down, making sure to be more careful than her friend, Charlotte mumbled to herself, "Why do I feel as though I am going to regret agreeing to this?"

~%~

On the walk home, the girls discussed how they would go about achieving their goal of teaching themselves to ride without anyone's knowing. Whenever one of their fathers was not in need of his horse, they would sneak it away from the stable. The girls would spend any free time they had watching the stable boys saddle horses so they could learn how to do it themselves.

Unfortunately, the saddles were too heavy for the girls to carry away from the stable and saddling a horse inside the stable would risk detection… but they were able to slip on a bridle quickly enough to prevent anyone's noticing them. So, their plan changed to learning to ride bareback.

After many trials, scraped elbows and knees—and bruised unmentionables—both girls improved and became quite comfortable riding bareback. As in all things, Lizzy was fearless and before long increased her speed from a trot to a canter, and then rather quickly moved on to a gallop, frightening poor Charlotte.

"It is a good thing that the prize money does not depend on posture, Lizzy!" Charlotte teased one day as Lizzy rode past her.

About a week before the race, they tested the plan for borrowing John Lucas's clothes. None of the clothing fit Lizzy very well, and it was a good thing Charlotte had thought to bring along a belt!

Lizzy soon discovered that the material of boys' clothing was much rougher than that of girls'. The next time the girls met, Charlotte offered her friend an old slip, and they spent the next couple of days sewing legs into it. Lizzy was not so well versed in sewing as Charlotte, but she helped as she could… and included the addition of a pocket in a very strange location.

"Why on earth are you sewing that pocket in such a place, Lizzy? I would think that is not very useful there!"

Lizzy raised one eyebrow and gave her a teasing smile. "You shall understand soon enough, Charlotte!"

The next time Lizzy tried on the trousers, they were much more comfortable with the new undergarment in place.

"Charlotte, why are you looking at me like that?" Lizzy asked.

"Well… um… Lizzy? There is something… *different* about your trousers than when boys wear them." Charlotte blushed furiously.

Noticing where Charlotte's gaze was directed, Lizzy exclaimed, "Oh! I almost forgot!" She went to her dress which was hanging off a low branch and pulled a handkerchief from the pocket. Charlotte watched with a curious expression as Lizzy proceeded to roll it up and open the waist of the trousers. "*This* is what the pocket is for, Charlotte!" she said as she stuffed the handkerchief down into the unusually placed pocket.

The girls' laughter rang across the meadow as they examined the resulting look of the handkerchief. It was some time before they regained control of their mirth, and when they did, they hid John Lucas's clothing in a nearby bush and then finalized their plans for the following day—race day!

~%~

Lizzy woke up early on the morning of the race, barely able to contain her excitement. Just as she and her father were about to leave, she doubled over and moaned repeatedly. "Oh, Papa! It hurts! My stomach hurts so much! What shall I do?" she cried.

At this point, the reader must be made aware that Mr. Bennet was no fool. It could also be said that Lizzy was no actress. One must also understand that Mr. Bennet's stable hands had indeed noticed the sudden increased presence of Lizzy near the stables as well as the regular absences of his favourite horse, Coeus, over the course of the past two months and had already reported these events to their master. Lizzy's father knew she was up to *something*, and he had been waiting patiently to find out just what bit of mischief these actions would reap.

Doing a fine job of holding back his chuckle, he offered his favourite daughter the support of his arm, guiding her toward the stairs. Mr. Bennet said softly, "My poor Lizzy! I am afraid you had best stay home today, my dear!"

Lizzy leaned heavily on her father's arm. "Oh, Papa! I *so* wanted to watch the race today, but I think you are correct. I feel so weak! I do not think I shall be able to get out of bed for the remainder of the day!"

"Ah, well, we shall miss you. Shall I tell Hill to inform your mother that you should be left undisturbed to sleep as long as possible, my child?" he replied, the corners of his lips twitching.

"Oh, yes, Papa! I do think I need a long sleep today and will feel much better later. Thank you, Papa," Lizzy said as she placed the back of her hand across her forehead and then sighed deeply.

"Do you need help ascending the stairs, my Lizzy, or are you strong enough to make it on your own?"

"Oh… I would like to make the attempt, sir," his daughter answered. With her eyes half closed and head hanging low, she made quite the show of pulling herself up the stairs by the handrail and sighing intermittently, and then turned at the landing and said, "I do regret my not being able to accompany you today. Please send the Lucas family my regards, sir," and then she let loose another loud sigh before slowing moving in the direction of her bedroom. Mr. Bennet heard her shuffle her feet down the hallway and close the door.

Holding his breath, Mr. Bennet rushed out the door and into the stables where he shocked the stable hands by bursting out in laughter. What an amusing show his daughter had put on for him this morning! Now having an inkling of what mischief Lizzy had been up to the past months, he told the stable boy to leave the stable unattended for a half hour after his carriage left the grounds, and that he should expect Coeus to be "missing" for most of the day today. Mr. Bennet then went to speak to Mrs. Hill briefly before entering the carriage, which would transport his party to the race.

As soon as she could no longer detect the sound of her father's carriage, Lizzy jumped out of bed, closed the drapes, and rearranged the bedding so that it looked as if she were under the quilt sleeping. She then slipped through the window that was very close to a tree, and with a practiced ease, Lizzy climbed out, carefully stopping to close the drapes and the window behind her. She then climbed down the tree and rushed off toward the stable.

What luck! There is nobody here! Lizzy thought as she made her way to Coeus. She slipped the bridle onto Coeus and led him out into the woods in the direction of her disguise. After tying up her hair as best she could and making a quick change into her "boy clothes," Lizzy rode across the fields so that she would get to Bramfield before her father and the Lucas family could by driving the road in the carriage. Deepening her voice, she told the judge her name was "Bennet." A group of contestants arriving behind her distracted the judge, and she was able to move away before any other questions could be asked. Afraid her father, Mr. Lucas, or his sons might recognize her if they saw her, she remained hidden until the race was about to begin.

Upon their arrival at Bramfield, Charlotte looked at the large crowd gathered to watch the race and thought as she shook her head from side to side. *I have a bad feeling about this!*

By the look on her face, Mr. Bennet knew that Charlotte was in on Lizzy's secret. He delayed handing her down until her father and brothers were out of hearing and asked with amusement dancing in his eyes, "So, how exactly does Lizzy think she will get away with it?"

Charlotte's eyes opened wider than they had in all her life! Her hand came up to cover her mouth as she exclaimed, "How did you know?"

"Lizzy's 'illness' this morning was not very convincing at all!"

"Are you very angry, sir? I did try to list the reasons why she should not do this, but she had an answer for everything!"

"*That* I can believe, Miss Lucas. Lizzy is very stubborn and once her mind is set on something, there is little anyone can do to dissuade her. Do not trouble yourself. But, please tell me… how does she think she will be allowed to race today?"

"We have been teaching ourselves to ride for the past two months, and she will be dressed in my brother's clothing and hat, Mr. Bennet."

His eyes became unfocused, and he rubbed his jaw with his hand as he pictured what his hoydenish daughter would look like dressed that way. Finally he nodded and said, "Well, Miss Lucas, if all goes well she just *might* get away with it."

Soon enough, the judges called for the racers to assemble at the starting line. As Lizzy pulled her hat down lower on her head, she heard a few boys laughing at the sight of her riding bareback. As always, any attempt at intimidation only caused her courage to rise. About to lash out at the boys with her sharp tongue, she was saved from her own impulsiveness when the starting shot fired. Right then and there, Lizzy decided that she would *win* this race against those arrogant, insulting boys!

Lizzy made very good time during the length of the race, keeping within the first three or four riders throughout. As the finish line came into view, Lizzy's excited energy seemed to have transferred to Coeus, and they took the lead and won the race, though it was very close indeed. A boy came to walk Coeus while Lizzy was led to the judges to receive her prize. Just then, a wind kicked up and blew off her hat. There was a collective gasp heard from the crowd as her waist-length hair came loose, spilling down her back.

Turning a bright crimson, she searched the crowd for Charlotte's reassuring gaze, but she first met with the sight of her father walking toward her instead. His proud expression and wide smile once again fueled her courage, and she straightened herself to her full height, jutting out her chin in indignation as she heard a judge call out that she was disqualified since she was a girl.

"Do the rules of the race specifically say the contestants must be male?" Mr. Bennet called out in a voice loud enough to be heard over the increasing volume of the crowd.

The three judges all looked at each other in confusion and had a quick, whispered discussion before one stood and said, "No, but it is assumed. Riding a horse in a race would be a disgrace to any female. She is disqualified!"

"Disgrace to the lady, did you say? Or do you mean the boys would feel disgraced if they were to *lose* to a lady, as they have today?"

At the judges' expressions of embarrassment, Mr. Bennet continued loudly while looking directly at his Lizzy with eyes sparkling with love and mirth, "Yes, yes, I see how it is. All right, Lizzy, let us go home now. Today all the boys in the county were bested by a *girl,* riding bareback at that, and everyone in attendance knows the truth of the matter. Well done, Lizzy!"

Mr. Lucas, unsure of his feelings about what had passed, decided he and his children would meet the Bennets at the carriage… but Charlotte had other ideas.

Mr. Bennet led Lizzy away from the crowd to retrieve Coeus as Charlotte met them and caught her friend in an embrace. "Oh, Lizzy! You were truly wonderful! Congratulations!"

~%~

It is said that the wagging tongues of gossips cause news to travel faster than a horse and carriage… and nowhere is this truer than in

Hertfordshire. By the time the Bennets had arrived, it was already known at Longbourn that a *girl* had won the race. Mrs. Bennet was thankful the *name* of the girl was not being spread abroad as she knew there was only *one* girl in all of England who would have the audacity to make such an attempt.

The onslaught of censure from her mother lasted many a week, and even then she never did let Lizzy forget the "disgrace" she had brought upon her family by "riding like a man."

Not willing to risk her mother's ire on the matter again, Lizzy did not learn to "ride like a lady" until years later when her loving husband offered to teach her to ride sidesaddle at their beautiful estate in Derbyshire.

Acknowledgements

To my editing team, who I have dubbed “Super-Betas”, you will always have my undying gratitude: Gayle Mills and Robin Helm.

I would also like to thank Barbara Tiller Cole for her support during a trying time.

There were quite a few people who helped with the first draft, which was posted at several online Jane Austen Fan Fiction forums between August and November of 2010. Jose, DebraMc, and Roxey, your input was vital. Brenna, your help at the beginning carried through to the end. Julia G, thanks for the read-through.

Linnea Eileen Smith, your pep talks always kept me going! If it weren’t for you and Gayle, this story would have been pulled off the forums after the original chapter ten.

A special thanks to Matthew Sotis, my very own Mr. Darcy, who painted the cover art!

To the entire Jane Austen Fan Fiction community—without your support, I would not have continued writing. I appreciate all of the comments you have offered throughout the years.

Of course, I must thank Jane Austen for authoring the fine works that have captured my heart for so many years and inspired my imagination.

To everyone who prayed, helped out, and chipped in to keep my family afloat during my hospitalization and rehabilitation in the aftermath of my life-threatening illness, you really made a difference.

All the doctors, nurses and physical, occupational, and speech therapists did a wonderful job.

I especially want to thank my mom Lillian Leisenheimer, my mom-in-law Viola Schwartz, and my sister Cindy Humpf (my sister) for all they did to help me and my husband, Matt, and my children, Katie, Luke and Maddie.

Also by Wendi Sotis

April, 1801 – London

William's distress was evident on his face. So confused was he by the turmoil of emotions churned up by this quest that he no longer knew how to find what he was looking for among the rows of publications on the shelves of the bookshop.

"Excuse me, sir, but you must stop!"

Surprised, the fifteen-year-old boy looked down to find a little girl of perhaps nine or ten years sitting on the floor with an open book on her lap. "I would curtsy, as my mama says is correct when meeting a gentleman, but you are standing on my skirt, sir."

He jumped back a step or two, and the girl rose and curtsied, saying, "Thank you, sir."

The boy bowed. "Please forgive me. If I have damaged your dress, please allow me to ask my father to compensate you."

"Oh, I do forgive you, sir. There is no harm done, only a bit of dust on the hem. Had I been at home, by this time of day my skirts would have been covered with dirt and most likely would have been torn already. I am certain that Mama would be scolding me right about now! I know that a proper young lady should not have been sitting on the floor in a bookshop, especially in London, but after finding the book I had been searching for, I could not wait to begin its perusal!"

They stood in silence for a few moments before she continued, "Do you live in London, sir?"

Taking in this girl's appearance more thoroughly, he realized she was most likely the daughter of a gentleman. Though it seemed she was in an awkward stage of development, there was something pleasing about her looks. She had dark hair that was more aptly described as a tumble of curls framing her face, tied back with a ribbon in an attempt to tame them. The healthy glow about her skin indicated that she spent more time outdoors than did her peers. She seemed more intelligent than her years… perhaps it was the indescribable sparkle in her dark eyes that assured him of this. "I have arrived only just yesterday with my father and sister from our estate in Derbyshire."

"Mama says I should always ask about the weather, so now I must ask you: how does the weather in Derbyshire? Is it as warm there as it has been here in London the past few days?"

Her polite look of exaggerated interest made him smile a little before saying, "It is never quite as warm in Derbyshire as in London, Derbyshire being so far north."

"And were the roads in good condition for your journey, sir?"

He pressed his lips together for a moment to hide the increasing urge to smile. Idle chatter had never been so amusing. "Yes, they were in as good a condition as could be expected after the unusually harsh winter."

"Capital! And had you a pleasant journey south to London?"

"Yes, we did. Thank you."

"I am glad to hear it… and I do hope I have covered the subjects of the weather and your journey well enough because I do not believe I can think of one more question to ask about either. I have heard much of Derbyshire, though I have never been there. Papa has a friend who lives in Derbyshire, and he visited his friend there many times while they attended Eton and Cambridge together. Papa says the area is very beautiful and promises to take me there some day."

Since the death of his mother several months ago, his father had allowed the boy to stay at home, but now it was time to return to school after a brief stay in London, and he was not looking forward to it. His mother's letters from home had always been the highlight of his week, and the idea that there would never be another was making his return all the more difficult. This little girl was very amusing and, it seemed, just what he needed right now to distract him from such somber thoughts. His generally depressed mood of late was lightening considerably. "Do you know where in Derbyshire your father's friend resides?"

"Yes, I believe the estate is called Pemley… no, I am not saying it right, but that is close to the pronunciation."

His eyebrows raised and he said, "Pemberley, perhaps? And what is the gentleman's name, do you know?"

"Yes, I think it is exactly that! His name is Mr. Darcy."

"Well then, I do know your father's friend very well as I am Fitzwilliam Darcy. Mr. George Darcy is my father."

Her smile brightened the room. "How wonderful!" She noticed the black armband he wore, which was similar to the mourning band her father had worn when her grandmother had died. Remembering what her father had told her, suddenly her smile faded, and she put her small hand on his arm. "Oh… then may I say how sorry I am to have heard about your mother's passing, Mr. Darcy."

He looked down to the floor and sighed before saying, "Thank you." It *had* been nice to spend a few minutes *not* thinking on that subject.

A very insightful child, she detected his pain and his need to change the subject. Her hand gently squeezed his arm before letting go. "Since our fathers know each other, I should introduce myself—though Mama would be very displeased with me for doing so, and I must beg that you do not tell her! I am Elizabeth Bennet, but most people call me Lizzy."

He bowed to her again, and she curtseyed in return. "It is a pleasure to meet you, Miss Bennet. I have heard my father mention Mr. Bennet often. You live in Hertfordshire, do you not?"

"Yes, at Longbourn." Elizabeth felt the subject was exhausted. "May I ask what book you were looking for, Mr. Darcy? I have an interest in botany, and since you are searching in this section… I wonder if I could help you find it. This is my uncle's bookshop, and I know where most everything is," she said, beaming proudly.

"I am looking for The Temple of Flora, a book by Robert John Thornton," said William quietly.

"Why does such a lovely book on botany make you feel so sad?"

Something about her made him want to tell her everything that was in his heart, but he restricted himself to saying only, "It was my mother's favourite; botany was her special interest. We have a copy at Pemberley and another in our house in London, but I wanted to take one with me to Eton…" he said, his throat tightened with emotion.

"I understand, Mr. Darcy." He looked up to see such a look of compassion in her dark eyes that it almost overwhelmed him. He blinked back a few tears. "It is just here." She moved past him to take the book from the shelf and then handed it to him. "It has the most beautiful pictures I have ever seen in any of these books. I hope it brings you comfort."

Swallowing the lump in his throat, William said, "What was it you were reading, Miss Bennet?"

She passed the book to him.

Flipping through the pamphlet, he said, "But this is not written in English. I believe it is in German! Are you able to read German?"

"Yes, my neighbour, Baron Leisenheimer, was originally from Prussia and he taught me his native language. I enjoy German more than French and Italian, though I like Latin about the same."

William's eyes widened, "*You* know all those languages? But you are so very young…"

"Papa says I have a special gift for languages. Mama says I should not show off so much, but I am not trying to show off. I just learn easily, and that is all; I am not trying to impress anyone. She also says I should not tell anyone what I can do because they will think I am odd, and that I will never catch a husband. Do you think I am odd, Mr. Darcy?"

He found himself holding back a smile again. "No, Miss Bennet, I do not think you odd. I think you very intelligent."

"Mama says I'm im…impernant. Do you think I will never catch a husband because I am impernant?"

"I believe the word is 'impertinent,' but from what I have seen today I do not think you impertinent. You are honest, and that is a fine trait to have."

"Yes, I am honest, but mama says I must learn not to be too honest because it is rude. I cannot understand this. Do you know how one can be too honest?"

"Well, I am older and can understand it a little better. For example, sharing that your mother is instructing you on how to 'catch' a husband is not an appropriate subject to discuss with a gentleman… or with any acquaintance, really."

"But that is almost the only subject she ever talks of… and she often repeats that if my four sisters and I do not marry well then we will all be thrown into the hedgerows to starve when my father passes. If that is all *she* ever speaks of, why should I not speak of it?"

William's raised his eyebrows, and he blinked a few times before asking, "Perhaps she speaks of it only when among intimate family?"

Elizabeth shook her head.

William did not know what to say to that and changed the subject slightly, "Why would you all be thrown into the hedgerows?"

"Because Mr. Collins is a nasty man who Papa had an argument with many years ago, and they have not spoken since."

"Mr. Collins?"

"Yes, I have no brother and my father's cousin Mr. Collins will take Longbourn when Papa passes."

"Oh, I see."

"Though Mama says he will 'steal' it because she does not believe in entailments away from the girls in the family. Mama insists that catching a husband is the most important thing we girls can do, but I have decided that I do not wish to be married at present."

William almost laughed out loud. "I do not think you will need to decide to whom you will be married for a few years yet."

She arched her brow. "One would not think I am too young the way Mama speaks of it!" She put her book back on the shelf.

"You will not be purchasing the book?"

"No, I have read it already, and so I do not need to."

"That is more of a reference book, is it not? You do not think you might need to refer to it at a later time?"

"I have it here, now." She pointed to her head.

"I do not understand."

"Every time I read something, I keep a perfect picture of it in my mind and can look at it later. It is like the book is in my hand, and I am reading it again."

"How interesting!" He opened his book to a random page, "You have read this book, correct?" When she nodded he asked, "What is on page number five of the book I have?"

She described the pictures and said the names, spelling anything that she could not pronounce.

Shaking his head, he said with a wide smile, "I think you are an amazing person, Miss Bennet!"

"Thank you, sir. I am glad you do not think I am strange. Mama tells me I should not tell anyone about that, either, because when I have, people have thought I was odd, and someday they might have me sent to Bedlam when Papa is no longer here to protect me."

William frowned deeply. "If in the future *anyone* wishes to send you to Bedlam for one of your talents, I beg that you contact me. I will protect you if your father is unable to do so."

Elizabeth smiled brilliantly. "Thank you, Mr. Darcy! That relieves my mind a great deal."

Just then the bell above the door rang, and Mr. Bennet came into view at the end of the aisle of books. "Papa!"

"Ah, there you are, Lizzy." Warily, he eyed the young man standing with his daughter, but his demeanor changed as recognition dawned on him, "And you, young man, are you perhaps related to Mr. George Darcy?"

William bowed and said, "Yes, Mr. Bennet; I am his son. My father is within as well, sir. I believe he can be found in the philosophy section of the shop."

"You certainly look very much like him when he was about your age." Mr. Bennet looked back and forth between the two children. "Has my Lizzy been entertaining you?"

"Miss Bennet is a delightful young lady, sir. She helped me find the book I was searching for, and we have been conversing these past minutes."

Mr. Bennet nodded, "Come, let us find your father. I have not had the pleasure of his company for these several years at least."

They found Mr. Darcy discussing his book purchases with Mr. Gardiner, the proprietor of the shop, while waiting for his son to join him. As Mr. Bennet approached, Mr. Darcy turned and said, "Bennet! What a surprise to find you here in London! It is good to see you!" The two shook hands.

"Darcy, it is good to see you as well. It seems my daughter has been assisting your son in finding a book, and I have just met him. He seems a fine young man. I am a bit shocked to see how much he has grown—when I had last seen you, he was only just walking! I cannot believe so much time has passed! I see you know Gardiner, my wife's brother?"

Mr. Darcy looked surprised, "I did not know you were related. I have been a patron of this superior bookshop for years, and it has only improved since Mr. Gardiner became proprietor last year."

"Yes, I quite agree. If not for the bookshops, London would be intolerable!"

"I see your opinion of Town has not changed, Bennet." Mr. Darcy laughed.

"Not in the least!" Mr. Gardiner replied. Mr. Bennet introduced Elizabeth to Mr. Darcy and then the three gentlemen began to speak of Cambridge. Mr. Gardiner had attended beginning the year the other gentlemen had left it, but they still had much to discuss.

"You said earlier that you attend Eton, Mr. Darcy.... do you like school?" asked Elizabeth.

"I like it very well, Miss Bennet." William felt a pang of guilt because he knew he was not being completely forthright with this very honest girl. He did enjoy learning, but he did not feel comfortable with the social aspects of living at school.

"I wish I could go to school."

"Perhaps if you tell your father, he will allow you to attend a school for ladies."

"I would not want to go to *that* kind of school! I meant that I want to go to the kind of school that boys attend. Girls learn silly subjects like embroidery, netting purses, and how to serve tea… and I already know more languages than they could teach me at a school for *ladies*. Papa says that I could probably teach the instructors a thing or two! I do like to dance and play the pianoforte… but embroidery!" Elizabeth rolled her eyes in such a way that had William attempting to hold back his smile again. "I want to learn about literature and mathematics and science and philosophy! Mama scolds me for reading so much for she says men do not like girls who know more than they do, but I want to *learn*! I am glad that Papa allows me to read anything in his library, and he does not forbid me from studying any subject I wish." She lowered her voice and said conspiratorially, "Well, except for the books on the uppermost shelf by the window on the left, at which I am *never* to look."

This time William could not stop a chuckle from escaping before he said, "It sounds as if you have many diverse interests, Miss Bennet, much like my mother did. She was an intelligent lady, and I applaud your wish to expand your mind past subjects you find silly." Thinking his praise might actually end up getting her in trouble, he thought to add, "Though embroidery does serve a purpose and would not be a bad thing to learn if it pleases your mother for you to do so. Do you enjoy only reading, or do you have other pursuits as well?"

"I love to be outdoors, sir, doing just about everything. I walk a great deal. Charlotte and Jane will walk with me, but they do not like to climb trees, or play army and pirates and bandits with the boys like I do, so they often go home after our walks. They like doing *girl* things much better."

"Are Charlotte and Jane your sisters?"

"Jane is my elder sister by two years, and she is an angel!" Elizabeth's smile was wide as she spoke of Jane, but it lessened as she continued, "I have three other sisters. The youngest two, Kitty and Lydia, are too young to go out with me, but I do think they will not be interested in what I like to do when they are old enough as they are very silly. Mary, the sister who is two years younger than I, is too serious to play at... anything. Charlotte is my friend and neighbour. Her father was just made a knight, and we must call him 'Sir William' now instead of 'Mr. Lucas.' It is mostly Charlotte's brothers that I play with, though there are other boys from the neighbouring estates and tenant farms that join us as well."

"And what position do the boys have you play during these games?" William asked, thinking they would have her pretending to clean up after the horses and swab the decks.

"I am not supposed to tell anyone... do you promise not to tell?" William nodded. "I am always the general of the army or the captain of the ship or the leading bandit, of course!"

"Of course!" William said with a grin. "And the boys do not get angry because they must take orders from a girl?"

"No, for I make up much better games than they do, and though they might not admit it to anyone else, they do say it to *me*. None of the boys play chess or read much, but I do, and I believe that is why I devise better strategies in our wars and conflicts. Sometimes we fight real battles as they were portrayed in history books or the newspaper—*not* with real weapons, of course. I am the best tree climber of the lot, as well as the best swordsman!"

At this point, William was not surprised by anything this obviously witty and adventurous young lady had to say. He saw his father looking at him with a small smile that reached his eyes—one he had not seen on his father's face since his mother had died. Little did he know his father was thinking that he had not seen his son laugh, smile or even take an interest in *anything* other than his sister since his wife had died… until now.

William overheard the men making plans to meet at Mr. Darcy's club for lunch the following day and expected them to soon be bidding each other farewell. "I am quite impressed with the many accomplishments already achieved by one so young. But I do believe you should try to work on the *girl* things as well. I know it is difficult to do things that one does not enjoy in the least, but we all must carry that burden. If you think of it as a challenge to improve yourself, as I do, it will make it more palatable." When Elizabeth looked doubtful, he added, "It does sound as if it would make living with your mother a bit easier if you showed her you were putting in a good effort, if nothing else."

Elizabeth made another face that reminded William of her age, and he almost expected her to stamp her foot and have a tantrum. He had been at first surprised and a little amused at hearing her converse with more intelligence than ever he had heard from young ladies twice her age, but soon he had become so comfortable with her conversation that he had forgotten just how young she was. Elizabeth sighed and relented, "Well… it does sound like a better idea when you put it that way. Since you do seem like a sensible young man, I will make the attempt to follow your advice. Perhaps I will ask my Aunt Gardiner to teach me a bit of embroidery while I am still in London. She has more patience with me than does Mama."

William could not help but chuckle. "That sounds like a very good plan, Miss Bennet."

Mr. Darcy approached and said, "It certainly was a pleasure meeting you, Miss Bennet. Your father will be having dinner with us in two days' time. Would you like to accompany him? Your father tells me you are interested in books, and I thought that William could show you our library; I hoped you might enjoy meeting my daughter as well."

Elizabeth looked at her father, and at his nod, she smiled brightly and said, "Yes, sir, I would like that very much. Thank you, Mr. Darcy." She curtsied.

Mr. Darcy bowed to her and said, "I look forward to seeing you again, Miss Bennet."

The Darcys took their leave, both happier than when they had arrived.

~ % ~

When the Bennets arrived at Darcy House, after the usual greetings Mr. Darcy suggested that William show Elizabeth the way to the nursery so that she could be introduced to Georgiana. After the children left them, Mr. Bennet said, "Good thinking to have my Lizzy meet Miss Darcy *before* seeing the library. We may never see her again after she has experienced the famous Darcy collection!"

"So she takes after her father in this way?" Mr. Darcy laughed.

"Yes, she certainly does, though I think she will surpass my abilities in many areas. I am afraid her mother feels Lizzy's thirst for knowledge is a liability, but I cannot deny her… and it has caused quite a bit of contention between us. Elizabeth is truly one of the most intelligent persons I have ever met, Darcy. She will be but ten years old next month, and she already knows more than do most boys upon entering Cambridge, and all from her own reading. The instruction I have given her is more guidance than teaching. Occasionally there is a concept that she has trouble comprehending, but to see how her face lights up with understanding when all becomes clear is reward enough to brave even my wife's disapproval! I think sometimes my wife is actually frightened of her. There is no doubt she is frightened *for* Lizzy, and at times I have to agree."

"Why would you be frightened for Elizabeth, Thomas?" When they were younger, the two had always switched to first names whenever discussing a serious matter, and though many years had passed since they had seen each other, Mr. Darcy easily fell into this old habit.

"If she were a boy, nothing would be able to stand in her way… but she is not. She will grow up someday, George—sooner than I am prepared for, in fact. To be honest, I do not know how she will manage. There could not be one in a thousand men who could be considered her equal in intelligence, and even fewer who would accept her for who she is and not insist that she pretend that she is something she is not."

From the moment George Darcy had seen his son interacting with his friend's daughter at the bookstore, he had had an idea of what Elizabeth's future would hold, but it was far too soon to bring that subject up with her father. "Do not fret, Thomas. I have a strong feeling all will be well for Elizabeth."

"You always did have a sense of what would work out well. I hope in this case you are correct."

Perhaps, though, he *could* plant a seed. "Actually, from what you have told me and from what I have seen, she reminds me of William at that age, but she seems to have an intuitive sense of other people's feelings that William has always lacked. She has gotten William to talk, and, believe me, that is a feat! He is even shyer than *I* was at his age, if you can believe it possible. Georgiana has been looking forward to meeting Elizabeth because William has mentioned her so often since we met you both at the bookshop."

"Really? No, I would not have guessed it! In fact, I had been thinking that while he *looks* very much like you did at his age, he does not *act* like you did at all, in *that* way at least. But then, I *did* come across them after he had already been speaking to Lizzy for some minutes, from what I understood."

"You always did have that effect upon me as well, Thomas, and I am certain you would have the same effect on William. With you, I always felt comfortable; it was with others that I became reticent. As far as I know, before two days ago the only person outside the immediate family with whom William was truly comfortable was my nephew Richard Fitzwilliam. He has had a difficult time at school and has had no Thomas Bennet to help him through it as I did. The headmaster tells me that while he is accepted due to his name, he does not really fit in with the other boys. Sound familiar?" When Mr. Bennet nodded, Mr. Darcy continued, "I was hesitant about sending him back to Eton after my wife's passing because he seemed so… lost, but I am sure you will agree that keeping him at home will do him no favors. He must learn to find his way in society, and Eton is a proper place to start. I keep hoping that perhaps he will find a true friend there, too. Seeing him the past couple of days has made me feel more comfortable with the decision. I now feel he will be all right."

After discussing a few other subjects, the gentlemen became curious as to what had happened to William and Elizabeth. Mr. Darcy invited Mr. Bennet to the nursery to see what they were about. Upon arriving they found William sketching and Georgiana entranced in Elizabeth's telling of the story, *Beauty and the Beast.* The gentlemen stood by the door, watching and listening for a few minutes before Georgiana noticed them and ran to her father with her arms open. Mr. Darcy scooped her up and gave her a hug before setting her down to introduce her to Mr. Bennet. Georgiana looked up to Elizabeth, who had joined them near the door, and Elizabeth nodded very seriously. Georgiana curtsied as well as a five-year-old could, and Elizabeth applauded. "You learn very quickly, Miss Darcy!"

"Very well done, Georgiana! Your curtsy has certainly improved since yesterday!" Mr. Darcy praised.

"Miss Elizabeth showed her a special way to accomplish it, Father."

"I thank you for your instruction, Miss *Bennet*." Mr. Darcy said with a sharp look at his son indicating that he was correcting him.

In a very serious tone of voice, Elizabeth said, "Mr. Darcy, I know I am supposed to be called 'Miss Bennet,' but 'Miss Bennet' is my sister Jane. I like to be called 'Elizabeth' or 'Lizzy' much better, but your son says *that* would be improper. So, we have decided to compromise and have settled on 'Miss Elizabeth,' if you do not mind, sir."

Mr. Darcy glanced at Mr. Bennet, who was stifling a laugh, and shrugged. "I suppose it is fine with me as long as your father does not object. But William, when you are in public, you should refer to her as 'Miss Bennet.'"

"Agreed, sir," Elizabeth said, "but may Miss Darcy call me 'Elizabeth'?"

"Perhaps when she is older she may, but for now I would be grateful for your assistance in teaching her to respect her elders by having her address you more formally."

Elizabeth's mouth formed into a silent, "Oh," and she nodded.

At a look from Mr. Darcy, the governess told Georgiana that story time was over, and it was time for a writing lesson. The remainder of the group said goodbye to Georgiana and headed toward the library.

As they walked, Mr. Bennet asked William what he had been sketching, and William handed him the pad, blushing. "This is very good!" Mr. Bennet said as he slowed to look at the beginnings of a sketch of Elizabeth. "Have you studied with a master?"

"A little, sir. I enjoy it, but…"

"But?"

"Mr. Bennet, at school the boys tease me, saying that drawing is a girl's activity, so I do not practice when away from home." William blushed again.

Mr. Bennet smiled. "Ah! Lizzy is often told she should not read so much, and that girls should not learn mathematics or science or ancient languages or play chess because they are all things that boys usually do. What is your opinion, Master William? Do you think I should not allow her to learn these subjects?"

William's look could be described as horrified. "No, sir, I would not change anything about Miss Elizabeth."

"What do you think Lizzy would say to anyone who dared to tell her that she likes boy's activities? Do you think that would stop her from doing what she loved to do?" Mr. Bennet said with a smirk.

William tried not to smile while saying, "I cannot imagine what she would say, but I know she continues to do what she enjoys as long as you do not forbid it, sir, and she is proud of her accomplishments. I do admire her spirit, Mr. Bennet."

"One would think that the father has much to teach the daughter, but Lizzy tends to teach me more than I could have dreamed possible. Perhaps you can learn a lesson from her in this regard as well?"

"Thank you, sir."

He clapped William on the shoulder, and the two picked up the pace to catch up to Elizabeth and Mr. Darcy.

When they arrived at the door of the library, Mr. Darcy allowed Elizabeth to enter first. She took a few steps into the room, and all eyes were on her expression. Elizabeth stood wide-eyed and open-mouthed as she looked around the room. She whispered, "*This* is your private *library*?"

"You do not have to whisper, Miss Elizabeth. We are the only people here. This is just a small sample; the true collection is at Pemberley," Mr. Darcy answered.

The eyes that none of the gentlemen thought could open wider, did. "This is but a *small* sample? But… there are more books here than in my uncle's bookshop!"

"I am very proud of our collection, Miss Elizabeth. It is the work of many generations of Darcys. Your father spent many hours ensconced in this room during his youth, as well as in our library in Derbyshire. Do you like it?"

"It is… *heavenly*, sir!"

Look for ***Promises*** at all your favourite online bookstores.

Thank you for your interest in Dreams & Expectations!

I do hope you enjoyed it!

Please stop by my website and read a

sample chapter of my next story:

All Hallow's Eve

https://wendisotis.wordpress.com/

Visit my author page on Facebook: *Wendi Sotis*

On Twitter, find me at *@WendiSotis*

About Wendi Sotis

Wendi is a graduate of Nassau Community College and Adelphi University, and holds a degree in Psychology. Following employment at private Long Island companies, she settled at the Town of Brookhaven before deciding to stay at home when her triplets were born in 2000.

Having always been an avid reader and adoring fan of Jane Austen, when the triplets were old enough that she was able to find a little time to herself, Wendi searched the internet and discovered a treasure trove of "fan fiction" written by fellow *Janeites*. At first, experiencing Austen's stories from several different characters' points of view caught her interest, but then she branched off into reading sequels, "what if" stories, and even modernized versions of Austen's tales.

Though she had always aspired to become a writer, it was not until Wendi awakened from a dream and realized that the story could become a terrific tale that she made a serious attempt. In the midst of penning a number of short stories, in 2010, she posted her first draft of a novel-length *Dreams & Expectations* to several online forums. Wendi then went on to write another novel-length story, *Promises*, published in 2011.

When asked why she continues to take Jane Austen's beloved characters on journeys in new directions, she points out that it is not much different than enjoying television programs that place the same characters in a different storylines during each episode.

Wendi continues to live on Long Island with her husband of twenty-three years, her son, and two daughters.

Made in the USA
Lexington, KY
13 October 2012